MEET THE MENAGERIE . . .

MR. DOYLE . . . Sorcerer and alchemist. A man of unparalleled intellect. When evil threatens to consume the world, he gathers those who will fight.

CERIDWEN . . . Princess of the Fey. Solitary and beautiful, she holds the elemental forces of nature at her command.

DR. LEONARD GRAVES . . . Scientist, adventurer, ghost. He exists in both life—and afterlife.

DANNY FERRICK . . . A sixteen-year-old demon changeling who is just discovering his untapped—and unholy—powers.

CLAY . . . An immortal shapeshifter, he has existed since The Beginning. His origin is an enigma—even to himself.

EVE . . . The mother of all vampires. After a millennium of madness, she seeks to repent for her sins and destroy those she created.

SQUIRE . . . Short, surly, a hobgoblin who walks in shadows.

continued . . .

TEARS
OF THE
FURIES

A NOVEL OF THE MENAGERIE

CHRISTOPHER GOLDEN
AND
THOMAS E. SNIEGOSKI

ACE BOOKS, NEW YORK

THE BERKLEY PUBLISHING GROUP
Published by the Penguin Group
Penguin Group (USA) Inc.
375 Hudson Street, New York, New York 10014, USA
Penguin Group (Canada), 10 Alcorn Avenue, Toronto, Ontario M4V 3B2, Canada
(a division of Pearson Penguin Canada Inc.)
Penguin Books Ltd., 80 Strand, London WC2R 0RL, England
Penguin Group Ireland, 25 St. Stephen's Green, Dublin 2, Ireland (a division of Penguin Books Ltd.)
Penguin Group (Australia), 250 Camberwell Road, Camberwell, Victoria 3124, Australia
(a division of Pearson Australia Group Pty. Ltd.)
Penguin Books India Pvt. Ltd., 11 Community Centre, Panchsheel Park, New Delhi—110 017, India
Penguin Group (NZ), Cnr. Airborne and Rosedale Roads, Albany, Auckland 1310, New Zealand
(a division of Pearson New Zealand Ltd.)
Penguin Books (South Africa) (Pty.) Ltd., 24 Sturdee Avenue, Rosebank, Johannesburg 2196,
South Africa

Penguin Books Ltd., Registered Offices: 80 Strand, London WC2R 0RL, England

This is a work of fiction. Names, characters, places, and incidents either are the product of the author's
imagination or are used fictitiously, and any resemblance to actual persons, living or dead, business
establishments, events, or locales is entirely coincidental.

TEARS OF THE FURIES: A NOVEL OF THE MENAGERIE

An Ace Book / published by arrangement with the authors

PRINTING HISTORY
Ace mass market edition / June 2005

Copyright © 2005 by Christopher Golden and Thomas E. Sniegoski.
Cover art by Christian McGrath.
Cover design by Judith Murello.
Interior text design by Kristin del Rosario.

ISBN: 0-441-01293-0

ACE
Ace Books are published by The Berkley Publishing Group,
a division of Penguin Group (USA) Inc.,
375 Hudson Street, New York, New York 10014.
ACE and the "A" design are trademarks belonging to Penguin Group (USA) Inc.

PRINTED IN THE UNITED STATES OF AMERICA

10 9 8 7 6 5 4 3 2 1

For Jim Moore, gentleman and friend.
Roll up for the mystery tour.

—C.G.

For Alice Sniegoski, my Mom.
She always said that this stuff would rot my brain.
She was right.

—T.E.S.

ACKNOWLEDGMENTS

Eternal gratitude to Connie and our crazy kids, Nicholas, Daniel, and Lily.

Much thanks to Ginjer Buchanan for her enthusiasm for all things weird and wonderful. As always, thanks to my family and to friends—scattered far and wide—especially Tom and LeeAnne Sniegoski, José Nieto and Lisa Delissio, Rick Hautala, Amber Benson, Bob Tomko, Lisa Clancy, Mike Mignola, Liesa Abrams, Allie Costa, and Ashleigh Bergh.

—C.G.

As always, I wouldn't be able to do what I do without the loving support of LeeAnne and my best pally, Mulder.

Special thanks are due to Ginjer Buchanan (in league with the monkeys, I'm sure), Christopher Golden, Dave "Don't touch my fan!" Kraus, Eric Powell, Don Kramer, Greg Skopis, Joseph Sniegoski, Liesa "Too Cute For You" Abrams, David Carroll, Ken Curtis, Lisa Clancy, Kim and Abbie, Bob and Pat, Jon and Flo, Pete Donaldson, Timothy Cole and the Legion of the Damned down at Cole's Comics. Be good to your parents, folks; they've been good to you.

—T.E.S.

PROLOGUE

A pale shroud had been drawn across the sky, softening the midday sun and filtering its rays through a layer of gauzy surreality. Billowing mist clung to the indigo waters of the Aegean Sea. This was the familiar, tangible world, yet in conditions like these, other worlds seemed close at hand, perhaps just a breath away.

It won't be long now, Nigel Gull thought. A thick bead of sweat slid from the top of his misshapen skull down the knobby flesh of his face, and he wiped it away with a silk handkerchief clutched in a contorted hand.

The cool haze lessened the heat, but only barely. Gull gazed up at the sun where it hid behind the drifting fog. It reminded him of the eye of some watchful deity, the once all-seeing orb glazed over with the film of death. He found it all strangely appropriate, to be observed from above by a god long dead.

He twisted around in his seat and narrowed his gaze as he regarded the skipper of the small boat. Though motorized, to his mind it was barely more than a skiff, certainly not large enough for the man to earn the title of captain.

"How much farther?" he asked.

The old man squinted into the haze as if he were able to somehow see what lay upon the sea ahead. "Not long now," he grumbled, his words thickly accented with the flavor of the isles.

Taki Spiliakos had been with Gull since his arrival in Greece nearly six months ago, assisting him in his pursuit of the most elusive of prizes. The fisherman—a resident of the tiny island of Giaros—had the reputation of being a madman, but of course, a madman was exactly what Nigel Gull required.

Born with his head and face enshrouded in a portion of his mother's amniotic sack, a caul as it was named by those who still remembered the ancient ways, Spiliakos was destined to be endowed with a powerful sensitivity to things of the preternatural. The superstition had proven true, and his unusual gifts had begun to exhibit themselves early in his seventh year. It was said that young Spiliakos could communicate with the spirits of the past, that he heard the whispers of ancient ghosts, and that he could see into the past the way others were said to be able to predict the future. That infernal chatter had driven him into isolation, and finally into the embrace of madness.

Gull sought a piece of antiquity, a fragment of myth with the ability to hide itself away from the most scrutinizing eyes. The ancients spoke to Taki Spiliakos, and through him Gull had gleaned many clues to the whereabouts of his elusive prize. There had been mishaps since Spiliakos had come to be in his employ, errant leads and tangents and false alarms. The spirits of the long departed were bored and thusly playful, but Nigel did not look at these moments as failures. They served merely as a process of elimination that would eventually yield his heart's desire.

And what about this time? Gull wondered, continuing to

gaze into the undulating fog, his body swaying with the swell of the sea. *What of today?*

The previous morning, after awakening from a particularly debilitating session with the restless dead that required half a bottle of scotch for recovery, the old man had finally recounted his most recent conversation with his ancient dead of the islands. This communion with the spirits had produced more than one mention of the object of Gull's quest, and a possible location as well.

Gull had immediately dispatched a reconnaissance team to the island of Kassos. As usual, his hopes were high, but his expectations were held at bay . . . until the field team failed to call in with its report. All attempts at communicating with his Wicked, as he enjoyed calling those in his employ, had been unsuccessful, and further investigation had found the entire island of some fifteen hundred inhabitants to be incommunicado.

Now, as the small boat cut through the uncommon mist—a perhaps unnatural phenomenon—Gull felt excitement roil in his gut. He had wasted no time gathering a crew for his yacht and setting sail for Kassos. Afraid of running afoul of the rocky reefs around the island in the uncanny fog, he had ordered his crew to drop anchor, deciding to go ashore by motorboat. His crew, loyal to a fault, had wanted to accompany him, but he had insisted on proceeding with only Spiliakos to guide him.

"How much farther can it be?" Gull grumbled, his patience beginning to fray, but as the words were leaving his mouth, he heard the sound he'd been anticipating, the surf breaking upon the shore.

Spiliakos cut the power to the motor, allowing the boat to drift toward the beach. It was as if a curtain of gray had been briefly lifted to reveal their destination. The old man leaped into the knee-deep surf, guiding the boat up onto the rocky shore. He extended his hand to Gull, who took it, allowing himself to be helped from the boat.

"Is this it, Taki?" he asked, his eyes frantically searching for any sign that this was indeed the place he had been seeking for so many years. "Is *she* here?"

Spiliakos touched his age-spotted fingers to the side of his head, rubbing at his temple. "That is what they tell me."

"Where?" Gull grasped the old man's thin, muscular arm in a malformed grip. "Ask them where she is to be found."

The sea mist clung to the shore, but a gentle wind blew, stirring the air, briefly revealing a second boat upon the beach before it was swallowed up again.

"Your agents' ship," Spiliakos said grimly. "I am sure that they could answer your question."

The island was eerily quiet, the fog-muted hiss of the surf the only sound, except for the pounding of Nigel's heart in his ears.

"Right, then," he said moving away up the beach. "Let's find them."

The fog churned and swirled as it drifted over the island, so that Gull was forced to move slowly, cautious with each step, peering ahead. The breeze off of the sea would occasionally tear through the gray mist, giving them fleeting glimpses of what lay before them. They had not traveled far before they found the first of the Wicked.

The figure in the distance stood with its back to them, remaining perfectly still as they approached. Gull was startled to see the man alive, and his expectations of success began to wane.

"You there," Gull called. But the man did not respond, and there was not the slightest hint of movement.

The mist coalesced about the figure once again, hiding him from view, and Gull cursed, quickening his pace. Nearly blind in the fog, he extended his hands, feeling his way through the cool, damp haze.

"Hello. Are you deaf, then?" he called into the mist, but there was still no response.

Spiliakos followed dutifully. Gull was vaguely aware of his stumbling pursuit as the rocky shore gave way to outcroppings of stone. Gull stumbled, the toe of his boot catching on an oddly shaped rock. Spiliakos tried to stop his fall, but the old man was not fast enough, and Nigel found himself pitching forward.

He flailed outward and managed to grab hold of an outcropping of rock, clinging to it as he tried to restore his balance. Gull was draped across the oddly formed stone configuration, and even as he recovered from the shock of his stumble, and he got his footing again, he became aware of the shape of the stone beneath his hands. It was not a natural formation, but the statue of a man.

Gull regained his footing, but his hands did not leave the statue. It was cool beneath his touch. His fingers traced the exquisite line of the statue's musculature and the way the stone had been made to replicate the folds of cloth. He moved around to the front of the figure, and the mist cleared enough for him to gaze into its face.

Nigel Gull had known this man.

His name was Colin Davenport, and he had been commander of the Kassos reconnaissance team, in Nigel's employ for nearly ten years. The expression frozen upon Davenport's face was one of supreme terror. A look that conveyed how aware the victim had been at the moment of his horrific transformation.

Gull reached a twisted hand out to Davenport's face to touch what his flesh had become. The tips of his fingers tingled as he caressed the smooth surface of the man's stone cheek.

"Has he answered your question?" Spiliakos asked, he, too, staring at the statue that had once been flesh and blood.

"Oh yes," Gull hissed, unable to look away. "He's absolutely extraordinary."

"But what of the others?" Spiliakos asked, turning away. The mist had again grown impenetrable, hiding what lay ahead. "Has the same fate befallen them?"

Gull finally tore his gaze from the stone man and stared into the swirling haze.

"Damnable fog," he growled, fumbling in his coat pocket

for his penknife. The blade was no more than two inches long, but it had proven its worth on many occasions, and he never went anywhere without it. "Should have thought to do this as soon as we first encountered the infernal brume," Gull griped as he opened his other malformed hand and ran the blade across the palm. Blood bubbled up from the gash, and he closed his fingers upon the wound, allowing his life stuff to trickle down the sides of his clenched fist and spatter upon the ground.

Gull closed his eyes, recalling an invocation taught to him by an ancient hag on the Russian Steppes. The words of the spell leaped from his mouth as if eager to escape. The blood that had dripped upon the ground began to smolder, vapors of red rising up to mingle with the fog that encompassed them. The gore on his hand had begun to fume as well, and he opened his hand, palm skyward, to expose the bloody cut to the elements. Blood no longer seeped from the wound, but instead streamed upward, scarlet strands that stretched from the gash to sway snakelike in the swirling vapor.

The wind suddenly picked up, responding to the ancient European magicks, and he watched as Spiliakos shielded his eyes from the dust and sand.

Gull extended both hands before him, the words leaving his mouth in a bellowing crescendo. With the last of the incantation spoken, Gull felt the power within him swell and reach out to take hold of the surrounding fog, clearing it from the sky above the island on an unnatural breeze.

Momentarily drained, he fell to his knees.

"May the gods protect us," Spiliakos said, muttering the words in Greek.

Gull shook off his disorientation and looked to see what had brought the exclamation to the old man's lips. He rose to his feet, surveying the island now that the mist had been dispersed. In the full light of day, with blue sky sprawling above and the Aegean crashing upon the shore, Gull at last could view the panorama spread out before him. Never in his long, accursed life had he seen anything quite so breath-taking.

A forest of stone figures. Statues as far as his eyes could see.

"I have to be closer," Gull said dreamily, walking forward.

Spiliakos was at first tentative, but then begrudgingly accompanied him. "They were fleeing her," the old Greek said, moving among the petrified men, women, and children. "The village of Panagia is that way, and Emborio is beyond it." He gestured in the direction from which the villagers had most likely come.

Gull stood before a cluster of men and women who had once been in his service. They, too, wore expressions of horror; two of the five had even drawn weapons.

"Bloody fools. I gave them specific instructions that she wasn't to be threatened," he said, shaking his head. "That she wasn't to be hurt." Gull pointed a crooked finger at the gun clutched in the stone fingers of one of his former operatives. "Does this look nonthreatening to you?"

"Look at their faces," Spiliakos said. "They were frightened."

Gull seethed. "None of this would have happened but for their stupidity! If they had followed orders . . . They caused this!" He threw himself at the stone figures of his men, knocking them over, shattering them upon the ground. He kicked at the broken limbs and body parts that now littered the ground.

"Mr. Gull, please," Spiliakos pleaded. "Calm yourself. It is not the time to—"

Then they heard it, soft at first but growing louder, and it froze them both in place. The air was filled with hissing, the sound made by a serpent when threatened. But it was not the sound of one snake, or even a dozen, this was the warning of serpents too numerous to count, and they were drawing closer.

"She's here," the old man whispered, and he blessed himself with the sign of the cross.

Gull wanted to laugh out loud, amused that the old madman had at this moment decided to embrace the Christian God.

"Oh, he'll be a lot of bloody help," Gull said with a shake of his deformed head. He scanned their surroundings. "No, sorry, old boy, but today is a day for deities far older and wiser."

The echo of his own words still in his ears, he caught sight of her and froze. She moved among the petrified bodies, and he felt his breath being taken away.

"It appears the ancients have whispered the truth at last," Spiliakos said, his gaze following the stealthy dartings of the figure that approached.

"A reward for being such a good listener, perhaps," Gull replied. "Now cover your eyes."

Spiliakos ignored him, moving into that forest of the stone dead for a closer look.

"There were two things the old voices told me last night," he said. "First, that you would find her at last, and second, that her eyes would be the last thing I would ever see." The old man stopped beside the petrified figures of an old woman and a little girl, frozen in midrun, their heads turned slightly to gaze back upon their pursuer. "I have always heeded the whispers of the ancients."

Gull would have ordered the man back to his side, but his voice would not come. She was slinking among the statues, and her progress held him transfixed. Her movements were filled with a predatory grace. Her hair was a nest of writhing green vipers, and her face—once so alluringly beautiful that the goddess Athena cursed her out of jealousy—was hideous. Monstrous. Not unlike Nigel Gull himself.

Medusa.

She swayed cobra-like before Spiliakos, a good deal taller than he was. Her gaze was eager, her beguiling movements urging him to raise his eyes, to look at her. The old man stared at the ground, at his feet.

Medusa reached out to Spiliakos, placing an alabaster hand beneath his chin, tilting his gaze up to meet hers. The old man complied with her gentle urgings, the snakes in her hair writhing and hissing excitedly, as their eyes locked, and Taki Spiliakos fell under her curse. There was a sound like twigs snapping, a gray hue spread over his flesh, and then the old man froze, immortalized in stone.

For a moment, Medusa stared down upon her handiwork in admiration. Then she twitched, her head rising as she remembered there was yet another to feel the effect of her stare. The object of his obsession turned her gaze upon Nigel Gull, moving swiftly toward him, the very air seething with the malice she projected.

Gull only smiled.

The Gorgon slowed, staring at him in confusion. Gull wondered how long it had been since she had been able to look into someone's eyes without harming them. It was a moment that would stay with him for the rest of his afflicted existence.

"I bear my own curse, miss. Yours cannot hurt me. We're much alike, you and I," he said to her, drawing her attention to his malformed visage. "I'm Nigel Gull," he said in his most gentle voice as he gingerly moved toward her.

He reached out to take her hand in his, pleasantly surprised to see that she did not pull away, and bent forward to place a tender kiss upon the back of her hand.

"And I have loved you for an eternity."

The monster—the woman called Medusa—began to cry.

1

NOW . . .

THE morning sun shone across the streets and squares and rooftops of Athens, from Lykavitos Hill to the Acropolis, but the daylight only made the shadowy alleys of the Pláka seem deeper. Yannis Papathansiou parked his car near Hadrian's Arch, propping a card identifying himself as a policeman onto the dashboard before locking it up. The heat was already oppressive, and Yannis took out a handkerchief and wiped his forehead. He stretched his back, showing off his voluminous belly, and then started off.

The Pláka was the oldest neighborhood in Athens, not far from the agora—the market—at the base of the Acropolis, right in the shadow of the Parthenon. It was a warren of streets so narrow the word *alley* was a compliment. All throughout the Pláka there were buildings with names from ancient times and monuments, which made the little neighborhood a tourist mecca. Yet there were still many Athenians who made their lives here and had shops and apartments, as though the true Greeks refused to surrender this one last little portion of their city to foreign visitors.

Yannis could admire that. But it didn't mean he had to

like the Pláka. It was so damned easy to get lost there, that was the biggest problem. He had lived in Athens most of his life, had been a policeman, and now a detective, in the city for three decades. It was embarrassing and a little unsettling to find himself lost anywhere in his home city. He was always careful to keep track of his path in the Pláka. And not only to avoid embarrassment. Athens was an ancient city, and this was its ancient heart. In his career as a policeman he had learned a great many things about what lay hidden in the shadows of the world.

And the alleys of the Pláka were nearly always in shadows. He didn't like it here.

Yannis grumbled and wiped his forehead again, feeling the dampness spreading beneath his arms and a trickle of sweat run down his back. He was too old and too fat for this job, but most days he managed all right. Most days, he didn't leave his car and walk blocks to get to the scene of a crime. But he didn't like to drive into this maze. Getting lost was only one problem. There were too many people, and some of the shopkeepers thought nothing of blocking part of the already narrow way. If he came upon an obstacle, he would have no way to turn around.

He reminded himself of all of these things as he marched along Thaloú Street. It was barely past breakfast, and yet already the restaurants were preparing for lunch. His stomach grumbled at the scents of souvlaki and loukanika cooking. Yannis began to plan his own afternoon repast, musing lovingly over thoughts of dolmodakia and a tyropitta as a small after lunch snack. A little cheese pie never hurt anyone. He smiled at the thought.

His smile was erased the moment he turned onto Pittakoú Street. The sun did not reach this far. The tops of the buildings hid the place away. Though the sky was blue and clear as the Aegean, down along this short road it was as gray as the black heart of a thunderstorm. Nothing but shadow. The scents of the food seemed to disappear. He could still see the faces of the tourists passing by, and the smiles of shopkeepers as they tried to draw people into their stores. It was the Likavitos Festival in Athens, now. A time of jubilant celebration, of music and wine, drawing families from all over Europe.

Bad luck, he thought. *Bad luck and bad timing.* Not that there was ever a good time for horror to slip from the darkness and taint the world of daylight. Murder was never good for business. Athens had more than its share of crime, mostly theft. But the murder of tourists was very bad for business. By lunchtime he would have his captain breathing down his neck. By the end of the day, the mayor would be laying it on Yannis as though he himself were the murderer. The newspapers would be starved for crumbs of information. But that was nothing to what he would face if the international press became involved.

CNN, he thought grimly. *Sewer rats.*

Yannis paused to push wispy strands of gray hair away from his face. Again he mopped his forehead, and he took a moment to rest. He lay his hands upon his belly as though he might relieve himself of the burden of carrying it for a moment. His father had been skeletally thin, but his mother . . . from her he had inherited his bulk and his shambling gait. She had been proud of it, the old witch. As though her size had been her greatest ambition and proudest accomplishment. Yannis was as heavy as he had ever been and was still half the weight that had finally killed his mother.

Water, he thought. He needed a drink of water. Although coffee would be an acceptable substitute.

At last, having no way to put off his venture into that gloom-dark street, he started on again. Halfway along there was yet another turn, this one barely an alley. It was a curving, cobblestoned path that at first glance could have passed as a delivery entrance for some of the buildings on Pittakoú Street. At the end of the path was the Epidaurus Guest House.

There were a few people out in front of the place, but not as many as Yannis would have expected. He grunted to himself. *Would you want to stand out here in the shade, with all the buildings far too quiet?* The answer was no. The sounds of the Pláka could be heard from here, even distant music, but it was as though he had stepped into another world and the way back to the other might be gone when he tried to return.

Ha! he thought. *You're getting morbid in your old age.*

His mouth twisted as though he had sucked on something bitter. Yannis had reason to be morbid. He had been witness to the monstrous and the terrible far too often in his life.

An officer in the uniform of the Athens police nodded to him and waved him in. Yannis did his best to hide the exhaustion he felt after wending his way through the maze of the Pláka. He said nothing to the officer, asked him nothing. The young ones hardly knew enough to fill an ouzo glass.

The Epidaurus was like many guest houses in the area. On the outside it was kept up reasonably well. The interior was barely passable. Its location near to the Acropolis brought in tourists who would consider it quaint, but though clean, the place was in disrepair. The walls needed painting, and the wooden floors were scuffed and faded. There was nothing beneath those high ceilings to bring beauty to the place. No art on the walls, no elegant furniture or drapes on the windows. The prices were too high, but people paid them, and the owners spent not a penny to improve their lodgings.

Yannis thought the owners were miserly and their guests were fools. But he had a low opinion of most people. He was a curmudgeon, well-liked only by other detectives, and only then because, despite his appearance, he was skilled at his job.

There were two other detectives there when he arrived, but Yannis had seniority. The two men, Dioskouri and Keramikous, were pale and seemed nervous. When they noticed him they immediately broke off conversation with a pair of uniformed officers and a crook-backed old man who must have been the owner, and came to him instantly, faces etched with relief.

"Lieutenant," Dioskouri said, adjusting his glasses and running a hand over his wiry black hair. "You've got to come in and see this. We don't know what to do."

It was all Yannis could do to sigh and not roll his eyes. Dioskouri was a broad-shouldered boy from the wine country, and his Greek was spattered with the dialect of his birthplace. It gave him away as young and naive, though he was past thirty.

Keramikous was altogether different. He was a tiny man, both thin and short, his stature barely that of a teenaged boy. Yannis was uncertain of his age, but he marked it at somewhere south of forty. Keramikous was balding, his hair already as gray as Yannis's. He seemed fragile and withered, the oldest young man Yannis had ever met. But he was a good detective and a family man, and for that Keramikous had his respect.

"Niko," he said, studying Keramikous, surprised at the pallor of the veteran detective. Despite the summer heat that brought beads of sweat out on his forehead, the man shivered as though in a fever. "Niko, tell me the story."

The tiny man shook his head. "It's useless to tell you." He spoke the Greek of a born Athenian, with the edge of the city in his voice. "Come and see for yourself."

His partner hesitated. Keramikous gestured to him, indicating that he should stay with the owner. The stooped old man seemed about to weep, his eyes red and moist, the skin beneath them swollen. The expression on Dioskouri's face was enough to embarrass even Yannis. He had never seen a man look so grateful.

Coward, he thought.

But that was before he saw what was in the breakfast room.

Keramikous led the way. It wasn't a very large room, just broad enough for half a dozen small tables and a sideboard laden with milk and juice, a bowl of fruit and boxes of dry cereal. There were pastries as well. This wasn't breakfast as far as Yannis was concerned, but it was enough for tourists.

The glass floor-to-ceiling windows in the rear of the breakfast room looked out upon the guest house's one bit of beauty, a large courtyard garden. The flowers were in full bloom, and their scent traveled in through the shattered windows on the breeze. Somehow the sunlight touched the garden, though it would not bless the street outside.

The only reason that Yannis had even a moment to notice any of these things was that at first his eyes could not make sense of the things that he saw in that room. His mind simply did not comprehend. Two of the tables, it appeared, had been given over to some strange artistic impulse. Seated in chairs were a trio of granite statues, intricately carved, startlingly realistic. There were cracks in the stone. One had a finger broken off, and it lay on the floor. Another had a real coffee cup raised to its lips.

Yannis frowned, shaking his head, confused by this oddity. What sort of attraction did the owners of this place think this would have for their guests.

It was a matter of a second or two, only, while these thoughts capered in his brain. Then he frowned, deeply.

Where's the body? Where is the murder that brought me here?

Next to the sideboard was another statue, this one of a young girl, perhaps ten or eleven. It had broken into half a dozen pieces, but mentally he rebuilt it, picturing what it would have looked like before it had broken, standing up.

It would have appeared to be reaching for something with its right hand. In its left it clutched an orange.

A fresh orange.

Understanding dawned on him. These *were* his bodies. The murders. Niko Keramikous must have seen it in his eyes, for the younger detective nodded in confirmation, unable to speak the words, his revulsion plain on his face.

Yannis's stomach churned. He thought he'd seen everything.

"Niko. Go and get the owner. I want to speak with him."

Keramikous sped from the room and closed the door behind him. Yannis cursed under his breath, the filthiest words he could dredge from his mind. He turned his back on the murdered family, on their stone faces, and reached into his pocket. The sweat on his back and under his arms was worse now, in spite of the breeze from the courtyard.

He withdrew his cellular phone and glanced around the room. There was too much sunlight in here. In a corner there was another door, and he opened it to find a closet used to store extra chairs. There were shelves of plates and glasses and silverware, but there was just enough room for him to step inside. He closed the door behind him, cloaking himself in near total darkness . . . in shadows. And he dialed a number.

Yannis Papathansiou had been on the job a long time and had seen much of what lay within and beyond the surface of this ancient city. The Athens police wouldn't have the first clue how to deal with something like this. But he knew someone who would.

EVERY shadow was a doorway. Not just anyone could walk through one, of course. To most—humans in particular—shadows were simple things, patches of darkness created when an obstacle came between the available light and any surface upon which it might shine. A woman walking her dog in the park on a sunny day would cast a shadow upon the ground. So would her dog. A jacket hung on the end of a child's bed might block enough of the illumination from her nightlight to throw a strange shadow upon the wall or ceiling. Yes, there were shadows everywhere. Beneath every bed and in every closet. On the far side of every tree. Under benches and buses and just around the corner of every building.

And every one . . . every single one . . . a doorway.

Beyond those doorways there existed an entire world, a

gray-black warren of pathways and tunnels, an interconnected maze that seemed infinite and yet turned in upon itself again and again. There were vast empty spaces in the midst of that shadow world, dark and barren places. The footing was uncertain, and the darkness seemed to breathe and to be very aware of those who walked within it. No one stayed in the shadows for very long.

Humans gazed at the shadows and shivered. They perceived the splashes of darkness with trepidation, their unconsciousness, the ancient, shared memory of their species reminding them that anything might emerge from the darkness, which was a place of the unknown, a dangerous place from which, once upon a time, many things might have escaped. Most of them were extinct, now. There might be a Norse *svartalf* or two still roaming the darkness, and if any of the tengu awoke, it was possible they would seek refuge there. But for the most part, the shadows were the domain of hobgoblins now.

And there weren't that many of *them* left, either.

All of which suited Squire just fine. He liked a party as much as the next goblin, but when he was working, he liked it quiet. Plenty of space to move around in, nothing to disturb him, and time to think.

Hobgoblins had an innate ability to navigate the darkness. He could dive into a pool of shadows in England as though it were water, and emerge from beneath a baby carriage in Los Angeles moments later. Many of the ancient races of the world had died out or were in danger of doing so. His own kind was not thriving, but they survived. To Squire's mind, this was because they were simply better at running away from trouble than any other creatures in existence.

Squire didn't like to run away. Not normally, in any case. He was more a lover than a fighter, but that didn't make him a coward. Fortunately, he spent most of his time around beings who were fighters. So aside from the occasional, unavoidable scrap, he could concentrate on the lovin'.

Well, that and the weapons.

One of the things about hanging around with fighters, and being employed by one, was that they needed weapons. Mr. Doyle had an unparalleled collection of weapons from every culture in the world, not to mention many from realms beyond it, and from every era in history. Some were museum quality and beautiful, others were ugly and efficient. When the muses called to him, Squire would forge new weapons of his own design. All of them needed caring for, and that was one of Squire's many duties in the household of Arthur Conan Doyle.

Driver. Valet. Weaponsmith. Armorer. His name was his occupation. He was Doyle's squire. And he loved his work.

Now, in his workshop in a lost corner of the shadow world, with the darkness pulsing around him, shifting and breathing, the gnarled little hobgoblin worked at the grindstone, pumping it with a foot pedal. The blade shrieked against the stone, and fiery sparks sprayed from the metal. The sound unnerved most people, like nails on a chalkboard, but Squire loved it. It was music to him.

He bared rows of tiny shark teeth in a satisfied smile as he held the weapon up, examining it in the illumination cast from the flames of his forge. The shadows did their best to swallow all light in this place, but the furnace of his forge was enchanted, and would have burned at the bottom of the ocean. The weapon was double-bladed . . . little more than a double blade, really. He had combined the concept of the ancient punching blade, katar, with the more Medieval double-headed battle-axe. The warrior grasped a handle in the middle of the two razor-sharp, rounded blades and thus could swing a cutting edge in any direction. The blades themselves were an iron-and-silver alloy that would have been impossible, save that his employer was an accomplished alchemist.

Iron was poison and pain to witches and the Fey. Silver was death to many of the creatures of the night. A good weapon. Squire was proud of it.

In the light of the forge's blaze he could see his reflection in the blade. His tiny eyes flickered in the firelight. There was a blemish in the metal, and the leathery brown flesh of his forehead wrinkled in consternation. He reached out a yellowed, cracked nail to scrape at it, to investigate, and then he chuckled softly with a rattle in his throat from too many cigars. It was merely a cut on his face, reflected in the pure mirror of the blade.

Squire drew his thumb along the edge, barely touching, but it cut him like a whisper, drawing a thin line of blood from his flesh.

He nodded to himself in satisfaction. A job well done. Now he only needed to fashion the leather sheath such a weapon would require. It was not complete without it, for the dual blade was too dangerous to carry unsheathed.

But the leather would wait.

Squire set the weapon on the wooden worktable, where he kept most of his tools, and stretched. He had been crouched over the forge, and then the anvil, and at last the grindstone. His back hurt like a son of a bitch, but it was worth it—just look at the beauty he had made. He sucked his injured thumb, but there was pleasure in it. To him it was only right that the first blood the weapon should draw would be his own.

"What am I going to call you?" he said aloud, brows knitting as he studied the weapon. The perfect symmetry of the twin blades impressed him. It was a nasty piece of work.

Twins, he thought.

"Gemini." That was the perfect name. It was a Gemini blade.

The hobgoblin patted the pockets of his coat and felt the reassuring bulk of his cigar case. He fished it out, spilling old candy bar wrappers into the shadows, then removed a cigar and set the case on the table. With great pleasure he bit the end off of the cigar and clenched it in his teeth, then went to the forge and leaned in, plunging the tip into the blazing furnace. The heat from the fire baked the skin of his face, but he was used to that. Hobgoblins had no particular fear of flames. Of burning to death, yeah. They weren't stupid. But not of fire. A little scorching wasn't going to do much damage to one of his kind.

With a sigh of pleasure he puffed on the cigar and glanced around at the shadow chamber. There were no walls, really, and yet the workshop did exist in a sort of void within the world of darkness. Black mist churned and pulsed all around, but there were openings in that breathing shadow, pathways that would take him anywhere he needed to go. Once upon a time, Squire had been like other hobgoblins . . . daunted by the constant feeling that the shadows were aware of him, that the darkness sensed his every move and thought. It still unnerved him at times, but he had come to know this place, and there was no danger in it. Not for hobgoblins. Not unless other things roamed the shadows.

When that happened, he closed his workshop up and fled back to the world of light.

But at times like this, with a job well done and a fresh cigar in his hand, Squire could relax. He took several more puffs on his cigar and blew a cloud of noxious smoke into the shadows.

At peace.

A soft, electronic melody broke the silence of the shadows. The tune was The Beatles' "Penny Lane." It was Squire's ringtone.

He reached into another pocket in his coat—it had more pockets than was possible—and answered. "Squire."

He listened to the voice on the other end, cursing a couple of times. "Yeah. Yeah, of course. No, that can't be good. You just sit tight there, spanky. Someone'll be in touch."

MR. Doyle strode along Hanover Street in Boston's North End, enjoying the warm summer day. Once upon a time the neighborhood had been subject to a constant drone of noise from the elevated interstate that ran through Boston's heart.

But the city had done something extraordinary, burying the highway underground. It was quiet, now, in the North End. Or as quiet as the neighborhood would ever be.

The North End was a warren of curving streets, lined with churches, apartments, bakeries, and restaurants. Early in Boston's history it had become the haven of the city's Italian immigrants, and it still reflected the best of that cultural influx. The spring and summer seemed a parade of festivals honoring the Italians' favorite saints, carnivals of food, and music. This was a corner of the city—of the nation—that still enjoyed simple pleasures.

The summer breeze swept off the ocean and blew through the narrow streets, picking up the wonderful aromas from the markets and the pastry shops. Mr. Doyle could not help himself, and he paused to peruse the small menus posted in front of several restaurants as he made his way along the street. Frank Sinatra's voice whispered through one propped-open door, Andrea Bocelli through another.

The sidewalks were busy with people out strolling, deciding on lunch, or making their way to the Old North Church to appreciate the history of the place. Like so many of Boston's treasures, the church was tucked away far from anything else, beyond even the limits of the touristy areas of the North End. Parts of that neighborhood did not share the appeal of its main streets. Beyond Prince and Hanover, there were other smaller, narrower roads where there were no expensive signs, no festival banners, no outdoor music. The shops on those backstreets catered only to local people. The faces of the buildings were in desperate need of sandblasting and refurbishing, and the windows were often cluttered with handmade signs.

Mr. Doyle left the brighter, more colorful heart of the North End and slipped into a gray side street with the sureness of one who had walked this way many times. He passed a shoe repair shop, a small butcher's, a used appliance store, and an antiquarian bookstore that looked tiny from a peek through the front window, but was unimaginably enormous within. Impossibly large, some might have said.

Ah, well. People had so little imagination. And other than the locals—who had a strong enough sense of community never to remark on anything odd—the only people who went into the bookstore knew what they were looking for, and that only a special kind of shop would be able to acquire it for them.

He inhaled deeply. The salt of the ocean was strong on the breeze. It had been a beautiful walk down here from Beacon Hill. It was June, the solstice imminent. The days were long, and the air shimmered with the heat of the sun. During the workweek there were mostly professionals about, but this was Saturday, and so he had passed many women in pretty summer dresses. It was the sort of day that inspired that kind of thing. On his walk back, he thought he might stop and buy a lemonade from one of the street vendors in front of the aquarium.

Mr. Doyle waved to a Sicilian grandmother pushing her daughter's child in an old-fashioned carriage. She nodded gravely in return. A silver Lexus prowled along the curving street. Someone looking for parking had lost their way. There were things he simply knew, things he intuited from the moment. It was a gift.

He twitched, pain lancing into his head from his empty eye socket. The patch that covered it was not a problem, though its strap itched the back of his head. For a moment, Mr. Doyle paused on the sidewalk and pressed the heel of his hand against that void, that eyeless hole. At times it ached profoundly.

Doyle had removed the eye himself. The pain had been like nothing he had ever felt. Worse, though, was the feeling of *tugging*, deep in his head, as he tore it loose from the optic nerve. It was a memory he would have very gladly erased. The man had done what he had to do, and it had helped to make the world safe—at least for a time. It was good, however, that he had not had any idea what it would feel like at the time. In retrospect, it wasn't something he would do again.

A dry laugh escaped his lips. What a sickening thought. Only a lunatic would do what he had done. But perhaps in that moment, knowing that it was the only way, he had been a lunatic indeed.

Now, the question was, what to do about it.

His shoes scuffed the sidewalk. The sleeves of his crisply pressed white shirt were rolled halfway to the elbow, and he wore black suspenders that did not go very well with his beige trousers. By his outward appearance, he would seem to most a librarian or a museum curator who'd lost his way, perhaps an eccentric academic. That was one of the reasons he loved Boston so much. The city was old enough to suit him.

For he himself was, of course, far older than he appeared.

Mr. Doyle rounded a corner and came in view of a small sign that jutted from the front of a building. Ancient neon blinked off and on, forming the letters *Rx*. The symbol for prescription drugs. It was a pharmacy, of sorts, at least as far as the neighbors were concerned. Many of them had their prescriptions filled at *Fulcanelli the Chemist*.

It was old-fashioned, of course, for the pharmacist to call himself a chemist. Still commonplace in England, it was unusual in the United States. But there were a great many things that were unusual in this little warren of old Boston. Fulcanelli carried most things people could buy at another pharmacy, and many things that could be purchased nowhere else in the northeastern United States.

A bell rang above the door as Doyle let himself in. He turned the hanging sign around to read closed and locked the door behind him.

There was no one at the counter when he entered, but in just a moment Fulcanelli emerged from the back of the shop, summoned by the bell. The man was bent with age, his pate bald on top, his white hair a thin curtain at the back of his head.

"Hello, old friend," Doyle said.

Fulcanelli nodded, grunting in the manner of the very ancient and very cranky. He waved a hand as if to say, let's get on with it.

"Come," said the chemist. "I've got what you need."

Shuffling his feet, the aged shopkeeper moved to a cabinet. Though his fingers were yellowed and covered with age spots and his knuckles were swollen, they moved with the dexterity of a prestidigitator as he reached into a pocket and withdrew a key.

"You're nearly there, aren't you?" Doyle asked, concerned.

Fulcanelli froze with the key nearly to the lock. He paused and regarded his visitor with moist, yellowed eyes. "Don't act as though you are overwrought with sympathy, Arthur."

Doyle stood a bit straighter, the hair on the back of his neck standing up. He hooked his thumbs in his suspenders and blew out a puff of air that ruffled his mustache.

"I take umbrage at your tone, sir. I take no pleasure in your pain."

The chemist studied him, the old man's face like that of a hawk seeking prey. "If you'd shared with me your own secret, I wouldn't have to suffer that pain at all."

The air grew thick with tension. They had had this conversation before. Fulcanelli had found an alchemical solution to the problem of his aging but it was complex. When his physical body aged and deteriorated to the point where it could no longer function, his skin would slough off and his bones would collapse and he would ignite in a burst of flame that would render his body nothing but ash. Then, from the ashes, a young man of perhaps sixteen would crawl, skin gleaming and new.

Fulcanelli had made himself a human phoenix. It was eternal life, of a sort, but the price was the agony of the process.

Mr. Doyle did not age. Fulcanelli envied that.

"We have been over this," Doyle said, narrowing his gaze. "Those secrets are not mine to share."

"So you say," the man said, sniffing in derision. But he scratched once at the side of his nose and then let the debate retire, bringing the key once more to the lock. "You have the money?"

Stinging from the man's bitterness, Doyle made no reply. Rather, he strode to the counter and thrust out one fist, palm downward. When he opened his fingers, a dozen gold coins spilled from his grasp. They had not been there a moment before, but now they clattered down onto the countertop, several rolling or bouncing off onto the floor.

Fulcanelli smiled greedily. "That'll do."

He opened the cabinet. It was filled with jars that contained strangely colored liquids, things floating in the cloudy contents of each jar. From an upper shelf, Fulcanelli drew down a jar filled with a viscous amber-colored fluid.

"Here we are," the ancient chemist said.

Mr. Doyle drew a deep breath and let it out. *At last,* he thought. The ache in his skull had been a terrible distraction to him. And the worst was when, late at night, the vacant socket would begin to itch.

"The patch," Fulcanelli instructed.

Doyle removed it gratefully, sliding the patch into his pocket.

The chemist whistled in appreciation. "That's a hell of a job," he said, staring at the ruined eye socket. "Someone did nasty work, taking that out."

"Me, the first time."

"The first time?" Fulcanelli replied. "You didn't mention anything about a second time."

"It's a long story. I replaced it with . . . another. A more useful eye. Like I said, a long story. But that one was taken away."

Fulcanelli sighed, shaking his head. "I don't know why you do it, Arthur. You could have such an easy, quiet life, and you make it so difficult for yourself. Set up a little shop, like mine. Salves and potions. Yours could have books and weapons as well. Much less dangerous. Less worry. Nobody tearing your eyes from your skull. Or even borrowed eyes from your skull."

Doyle smiled. The old man's bitterness had receded, as it always did. They had known one another too long.

"I could do that," he agreed. "But then who would do the worrying?"

The ancient chemist clucked his tongue and unscrewed the top of the jar. He thrust two withered fingers into the amber liquid and withdrew, dripping, a tender, gleaming eyeball. The optic nerve hung from it like a tail, twitching and swaying, searching for something to latch onto.

Fulcanelli's hand was shaking as he raised it toward Mr. Doyle's face.

"Hold still," the old man said.

Doyle did not point out that he was not the one who needed to be still.

After wavering for several seconds, the chemist's hand steadied and he slid the eyeball into Doyle's empty socket. The optic nerve shot into the open space, and into the raw flesh beyond, like a striking cobra. A jolt of pain spiked through Doyle's skull and he recoiled, cursing. He gritted his teeth together, groaning, and clapped his hands over his eyes. It felt like his whole head was going to split open, like that nerve was worming its way through his brain, tearing it to tatters.

Slowly, the pain subsided. He pulled his hands away and blinked.

Both eyes.

Relieved, and with only the memory of that terrible itch, he glanced at Fulcanelli. "You do good work, old man. You're an artist."

The chemist beamed. "It is my calling."

Something thumped to the floor in the back of the shop.

Alarmed, Fulcanelli spun, his fingers curved into terrible claws, and he reminded Doyle even more of a hawk. The door to the back of the shop was still partially open, but there were no lights on back there. The only illumination in that room was what little reached it from the front. Otherwise it was only shadows.

The door creaked as it swung open.

Squire stepped out. The hobgoblin was only slightly taller than the counter, so it was not until Squire had emerged fully into the shop that Doyle saw that he clutched a piece of notepaper in his gnarled fingers.

"Just got a phone call, boss. You're going to want to hear this."

2

BOSTON'S Newbury Street was abuzz with life and laughter, the sun glinting off of the plate glass windows of trendy clothing boutiques, art galleries, and bistros. Those who strolled along Newbury Street were either the idle rich or those who longed to be. College girls roamed in perfectly styled packs, and business types marched to lunch with tiny cellphones clapped to one ear. The buildings were comparatively old by American standards and yet the brick and stone had been sandblasted and treated and restored so that the entire string of blocks seemed to have been only recently erected. The sidewalks were in perfect condition. Even the cars that were parked along the curb gleamed new in the sun. BMW, Lexus, and Benz, *oh my*.

Milano's Italian Kitchen was among the trendiest of the new bistros, with a sidewalk café in front and a menu of nouvelle cuisine, despite the homey name of the place. Clay knew that if he had wanted more authentic Italian food he could have chosen any doorway in the North End, where dozens of restaurants awaited that were less expensive and more generous with their plates. But the idea today was to spend a little time with Eve, and if he wanted to get her out—

particularly when the sky was blue and the sun shining—he would have to lure her.

Newbury Street was irresistible to her.

They sat at the outdoor café, in the cool shade of Milano's wide awning. Eve was always aware of the position of the sun. She had to be. It could kill her.

Though the weather was warm, a typical mid-June day in Boston, she was covered from head to toe. Ample sunscreen had been rubbed onto her face, and a red silk scarf tied in a knot at her chin covered her head. She wore a blazer-cut black leather jacket, a pair of thin calf skin gloves, and completed her ensemble with dark moleskin trousers and Tony Lama boots with a severely pointed toe. Eve was stunning. With that scarf and her designer sunglasses, she looked like a movie star trying desperately not to be recognized in that ridiculous, conspicuous Hollywood way. She drew a lot of attention, but Clay had been out with her at night as well as during the day, and Eve drew appreciative stares no matter how she was dressed.

His appreciation of her beauty was objective, however. There was no romantic entanglement between them. Clay and Eve were associates. Perhaps they might even be friends. He considered her a friend, certainly, but often felt an odd reticence in her when they worked together. That was part of the reason he had invited her to lunch today.

They had been sharing observations about Conan Doyle and some of his other operatives when the waiter brought appetizers to the table, including a white plate laden with stuffed mushroom caps. Clay smiled and reached for one.

"Alexander loved these," he said as he popped it whole into his mouth.

"Alexander? As in, *Alexander*?" Eve asked, using her salad fork to help herself to one of the four remaining mushrooms.

Clay nodded. "Absolutely. He was obsessed with food," he said, trying not to be grotesque though he spoke with his mouth full. The mushroom caps were not the best he'd ever had, but far from the worst. That honor went to the Angry Boar, a restaurant not far from the highlands of Scotland, in the village of Poolewe, where the ultimate in fine cuisine was served from a fryolator. Clay shivered inwardly at the still disturbing memory of fried pizza.

Eve had sliced a small piece of stuffed mushroom and used the fork to bring it to her mouth. Now she swallowed before continuing. "You expect me to believe that?" She smiled slyly. "You hung out with Alexander the Great and ate mushrooms?"

Clay helped himself to another mushroom, this time showing some manners and bringing it to his plate where he broke it in half with his fork. He shrugged.

"Everybody has to eat."

The expression on Eve's face said she wasn't certain whether or not to believe him. Clay was having some fun with her, but in truth he *had* known the Macedonian legend. Many of his memories were lost to him, shifting in his mind like a deck of cards, with far too many missing or obscured. But others were intact and crystalline in clarity. He had been many things in his eternity of life—warrior and monster, hero and assassin. Clay could alter his flesh, could become anyone or anything he wished. In the year A.D. 331 he had used that ability to help Alexander defeat the Persians. Those had been simpler times, violent times, and often it disturbed him how much he missed them.

"Why is that so hard to believe?" he asked, staring at his twin reflections in the lenses of her dark sunglasses. "Don't tell me you've forgotten your past."

Eve was a bit younger, give or take a millennium, and had lived a life equally fascinating, but he knew she had also experienced a fair amount of pain and anguish.

A waiter came over to refill their water glasses and inform them that their lunch would be brought out shortly, before excusing himself with a slight bow and a genial smile. Eve removed a packet of sugar from a container on the table and began to play with it.

"I remember quite a bit, actually. Some things I've let go of, but other things . . ." Her voice trailed off, and a look of heartbreaking sadness flickered across her face.

Clay wished he had never brought it up, never caused her to examine the memories she wished she could abandon. But as quickly as it had appeared, the telling look was gone and Eve managed to summon a smile as she changed the subject.

"So, tell me something else about him," Eve said, taking a sip of water. "Something we couldn't pull from a history book. Or is his love of stuffed mushrooms the only thing worth knowing about the man who once conquered the entire civilized world?"

Clay set down his fork and pulled the white napkin up from his lap to wipe his mouth. "He was a pretty good dancer," he said with a straight face. "Man, could that guy cut a rug."

Eve burst out laughing, almost spilling her water. An ice cube had escaped over the rim of the glass and dropped onto the tabletop. She plucked it up with her gloved fingers and tossed it at him. "Asshole," she said, a lingering smile on her face.

He could probably have counted on one hand the number of times he'd seen this woman look genuinely happy. *It's nice to see her smile,* he thought, brushing the cube from his lap to the ground.

"You don't believe me," he said, doing his best to stifle his amusement. "Fine, be that way. I'll just keep my candid recollections of history to myself, though I think you might have been very interested in Genghis Khan's phallus-shaped vegetable collection."

When Eve glared at him, Clay couldn't hold it back any longer and burst out laughing himself. The life he led did not often give him the opportunity for laughter, and he held on to the moment with both hands, truly enjoying himself.

Eve grinned. "Think you're pretty funny, don't you?" she said.

He nodded, wiping the tears from his eyes.

"We'll see how funny you think it is when I stick you for this bill."

Clay had regained most of his composure by the time their food arrived. Two waiters brought their entrees: his the linguine with clam sauce, and Eve's a Caesar salad. They were silent through their meal, and he could see by the way her brow furrowed, that she was thinking hard about something. This happened too often when they were together, but for once they were in a situation that allowed him to inquire about it.

"Penny for your thoughts," he said finally, spinning the last of the linguine onto his fork.

Eve shrugged, placing her napkin on top of the table, and pushed her salad plate away from her. "Don't know what it is, but every time I'm with you, I end up thinking about things I'd rather not."

"Such as?"

She glanced away. "It's hard to explain."

"Then let's distract you," Clay said, pushing away his own empty plate. "How about some dessert?" he asked, removing a menu card from the side of the table. "I hear they make an amazing brownie sundae, and I'd even be willing to share."

There was a tinge of desperation in Eve's gaze when she met his eyes.

"I can't remember . . ." she said. "I can't remember what the garden . . . what Eden looked like." Eve turned her head away to watch the shiny, happy people stroll down the crowded sidewalks of Newbury Street. "I often wonder if this is another way that *He* intends to punish me, to take away the memories of the things I cherish, one by one, so only the bad stuff is left."

Clay was at a loss. The Creator had a gift for punishment, there was no doubt about that. The punishment He had meted out to Eve had led to the horror that had made her what she was now. She had been raped and defiled and driven over the edge of madness by demons, and turned into a monster. Wasn't that enough?

"We're old, Eve," he said. "Time steals everything eventually, memories in particular. You forget. And, in truth, I'd like to think that God has more important things to do with His time than to keep fucking with you."

For a moment, Clay thought he saw the slightest hint of anger bloom on her face, her canine teeth elongating to nasty points. But as quickly as it was there, it was gone.

"Do *you* remember?" she asked him.

He didn't want to lie to her. "Yes."

"Not right now," she said, "but maybe sometime, we can talk about it . . . maybe jog my memory. It just seems . . . I mean, to be unable to erase the memories I wish I could forget, and not to be able to have even a glimpse of that in my mind . . . it just hurts."

Clay reached out and laid his hand atop hers. He was not always comfortable with intimacy, but he could not ignore her pain. "I remember that there were a lot of plants, if that helps you any."

He gave her a wink, and they both laughed softly.

"Thanks," she said. "That's a big help."

"Seriously. Any time. We'll go somewhere humanity hasn't completely destroyed nature, and we'll talk about it. I'll share everything I can recall."

Eve took a long breath and let it out. "That would be wonderful." She fluttered one hand in the air. "Meanwhile, though, back to ancient conquerors and penis-shaped vegetables."

"Actually, we were moving on to dessert. Now, about that brownie sundae—"

He felt a sudden tug on the cuff of his pants and on reflex shifted the skin on his legs to resemble that of a prehistoric sea urchin, nasty spines rising up out of flesh as defense.

"Shit!" he heard a familiar voice hiss from beneath the table.

Eve heard it as well, rolling her eyes, and they both bent

forward, carefully lifting the white linen cloth. From within a pool of shadow under the table, the gnarled, leathery features of the hobgoblin peered up at them. Squire was sucking on one of his sausage thick fingers, pricked by Clay's defensive metamorphosis.

"What do you want, you little creep?" Eve asked.

"Nice to see you too, bitch," he snarled, turning to address Clay. "Sorry to cut into your lunch, but the boss wants you back at the house right away." He scrutinized his finger, squeezing a bead of blood from the wound. "Gave me a nasty prick there," he said, placing the injured finger back into his mouth.

"How apropos," Eve remarked, dropping her side of the tablecloth. "A nasty prick for a nasty prick."

DANNY Ferrick studied his reflection in the mirror over the bureau. "I think they're getting longer," he said, touching the curved horns growing from his forehead. He turned to glance at his mother.

"What do you think?"

Julia didn't *want* to think about her son's horns, let alone look at them, although it was impossible to ignore the black protrusions. "Could be," she said offhandedly, taking an overlarge New England Patriots shirt from the suitcase on the bed, folding it, and placing in a dresser nearby.

Danny was almost completely unpacked, except for some cargo pants and his toiletries, and she found herself slowing down, stalling, not really wanting to complete the task.

"You're not even looking."

Julia slid the drawer closed and reached for the cargo pants. "I looked, trust me, I just can't say."

Danny was suddenly at her side, his hand closed around her wrist, pulling her away from her task. "Look at me."

Her heart skipped a beat as she let herself see him again. He looked like something out of a bad dream; completely hairless, with horns sticking from his scalp, skin the color of burgundy wine and yellow, hypnotic eyes. This couldn't be her child—her baby boy—this was some kind of monster, a demon. But when he spoke, or looked at her in that certain way, there wasn't a doubt in her mind that this was indeed the child she loved.

A changeling. That was what Mr. Doyle had called him. A demon child, left in place of a human baby at birth by mischievous devils. The child she had given birth to was gone, long ago. Mr. Doyle insisted that her biological infant had likely been dead since shortly after his abduction. The weight of that knowledge might have killed her, the sheer black burden of it, if not for the presence of the boy left in his place. A demon child, to be raised as a human. How surprised those monsters would have been to learn that she had done exactly as they planned, and that she did not regret it. She grieved for the infant she had lost, but she loved her son, no matter how he had come to be hers.

She loved him.

Danny Ferrick was a demon, but he would always be her son.

"I'm sorry, baby," she said, pulling him into her arms and kissing the side of his bald head. His skin felt different now, like the soft leather of an expensive car seat, and she was careful not to scratch herself on his horn. "I'm being rude to you, even though I don't want to be."

He hugged her back, and she could feel a frightening strength in those arms, but also a tenderness that proved she was loved, despite what they had learned about his origins.

"Did I do something wrong?" he asked, gently removing himself from her embrace.

Julia laughed and shook her head. "If only it were that easy." She again reached for the pants in the open suitcase and removed them, refolding them. "I don't like this, Danny, any of this; your physical change, leaving home, living here." She turned toward the bureau, feeling his gaze on her.

"But you talked to Mr. Doyle. It's best that I'm here, to

learn about what's happening to me, what I am. I thought you understood that."

She pulled open the bottom drawer, where she had put his jeans earlier, and shoved the cargo pants in beside them. "It's not that I don't understand, Danny. I just don't like it."

"What's not to like?" he asked, his voice louder now, his volatile teenage temper rearing its ugly head. "Look at me, Mom. These people actually *want* me here."

She felt him move closer and, for the briefest of moments, actually felt afraid, and this angered her.

"You don't think I want you at home?" she demanded.

He sighed. "You know that's not what I meant. It's just . . . with the assholes at school, and the neighbors . . . you know I'm better off here. It'll be easier for both of—"

"I didn't raise my son to become part of some freak show," she snapped, turning to face him.

Danny chuckled humorlessly and ran a hand over his deep red pate. His fingernails were black now, like the claws of an animal.

"Okay, so I don't stay here, I come home with you, and then what?"

She didn't have an answer, so she folded her arms defensively across her chest.

"I go back to Newton and everything's just fine, is that what you think?" He laughed unhappily. "How long do you think it will be before the villagers are surrounding the house with torches?"

"Stop," Julia said. "Please, stop it." She closed her eyes, listening to the pounding rhythm of the blood in her temples. She was getting a headache; the kind that usually sent her straight to bed with all the lights out and the curtains drawn, not quite a migraine, but a bad, *return to the womb* kind of headache, as her ex-husband used to say.

"No, I won't," he said defiantly. "Things are different now—*I'm* different now." He pointed to one of the room's windows with a clawed finger. "I don't fit out there anymore."

She still had her eyes closed, the pain in her head growing with every pulse of her heart.

"Look at me!" Danny roared, and she had no choice but to open her eyes. He stood before her, arms spread, displaying what he had become. "Look at me and tell me I'm wrong."

Julia didn't know what to say. Deep down she knew he was right, but damn it she couldn't bear to let him go, to release her only child into the care of Arthur Doyle, someone she barely knew—to become part of his . . . what did he call it? His *menagerie*.

"What do we actually know about this Mr. Doyle?" she blurted out. "And the people who live here with him—don't even get me started on them. I'd just feel better if I knew . . ."

"He saved the world, ma," Danny interrupted. "And I helped." He touched the front of his Eminen T-shirt with a taloned hand. "I really don't think you need anything more by way of character references."

The world was pretty much back to normal since the bizarre occurrences of almost three weeks before, when a crimson mist had blanketed the region and the dead had crawled from their graves. Julia shivered with the memory, the hair at the back of her neck prickling to attention. It was hard to believe that everything that happened was anything other than a very bad dream, but when she looked at her son, she knew it was real.

"I want to stay here," Danny said taking a step toward her. "I need to be here."

There was a desperation in his voice that made her want to cry, as if the answers to all of his problems were right here, and she was the only obstacle standing in the way of his total fulfillment.

"Danny, please." She weighed each word carefully. "Look at this from my perspective."

"This isn't about you!" Danny bellowed, and Julia could have sworn she saw sparks of orange flame leap from his eyes. He spun away from her, bounding across the room, and brought his fist down on the mahogany dresser, splintering the top.

Julia was horribly torn. Motherly instincts told her to go to her son, to comfort him, but another voice inside her head, more attuned to self-preservation, whispered that it might be wiser to keep her distance. The moment was broken, however, and her quandary solved, when a spectral figure emerged from the ceiling, drifting down to float eerily in the center of the room. The temperature dropped several degrees, and she shivered.

No matter how many times Julia saw the ghost of Dr. Leonard Graves, she couldn't get used to it. He was a kind man, and had been a noble example of humanity while he lived, but that was the problem. Dr. Graves was dead.

"Is everything all right?" the specter asked, his gaze shifting from Julia to her son, who now knelt before his demolished dresser.

"Danny?" Graves drifted closer to the boy, and Julia noticed how much warmer it was without him near.

"I'm cool," Danny said, reaching down to touch the broken dresser. "My mom and I were just discussing how it would be best for me to go back home with her and live in the basement."

Julia sighed. "I said no such thing," she said wearily, bringing her hands to her temples in an attempt to massage away the throbbing agony in her head.

"It's completely understandable if you don't quite trust us yet," Graves said, turning his focus on her and drifting closer. "We are quite the unusual bunch."

"It's not that I don't trust you per se . . . damn it this hurts," she moaned, and stumbled slightly to one side, sitting down on the end of the bed.

"She called you all a freak show," Danny said with contempt.

Julia started to deny it, but gave up, the pain inside her skull taking away her strength to defend herself. She grimaced. "If you can believe it, I meant it in the nicest way possible."

Her eyes were closed, but she felt Graves approach, the temperature in the air dropping dramatically as he drew nearer to her.

"No offense taken," the ghost replied. "You have another headache, Mrs. Ferrick?"

She slitted her eyes open and saw that he was leaning forward to study her. Though a ghost, Leonard Graves was still quite handsome. He was a man out of time, a man of another age, but he had rugged, determined features that reminded her of Denzel Washington . . . only transparent. Julia couldn't believe she was thinking such things about a dead man and chalked it up to insanity caused by the pain inside her head.

"It's Julia, Doctor, and yes, I've got a hell of a headache."

Danny stood, holding a piece of the dresser top in his hands, and looked at her with concern. "She gets them when she's stressed out. Mom, do you want us to pull the curtains and let you lie down for awhile?"

"No, I'll be fine. Maybe a couple of Aleve from my purse will—"

"Squire often gets tension headaches," Graves stated, "and I've developed a slightly unusual, yet effective technique that helps to diminish his pain."

She began to feel herself growing nauseous. "Does it involve sacrificing a virgin or cutting the head off a chicken?" She ventured a tremulous smile.

The ghost chuckled. "Surprisingly, it doesn't."

"Would I be a candidate for this treatment, or does it only work on trolls?"

"Squire is a hobgoblin," Graves said. "Quite different from trolls actually, far better hygiene, and, yes, if you're willing, you would be a candidate."

"I'm willing," she croaked, the acid in her stomach churning from the intensity of the ache in her skull.

"All right," the ghost said. "If you'd be so kind as to remain seated and lean forward."

Julia did as she was told. The headache was coming on hard and fast now, and the pain was such that if Graves had said that a very sharp axe would now be needed, she would have helped him search for it.

"Now don't be alarmed, you're going to feel something a little strange."

The icy sensation at the back of her neck was almost pleasant, at first numbing, but then it grew intensely warm. Five points of heat pressed on the cluster of pain inside her skull. Though her eyes were closed, Julia suddenly understood what Dr. Graves was doing to her; she could see it in her mind. He had put his hand—his ghostly fingers—inside her head and was taking her headache away.

"That should do it," the doctor said, as she slowly straightened.

Julia opened her eyes and ran a cautious hand along the back of her neck. "It's gone," she said, not without a little surprise. "That's incredible." She smiled. "I feel great."

Danny stood beside the apparition of the former adventurer. "Not bad for a freak, huh, Ma?"

"Most headaches are caused by constriction of blood vessels inside the skull," Graves explained. "A little hot and cold therapy applied directly to the clusters is usually enough to alleviate the symptoms."

"I feel as though I should write you a check or something," Julia said, relishing the relief from her agony.

"The only payment I ask is that you extend the trust you gave to me to the others of this household."

What he was asking her to do was likely to pain her far more than any headache ever could, but deep down she knew that it was indeed best for Danny. Besides, how could she be steered wrong by the one of the world's most famous scientists and adventurers? Ghost or not, this was Dr. Leonard Graves. Not trusting him would be like calling Elliot Ness a crook.

Julia smiled at the comparison, these two men from the annals of twentieth-century American history.

"You'll have to call me every other night," she told her son.

Danny nodded. "I can do that."

"And I want to be able to visit. Nothing crazy, just to be able to see that you're doing all right."

"That can be arranged as well," Graves responded. "I'll see that you are given a key. And you'll have a guest room at your disposal whenever you like."

"So does that mean I can stay?" Danny asked.

"Let's just say I'm willing to try it," Julia answered, trying to quell a slight twinge of unease.

There came a knock at the door, and it swung open. Squire ambled into the room without an invitation.

"Sorry to interrupt. Hey, love what you're doing with the place," he said sarcastically, nodding his potato shaped head at the dresser. "Fuckin' kids today," he added with a disgusted grumble.

"What can we do for you, Squire?" Graves asked, distracting the hobgoblin from glowering at the boy.

"Mr. Doyle wants to see everybody in the study."

Danny pointed to himself.

"You, too, horny Joe," the hobgoblin said, turning to leave. "Go a little easier on the furniture downstairs, would ya?"

Danny followed Squire into the hall. "I'll talk to you later," he called, waving to Julia, leaving her alone with Graves.

She didn't know how to feel. "I love you, Ma," she muttered as she stood up from the bed looking for her purse, preparing to leave.

"Mrs. Ferrick . . . Julia," Leonard Graves said. She found her pocketbook and slung the strap over her shoulder, turning toward the ghost. He smiled at her reassuringly, raising his hand to hold a forefinger and thumb slightly apart. "Only a little bit of trust."

"It's the least I can do," she answered with a smile, and then watched as his body became even more immaterial, dropping down through the floor until he was gone.

Leaving her alone with the weight of her decision.

FROM the window of his study, Conan Doyle watched Julia Ferrick leaving his home and striding purposefully toward her car, which sat in one of the few legal parking spaces in the affluent Beacon Hill neighborhood of Louisburg Square. His sight was perfect again, perhaps even a bit better than that. He was glad that he had decided to pay Fulcanelli more than was necessary for his efforts; the chemist had outdone himself.

He let the heavy curtain fall back into place and turned just as young Daniel Ferrick entered the room. Eve and Clay, the eldest of his menagerie, sat side by side on the sofa. Dr. Graves stood behind them with his arms crossed, not quite as translucent as usual. Graves was focused at the moment on the substantial world. Danny glanced around for a moment, an odd expression on his face as he regarded the furniture, before sitting himself on the floor, his back against the sofa.

The only one who had yet to arrive was Ceridwen, and Conan Doyle felt his pulse quicken at the thought of her. *Silly git,* he chided, surprised that the Fey sorceress could still have such an effect upon him after so long. What had been between them once was no more. They had become allies again, but it went no further. *Must be getting soft in my old age.*

Squire entered the room carrying a long serving tray laden with a pitcher of ice water flavored with lemon slices, red grapes, crackers, and a selection of cheeses. He set the tray down upon a wheeled cart just inside the door.

"Have you seen Ceridwen, Squire?" Conan Doyle asked.

The goblin snatched up a piece of cheese from the tray and popped it into his mouth. "Saw her on the top floor about ten minutes ago and told her there was a powwow," he said, chewing noisily. "She was still working on reestablishing that doorway between the house and Faerie, ironing out the wrinkles and all. Said she'd be right along."

Conan Doyle nodded. It was powerful magic she was attempting alone, and he wondered if the sorceress might require his assistance. As soon as this meeting was concluded, he would seek her out.

From a cabinet of dark wood, he retrieved a crystal decanter of scotch and a glass tumbler. "May I interest any of you in something with a bit more bite?"

Clay declined as he rose and went to fill a plate with crackers and grapes.

"I'd love a jolt, thanks," Eve said from the couch.

"Me, too," Danny added.

Graves glared down at the boy from where he hovered. "I think not," he said coldly.

"It was worth a try." The boy shrugged, getting up and going to the cart for some water.

"I'll pass," Squire said, perching on the edge of the loveseat with a plate stacked with cheese. "Make it a point not to drink any hard stuff until after five." The hobgoblin had a bite of one of the cheese wedges. "Unless I'm already shitfaced, that is."

Conan Doyle sighed and rolled his eyes as he crossed the room to bring Eve her drink.

"Here's mud in your eye," she said with a sly smile, raising the tumbler in a toast. "And speaking of eyes, the new one looks fabulous. Who did it for you, Agrippa?" She tossed the scotch back in one go, then ran her tongue over her lips comically. "Not as nutritiously satisfying as the red stuff, but not without its merits."

"Always the lady, Eve," Conan Doyle said. "No, Agrippa and I had a bit of a falling out, so I decided to go with someone local. Fulcanelli in the North End; do you know him?"

"Only by reputation." She studied his newly acquired eye. "He does nice work."

Clay returned to the sofa and offered her a cracker. She declined with a wrinkling of her nose.

"So, what's the scoop?" she asked Conan Doyle. "I'm sure you didn't call this little meeting just to chitchat and show off your new peeper."

Conan Doyle crossed the room to an empty wing back chair in the corner, *his* chair, and sat down. He set his drink down and picked up a file folder from a small table beside him.

"I received a phone call from one of our informants in Athens," he said as he opened the folder. "As well as these digital photographs over the Internet shortly thereafter."

Squire got up, took the printed photos and brought them to Eve. "Pass 'em down when you're done."

She glared at him.

"Hey, if those don't do anything for ya, I've got some back at my room that might be more to your liking," the hobgoblin winked salaciously.

"I think I'm going to be sick," Eve said, as Squire sauntered back to his seat.

"Before that, please peruse the pictures, if you would be so kind," Conan Doyle said picking up his glass and taking a sip of scotch.

Eve still had her sunglasses on, but now she removed them to examine the pictures more carefully. "Okay, I'm game. What's up with the statues?" she asked, passing the digital printouts to Clay.

"They weren't always statues," the shapeshifter said grimly, looking up to meet Doyle's eyes.

"Precisely."

"Any idea what's responsible?" Clay asked, rising to give the pictures to Graves.

Conan Doyle shook his head, resting his glass on the arm of the leather chair. "Nothing as yet. There are any number of supernatural causes ranging from a transmutation spell gone horribly awry to Basilisk poisoning."

"Let me see," Danny said, pulling the pictures away from

Graves. "Oh, damn," he said, his red eyes growing wide. "These used to be people?"

"Tourists," Conan Doyle explained.

"Almost like people," Eve added.

"So I'm guessing we're going to Greece," Clay said, rising from the sofa to set his empty plate on the cart.

Conan Doyle downed the last of his drink before answering. "Not all of you," he said. "I'd like you, Clay, to go to Athens to investigate, with Dr. Graves and Squire."

Clay nodded his acceptance of the mission, as did the spectral Graves.

"That sucks," Danny grumbled as Doyle got up to refill his glass. "I wouldn't mind a trip to Greece."

Conan Doyle studied the boy a moment, still evaluating him. "Perhaps another time."

Eve cleared her throat. "So what about the rest of us?" she asked, crossing her long legs. "Are we free to go about our business?"

The ominous words of his old teacher Lorenzo Sanguedolce echoed through Conan Doyle's mind. *The clock is ticking toward the fate of the world,* the mage had warned, and Conan Doyle believed this to be true, but did not know when the metaphorical clock would chime. He did not want to be caught unawares.

"No," he responded. "The rest of you will remain here with me."

He poured himself another scotch. A double this time.

"Better to be safe than sorry."

3

NIGEL Gull stood in the customs line at Logan International Airport and waited to show his passport to a security guard. The long flight from Athens had been a test of his patience, thanks to the rudeness of his fellow passengers, but he had been relatively comfortable in the first-class section. Over the years he had grown inured to the stares of those who were ignorant or insensitive. He did not need a mirror to remind him how freakish his appearance was, his skull so misshapen that his face looked more like a horse's than a human's. No, every idiot who stared at him was his mirror. He saw himself in and through their eyes. Once upon a time there had lived in England a man named John Merrick who was publicly referred to as the Elephant Man, because it was believed he had a rare condition called elephantiasis. In subsequent years Merrick's actual ailment had been debated, but the name remained.

The Elephant Man.

Gull had been repulsed by the circus that had surrounded Merrick. He knew the source of his own freakish appearance but had no desire to be paraded around London as the Horse-headed man, or some such. He was a human being, despite the equine influence that was evident in his eyes and ears and the length and shape of his head.

No, all in all, the flight had been innocuous enough. Now, though, as he and his two traveling companions made their way down the long corridor toward the customs area, they were herded along with the rest of the passengers, as well as those from two other flights that had arrived nearly simultaneously. Logan Airport was the hub of air travel not only in Boston, but in all of New England, particularly for overseas travel. There were plenty of gawking children, adults who alternated between open astonishment and averting their gaze, and a pair of teenagers with so little breeding that they actually clutched one another, pointing and laughing.

"Oh, shit. What is up with that?" one of them crowed, a dark-skinned boy in an oversized basketball jersey.

Gull ignored them. He felt his companions stiffen, however. They walked on either side of him as though they were his bodyguards, when in fact they were his friends and associates. On his left was a distinguished, silver-haired gentleman, well-dressed in a sport coat and trousers. Nick Hawkins looked as though he had just left a fitting at the tailor's rather than just disembarked from a six-hour transatlantic flight. At first glance, women were taken by the man's chiseled features and insouciant smile. Then they saw the cold emptiness of his eyes.

Hawkins had proven himself an asset time and time again. He had gifts he had only begun to tap in the employment of the British government, but he had chosen to work with Gull instead. The benefits were far greater. Anything Nick Hawkins could imagine, his association with Gull could enable him to achieve. And Hawkins had quite an imagination.

Gull's other companion drew nearly as many stares as he did himself, though for far different reasons. The girl was fifteen—or perhaps sixteen, he could not recall her age at her last birthday—and quite stunning. Her hair was a rich cinnamon, her eyes ocean green, and she walked with the confident strut that was part dancer, part prizefighter. Her jeans hung so low on her hips it seemed impossible for them to remain in place, and her top came down to just beneath her breasts, leaving what seemed to be yards of beautiful pale abdomen and a tiny dimpled navel exposed for public view.

Jezebel was a force of nature. Gull's heart filled with pride at the sight of her. She swept the attention of others in her wake, commanding them without a glance. But even her radiance was not enough to draw all eyes from Gull's hideousness. When the pair of teenaged boys laughed and pointed at him, she and Hawkins had both tensed. The suave gentleman turned gray, soulless eyes on Gull, who shook his head. But Jezebel was not so easily discouraged.

"Come on, then," she said playfully, linking her arm with his as they moved up in the customs line. "Let me hurt them. Just a bit of a scorching ought to do for the lads well enough."

Gull frowned. "Do nothing, Jez. You cause any trouble and we may have to wait 'round till it gets sorted. I can't have that, yeah? You just be my good girl. I promise you'll have plenty of fun later on."

Jezebel rolled her eyes, tucked a lock of cinnamon hair behind her ear, and spun around to face him, walking backward in the line. "As long as you promise. I'll be good. I'm always good, aren't I, Nick?"

The girl enjoyed baiting Hawkins, but the man was stone-faced. His years with British Intelligence had honed him to such a fine edge that he was too sharp, too dangerous, even for them. One nubile girl was not going to dull his edge. No matter what else she might be capable of.

"You're always good, love," Hawkins replied at last, but Jezebel had already turned to hand her passport to the customs agent.

Gull waited for his turn, Hawkins taking up a position behind him. The teenagers continued to snicker and made rude comments under their breath. The tall, malformed man lifted a large hand and scratched at his chin. His brows knitted in consternation. For well over a century he had endured such idiocy. But sometimes he ran out of patience. He glanced back at Hawkins and nodded. The handsome man remained expressionless as he reached into his jacket pocket in search of his British passport. As he withdrew it, he fumbled it, and it dropped to the floor not far from the two boys.

Hawkins stepped out of line, closing the distance between himself and the teens. He crouched to pick up his passport, and as he did, he let the fingers of his left hand brush the shoe of the nearest, a slight boy with delicate features.

If Gull had not had exceptional hearing and been paying close attention he would have lost Hawkins's words in the susurrus of voices in the terminal. But he was able to decipher them, lagging a bit even as Jezebel finished with the customs agent.

"Your friend here is going to get pinched for smuggling drugs later this year. He's going to sell you out. In prison, you'll be shanked in the shower, cut wide open so your intestines are hanging out, and while your blood runs down the drain, they'll take turns raping you, so the last thing you know will be the pain of your rectum tearing and the weight of a murderer with heinous breath upon your back."

The silver-haired gentleman held up his passport, brandishing it so that Gull could see it, as if letting his companion know there was no problem. As if he had said nothing. He smiled an empty smile and returned to the line, even as Gull handed his own identification to the customs agent.

"Fuck! You're a fucking nut! Sick fucking freak!" the teen was shouting.

But no one else had heard Hawkins speak, and all they saw was an ill-mannered lout of a boy screaming at a distinguished businessman. Hawkins shook his head as though the boy's behavior was beneath him to even acknowledge and waited patiently for his turn with customs.

Fifteen minutes later they had retrieved their luggage

from the baggage claim. Jezebel secured a cart and helped Hawkins load it, and now they wheeled it in silence through the busy terminal as travelers moved out of their way. The electronic doors parted to make way for them, and they emerged onto the sidewalk in front of the airport, where a line of limousines and taxicabs waited.

Cold rain swept down from dark skies heavy with thunderheads. It was midafternoon, but the gloom pretended evening. The cars that rolled beneath the overhanging roof that kept the emerging travelers dry dripped with rain, leaving damp tire tracks in their passing.

Nigel Gull paused on the sidewalk, his distended nostrils widening. It had been raining lightly when they landed, but the storm had gotten much worse in the subsequent forty minutes. He snorted in displeasure.

"A singularly unlovely day."

Jezebel had slipped on her burgundy leather jacket. Now she left the luggage cart and stood beside him, gazing out at the storm. Her left hand gripped his arm, and she lay her head against his shoulder.

"No," Gull began. "Jez, love, you don't have to—"

"Hush," the girl said.

Gull's heart swelled. Such a sweet child. He would never have a daughter of his own, but in Jezebel he had found a girl who was everything he could ever have wanted as a legacy. How he loved her. As he watched, her beautiful, delicate face became dark and cruel. Her eyes were closed tightly, her features lined with intensity. She shook, and her grip on his arm tightened. A drop of blood bubbled out of her right nostril, steaming, and when it fell to the sidewalk it evaporated on contact with the concrete.

Her eyes flickered open. A mist seemed to rise off of those orbs, the same ocean green as her irises. Then a smile blossomed on her face and she went impossibly rigid beside him. Gull was at once fearful for her and enchanted. She was never more beautiful than in the throes of her power. Her personal magic.

Her grip relaxed, and she slumped against him. Gull put an arm around her shoulders and at last tore his gaze from her. As far as he could see, the rain had ceased. The black clouds were thinning, burning off, and in several places the sun peeked through, revealing a hint of blue sky beyond.

"It will be nice now," Jezebel said, her words slurring. "Spectacular, even." She glanced around for Hawkins and spotted him a few feet away, studying the line of limousines that stood at the curb, their drivers standing in front of them, each holding a sign scrawled with the name of their client.

"Nick, lovey, get us a car, won't you? I need somewhere to fall."

Hawkins glanced at her, then at Gull. He said nothing, for Jezebel was irritating him on purpose. She knew full well that he was already in the process of choosing their transportation. Women passing by watched him appreciatively as they dragged their wheeled baggage toward waiting taxis. But despite Jezebel's exhaustion, Gull had no interest in a taxi. He would not ride in one in London, nor would he do so here in the States.

"Only a moment, Jez," Gull promised her.

But the girl had already closed her eyes again and seemed on the verge of falling asleep where she stood, leaning on him.

After another moment, Hawkins began to walk along the line of limousines, idly brushing his fingers against each of them as he passed. At the third—a long ghost-white model—he paused. Gull thought he saw a tiny smile flicker across Hawkins's face, but it might have been his imagination.

"Mr. Gull," Hawkins said, beckoning to him.

With Jezebel staggering somnambulently at his side, Gull grasped the handle of the luggage cart and wheeled it toward the limousine. He reached it just as Hawkins was approaching the driver, who stood in front of the vehicle holding a small white cardboard sign stenciled with the name E. POWELL.

"Hello there, are you Bob, then?" Hawkins asked the driver.

The young man with the black suit and the E. POWELL sign flinched and then looked Hawkins up and down in frank appraisal.

"Can I help you, sir?" the driver asked.

"You are Bob, yes?"

"Yes, sir?"

"Ah, excellent," Hawkins said. "I apologize for keeping you waiting. I missed my flight and had to take the next one. I know you've been here for quite some time . . . two hours, is it? I'll make sure to add a large gratuity to the company charge."

Bob smiled in relief. "You're Mr. Powell," he said. "I was beginning to wonder if I was in the wrong place. I called in, and they said to wait another twenty minutes or so. Truth is, I was about to leave."

Hawkins glanced over his shoulder at Gull and Jezebel. "Well, then it seems we've arrived just in time."

The driver frowned, glancing once at the others but then trying his best not to *see* them, Gull because of his hideousness, Jezebel because of her beauty. "Oh. I didn't realize there were three of you. The slip said one passenger."

"Is that a problem?"

"No. No, of course not. There's plenty of room, Mr. Powell."

Then he smiled and opened the door for Gull and Jezebel. They climbed into the expansive rear of the limousine, and she stretched out full length on one of the seats, instantly asleep. Moments later Bob was sliding behind the wheel and Hawkins was climbing into the rear of the limousine, and then they were drawing away from the airport.

Above them, the clouds had all but disappeared. The sky was clear and blue, and the sun shone warmly down upon the limousine as it made its way toward the heart of Boston.

"Oh, Bob," Hawkins called.

"Yes, Mr. Powell?"

"Change of destination, my boy. We're going to be staying with a local associate this trip."

"Whatever you say, sir. So, where are we headed?" the driver asked.

"Beacon Hill," Gull replied, his mind darkening with memory now. "Louisburg Square. I've come to visit an old friend."

"Yeah," Bob said, nodding sagely. "That's nice. Visiting old friends."

Gull gazed out the window, but he could no longer see the beautiful day that Jezebel had given him. His eyes stared, instead, into the shadows of the past.

THE ninth of August 1902. Coronation Day. But Nigel Gull had neither the inclination nor the invitation to attend Edward's installment as king. Even if he had, he had spent the day and the evening performing a different service to the Crown. It was long after dark, now, when sensible people were in their beds. Gull rarely slept.

The rail station at Clapham Junction was dark and deserted as he made his way along the platform, gaze plumbing the shadows all around. It had begun to rain an hour or two before, and the storm cast a shroud upon everything it touched. Gull's eyesight was keen, however, and the rain would not inhibit him. He could see, for instance, that nothing moved in the gallery on the far side of the tracks, where passengers would await the morning train come dawn. Within the station itself, all seemed still and undisturbed. Yet he could feel it. In the damp air there were traces of malign magick, echoes of a sinister presence. Gull thought the author of such dark deeds was no longer at the scene, but caution guided him, nevertheless.

Three separate sets of rails ran through Clapham Junction. On the center track there sat a charcoal black steam engine with the number one painted on its face in silver. Rain pelted it, making it gleam even in the dark. No steam rose from the engine, but it seemed a watchful thing, just the same, as though it might burst to sudden life at any moment. Behind it was a single coal tender, and attached to that, two elegant Pullman cars with crimson wooden panels beneath each window and gilt stenciling above. It was a private train and spoke of powerful wealth.

Gull leaped from the platform into the rain. It streamed down his misshapen face, a moist caress that only served to remind him of his appearance. He shook off the rain and dipped his chin, feeling the storm at his back as he crossed the first set of tracks. The engine's cab was dark but that was his first stop. Gull climbed up inside Number One and found it empty as he had expected.

He moved more quietly now, slipping out of the cab to the ground. The rain was cold and cruel, punishing him as he crept slowly along beside the tender until he reached the steps up onto the first Pullman. Hand on the rail, he went up and then found himself before the ornate door of the car. Gull muttered to himself a few words of ancient Aramaic, and the fingers of his left hand began to burn with a tainted yellow light. For illumination, and for defense, in case his instincts were wrong and the culprit remained.

The door swung open easily. Gull moved into the car and raised his hand, splashing a sickly golden glow across the car. His breath caught. The opulence of the Pullman was startling. The floor was covered with Oriental carpet, the windows curtained by velvet drapes. A trio of crystal chandeliers hung from the high ceilings, and the windows were etched glass. The wood gleamed richly.

The car was empty.

Gull would have sensed anything lurking in the shadows through his light. There was nothing beneath the tables here.

He hurried, now, moving through the Pullman as swiftly as he was able. When he reached the door at the other end he paused only a moment before drawing open the door.

The dead girl lay on the platform between trains. Her hair was dark, but might have been lighter were it not sod-

den with the rain. Her body had been forced through an opening in the ornate railings, and she was splayed there, her arms spread out, her head hanging several inches from the platform, thrown back, mouth wide open.

She was unclothed, her flesh pale, save where arcane symbols had been carved into her. The storm had washed the blood away. Tiny puddles of rainwater had accumulated in the hollows of her eyes, and the storm had filled her open mouth as well. Rain dribbled from one corner of her lips, sluicing down her cheek and falling down into the space between cars.

She was no more than seven.

Nigel Gull knew his own heart. There was little therein that was spectacularly noble. Yet the sight tore at him. The villain was gone, the one responsible for the girl's death, who had killed her in ritual sacrifice as part of some spell to hide himself. He had attempted to murder King Edward on this eve of his coronation, not expecting other mages to be there to prevent it. Then he had fled here.

Had he found the girl somewhere along the way, or kept her awaiting her demise as a prisoner in the luxury of his private train . . . just in case he needed her life? Gull found he did not want to know the answer.

But he needed to know.

And though it made him shudder to think of it, though his spirit cried out that it was an abomination in itself, he realized he knew a way to retrieve that information. Nigel Gull had learned from the greatest of mages, Lorenzo Sanguedolce—the man many called Sweetblood, the literal translation of his name. The mage's other apprentice had been horrified, but Sanguedolce himself had not passed judgment at all, when Gull had looked too deeply into ancient Egyptian magicks that had been forbidden even to the high priests of that age. He had acquired certain hideous • skills on that night, at the cost of his face, and he had never yet employed them.

But this . . . it seemed almost as though his sacrifice on

that evening several years past had been in preparation for this. For one of those skills was The Voice of the Dead.

Sickened, stomach churning, but more determined now than he had ever felt, Gull stepped through the opening in the railing and straddled the platforms between the two Pullman cars. He clutched the railing and leaned over far enough that he could slide his free hand beneath the dangling head of the dead girl. Rain spilled off of her eyes, and some slid from her mouth. One of the sigils sliced in her chest opened slightly, the wound resembled an eyelid, leaking pink tears.

Gull stared into her face. Perfect, shattered innocence. He closed his own eyes tightly and drew a breath to steady himself. Then he pulled her head toward him and placed his lips over hers in a grotesque kiss. Lifting and tilting her head all at once, he drank the rainwater from the mouth of the dead girl as though her skull was his goblet.

"Dear God, Gull! What are you doing?"

Startled, he let the girl's head drop, leaving her wedged into the railing, and crossed over the small gap above the coupling to the second Pullman car, turning all in the same motion to face the figure who had appeared so suddenly behind him. The horror and disgust in the new arrival's tone was engraved upon his features as well, but the man did not seem surprised. It was, rather, as though his discovery of Gull in the midst of such an apparently odious act only confirmed what he had always believed.

"Well, well, well . . ." Gull said, feeling the magick working within him, feeling the thoughts and feelings of the dead girl fill him. Her name had been Carolyn but everyone called her Cass. She was from Derbyshire. The sorcerer had stolen her from her own bed before coming to London to kill the king.

"Speak up, man!" the other demanded.

Even as Gull continued on. "If it isn't Sir Arthur."

Conan Doyle flinched. Rain dripped from his mustache, plastering it to his face. Gull wanted to smile at the sight of *the distaste in his eyes, but he was too connected now to the echo of the girl that was inside him. Still, he saw it. Even as he tried to make sense of what he'd found Gull engaged in, Conan Doyle was bristling at the insult. For during the coronation ceremony, he had been knighted by the king. The man had spent his life in service to his country as a doctor, a writer, and an outspoken private citizen, working tirelessly against the enemies of the Crown, but disdained the idea of a reward. In truth he had accepted only to avoid insult to the king, and the wrath of his aging mother.*

Gull knew this, and it made him all the more bitter. Conan Doyle was his friend and his fellow apprentice to Sanguedolce, but he had not the other man's station or experience. He would have sacrificed almost anything for such an honor.

"I'll have an answer," Conan Doyle said, the suspicion in his gaze now burning with a crackle of blue magick. The energy misted from his eyes and sparked around his fingers.

"Ah, you think me the villain now," Gull said. "Of course. The freak, the twisted one, is tainted so he must be evil. You're so very predictable, Sir Arthur."

"Stop calling me that!" Conan Doyle snarled.

A fight was in the offing. But Gull knew they could not afford the indulgence. The true villain was escaping, and the dead, violated flesh of the innocent he had destroyed was only growing colder.

"My name is Cass," he said . . . but it was not really Gull who spoke. His mouth moved, and he generated the words as if reading them from the echoes of the dead girl's spirit that moved within him, but it was her voice.

The Voice of the Dead.

"He is a tall man, thin, and he wears spectacles. His jacket is long and fancy. His name is Graham," Gull went on, the sweet, angelic voice of the murdered girl issuing from his lips.

Conan Doyle recoiled, taking a step back into the open door of the Pullman. "What black sorcery is this, Gull? This is the gift you received from Anubis, the power for which you let yourself be disfigured?"

"Only one of them," Gull replied, still in the voice of the dead girl. "Only one. And would you not listen, now, Arthur? Is your disdain so great you will not hear the voice of this savaged child, so that we might find her defiler?"

Conan Doyle's mouth opened, his expression revealing his intent to deliver a righteous tirade. But then his gaze shifted to the naked, carved body of the girl, and he faltered. Anger burned in his eyes but the spark of magick in them receded. His fists clenched at his sides, and he nodded once.

"Go on."

Gull felt for the echoes within him again and once more spoke in the Voice of the Dead, searching the fragments of her spirit for the clues that would lead them to her killer. He felt confident it would work. It must work. The friendship he had shared with Conan Doyle, tenuous as it had always been, would never be the same after this. Gull knew it even then. But he was no stranger to sacrifice, when the stakes were high enough, and he accepted this loss without hesitation.

"He spoke of Norwich as home," said the dead girl's voice.

Conan Doyle nodded. "That may be where he's headed."

AFTER he had finished conferring with his agents about their assignment in Greece, Conan Doyle excused himself and retreated deeper into the house. It was pleasant to have them all together beneath his roof, and he knew they would take some small time to socialize. This was only right and natural. And it was important, as well, for them to continue to get to know one another better, to develop their relationships. Sanguedolce had issued dire warnings upon Conan Doyle's last encounter with him, and there was no doubt that the Menagerie would be needed once again before long. He had not revealed to them all of what Sanguedolce had said to him about The DemoGorgon, an entity of cosmic evil that was, even now, making its way across the universe toward this world. He would bear the weight of that threat himself, for the moment, and do all he could to see that when the DemoGorgon arrived at last, they were prepared.

But that was for another day, another year. Perhaps even another lifetime. For now, there were other threats and other concerns.

Smoothing his jacket, tugging at his sleeves, he stood a bit straighter and made his way up the stairs. The banister was smooth under his touch. Upon the wall beside the stairs hung portraits of long ago friends such as Houdini and Barrie and Colonel Cody. Elsewhere in the house there were portraits of Innes and Jean and the Ma'am. All were remnants of another life, melancholy echoes of another age. Yet rather than sadden him, their presence comforted him and lent him strength.

A smile pushed up the ends of his mustache as he crested the landing. Conan Doyle made his way down a long corridor, turned and followed another, and with every step he could feel the electric tingle of magick in the air. He breathed deeply, and on the air he caught the scent of flowers so sweet they could only grow in Faerie. That alone soothed him, the air of Faerie filling his lungs, refreshing him.

Ceridwen stood at the end of the corridor, her long, lithe form draped in sheer silk the deep blue of the horizon just before sunset. The wind from Faerie blew through an open door, each gust causing the silk to cling to her sensuous form in such a way as to make his breath catch in his throat. The pain of regret still lingered between them, and he had not dared to suggest that they might put aside the harms of the past, but there was no denying the emotion that remained.

The door was the very one Conan Doyle had once used to leave her, to leave Faerie—he had thought forever. He had sealed it behind him, this passage between worlds, and only recently had been forced by circumstance to open it again, to return and plead for her aid. In the crisis that ensued, the passageway had been destroyed.

Now, Ceridwen had rebuilt it. The question in Conan Doyle's heart was, to what end?

"You can return home, now," he said, damning himself for the quaver in his voice.

Ceridwen stared a moment longer through the door. As Conan Doyle joined her, he could see the trees and hills of Faerie and a stream that flowed gently along a curving path, burbling over stones.

Then the elemental sorceress, the niece of King Finvarra of the Fey, turned to him. Her features were fine and noble, cheekbones high, violet eyes wide and commanding. Yet he knew her. Loved her as no one ever had. And he saw the sadness and doubt in her gaze.

"I could," she agreed. A glint of magic sparkled in her gaze. "And I could return, from time to time. This passage makes it convenient enough. For now, though . . . it seems to me that the recent troubles in Faerie were inextricably tied to the misery that befell this world. The connection between the two seems stronger than it has been in quite some time, so that what threatens one realm threatens them all. It may be that a new dark age is imminent. If so, I believe that I will do more good working with you and your clan here than at home."

Her proud gaze faltered a moment, and she glanced away. Then she lifted her chin and met his eye. "That is, if you have no objection."

Conan Doyle wanted to reach out to her, to pull her into his embrace and feel the soft silk of her robes beneath his touch. He wanted to laugh with surprise and pleasure. But Ceridwen would not have approved. He had hurt her badly, once upon a time. Perhaps there would come a time when all the detritus of their past could be brushed aside and the simple adoration they had once felt for each other could be reborn. For now, though, they were separated by the ruin of things that might have been. But Ceridwen wanted to stay, and that meant there was hope.

"My dear, you are welcome in my home from this night until the last night of the world."

Her pale, blue-white marbled skin flushed slightly pink, but only for a moment. Ceridwen nodded, softening. "I am pleased. We may be at the forefront of a new round of Twilight Wars, and there is no one at whose side I would rather fight."

The blush of a smile whispered across her face and in her violet eyes he saw the innocent heart he had known, years before. It was gone, then, hidden beneath the hardened wisdom of the time since, but as Ceridwen nodded her thanks and then set off down the corridor away from him, Conan Doyle found happy contentment in the knowledge that it was still there, within her. Regardless of what might or might not happen between them in the future, he silently vowed never to disappoint her again.

THE roads were still slick with recent rain but the sky was crystal blue, the kind of day that seemed like a gift. Nigel Gull did not like the rain. It spoke to him with the voices of the dead, yet only in unintelligible whispers. The ghosts of words he couldn't really hear. Now he sat in the back of the limousine and glanced at Jezebel, sleeping soundly where she lay sprawled on the seat, and he cherished her. She was always looking out for him, poor girl. Gull intended to return the favor.

The windows were down slightly, and there was a salty tang to the air that blew in. A stranger to Boston, he had known it was near the ocean but had not understood exactly how integral was the relationship between city and harbor. Gull breathed in deeply, savoring the breeze.

"We're coming up on it now," the driver reported.

Gull raised an eyebrow. Jezebel did not stir, but Hawkins glanced curiously out the window. Gull leaned over Jezebel and caught sight of a row of well-kept brownstones on one side and a perfectly manicured little park on the other.

"Which one is it?" Hawkins asked, his voice a rasp. He stared out through the glass like a caged lion, confident that one day he would be free.

The brownstones had been built so that they shared a single face, and yet those faces had been individualized over the years. Some had flowers in window boxes. Bright curtains hung in the windows of one building. Another had the frames around every window painted a bright yellow, and a door of the same color. But at the corner was the one Gull was searching for. He could sense the magick emanating from it, could taste it on the air even more strongly than the salt of the ocean.

"There," he said. "That one."

Hawkins leaned toward the front seat and instructed the driver, and a moment later they parked beside the curb in front of the home of Arthur Conan Doyle. At last Jezebel came around. Her eyelids fluttered, and she turned to give him a sleepy smile.

"That was fast," she mumbled.

Gull patted her shoulder. "Rest a while longer, Jez. Think I ought to have a word before we drag out the luggage." He glanced at Hawkins, who nodded and leaned forward to explain to the driver. Gull paid little attention to the words as he opened the door and stepped out.

For several seconds he only stood there, staring at the house. It was solid and respectable—precisely the sort of place Conan Doyle had always favored—but otherwise unremarkable, save for the magickal defenses around it. They were substantial. Gull thought that they might pose a challenge even to him, should he be inclined to try to force his way in. But he thought that he ought to try things the easy way first.

Basking in the coils and jets of magick that swirled around the house he approached the steps. It was very much like walking under water. An ordinary man would not even have noticed, but Gull was a powerful mage and the defenses dragged at him. Had he any ill intentions they would already have immobilized him. Or he would have destroyed them, one way or the other.

It was so much simpler to walk up those steps and knock on the door.

He never got there.

Even as he approached the stone steps, a lithe, dark shape darted across the front of the house, low to the ground. It leaped up onto the stairs, joined immediately by another from the opposite side. From around the far side of the brownstone was yet another. A fourth emerged from the sewer grating in the road and slunk over to join his brothers and sisters upon the stairs, blocking his way.

Cats. Each of them black as midnight. Others darted for the stairs as well. One slunk out from beneath the limousine, as though it had been waiting there for his arrival. The moment it reached the steps—making nine of them in total—all of the creatures froze, focusing on Gull with their yellow eyes slitted in warning. As one, they hissed, fur standing up as they arched their backs.

Gull paused five feet from the bottom step, regarding the felines. Their hissed warning bothered him not at all. What caused him to hesitate was the way the cats moved so intently and with such single purpose. They were spread all across the brick stairs, nine pair of jaundiced, cruel eyes. And then they began to change.

It was subtle, at first. Their jaws stretched wider and the fangs inside grew longer, gleaming in the sunshine of the perfect day. The vicious pools of shadow began to grow, then, fur rippling like cornfields in the breeze as the cats stretched their backs and scraped claws on brick, doubling in size.

The growth stopped them. It was startling, but not so much so that a passerby on the street would have believed he had seen anything impossible. *Unsettling*, yes. But not impossible.

Until the cat in the center—Gull believed it to be the one that had slipped from beneath the limousine—stood up on its hind legs. Its bones and muscles popped as its body was altered. Gull's breath caught in his throat. It was a terrible thing, the size of a panther but its eyes full of sentient malignance. Saliva slid in thin strings from its open jaws with their glistening fangs.

"Well, well," Gull said, cautious and admiring. "Nice kitty."

It appeared that Conan Doyle was not relying merely on spells and wards to protect his home.

With a chorus of hissing, the cats started down the stairs toward Gull. Several of the others had started to grow again, and their leader was becoming more hideous looking, more demonic with every passing moment.

The front door of the house opened with a clank of the latch and a creak as the heavy wood swung wide. Conan Doyle stood on the threshold and gazed down at his visitor. After a moment he made a gesture. All of a sudden, the cats were only ordinary things once more, at least on the surface. Just cats. They scattered, disappearing beneath cars and beside stairs, one of them running into the house.

Conan Doyle did not seem at all surprised. He only stared, grim and unsmiling.

"You might have saved yourself some trouble if you'd called before paying me a visit."

"It's no trouble," Gull assured him.

Conan Doyle's eyes darkened, flickering with promised danger like lightning in the night sky.

"That, old friend, remains to be seen."

4

I N Nigel Gull's experience, there was an element of the surreal in living long past the ordinary human life span. He could not imagine what it must have been like to be truly immortal, but was not at all certain he would have liked to find out. Once he had outlived the era of his birth, it had begun in earnest. Gull was an anachronism, and he knew it. A man with the sensibilities of another age—a time both more genteel and more savage—and yet he was also hungry for evolution, for the experience of the future.

Conan Doyle was the only one of his contemporaries still alive and one of the few men in the world who could have understood what he was experiencing. Once upon a time they had been like brothers, in both the best and worst sense of the comparison. Now they were estranged.

How odd, then, to find himself sitting on the sofa in Arthur's study—a room whose decor seemed designed to replicate the past—as though they had stepped back in time and were allies once more, fellow students of the great Sanguedolce, whom the British occult masters had called Sweetblood as a dismissive sobriquet, as though he were beneath them. They had all learned who was the master, but only Conan Doyle and Gull, dabblers in the craft, had become his pupils.

Gull watched his old associate across the room. Doyle was fixing drinks, exuding an air of calm and civility as he acted the perfect host, though in reality the tension in the room was so thick, it was almost palpable.

And this will not do, not at all.

"Lovely house, Arthur. Bit of old King George, isn't it?" Gull asked genially. "Getting nostalgic in your old age. And what were those delightful creatures that greeted me at your doorstep?"

Jezebel snuggled closer to him on the sofa, resting her head adoringly on his shoulder. Her eyes were closed as though she were napping. She had a tendency to become clingy in the presence of strangers, but Gull didn't mind. The girl was loyal to him. That was the vital part.

"Were-kitties," she said into the crook of his neck and began to giggle.

Conan Doyle crossed the room, a tumbler of scotch in each hand. "Actually, they're Krukis, recently immigrated from Romania," he said handing Gull his drink. "It's startling what one can employ for a warm saucer of milk and an occasional can of tuna fish."

He took the other glass of scotch to Hawkins, who had stood since his arrival at the northernmost window in the room. As a former soldier and spy, Nick Hawkins could not help himself, and he glanced out at Louisburg Square every few moments, watching the main entrance to Conan Doyle's home.

"Thank you," Hawkins said as he took the tumbler from their host. Gull saw his eyes narrow as the man studied Arthur. "You having security issues, Mr. Doyle? Mage of your stature, I find it hard to imagine there's a lot you're afraid of."

Gull smiled as he brought his drink to his twisted mouth, careful not to dribble. Hawkins was a complete sociopath, and yet somehow managed to navigate complex dynamics well enough. Even now he was somehow mocking Conan Doyle, plumbing his current status, and massaging his ego, all at the same time.

Well done, Nick, Gull thought, watching as Hawkins at last took a seat in a wing back chair in the corner of the room.

"One must not fall prey to the curse of overconfidence," Conan Doyle said as he turned away from the liquor cabinet, having poured himself a scotch as well. "There was a recent incident that forced me to take a closer look at the brownstone's defenses and—" He stopped mid-sentence, casting an icy stare at Hawkins.

"Is something wrong, Arthur?" Gull asked.

"Not at all," Conan Doyle replied, his tone clipped, his feathers seemingly ruffled. "I'll just have a seat over here."

Gull wanted to laugh out loud. *So Hawkins is sitting on Arthur's throne.* The annoyance poured from the man in waves.

"So, Nigel," Conan Doyle began, swirling the golden brown liquid in his glass. "It's been quite a long time."

"A dog's age," Gull agreed, and then chuckled. "Or an entire litter's. When was it that we last saw each other?" he asked, knowing the answer well enough.

Conan Doyle took a moment to think, and Gull felt his own ire begin to rise. Though it had been more than twenty years ago, he was certain that the arch mage had not forgotten. They were fencing, and Arthur had just parried.

"Was it that tawdry business with the phoenix egg?" Conan Doyle asked finally.

"I believe it was," Gull said with a nod and smile that he hoped appeared pleasant. "I can still see the look on my client's face as you and your Menagerie stormed into his citadel to relieve him of his prize."

Conan Doyle nodded at the memory, resting his tumbler on his knee. "A shame that I had to step in and prevent that transaction." He straightened the crease in the leg of his dark trousers. "But as you well knew, the phoenix was at the top of the endangered mythical species list, and I couldn't allow it to fall into the hands of some boastful Middle Eastern death cult." He took another sip of his drink. "Your client did eventually understand, did he not?"

Gull smiled knowingly and shifted his position on the couch. "You killed them all, Arthur, down to the last mad-eyed lad. You and your followers sent their spirits into the embrace of the Sumerian death goddess they so devoutly worshipped."

Conan Doyle gazed thoughtfully over the lip of the tumbler. "I guess we did at that. So long ago, I didn't quite remember."

Like hell, Gull thought. But he kept the smile on his face. "No matter," he said. "Since they were all dead, there was no need to refund any money. It worked out for the best."

Hawkins chuckled darkly and lifted his glass toward Gull in a toast, then polished off what remained of his drink. At her mentor's side, Jezebel cozied up closer to the nearest thing to a father she'd ever had.

Conan Doyle had finished his drink as well and balanced the empty glass on the arm of the chair. He fixed Gull in his gaze.

"I'm certain this isn't a social call, Nigel," he said. "So why don't we cease the rather uncomfortable pleasantries, and you can get on with your business."

Gull leaned forward, placing his drink on the floor at his feet. Jezebel frowned and sleepily opened her eyes, looking up at him with a certain petulance. One moment she was full of sexual swagger, fully in charge of her charms, and the next she was uncertain and awkward. He cherished her for her complications.

"Not very subtle, is he?" Jezebel asked, her eyes fluttering closed again as she settled back.

Gull smiled. "No. He never was." Then he turned his focus back to Conan Doyle, placing a hand over his heart. "You wound me, Arthur. After all this time, you still cannot see the ties that bind us? We are brothers, not defined by biology, but by something far more powerful than mere parentage. We are brothers in magick."

Suddenly Jezebel bolted awake, startling green eyes wide in shock. "Why can't you just leave me be!" she shrieked, jagged bolts of electrical force arcing from her fingertips.

"Lovely," Hawkins muttered, dropping from his chair— *Arthur's chair*—to the floor as the tendrils of electricity seared through the air above him, blackening the wall behind the seat.

Gull placed a gentle hand on the girl's cheek as she gazed around the room, wild-eyed.

"It's all right, Jezebel," he whispered. "It was a dream."

She slapped his hand away. "Don't touch me—don't you ever touch me!" Her right hand shot out, a swirling ball of lightning collecting in her palm, and Gull instinctively began a spell to counter her destructive force.

With a piercing scream Jezebel unleashed her collected power, but it did not travel far. Before Gull could stop her, he was staggered by a blast of magick that traveled past him and encircled Jezebel in a sphere, her own power exploding within the containment field. This had been a recurring problem, nightmares of her time before coming to join him. He thought that they had made better progress than this.

Gull's heart nearly broke as he watched the pretty young thing convulse, tossing her red hair around like fire. The elemental power that she had summoned struck at her like a cobra, trapped within the sphere with her, and after jittering for a moment with the shock of it, Jezebel slumped to the sofa, unconscious. He turned away from the disturbing sight to see Arthur standing in front of an upended chair, his hand extended and the residue of his spell still trickling from the tips of his fingers.

"That will be enough of that," Conan Doyle said sternly.

The magickal sphere dissipated as suddenly as it had appeared, and the unconscious Jezebel moaned in discomfort. Gull was relieved to see that she was not badly injured.

"My thanks, Arthur," he said. "She has a bit of a problem with night terrors."

"Still choosing the cream of the crop, I see." Conan Doyle glanced briefly at Hawkins, before returning his steely gaze to Gull. "Now, then, Nigel, no more foolishness. What do you want? And be quick about it, I grow weary of your company."

Gull bristled, longing to reply with equal candor. But there were other things at stake here than his pride.

"Right, then. How foolish of me to attempt to be polite. As you no doubt are aware, there are people dying in Greece from most unusual causes."

He watched Conan Doyle's face. A tick of familiarity danced at the corner of his old friend's eye. Arthur knew exactly what he was talking about.

"Go on."

"I intend to stop these horrid killings, and I thought it would be best if we were to work together."

Conan Doyle's eyes narrowed with suspicion, and he brought a hand to his face, smoothing his mustache. "You haven't the best record of selfless heroism, Nigel. What's the catch?"

Gull feigned surprise. "No catch. Simply put, I need your help."

WITH Nigel Gull, there was always a catch.

Conan Doyle had encountered him many times over the years since they had parted company, and though Gull was not precisely evil, he had certainly been tainted by the dark magick he employed. Or, perhaps more accurately, he had become the epitome of the old adage that the ends justified the means. Deceitful, ambitious, and amoral, with Nigel Gull, nothing was ever as it seemed. The man referred to those in his employ as his Wicked. That was signal enough that he was not to be trusted.

"I think not," he said with a shake of his head.

"Oh, come now, Arthur," Gull replied. "I'm fairly certain *I* can learn to play nice. I'd assumed no less of you." The deformed man smiled, and Conan Doyle was chilled by how horribly wrong it looked.

Conan Doyle righted the chair he'd upended and took his seat once more, crossing his arms and staring at Gull. "Since when have you had a concern for anything or anyone other than yourself?"

Seated beside the unconscious Jezebel, Gull began to gently stroke her face, just as a father might have done. "You're quick with the barbs, aren't you? I've put the past behind me. Pity you can't say the same," he said with a sad shake of his misshapen head.

Conan Doyle was unsure if it was a symptom of the man's malady, but he could have sworn that Gull was even more deformed than the last time they crossed paths. *Perhaps the result of further dabblings in dark magick,* he thought.

The man named Hawkins stood and went to the liquor cabinet, distracting him from his musings. He gestured toward the decanter of scotch with an empty glass. "Mind if I help myself?"

"Please be my guest." Conan Doyle wanted to focus on his verbal sparring with Gull, but could not help watching as Hawkins removed the glass stopper and poured the drink. There was an unusual tremble in the man's hand.

"Is something wrong?" Conan Doyle asked.

Hawkins carefully returned the stopper to the bottle. "Not really, it's just that the poor sod who made this crystal decanter died by inches, poisoned by his wife's lover. That's a terrible way to give up the ghost."

Gull cleared his throat. "Hawkins is psychometric."

Conan Doyle frowned. He didn't like that. Not at all. A psychometric was able to read the psychic residue imprinted upon any object he touched. Having such a man in his house could be unpleasant and inconvenient. The invasion of his privacy made Conan Doyle even more sour.

Hawkins sipped his drink, returning to the chair he had claimed as his own. "Not even going to tell you what I've learned about you sitting in this chair," he said with a disconcerting smile.

Conan Doyle was not amused. "Perhaps that's best," he said dryly, returning his attention to Gull. "I'm sorry, Nigel, but I'm afraid the answer is still no." He stood. "Now, if you will excuse me, I have a rather full agenda today . . ."

He gestured politely toward the doorway.

"Don't be so rash. How many more will die before you finally stumble across the answers you seek?" Gull demanded. "Simply because you cannot put aside past animosity."

Conan Doyle did not respond, so Gull stood, bending down to haul the still unconscious Jezebel into a sitting position. "Come along now, Jez, it seems the old boy's even more arrogant than I remembered."

The girl moaned, beginning to come around. Hawkins moved to assist Gull, slipping the girl's arm around his neck and lifting her to her feet.

"Thanks, Nick. She's heavy for a little bit of a thing."

They were ready to leave, and Conan Doyle struggled with his decision to let them go. He had the utmost faith in the team he had dispatched to Athens, but he knew that Gull was right. If his old adversary had information that could save the lives of innocents, how in good conscience could he let them leave?

"A pleasure to see you again, Arthur," Gull said as he reached the door of the study.

"Nigel? Crickey, Nigel, what happened to me?" Jezebel asked softly.

Gull shushed her, reassuring her that everything was fine.

It pained him, but Conan Doyle cleared his throat and clasped his hands behind his back. "If we were to work together," he began, drawing the attention of Nigel Gull and his operatives, "you would have to follow my instructions completely."

Gull smiled. There was a twinkle in his dark, animal eyes, and for a brief moment, Conan Doyle could not help but feel as though he had stepped into the lion's den.

"To the very letter," he agreed. "My Wicked and I will be at your beck and call." And he bowed his wrongly shaped head in complete obeisance.

"Fine," Conan Doyle agreed, nearly choking on the word.

Gull strode back across the room and gripped Doyle's shoulder with a gnarled hand. "You won't regret this, Arthur."

Doyle's nostrils flared with distaste. "Time will tell. For now, you can begin by telling me everything you know about the threat we face in Athens."

"Very well." Gull released him, turning to his Wicked. "Take Jezebel to the car," he told Hawkins. "Arthur and I will finish up here, and I'll be down shortly."

Hawkins did as he was told, helping the girl, who was still unsteady, from the study.

"Don't be long," Jezebel called over her shoulder, weakly lifting a hand to bid her master good-bye.

"A charming girl once you get to know her," Gull noted.

"Athens?" Conan Doyle prodded.

"Of course," Gull responded, bowing his head again. "I was doing some research on the Greek Isles for a potential client, when I stumbled upon them—Gorgons, Arthur. There are Gorgons loose in Greece."

Conan Doyle reached up to again stroke his mustache. *Gorgons.* It certainly was a possibility. "Those creatures haven't walked the earth in millennia. Why now?"

Gull tilted his head. "That I don't know. But the second I realized this, I knew I couldn't deal with it alone, even with my operatives to back me up. There was a time when I had plenty of agents, but now there's only Hawkins and Jezebel. Coming to you was the logical decision, but it had to be in person. You would never have trusted me if I'd just sent you a letter in the post or rang you up."

Conan Doyle crossed his arms across his chest. "And I'm supposed to believe you've done all this out of some sudden nobility? You've always got an angle, Nigel. What's in it for you?"

Gull chuckled, walking toward the window, then turning to look at his friend. "Quite a bit, actually. Never claimed I was a model of virtue. I was trying to find the remains of a Gorgon. Then I stumbled upon the real thing. Point is, there are a few items I've got to acquire from the creatures. For a client, you understand."

"What sort of items?"

"Do you know how much a mere drop of Gorgon blood is worth on the black market? A lock of its hair? A claw? Or one of its eyes? Priceless."

"You always were quite the humanitarian," Conan Doyle said with a shake of his head.

"Do not condescend to me, brother," Gull said, leaving the window. "You'll get what you want, yes? Another supernatural threat eliminated from the world. And I'll have what I need as well. Everybody wins."

Conan Doyle had heard enough. "I believe I've had my fill of your company for now, Nigel," he said, turning to leave the study. "You can show yourself out."

"Will you be assembling your team?" Gull asked. "Your Menagerie?"

Doyle pretended not to hear the question, continuing on his way.

"I'm so looking forward to working with them."

YANNIS Papathansiou sucked on the end of a fat cigar, savoring the thick, oily smoke. It had been nearly six years since he'd last partaken of what his late wife had called a filthy habit. He had forgotten how much pleasure it gave him.

Away from the city, the night was quiet except for the chirping of crickets. If he closed his eyes and cleared his mind, he could almost imagine that the world was a beautiful and sane place. Almost. But he doubted he would ever be able to convince himself of that again, not with the images of the victims at the Epidaurus Guest House seared into his mind.

Yannis opened his eyes to gaze out over the field behind the Moni Pendeli monastery. It was used as a private landing strip for some of the wealthier visitors to the popular weekend retreat. Tonight, he waited for an altogether different kind of guest.

He glanced at his watch. It wouldn't be long now. He had received an in-flight call from his visitors, estimating that they would reach Athens's airspace within the hour. He opened his car door, then switched on the headlights to better illuminate the grounds. Moths danced in the twin beams of pale white light, entertainment as he waited.

He recalled the day that he had first learned of the shadowy group of investigators that dealt with only the most unusual cases. It had been at a retirement celebration for a fellow detective. The departing officer, Stavros, had pulled Yannis aside and asked if he would like to make some extra money from time to time. Of course he had been interested. A new detective on the Athens police force did not make a great deal of money. Even so, he had been cautious, asking if he would be required to do anything illegal. The retiring detective had laughed oddly and handed Yannis a worn piece of paper on which was scrawled an international phone number—one from America. In retrospect, he thought that Stavros had seemed almost happy to be rid of it. The old detective had explained that the number was to be dialed only when there was an unusual occurrence in the city. Something unnatural.

At first Yannis had suspected that Stavros was pulling his leg, one last joke on the still-green detective before heading out to pasture. But there came a time not so long after Stavros left the force, when Yannis had an opportunity to dial the mysterious number. Someone had been digging up the recently buried in the First Cemetery of Athens, and feeding on the corpses.

Yannis's bulbous belly churned, sickly with the memory—the overturned earth, splintered coffin pieces strewn about the beautifully peaceful setting, and the condition of the helpless dead. The old man belched, the stifado, a spicy beef stew with baby onions that he'd had for supper, repeating on him. Popping the cigar into his mouth to free his hands, Yannis rubbed his large stomach in an attempt to calm it.

Just the memory of the odor from those open graves was enough to make him feel queasy. The air had been filled not only with the stench of the disinterred, but with swarms of flies, feasting and depositing their eggs on the scattered remains. As he stood there with the other officers and the grief-stricken families of those whose graves had been violated, he had thought of the number scrawled upon the worn piece of paper in his wallet.

Something unnatural.

The hum of an approaching plane stirred him from his recollections, and he squinted into the nighttime sky. The plane descended in the distance, touching down expertly in the field that was once rife with olive trees. But that had been long ago, when Yannis still believed that the world was sane. He chuckled as he took another puff on his cigar, amused that he could ever have been so naive.

In that case, years past, he had called the number, and a strange gravelly voice had answered. In broken English, Yannis had described what was happening in Athens, about the desecrated graves and the cannibalized bodies. The voice on the other end had grown silent, the open phone line hissing in his ear, and for a moment, Yannis thought he had been cut off, but then the voice returned and said that someone would be along to help.

Yannis took a final pull on his cigar, and for the sake of his upset stomach, tossed the remains to the ground. The plane rolled toward him, its landing lights pulsing as if to the beat of the craft's mechanical heart, and again his mind traveled back through the years, to a time and place when he had met another plane.

He hadn't been sure what to expect, but the man who stepped from the small private plane certainly was not it. He had imagined a wild-haired scientist, with thick glasses and perhaps a German accent, but as the man approached him, Yannis realized that perhaps he had seen too many American horror films. The stranger was a fine looking gentleman, handsome as far as Americans go, with dark, close-cropped hair and an air of authority that seemed to radiate from him in waves.

There had been very little by way of formalities. The man had instructed Yannis to take him to the First Cemetery immediately, and once there had told the detective to remain in the car no matter what he heard or thought he saw. It had all seemed very unusual to Yannis, but he had accepted the orders, especially since the man had given him an envelope full of cash before leaving the car. For that kind of money he would have spent the entire night there if need be.

The plane's engines whined down and he ambled toward the craft, adjusting his clothing as he went. The bottom of his shirt had come undone, the pull of the material across his expanse of belly making it difficult for the last buttons to remain fastened. But he quickly lost interest in his appearance as the door to the craft swung open and a set of collapsible stairs unfolded from within.

The first person to exit was very small, almost dwarf-like. Yannis wasn't sure if he had ever seen anyone quite so strange.

"How's it hanging?" the tiny man asked him in a voice that could have been the one to answer that first call he had made, years past.

Yannis simply stared. The man's eyes were a sickly shade of yellow, and both his ears and teeth came to points.

"What? No speaky da English?" the ugly little man

asked, before bursting out in a braying laugh. "Don't worry about it, pally. I don't speak Greek."

Next off the plane was a handsome black man whose movements reminded Yannis of someone floating underwater.

"Pay him no mind, sir," the man said in a low, tremulous voice.

Yannis could have sworn that for the briefest of moments he was able to see right through the stranger, but he blinked and the gauzy effect went away. He told himself it must have been a trick of the light.

"Yannis Papathansiou," called a strangely familiar voice from inside the plane, and the police detective looked up to see another figure emerging.

The man looked exactly as he had more than twenty years ago. Exactly.

Something unnatural, he thought again. It was almost funny. He called this man when the extraordinary presented itself . . . but who was he to call about the passengers of this plane? No one, of course. They were the solution, not the problem.

"It's a pleasure to see you again, sir," the ageless man said in Greek, extending his hand, and Yannis remembered how he had disobeyed this man's instructions that night so many years ago.

He had been dozing behind the wheel of the car when the screaming began. It had been unlike anything he had ever heard, and he had immediately reacted, climbing from his vehicle and running into the cemetery before he even realized what he was doing. After all, he was a policeman.

It had been dark that night, and he had strained his eyes to see what was happening, and then the clouds parted for an instant, and beams of moonlight shone upon the burial grounds. Then Yannis had seen what he would never forget.

The man he had brought from the airfield, the man whose hand he now shook, had been in the midst of battle with a creature the likes of which Yannis had never seen. Its body was covered in filthy, matted fur, its eyes glowing red, like burning coals. Strands of dead flesh dangled from its gnashing, snapping teeth. Yannis had never believed himself a particularly brave man, but he had found himself moving toward the struggle, weaving around the tombstones to help the stranger.

When he had been only a few feet from the battle, the man had noticed his approach and ordered him to stop. Yannis had frozen in his tracks and watched in awe the scene that played out before him. The creature tore at the man with its claws, rending his clothing and flesh, but the man seemed unharmed. Then he had begun to change, to grow, his body transforming into something of great ferocity, his flesh as malleable as clay.

THE years have not been kind to Yannis Papathansiou, Clay thought. He was sitting in the front seat of the detective's car as they drove toward Athens. He remembered a much different man than the one beside him now, but then again, twenty years had passed. The blink of an eye for Clay, but not so fleeting for humans.

"So, Yanni," Squire said, leaning forward from the backseat.

"It is Yannis," the detective corrected, eyes still on the winding road before him.

"Yeah, yeah, that's what I meant. So, you had any other tourists turn up petrified?" the hobgoblin asked.

Yannis shook his head, jowls wiggling. "No, the bodies found at the Epidaurus are the only ones."

"So far," Squire added, sliding back against his seat. "But I'd bet we get a few more statues before this is over. Crap like this is never easy."

The detective grimaced at Squire's words, and Clay wondered if he was remembering the last time he had phoned Conan Doyle for assistance. On that night, years past, he had specifically told Yannis to stay in the car. The man was never meant to witness what transpired in the cemetery. Clay's battle with the corpse-eating Mormolykiai was not for human eyes, but Yannis had seen it, and there was nothing Clay could do to change that.

"What . . . what is responsible? What can turn a person to stone like that? How can it be?" the detective asked, steering the car around a sharp turn that would lead them to the first of numerous side streets in the crowded city.

Clay gave him a reassuring glance. "That's what we intend to find out."

"You must suspect that it is bad," he said. "To have come with others." He fixed Clay with large, watery eyes.

Clay had wondered if what Yannis Papathansiou saw those years past had changed him in any way. Looking into those eyes now, he had his answer.

"Better to be safe than sorry." He glanced over his shoulder to see Squire looking out the window like an excited pet, happy to be off the plane and to have somebody else doing the driving for a change. Graves appeared lost in thought, but Clay suspected the ghost was probably already beginning their investigation, listening to the whispering voices of the dead prevalent in this ancient city.

"We'll try to get this done as quickly as possible," he reassured the detective. "You won't even know we're here."

Yannis chuckled, a wet burbling sound that gave Clay the impression that the Greek was filled with fluid. "I will know," he said, taking a left turn in the Athenian West End, heading into the Kerameikos, the pottery district. "And I will not sleep peacefully until I know that you, and whatever it is that plagues this city, are gone."

"Nice," Squire squawked. "Is that an example of Greek hospitality? No wonder I've been feeling all warm and tingly since I got here."

The detective did not respond. Moments later he brought the car to a stop in front of a dilapidated building at the far end of a darkened street. All the other buildings around it appeared to be in an equal state of disrepair, but scaffolding had been placed around some of the structures, hinting that some form of renewal was on its way.

"We are here," Yannis said, unceremoniously throwing open his door and extracting his large frame from the driver's seat.

"And here is . . . ?" Clay asked.

"The man who owns this building is a former police officer," he explained, lapsing into Greek now. "He has allowed us to store the bodies here, away from curious eyes." The detective fumbled in his pockets and produced a key. "This way."

They followed him to a padlocked door. Clay noticed that the man's hands were trembling as he inserted the key into the lock.

"I think we can take it from here," Clay reassured him, also in Greek.

Yannis looked at him with those eyes again, tired eyes that had seen too much, and could never forget. "They are in the back—three of them—a family," he said as he tugged the key from the lock and handed it to Clay.

"You look tired," Clay said.

Yannis nodded, saying nothing.

"Let me see about getting this taken care of so that you can sleep peacefully again."

The detective took a long breath and let it out, then shuffled back to his car. "Lock it up before you leave," he called to them as he forced his stomach behind the wheel, turned over the engine, and drove off into the night.

"Nice guy," Squire said sarcastically. "A real life of the party; bet he's a hoot at funerals."

"Give him a break," Clay said as he removed the padlock and pushed open the wooden door into complete darkness. "We deal with this kind of thing all the time, but ordinary people aren't prepared for what happens when the nasties come out of the shadows."

"Mewling babies," Squire growled, squeezing past him, having no difficulty at all maneuvering in the dark.

The place smelled of dampness and rotting wood. Still standing in the doorway, Clay's eyes shifted to those of a night predator, the darkness becoming as bright as day. Graves floated by on his right, eager to begin their investigation.

"Yannis said they're in the back," Clay told them, and they proceeded across the open space. The large room appeared to be used for storage. Clay noticed signs of decorations that would be for some kind of celebration or religious festival, as well as pallets of building materials.

Squire was the first to reach the victims.

"Here we go," he said aloud, carefully removing a tarp that had been thrown over them. "Oh, shit, look at this," he said, walking around the three stone figures, frozen in the act of having breakfast.

Graves drifted closer, his face mere inches from a petrified woman's. He reached out, touching her stony cheek with ghostly fingertips.

"Any thoughts on what did this?" Clay asked, his heart aching at the sight of a child whose granite body had been broken. The pieces of her had been laid out on a tarp beside her parents.

"Nothing of the natural world can lay claim to this," the ghost said.

Clay thought he heard the slightest hint of disappointment in the spirit's voice. Graves had an extreme distaste for the supernatural, preferring to work on cases that could be solved with the art of science and deduction. This was not to be such a case.

"Ya think so, spooky?" Squire said, kneeling on the tarp that held the remains of the young girl. He picked up the girl's broken stone hand. It still clutched what appeared to be a piece of fruit—an orange. "I was thinking that maybe this might be the result of some bad baklava or something." The goblin waved at them with the hand. "Hi everybody," he said in a squeaky high-pitched, voice.

Graves showed his distaste by folding his arms across his chest, shaking his head from side to side.

"Enough of that," Clay snapped. "Have a little decency. If you don't have anything to contribute, let us do our work."

The hobgoblin still knelt at the girl's remains. He'd put the hand down and was rummaging through the other, fragmented pieces. "I can pretty much rule out a basilisk attack," he said. "Those sons of bitches just solidify the outside, leaving a soft, chewy center. These poor folks are stone through and through."

Abruptly the hobgoblin stiffened, looking about the darkened space as if he had heard something.

"What's up?" Clay asked.

"Think I'm getting a call." Squire climbed to his feet and strolled from the room. "Give me a minute."

Clay and Graves remained silent, both staring at the remains before them. Clay had been walking this world for thousands of years, dealing with all manner of paranormal manifestation, but the sight of this family transformed to stone disturbed him profoundly.

"Can you trace them?" Graves suggested quietly.

The souls of murder victims never passed on to the afterlife immediately. Always, they clung to their old shells for a time, crying out for vengeance, hoping that someone would hear their anguish. The Creator had touched him, and over time, as he saw the sins of humanity evolve, Clay had developed the ability to see the ectoplasmic trail left behind by a murdered soul. The victim's spirit clung to the murderer, creating a tether of soul stuff that connected corpse to killer, and if he reached the dead soon enough, Clay could follow that trail. He could catch the killer.

But this . . . he did not know.

The shapeshifter moved closer to the stone bodies, his eyes searching for signs of their tethers.

"Well?" Graves asked.

"Nothing," Clay replied. "It's as if they've always been

nothing more than inanimate objects. Maybe because they're no longer flesh, but there's no connection to the killer that I can see."

"Curiouser and curiouser," Graves whispered.

Squire returned, a quickness to his step as he crossed the room.

"Just got a call from Mr. Doyle," he said.

"I didn't hear any phone ring," Clay commented.

"He doesn't have to use a phone," Squire explained. "Me and the boss, we got this system set up so that he can contact me through the shadows. All he has to do is find a nice patch of darkness and speak in my native tongue to make the connection."

Interesting, Clay thought. Here was yet another unique talent the little goblin had never exhibited before. Squire was always full of surprises, which was probably why Conan Doyle kept him around.

Graves's spectral form shimmered in the gloom. "What did Conan Doyle want?"

"He and the rest of the crew are coming to Greece. An old acquaintance dropped by the brownstone and filled him in on what's really going on around here."

"And?" Clay prodded him.

"The Greeks've got a fucking Gorgon problem."

5

CERIDWEN stood naked in the empty rooms that were to be her quarters, now that she had decided to stay. In recent days she had used one of the many guest rooms on the upper floors, but if she was going to live here, she desired a more permanent and more personal space. Conan Doyle had recommended this suite of rooms because of their location. There were half a dozen high windows along the rear wall of her bedroom, three each on either side of broad French doors that opened onto a small courtyard garden behind the house. The doors were wide open now, and a cool breeze swirled and eddied about the room, caressing her skin, bringing up gooseflesh and hardening the nubs of her breasts. It was a delicious sensation, and she shivered in pleasure.

She swung out one long leg and did a spin on the smooth wooden floor, her bare feet rejoicing in the feel of the wood. There would be no carpet for Ceridwen. The smell and feel of wood was her preference.

The sun shone upon the cut edges of the many glass panes in the French doors, and it glinted there, refracting, throwing a scattering of tiny rainbows across the natural maple floor. The rooms were bright with sunshine and had been cleaned recently. She wondered if Arthur had used magick to tidy up, or if he had had Squire clean the suite earlier, presuming she would stay.

No. He didn't know I was going to choose to remain here, she thought. *Though perhaps he hoped.*

And it had been clear that he was glad Ceridwen was staying behind, and not solely because she was a staunch and valuable ally. That was all right, though, for she had not been forthcoming about the entirety of her reasons for that decision. The Faerie sorceress had not lied. She had simply not provided the whole truth.

Fighting at Arthur's side made her feel complete, somehow. As though it was meant to be. Such attitudes toward destiny were common among her kin, but she had always eschewed such ideas as flights of fancy. Now she could not decide what to think. But, then, Conan Doyle had always had that effect on her.

A tiny smile played upon Ceridwen's lips, and she shivered again at the caress of the cool breeze upon her flesh. *I think it must be his eyes,* she thought. *Yes. His eyes. There's iron there.*

She danced over to the open doors and stepped into the warmth of the sun. Her flesh absorbed it, the heat radiating down to her bones. Ceridwen went to her knees on the stone patio and glanced around the garden. It was a pitiful thing, with little variety and less vigor, but she would soon see to that. With a satisfied sigh she plunged her fingers into the soil, and she felt the life there. The earth responded to her touch, quivering beneath her. There was so much she could do here. The garden needed color and wild scents. And water. She would want a fountain, built of stone and with the water summoned from deep within the earth, a spring she would create by simply asking the water to flow upward.

Elemental magick was her very pulse.

As Ceridwen smiled, sprouts burst from the soil, a trio of small buds that grew rapidly to full-fledged flowers, the same violet as her eyes. They smelled of vanilla and oranges, and they grew only in Faerie, only within the walls of Finvarra's kingdom.

Unless she willed it.

They were the merest fraction of the color and life she would bring to this garden. But now she had other duties to attend to. A different sort of summoning to answer. Ceridwen stood and stretched, enjoying the sun on her body. The walls around the garden courtyard were high. Anyone inside Conan Doyle's house might see her, but she knew he had thrown up wards to keep away the attentions of prying neighbors. Not that she minded. Women of the Fey were never coy about their bodies. In its way, the flesh was the fifth element, after fire, air, water, and earth. She only wished she could control her flesh as easily as she did the others.

With a sigh she slipped back into her bedroom, calling a small breeze to blow the French doors closed, just softly enough not to shatter the glass. The only things of hers she had already brought into her suite were some of the clothes she had kept in the guest room upstairs. Now she examined the closet and chose a light gown the color of the winter sea. Once she had slipped it on she also donned a hooded cloak of a blue deeper and richer than the gown.

Eve wanted to take her shopping for clothes more appropriate for the modern human world. Ceridwen felt that since she had decided to remain for a time, perhaps she would take the vampire up on this offer. At the very least, it ought to be an entertaining evening out. Beyond their fondness for Arthur, the two women had little in common.

Ceridwen retrieved her elemental staff from its place by the door, the wood cleaving to her grip and the fire within the icy sphere at its tip glowing brightly within. Another wind blew up and closed the door behind her as she went out into the corridor.

This part of the old house was silent . . . what Arthur and his former associate, the disquieting Mr. Gull, were doing on the roof had no echo down here. Ceridwen liked it this way.

In Faerie, everything was alive and vibrant. There was a beauty and sublime rightness to the dwellings of the Fey, particularly the homes constructed in the boughs of trees, but something about mortal houses brought her an inner peace. There was an elegance and a sense of artistry in a dwelling such as this one that she could appreciate in quiet moments.

Now, though, was no time for reflection.

Ceridwen swept along the corridor, a blue mist swirling around the ice atop her staff, her cloak nearly brushing the floor. They would all have gathered upon the roof by now and might already be awaiting her. Yet even as she thought this, Ceridwen passed a pair of large doors that had been thrown open and saw within the vast spectacle of Conan Doyle's library. Nostalgia bloomed within her, a feeling rare for one of her race. Yet it was powerful enough to pause her in her purpose and divert her into that massive hall. For calling it a room would not do it justice.

The library was a glorious place, fully four stories high with nothing but bookshelves along the walls, save for the large skylights far above. The center was open and filled with comfortable chairs in which to cozy up and read. Stairs led up to the second floor, which was little more than a balcony that ran around the perimeter, looking down upon the first. The third floor balcony was slightly narrower, and the fourth the narrowest of all, so that the vast open air of the library grew wider the higher one climbed.

"Wonderful," Ceridwen whispered to herself. She could recall long hours spent here on the occasions when she had come back to the mortal world—what her people called the Blight—with Arthur.

Yet the immediacy of their situation beckoned. She turned to leave, but even as she did so, she caught sight of another figure moving across the balcony on the second story. It was only a glimpse, as he moved into one of the many alcoves of bookshelves, but there was no mistaking the leathery skin and small, sharp horns.

Ceridwen went softly up the stairs to the second floor and moved around the circumference of the room, along the balustrade, to the alcove where he had disappeared. Danny Ferrick had his back to her and wore small silver headphones. She knew that music somehow came from such things but she could not see its source. The demon boy nodded along in time with the rhythm and had not noticed Ceridwen's arrival. For several moments she watched him curiously as he withdrew certain volumes from the shelves and perused them. Conan Doyle had one of the most extraordinary libraries in the world, replete not only with the summary accumulation of human wisdom, but with the secrets of the occult as well. The true histories of the world. Revelations of ancient societies. Lost worlds. Other dimensions. Many of the books in the library were unique and thought to have been lost at the time of the burning of the library of Alexandria.

A young man with an interest in the supernatural could learn a great deal in this hall.

She tapped him on the shoulder. "Danny."

"Jesus!" he snarled, spinning to face her and backing away at the same time. Fright and aggression warred in his eyes, and then he saw who had disturbed him, and he let out a long breath, relaxing into his sagging, teenager posture.

"You wear the face of his enemy and yet still call upon the man-god of your parents' religion?" Ceridwen asked.

The demon boy leaned back and gazed up at the sunlight streaming in through the windows in the ceiling high above. He waved a clawed hand. "Well, He hasn't struck me with lightning yet, so either He isn't listening or I'm getting the benefit of the doubt. My guess is, you don't get judged on your gene pool, but how you swim in it."

"I am amazed at how often I have no idea what you're talking about."

Danny looked at her and shook his head. "Damn. You and everyone else around here. Squire's the only one who doesn't give me that confused look, and that's because he's more of a kid than I am. If he's got a mom somewhere, I got a feeling she's pretty horrified. Maybe that's why we get along."

"You do yourself a disservice, Daniel. You have earned the respect and fondness of every resident of this house. Dr. Graves in particular."

The teenager shrugged. "He's cool. You've all been pretty much all right by me. Except maybe Mr. Doyle. I don't think he likes me very much."

He gazed over the edge of the balustrade, down at the first floor, and he said it carelessly. But Ceridwen could see in his eyes that he did care, quite a bit.

"You might be surprised. I think Arthur fears for you, Danny. That is the concern you see in him."

The demon boy did not respond to that. He appeared to think it over a moment and then only nodded, keeping his own counsel. At length he walked past her and started perusing the shelves again, but halfheartedly, including her in his observations.

"This is a pretty amazing place, isn't it? I mean, it's so giant I have a hard time figuring out how it fits inside the house. From the inside it seems big enough that there shouldn't be room for anything else. No bedrooms, no parlors, no dining room. It's weird. Maybe it's an optical illusion or something."

Ceridwen smiled. "Something like that."

Danny had begun to run his fingers along a line of books, reading the titles silently to himself, but at her response he paused and regarded her.

"No. Uh uh. Don't do that. I know that tone of voice. Okay, so there's stuff I don't know. I'm a mo-ron. Well, un-idiot me. Fill me in. What's the secret of this place?"

She lost her smile. "You're right, of course. You are young, but you've earned the right not to be treated as a child. My apologies."

Danny grinned. "Well, you don't have to be *so* fucking serious about it."

The mischief in the boy's eyes was contagious. Ceridwen found herself laughing softly along with him. As they spoke their voices echoed in the vast chamber. She gestured upward.

"You are correct. It is much too large to fit inside Arthur's house. The truth is that it isn't inside the house at all. It's . . . elsewhere. And the door is just a door that leads to that elsewhere. If you were to go up through that skylight, it wouldn't be Boston unfolding around you."

"Where are we, then?" Danny asked, sounding more than a little concerned.

Ceridwen considered a moment before replying. "I don't know. I also don't know how the library is summoned. Sometimes it is here, and sometimes it isn't. The doors appear wherever they like in the house. The library is only available when it is needed, even if your need is only for pleasant distraction, for there are storybooks in here as well."

As she spoke, the two of them strolled along the second-floor balcony. Ceridwen held her staff in one hand and ran her fingers over the smooth mahogany of the balustrade with the other. She could not help admiring the simple luxury of the great library. Danny kept moving along the shelves. They came to another, far larger alcove, set into the wall. There was an identical alcove on each floor of the library. The books here had a certain scent to them . . . a kind of wild, musty odor. Some of them were bound in leather as ancient as Eve herself, others in materials that could only be found in Faerie, or in other worlds.

Danny slid one of the books from the shelf, a heavy, dusty tome with a weathered cover and a lock that fell away at his touch. He began to lift the cover.

"Stop!" Ceridwen shouted, lunging for him and swatting the book from his hands with a swing of her staff. She watched breathlessly for a moment as it tumbled to the floor and slammed closed upon impact.

"Hey! What's up with that?" Danny demanded.

"This section," she said, gesturing with her staff toward that wide alcove, fingers of blue fire shooting from the ice sphere atop it to touch the rest of this particular collection on the first, third, and fourth floors. "This is the bestiary. And it is off-limits to you."

"Why?" The boy was clearly angry. He crossed his arms. "Is the old man afraid I'll do something stupid? Or something evil?"

Ceridwen flinched. So that was what the boy thought? That Arthur believed he would cleave eventually unto his father's demonic nature. Well, and perhaps it was so, but only time would tell.

"Neither, Daniel," she said. "Do you know what those books contain?"

He rolled his eyes. "Hello? You wouldn't let me open one to find out. But from the titles, I'm guessing Monster 101. Bestiary, right? So pictures of giants, vampires, goblins, trolls, all that kind of stuff. Big deal. Why are they off-limits?"

Ceridwen frowned. "They are indeed full of monsters."

"They're *pictures*!"

"Yes," she agreed. "But sometimes they get loose."

The boy stared at her with wide eyes. Ceridwen only nodded in confirmation and took him by the arm to lead him down the stairs to the first floor. As she escorted him out into the hallway and then toward the front of the house, she lowered her voice.

"We must move along, now. Arthur will be expecting us. Off to Greece, he said?"

"Yeah," Danny agreed. "Some island of lesbians."

Ceridwen arched one thin eyebrow. "I believe it is called Lesbos."

"Okay. That's not nearly as much fun, but okay."

They started up the main staircase toward the roof. She let her senses become attuned to the air, moved it around, felt for the presence of others, just in case Gull's associates

were lingering nearby. Though there was no sign they were
not alone, still she lowered her voice.

"From the moment we set off on our journey with Mr.
Gull, you will have an assignment of your own."

Danny paused on the stairs and gave her a secretive
glance. "Yeah?" he asked in a whisper.

"You must do something for Arthur and me. You must
keep watch over the girl, Jezebel, to see if there is any sign
of duplicity among Gull and his companions."

"Jezebel?"

"It shouldn't be difficult, Daniel. You can barely keep
your eyes off of her," Ceridwen said, smiling sweetly.

He grinned. "It'll be pretty painless. But why Jezebel and
not that Hawkins guy? She's pretty wacko, but he seems
way more slimy."

Ceridwen nodded. "Eve will be looking after Mr.
Hawkins for precisely that reason. He is too dangerous for
you to make an enemy of him. Should he take a dislike to
you, Hawkins could kill you out of sheer boredom."

She started up the stairs once more, but Danny did not
move. Ceridwen looked back down at him. "What is it?"

He shrugged. "Just trying to decide if I'm insulted by that
or not." After a moment he seemed to determine that he was
not, for he started up after her.

They made their way to the roof with no further incident.
There was a small stairwell that went up from the east end
of the fourth floor corridor, and at the top was a door. It
stood open, and a cool breeze swept in from outside. Sunshine splashed onto the threshold, and when Ceridwen and
Danny stepped out onto the roof, they found a glorious blue-
sky day. Jezebel's weather manipulation had been only the
beginning, creating a chain reaction that altered the weather
pattern for the entire city.

"Her magick is sort of like a minor league version of
yours, huh?" Danny muttered to her as they joined the others.

Ceridwen shot him a hard look. Jezebel was nothing like

her. The girl bent the weather to her will, instead of cajoling it, nurturing and loving it. And Ceridwen was bonded to the elements, not the weather. Yet the comparison grated on her.

"I was beginning to worry about you," Conan Doyle called as he started toward them. He was neatly attired, and his clothing was extremely old-fashioned, but he did not look as proper as he often did.

Gull was with him, and beyond the misshapen man were Hawkins and Jezebel, watching like carrion birds awaiting the demise of their feast. But the show really belonged to Gull and Conan Doyle. Each of the two men held an object in his hand, a heavy stone carved into the shape of a pyramid and engraved with strange sigils unfamiliar to Ceridwen.

"All right," Eve said, "how does this thing work, exactly?"

Ceridwen stared at her in surprise. She was sitting on the far edge of the roof with her skin-tight natural denim-clad legs over the side, propped back on her arms with her face upturned toward the sun.

The mother of all vampires, basking in the light of day.

"Eve?" Ceridwen said. "What are you . . . how?"

The wind swept Eve's hair across her eyes, and the vampire tossed her head like some Hollywood starlet and gave them all a Cheshire cat grin. She stretched backward, obviously relishing the sunlight. The dark green sweater she wore rode up, exposing the smooth flesh of her midsection.

"How, what how?" she asked coyly.

"How come you're not crispy fried?" Danny put in.

Conan Doyle cleared his throat, and when Ceridwen looked at him he gave her a meaningful glance. "Mr. Gull has come to us armed with one of the things Eve most desired. A spell that cloaks her in hidden shadows all day long. The sunlight never reaches her skin."

Ceridwen frowned and left Danny to watch the mages at work, while she walked over to join Eve. She did not sit on the roof's edge, however. Instead, she stood and stared down at the vampire.

"That was rash, don't you think? Accepting his help? You owe him, now. You've made a deal with the devil."

Eve snorted derisively. "I've made deals with lots of devils in my time. I'm already damned."

For a long moment Ceridwen only stood there. "All right. Just watch him. And watch yourself. You never know what you've agreed to without realizing it."

"Eve?" Gull called.

Ceridwen eyed him cautiously. He was malformed, and she most clearly found him hideous, but she saw something tragically noble in his features and bearing. That and his charm combined to make him far more dangerous than any mere mage.

"Yeah?" Eve replied. She did not turn toward him.

"You asked how it worked. Quite simple, really. Or relatively so." He gestured at an oval ring of shimmering energy that opened like an iris on the rooftop. "Scattered across the world are loci that Sweetblood and his acolytes—Doyle and I—placed there well over a century ago. The one nearest the isle of Lesbos is in Istanbul. There must be three loci for a Blackgate to function. One to open it on this side, like a key. The second, at our chosen destination. In this case, Istanbul. The third to follow after, closing the Blackgate. Leaving such portals open is bad magick to begin with, but leave enough of them open, and the entire time-space weave could come undone and collapse."

"Don't cross the streams," Eve muttered, eyes closed, head still thrown back. "Thanks, Egon."

Ceridwen ignored her. Gull seemed puzzled but said nothing.

"Blackgate?" Danny asked.

"As you see," Conan Doyle replied, and he gestured to Gull. The two mages had used a spell to create the foundation for the portal, but now they separated, one moving to the left of the shimmering oval and the other to the right.

Then, simultaneously they raised their loci and touched the tips of those runic pyramids together. At the moment of contact, the portal ceased its shimmering and became a sheer, vertical oval of solid blackness. Like an oil spill painted on air.

"Right. Blackgate," Danny repeated.

"Mr. Gull will go first," Conan Doyle said, glancing warily at Gull. There was clearly a part of him that saw this as a trap, and Ceridwen could not blame him. "Then the rest of you, one at a time. And I will follow behind, closing the gate."

"Let's saddle up and get a move on, then," Eve said, climbing to her feet, picking up her long, dark brown leather Ana Sui coat and striding toward the Blackgate. The metal tips on her ankle length, dark brown boots shone in the sunlight. "I could use a shot of ouzo."

Ceridwen exchanged a glance with Arthur, a look rife with meaning. She would go second, right after Nigel Gull. And if anything should go wrong, if somehow Arthur was killed in transition or magickally rerouted or something equally unpleasant happened, she would slit Gull's throat and stay by his corpse to make sure it remained dead.

"As you say, Eve," Conan Doyle agreed. "As you say."

AS night fell over Athens, she lingered in the darkness between two of the columns of the Thesseion, the temple dedicated to Hephaestus. The progeny of man wandered in and around the temple as though the whole of the city were some hideous beehive. Yet there was no veneration in their visits, not an ounce of worship. The Doric columns of that proud temple stood as a faded testament to an ancient way, and all that remained of the mystical power that once had held sway here was the brittle residue that sifted down from the ceilings and columns.

Time had moved on and left a void within her, an ache in her heart. Once upon a time there had been great deeds performed in this city, by both gods and men. Now there was merely aimless meandering. What little she understood of the modern age told her that mortals aspired to very little beyond their own mortality.

Fools. She wished she could erase them from the land, or at least instill within them the sense of awe that their ancestors had once had for the gods and monsters of old.

She did not want to die. Yet if she were to live, she wanted at least not to be so alone. Somewhere in this ancient seat of power, she reasoned, there must be pieces of the Old World lingering, some tangible connection to the past. If she could touch that bygone age, taste it, she knew it would sustain her. For there in the modern city with pollution in the air and cars roaring on the roads, she felt like a wisp. Like a memory. Like a myth. As though at any moment she might simply disappear into the mortals' collection of legends, becoming nothing more than a story.

Yet she was not a story. She was flesh and blood.

And venom.

There in the darkness between the columns of Hephaestus's temple, she stared out across the Agora, a massive open area ringed with buildings and thronged with mortals. Yet they did not thrive there. They only survived and observed. They entered the buildings as though the city was a living museum. Once the Agora had been the center of life in Athens, the seat of its lawkeepers and administrators, with its temples and arcades and shops, and the mint where the coin of the ancient city had been struck. There had been a library there, and houses of education. But if all of those structures that lined the edges of the Agora were the mind of Athens, its broad open expanse was the city's beating heart.

The memory was fresh. So much so that if she narrowed her eyes just a bit she could still see the carts and the vendors shouting at passersby, the hagglers at the booths and the children running in among the crowds. A shudder of nostalgia passed through her. The Agora of Athens had once been the crossroads of the Aegean. In her mind's eye she could see Socrates orating in the street. She could smell the honey and spices permeating the sweltering air, hear the voices of slave traders as they boasted about their chattel. She could taste an olive upon her tongue, its perfect flesh crushed in her mouth, flavor spreading over her palate.

What mortals did not understand was that the ancient world faded but it never disappeared. If she could peel back the layers of time that had transpired since then, she could touch that world. Just for comfort. Her mind roiled with confusion. Immortal life was wasted if she could not decide how to spend it. Certainly not like so many others from her age. She had convinced herself that a taste of the past was all that was required. Then she would know what to do. How to live.

And none of these mongrel offspring of the once-proud human race were going to stand in her way.

In the darkness, her hands caressing the perfect beauty of the Doric column beside her, its marble cool against her skin, she hissed softly. It was only her voice for a moment, and then her hissing was joined by a chorus of angry whispers from the nest of snakes atop her head.

"Excuse me?" asked a voice from behind her. The language was Greek, but so mangled that she knew he had not been born here.

A curious tourist who'd lost his way, perhaps, and heard the hissing in the shadows. With an expression half smile and half sneer she turned to face him. He recoiled in horror, and his eyes froze, his features a mask of revulsion and terror that would remain for all eternity, etched in petrified stone.

THE passengers of the Range Rover had traveled in silence ever since setting out from Mitilini, where two of the vehicles had been awaiting their arrival. Eve was behind the wheel, with Conan Doyle in the passenger seat, and Danny and Ceridwen in the back. The kid still had his headphones on, but when she glanced in the rearview mirror, Eve could see he was alert and anxious, his eyes darting around, watching the sides of the road . . . not to mention the road in front of them. He was guarded and suspicious.

That was good. Healthy.

The other Range Rover was ahead of them. Hawkins was driving, with Gull riding shotgun and the wild-eyed Jezebel in the backseat. Eve had taken a liking to Jezebel, perhaps because of the madness in the girl's eyes. She knew what it was like to feel that unchained and how dangerous it could be. Eve figured the girl's instability was a liability, but she was Gull's problem, for now.

Conan Doyle had a map spread on his lap and the interior light on. Eve had enjoyed the sunshine, thanks to Gull's spell, but she was relieved that night had fallen. She was comfortable in the dark. At home.

"We're nearing Sigri, now," Conan Doyle reported.

Eve shot him a sidelong glance. "Let me guess. Cute little fishing village, like we stepped back in time, full of hardy Greek men and sensuous full-bodied women?"

Despite the tension Gull's presence was causing, Conan Doyle had not apparently lost his sense of humor. Most people would not believe he had one, but Eve knew it well. Even now, the mage pretended to be surprised.

"However did you know that?" he asked.

"I'm psychic. Didn't you know?"

In the back, Danny laughed softly. A quick glance in the mirror confirmed he had pulled the headphones off. Eve realized that, just as she had, the kid sensed they were approaching their destination. That there was something supernatural nearby. Something big.

Even Ceridwen smiled at her words. Eve was far from psychic, of course. But they had been driving the coast of the island of Lesbos for a while now, and every place they came to was just a more rustic version of the last quaint fishing village.

"I wish we coulda spent some more time in Istanbul,"

Danny said. Now that the silence had been broken, he seemed to want to engage the rest of them. "It was really beautiful. Dirty, yeah. But still . . . squint your eyes just right and it feels like you're walking through history. Those were maybe the only lectures I ever stayed awake for in my history classes . . . about the Byzantine Empire and the Turks and all of that."

"Perhaps we can return one day," Conan Doyle offered. "When other matters are not so demanding of our attention."

Danny seemed surprised. "Do you think?"

Ceridwen replied instead of Conan Doyle. In the mirror, Eve could see the Fey sorceress turn to the boy. "I don't see why not. You have the resources now to explore not only this world but others as well. You'd do well to take advantage of the opportunity to enrich yourself."

"Or you could just have fun," Eve added. "You know, learn about different countries by experiencing their pubs and whores."

Conan Doyle sighed but said nothing. Eve gave him a devilish smirk. She was glad that he and Ceridwen seemed to be healing the rift between them and maybe there was a future there. They certainly loved one another, and that in itself was rare. Even with the resentment of the past still lingering, the two of them would obviously have sacrificed anything for one another. But Eve was going to draw the line at the idea of their trying to parent Danny Ferrick. The kid needed friends and mentors, yes. But he had a mother. An ordinary, wonderfully human mother. Eve didn't want any of them distracting the kid from how lucky he was to have her.

They followed the Range Rover in the lead as it veered away from the village they'd been approaching. The land around them quickly began to change. The ground was rutted. Hawkins was driving like he had a death wish or just didn't care. Eve thought that was pretty sexy, actually, and had no problem doing the same. They bumped over ruts and cut corners too close, sending up swirls of dirt clouds that rose into the night as they passed.

Soon it was not only the terrain that had changed.

"Holy shit," Danny muttered in the backseat, voice so low he seemed unaware he had even spoken. "What *is* this?"

"Yes," Ceridwen agreed. She shuddered and drew her cloak more closely around her as she stared out her window. "It is like a tomb of trees."

Up ahead, Hawkins slowed. Eve did the same. She had to cut the wheel to swerve around a tree that had fallen across their path. But, then, it wasn't really a tree, was it? All around them now was a gray, charcoaled landscape. The trees did not blow in the breeze. The plants did not give off the perfume of flowers. Each trunk that jutted up into the shadow of the night seemed like a withered husk, a corpse, and their branches were skeletal figures pointing accusingly at the sky.

"That's exactly what it is," Eve told Ceridwen. "Exactly."

Hawkins turned off the road now and Eve followed slowly, very careful not to knock down any of the trees. The smell of the ocean came on the breeze through the window, but there were no other scents. Nothing.

"The forest is petrified," Conan Doyle explained, glancing back at Danny and then leaning forward to see out the window. "Nature as cadaver, if you will. In prehistoric times there was a great deal of volcanic activity here. Eruptions produced lava and ash that filled the air so quickly that instead of burning the vegetation here, it was coated with a layer of ash and preserved, just as you see."

Even for Eve the trees were haunting to look at, and they were deep among them now.

"So, the original trees are still under that ash?" Danny asked.

"No. Actually, they were fossilized from the inside out during that same process. You're in a sort of fossil diorama at the moment. It's a remarkable place, actually. A window on the past."

"I'm more concerned about the future," Eve said grimly. Up ahead, Hawkins had stopped the lead vehicle. There appeared to be some kind of clearing beyond.

Eve pulled behind and killed the engine. She was the first one out of the Rover. Conan Doyle and Danny got out. Ceridwen was slow to follow. The destruction of this primeval forest seemed catastrophic to her, or so her expression implied. The Fey sorceress reached out to touch a nearby fossilized tree, but she drew back her hand quickly and lowered her gaze in sadness.

"And this is where we will find the grave of Phorcys? The Gorgons' father?" she asked as she looked up.

Conan Doyle and Danny were already walking toward Gull and his associates, all of whom were out of their vehicle. Eve was the only one who had waited for Ceridwen. She did not dislike the Faerie woman. In fact, Ceridwen had earned her respect many times over, and she appreciated that Conan Doyle loved her, and that the feeling was mutual. But they just didn't have a thing in common. Despite the horrors she had seen in her life, Ceridwen remained in some way innocent.

Eve was the furthest thing from innocent. She was tainted, forever and always, by her sins and by the touch of unclean hands.

Yet Ceridwen always treated her with deference and a quiet camaraderie. So Eve waited for her, and it was she who answered the elemental's question.

"Maybe we'll find it, and maybe we won't," Eve told her. "Phorcys was a myth. A legend. Some of them are true and some of them are bullshit. But even if he was real, and the story of the Gorgons is true, that doesn't mean this is his grave right here. If there's one thing I know about Nigel Gull, it's that the truth is open to interpretation when it's coming from his mouth."

"Yes," Ceridwen replied. "I had that sense."

She glanced once more at the tree she had touched and rubbed her fingers together as though some residue remained on her skin. Eve wore her jeans and boots and her long leather coat over the dark green cashmere top. Her hair was perfect. Her dangling earrings, jade and amber set in gold, had come from a jeweler in Paris. Ceridwen wore a dress that was little more than a layered veil and a robe more suited to Medieval times. And yet there was no question that the sorceress seemed the more at home here, in this ancient place, despite what had befallen the forest.

"I think we're going to have to work extra hard to keep your guy out of trouble this time," Eve told her.

Ceridwen's violet eyes flashed defensively, but then she must have seen something in Eve's own gaze, for she smiled instead. "Where would he be without us?"

Eve glanced around and laughed. "A fossil."

The two of them caught up to Conan Doyle and Danny, Eve noting with admiration that the kid was handling himself well. Hawkins and Jezebel were standing back from the others slightly, and so Eve also hung back to keep an eye on them.

"You are certain this is the place?" Conan Doyle asked, glancing around. Despite the heat, he wore one of his dapper, old-fashioned suits. Thus far his only concession to the weather had been to remove his tie. Any moment she expected him to doff the jacket and roll up his sleeves. But, then, he was locked in this battle of wills with Gull, and that might be construed as a sign of weakness.

It was all ridiculous as far as Eve was concerned. Gull was deformed because he played with magicks he should have left alone. She figured Conan Doyle ought to be satisfied with that as a victory.

"Am I certain?" Gull asked. His wide nostrils flared. "Would I have dragged all you lot out here if I wasn't? You know me better than that, Sir Arthur."

Their mutual dislike and rivalry was buried beneath the chivalric code of another era, but it was there nevertheless.

"How did you determine this to be the site of Phorcys's

grave? What led you here?" Conan Doyle asked, his tone modulated, more reasonable, as he stroked his mustache.

Eve glanced around the petrified forest. The place was impossibly quiet. In that moment it seemed the whole world had been fossilized. Something was not right. She had felt the supernatural force growing here and had told Conan Doyle as much. It was obvious that *something* was here. But despite the look of the place, it did not feel like a grave to her.

It felt *hungry*.

And no one knew what hunger felt like better than she did.

"I've been mapping the real-world locations of mythology for decades. You know that well enough. In my travels I located stone statues . . . victims of a Gorgon's eyes. The Gorgons were Phorcys's daughters. That in mind, it wasn't difficult to find a spell that would use the stone remains of his daughters' victims to create a Divination Box."

He reached into the first Range Rover and withdrew a small wooden box with no cover. On its sides were markings similar to others Eve had seen once before, ages ago in Babylon. Gull held it low so that they could all see inside. There were bits of stone within that must have come from one of the Gorgon's victims as well as the small bones of some kind of bird and several dark-shelled nuts.

Gull shook the box. The contents rattled and jumped a bit, and then all of them rolled of their own accord across the bottom of the box, clicking on the wood as they gathered in one corner.

"Good as any compass," Danny noted, standing between Eve and Conan Doyle.

Gull's misshapen face beamed at the kid. "Precisely, my boy. Precisely."

The bones and stones and nuts began to rattle again. At first Eve though nothing of it. Then she saw the alarm on Gull's face. An instant later the contents of the Divination Box slid up the inside wall and jumped out, flying to the ground and bouncing and rolling across the barren earth, as if drawn by a magnet.

The ground began to buckle and quake. Eve was thrown against the Range Rover. Her companions began to shout but she ignored them all, her eyes searching the darkness among the petrified trees for the place where those bones and stones had gone.

The earth heaved, shattered, and sprayed, and then collapsed in upon itself, a massive hole opening in the ground.

From it came a noise . . . hissing, as if of a thousand snakes.

Then the first hideous head began to rise, sickly yellow eyes glowing in the night as it sought them out.

6

A Hydra.

Danny Ferrick didn't need one of Doyle's musty old books to tell him what it was that had emerged from the dry, barren earth, its multiple heads snapping and hissing. He'd seen enough movies to know exactly what now attacked them.

"Holy shit. A Hydra, a fucking real Hydra," he whispered with awe, frozen where he stood. He could not take his eyes from the serpentine monstrosity, its nine heads swaying hypnotically, as if trying to decide which of their number it would strike at first.

Conan Doyle stood beside Danny, his hands held up, a spray of emerald light flashing from them spreading in front of the two of them like some sort of shield. The old guy seemed way too proper most of the time, but the second the magick started to spark from his eyes and that weird nowhere wind buffeted his clothes and ruffled his hair, he was almost more frightening than any monster. Power simmered in him, flowing off of him in waves.

"Eve," Conan Doyle called. "If you would be so kind as to get off your behind and lend a hand . . ."

The vampire had been thrown back against the Range

Rover when the Hydra erupted from the ground, and now she pulled herself to her feet. "Right away, boss man," she said, shooting him the middle finger. "I live to serve."

The ground shuddered again, a tremor that all of them rode out as though they were onboard a ship. The earth collapsed around the Hydra, huge chunks of volcanic soil sinking inward, entire stretches of the dusty ground erupting upward as the Hydra bucked and hauled its body out of its den beneath the dead earth. Each head was as hideous as the first, jaws gaping open, slavering venom spilling out onto the ground to sizzle like acid as it touched the earth. Beneath its scales moved thick, ropy muscles, and its nine tails thrashed on the dusty ground.

Danny started forward, despite Conan Doyle's magickal defenses. The mage reached out a hand and grabbed his shoulder.

"Not yet, boy."

Eve cautiously moved toward the monster that now swayed on its thick, muscular trunk. She drew its attention, and nine pair of eyes focused on her.

"What's she going to do?" Danny asked.

Conan Doyle ignored him, muttering an incantation under his breath, even as Ceridwen entered the fray. The elemental sorceress pointed her staff toward the beast, the sphere of blue ice atop it crackling with growing power. Her violet eyes sparked, and she raised her arms.

The Hydra struck. Despite Eve's distraction, one massive head turned away from the vampire, and its jaws opened wide, vomiting a gray, noxious vapor. Ceridwen tried to ward off the billowing cloud, but it clung to her, coating her in a layer of ash.

Conan Doyle shouted her name, his face etched with fury as he unleashed a bolt of pure magickal force. But he had been distracted, and even as he ran to her side, the blast went wild, missing the monster and shattering a fossilized tree nearby.

Three of the Hydra's heads twisted around to stare at the

tree that the spell had destroyed. One set of jaws gaped open and hissed in the general direction of Conan Doyle and Ceridwen, but the others still focused on Eve. It had identified her early on as its main prey, and now it began to slither across the barren earth toward her.

This whole thing is going to shit, Danny thought. *Deep shit.* He started after the Hydra, but he remembered Conan Doyle's caution, and he turned to glance back at the man who led them. What the *hell* was he supposed to do?

Eve snapped a branch off of a petrified tree, and as the Hydra twisted its body across the earth toward her, she prepared to use it as a club. "Is she all right?" she yelled to Doyle, who knelt at Ceridwen's side, trying to remove the solidified ash that was crusted on her body.

The vampire had no time to wait for an answer. The Hydra darted toward her, quickening its speed, and while two of its heads feinted, a third lunged toward her, jaws spreading, venom drooling out.

Eve danced aside and swung the thick tree limb at its head. "Take that, you ugly prick."

The Hydra screeched in pain and fury, but even as one head sagged, disoriented, another long neck shot forward, jaws snapping. Once more Eve evaded the Hydra, but this time she jabbed one of its eyes with the end of the branch. The eye punctured, and putrid, gray fluid squirted out. But the Hydra was not nine separate beasts. Its injured heads had distracted Eve, and perhaps they had been meant to, for now a third and fourth serpentine mouth belched clouds of that noxious clinging vapor rather than attacking outright. Danny held his breath, his heart pounding in his chest, every muscle tensed to join the fray. But Eve amazed him with her speed as she dove to the ground, rolling beneath the vapor, right up to the belly of the beast. She swung her club, this time striking the monster's body. All nine heads bellowed its rage as the creature swiveled around and lashed at her with a pair of whip-like tails.

Eve could not dodge the monster forever. One of the tails

caught her in the chest with such force that the pop of cracking bone echoed in the air. She was thrown forty feet, landing in a tumble of limbs. She grunted with the pain of
broken bones as she spilled end over end and at last came to
a sprawling stop.

The Hydra eagerly moved toward its fallen prey.

This was a whole new life for Danny, this world of magick and monsters, but new as it was, it was *his* world. He
was part of it. No matter what Conan Doyle said, he had to
help Eve. The mage was with Ceridwen, and Eve's battle
with the Hydra was slipping by in heartbeats, so quickly that
it might be over before Conan Doyle returned to the fight.
Danny had to do something.

He looked around. *Where are Gull and his people?* He
saw them in the distance and shouted for them, but they ignored him.

A groggy Eve had just climbed to her feet when the
Hydra attacked again. A head struck her, its mouth clamping
onto her shoulder, long venomous fangs digging into her
flesh. She clawed at its face with taloned hands to little avail
and shrieked in pain as the creature held fast, sinking its
teeth deeper, driving her to her knees. Another of the heads
lunged, biting into the opposite arm, followed by yet another
that saw the potential for a strike upon one of her thighs. She
fought valiantly, but the serpent's heads would not release
her, lifting her from the ground, trying to pull her apart.

Danny breathed deeply, mustering all his courage, and
sprinted across the hard, dusty ground, volcanic ash rising
around him. One of the Hydra's heads whipped around, and
its hideous eyes locked on him. It bared its fangs and hissed.

The demon boy hissed back, and lunged for the monster.

THE man who arrived at the scene of the second atrocity
in Athens looked exactly like Yannis Papathansiou, walked
and talked like him, even smelled like him. But the detective
was elsewhere. It was Clay who wore his face, and he en-

tered the building with Squire in tow. The hobgoblin was hideous, but he had passed for human before, primarily because people saw his ugliness and tried to avert their eyes out of politeness. When they did stare, they thought him some kind of freak. There would be those who would wonder about the gnarled little man with Detective Papathansiou, but no one would say a word in front of Squire.

"Let me handle this," Clay whispered to the hobgoblin.

"I think we've finally found the perfect look for you," Squire whispered, peering over the top of his dark sunglasses, even though dawn was hours away. The hobgoblin was wearing a baseball cap that had *Kiss Me I'm Greek* embroidered on it, with a pair of red, luscious lips below. Clay had considered asking where he'd gotten such a hat, but knew he would probably regret the question, so he let it go.

The detective had called them at the hotel to inform them that another stone body had been found. Clay had instructed the old man to stay home, that he and his associates would handle the investigation. Yannis had at first protested, but when Clay had explained that a fresher victim might provide better clues to lead them to their quarry, he had at last acquiesced.

Clay and Squire moved past the Thesseion temple toward the small gathering of police officers and detectives. "Not a word," Clay warned the goblin again, as a broad shouldered man with glasses approached them. Papathansiou had told him that this detective was named Dioskouri, and the other, smaller man, who had yet to notice their arrival, was Keramikous.

"Lieutenant," Dioskouri said.

"Detective," Clay acknowledged dismissively, channeling every nuance of Lieutenant Yannis Papathansiou's personality and body language. They were speaking Greek, which Squire did not understand very well, but in his masquerade, speaking English would have raised suspicions. He looked past Dioskouri, searching for the crime scene. "The body is where?"

The detective nervously adjusted his glasses as he turned and pointed through the darkness to a section of columns. "Back there. His wife found him."

"Time's a wastin', Zorba," Squire said, heading toward the crime scene.

"And you are?" Dioskouri asked in English, moving to block Squire's way.

Squire sighed in exasperation. "Would you mind telling him who I am, Yannis, old chum?"

"This is Professor Squire from the Institute in Vienna," Clay explained in staccato Greek. "He's been vacationing on the islands and was kind enough to offer his assistance."

Dioskouri looked down at the tiny man in confusion. His English was rough, but understandable. "I mean no disrespect sir, but you are an expert on the impossible? On men and women turned to stone?"

Squire clasped his stubby arms behind his back and rocked on the heels of his high top sneakers. "You'd be surprised, my boy, you'd be surprised."

Clay decided that it would be wise to get them to the body as quickly as possible and pushed past Dioskouri and Squire. "Keramikous," he called to the other detective, who was still conversing with two, uniformed patrolman.

"Yes, Lieutenant?" the man responded quickly, stepping away from the officers.

"Secure the area. Professor Squire and I are going to look at the crime scene."

Keramikous looked momentarily confused. "Professor Squire?"

"He's from the Institute in Vienna," Dioskouri snapped, with an air of superiority.

"Carry on," Clay said, waving them away as he and Squire carefully navigated the stone pathway that would take them to the body.

"Where exactly is this Institute in Vienna?" Squire asked in a whisper from the corner of his mouth, amusement in his voice.

Clay shrugged. "I made it up. But neither of them seems interested in second-guessing their lieutenant."

"Did you know I'm this much shy of a degree in massage therapy?" the hobgoblin asked, holding his sausage-sized thumb and forefinger apart less than an inch.

"You don't say," Clay said as they approached the Doric columns around which yellow crime scene tape had been wrapped.

"Couldn't find any place to accept my internship though," Squire grumbled. "I think it's because I'm a guy trying to break into an industry dominated by chicks. What do you think?"

Clay pulled away the tape, maneuvering around the column, searching for the latest Gorgon victim. "I think I might be able to find you something in New Orleans, if you're interested."

An unusually wide, toothy grin spread across the hobgoblin's face. "Hey, you'd do that for me? That'd be sweet."

"Here we go," Clay said as they came upon the petrified body. It was just as disturbing as the others, the features wide with fear and despair.

"All right, let's deal with this Gorgon bullshit and get home to the important stuff." Squire began to move around the crime scene, examining every shadow.

Clay smiled to himself. Now at least Squire would be focused. He wondered briefly how Graves was faring in his more spiritual investigation, haunting the streets of the ancient city for a spirit or two that might give them some information about the Gorgon's whereabouts. Hopefully, working both the physical angle and the ethereal, they could make some progress and find the creature before it caused any more harm.

Still wearing the shape of the overweight detective, he turned his attention to the ossified figure before him. Its terrified gaze was frozen, staring blankly in the direction of the two columns. "The Gorgon must have been standing somewhere over there," Clay said, turning toward the columns.

"Let's see if it left anything of interest behind." Squire walked over to the columns, surveying the ground around them. "No conveniently dropped cigarette butts or anything," the goblin observed, "but that doesn't mean it didn't leave a scent behind."

Clay took that as his cue to alter his form again. To track by scent he summoned the shape of an animal with an incredibly acute olfactory sense. The shape of Yannis Papathansiou melted away with a sound very much like the flapping of bird's wings, to be replaced by a far more beastly form—a Dire Wolf, prehistoric relative of the common gray wolf, larger and more sturdy than its modern counterpart.

"Nice doggy," Squire said, stepping away.

Clay smelled it immediately, the aroma of something ancient and dangerous, hinting of desperation and unpredictability. It made the hackles of fur at the back of his neck stand on end.

"I've got it," he growled, altering the structure of the wolf's mouth slightly to allow him to speak.

Squire jumped onto his back, grabbing a handful of thick, grayish fur. "Go fetch."

It was no simple thing to avoid the police already in the area, but Clay maneuvered in the shadows and soon found the route of the Gorgon's escape, near the back of the ruins. Its scent was all over the place. The Dire Wolf leaped into the darkness. They paused a moment, waiting for voices to shout at them, but no one had noticed their exit.

Clay placed his nose closer to the ground and began to follow the trail, a path so obvious it was like following bread crumbs, or a line drawn with bright red crayon. The Dire Wolf and its passenger padded across the timeworn ground of the Agora, leaving the murder scene behind. The spoor was strong. At this rate, it would only be a matter of time before they found their prize.

A sound like the crack of a bullwhip filled the air as a bullet exploded from the barrel of a rifle. The steel-jacketed projectile slammed through the thick fur and muscle of the Dire Wolf's neck, turning several of its vertebrae to powder. Clay flipped backward on his side with a roar of pain, bucking Squire from his perch. Already, the flesh was knitting as the shapeshifter assumed a more familiar guise, a human face.

"Squire, are you all right?" he hissed, altering the structure of his eyes, turning the darkness of night to the light of day and scanning for signs of their attacker.

Squire slunk up next to him in the shadows, an inch-long gash in his forehead. The two of them moved quickly against the face of a building, gauging the location of the shooter as best they could and hoping they would be out of the line of sight. Without another shot, Clay could only guess about the sniper's location, and guessing would be dangerous.

"Think he's still up there?" Squire asked, craning his neck back as though he might spot the sniper from their vantage point.

"Only one way to find out. Stay here."

The hobgoblin did not protest as Clay stepped away from the building and out into the open. No matter how destructive, a simple bullet wasn't going to do more than tear him up a little, and Clay could always knit himself back together.

No second shot came.

Peering into the darkness at the tops of the neighboring buildings, even with his eyes adjusted, he saw only architecture. Nothing moved.

"He's gone."

Squire grunted, cursing under his breath as he touched the wound on his head and stepped away from the wall. "What the hell was the asshole doing? If he thought he could pop us, he would've stuck around. But if he knew it wouldn't be that easy, why bother?"

The question troubled Clay. He shifted into the form of the Dire Wolf again, but this time Squire trotted along behind him. Clay was moving more slowly. They passed through a narrow alley, tracking the scent, but on the next street over, a cobblestoned road that seemed almost abandoned, the Dire Wolf sniffed and flinched away from the ground, nostrils searing and eyes watering.

Once more Clay metamorphosed into the familiar, human face he so often wore. He rarely revealed what he thought of as his true appearance. There was nothing human about him.

"He's gone, all right. He shot me just to buy time."

Squire dabbed at his wound with a filthy handkerchief. "To do what?"

Even in human form, Clay found the strength of the pungent aroma nearly overpowering. "Do you smell it?" he asked.

Squire sniffed, and his brow furrowed, causing a fresh trickle of blood from his wound. "What the fuck is that?"

"Ammonia," Clay answered. "To eradicate any trace of the Gorgon's scent. I could pick up the trail again if I searched long enough, but there's no way to know if it'll be a fresh trail, or the path the Gorgon took getting to the ruins, instead of away."

Squire placed his hands on his hips. "Are you suggesting that our monster has a guardian angel looking out for it?"

"I'm suggesting that somebody else has an interest in our quarry," Clay responded, his dark animal eyes scanning the darkness. "And they're willing to kill to keep us from getting to it first."

"QUICKLY now," Gull ordered as Hawkins sunk the blade of the shovel deep into the dry, black soil.

He chanced a glance over his shoulder at the commotion in the not-too-far distance.

Conan Doyle and his people are putting up quite a fight,

he thought, the Hydra's angry wails echoing through the night. Gull felt a momentary pang of guilt as he watched them fight for their lives against the many-headed beast, but then realized their lives meant nothing compared to his objective.

"Did you know it was there?" Jezebel asked, distracting him.

He turned from the battle in the distance. Hawkins was still digging, making excellent progress, each shovelful of dead earth bringing them closer and closer still. Jezebel was staring at him, large, green eyes glistening in the darkness, red tresses blowing across her face.

"Did you know the monster was under the ground?" the girl asked again, reaching out to touch Gull's sleeve, urging him to reveal his duplicity.

She was a fragile thing, filled with such rage, sadness, and fear. He hated to show her the lengths to which he would go to achieve what he most desired, how easily established trusts could be torn asunder, but there was far too much at stake to concern himself with such flimsy concepts as loyalty and honor.

"Nothing must sway us," he told her, nodding grimly. "There was no way the Hydra would have allowed us to reach the grave."

Jezebel looked from Gull to Hawkins, who continued to furiously dig, and then turned her attention to the Hydra and its prey. "They trusted you," she said, her voice no more than a whisper.

Gull chuckled. "I seriously doubt that. But there was no choice, my dear Jezebel. If Conan Doyle knew who was actually buried here, and my intentions for him, well, let's just say I doubt we would be where we are right now."

For a long moment, Jezebel only looked at him, one hand on her outthrust hip, ever the rebellious teen. Then she shrugged, her T-shirt riding even higher up on her exposed abdomen. "I didn't like them very much anyway," she said with a darling shake of her head, a sly smile creeping across her delicate features; her faith in him seemingly restored.

"That's the spirit." Gull pulled her close and placed a gentle kiss on her brow, then turned his attentions to Hawkins. "How're we coming along, Nick?" he asked, the crackle of anticipation in the air.

"Would be further along if one of you would lift a bloody finger to help," Hawkins grumbled, tossing another shovelful of dirt over his shoulder. The man was making excellent progress. He had dug down at least four feet into the dusty soil.

"We all have our parts to play, Mr. Hawkins," Gull reassured him. "Soon your part will be done, and it will be our time to shine."

"Yay!" Jezebel said, clapping her hands.

Hawkins sunk the blade of his shovel into the earth again, but this time it was met with a strange, hollow thud. Gull gasped as the man looked up and smiled. Hawkins leaned his tool against the side of the hole and, kneeling down, began to carefully brush away the dry, black dirt. Even this far down the soil was like dust, as if all moisture had somehow been removed from the ground.

Gull moved closer to the hole's edge, watching the man as he worked. Something wooden was gradually coming into view. He held his breath as Hawkins placed the flat of his hand against the top of the buried box to read its psychic impression.

Hawkins gasped, falling backward as his body was wracked with trembling spasms. Gull frowned and knelt to reach for him, but Hawkins waved him away, catching his breath.

"This is it," he said, struggling to his feet and retrieving his shovel.

"Let's have it, then, Nick," Gull ordered, his heart racing. "But be careful, yes? It'll be useless to me if the contents of our little box are damaged."

Hawkins jammed the point of the shovel into the rotted

wood, splintering the top with ease. He tossed his shovel aside to squat down at the box. Carefully he pulled the cover away, the ancient wood crumbling in his hand, to expose a filthy, burlap sack. Hawkins reached inside and hauled the sack out of the box.

"Give it here," Gull said, his twisted hands reaching eagerly as Hawkins handed it up to him.

Gull gently laid the sack on the ground and knelt beside it as if preparing to pray. The burlap was as rotted and dry as the earth in which it had been interred, and he grabbed hold of the coarse cloth, tearing open the sack to expose its contents.

A single human skull.

Jezebel knelt breathlessly beside him, and Hawkins peered out over the rim of the hole.

"Here we are," he said as he raised up the perfectly preserved skull. It still wore a paper-thin covering of dried flesh, and tufts of downy hair clung to the top of its head, like some grotesque baby chick. "What a handsome devil you are," Gull cooed, first showing the face of the skull to an appreciative Jezebel, and then to Hawkins.

"A real looker," Hawkins agreed as he began to haul himself from the hole.

"He has a kind face," Jezebel said, reaching out to gently feather the tufts of hair with her long, delicate fingers. "I think I would have liked him quite a bit."

"And he you, I'm sure," Gull said as he climbed to his feet, skull in hand. "But as of now, our disembodied friend has much to share with me, and I require your special talents."

The girl smiled, planting her feet on the ground and moving her head around, stretching the muscles in her neck in preparation. "Your wish is my command," she said, closing her eyes.

Jezebel's brow furrowed as if she were suddenly in the throes of deep thought, and her breathing became heavier. Desiccated skull still in hand, Gull watched as a visible tremor passed through her body, and she gasped, eyes opening wide as she turned her gaze to the evening sky. Twin trickles of scarlet began to leak from her nostrils.

"Here it comes," she said in breathless whisper, shivering uncontrollably as the full force of her personal magick was unleashed upon the environment.

Thick, billowing clouds of white coalesced in the sky above them, but nowhere else. A rumble of thunder heralded the arrival of their own private storm. A flash of lightning slashed the night's black tapestry, followed by an even more severe clap of thunder, and then the rain at last began to fall.

Jezebel fell to her knees, then began to giggle as she curled herself into a tight ball on the ground and promptly fell asleep.

"Mr. Hawkins," Gull called over the sound of the torrential rainfall. "If you would be so kind as to bring Jezebel to the truck."

The former SAS man complied, picking up the soaking girl and carrying her to the Range Rover parked not far from them.

Gull stood in the rain and reached out to grasp the fabric of the very air itself, plumbing a darkness that lurked beneath the ordinary shadows of night. It was an ancient Egyptian magick considered too powerful for even the high priests of that venerable age, a talent he had not used since that rainy, late summer night in 1902 when, much to the disgust of Sir Arthur Conan Doyle, he had spoken with the voice of a murdered child.

Oh, what things the dead can share, Gull mused as he gently pried the jaw of the skull open, the dried skin crackling like autumn leaves, and then holding it up for the rain to collect within the hollow of its mouth.

In time he lowered the skull, careful not to spill its contents, and brought it to his mouth. Gull pressed his lips gently to the jaw bone, tipping it back, drinking deeply, cool rainwater cascading down his throat. Then he dropped the now empty skull to the muddy ground, waiting for the magick to fill him. He did not have long to wait.

The voice of the dead man was in his throat, bubbling up and out of his yawning mouth, a voice raised in a song long silenced.

Until now.

CONAN Doyle's worst fear had become a reality.

The cloud of ash spewed by the Hydra had formed an unyielding shell on Ceridwen's body. Frantically Doyle clawed at the thick soot that had solidified on her face as she thrashed against him, desperate to breathe. He could hear his Menagerie in the midst of combat with the many-headed serpent and knew that he should be helping them, guiding them, but he couldn't. Not now. Not when a heart he had long thought shriveled and cold had begun to beat again.

The thought of losing Ceridwen again had frozen him, crippled him in this battle, and it might have doomed them all.

Her struggles were slowing, and Doyle cursed himself. This was not the time for panic, but for action. His fingertips, raw and bloody, tingled as he began to summon a spell. The magicks he was attempting to wield were not meant for such delicate matters, but he had no choice. The power coursed from his fingertips, and it took all his strength to keep the flow to a trickle, directing the magick where it was needed.

The ashen shroud broke, falling away from Ceridwen's face, and she gasped, sucking the air greedily. She began to cough uncontrollably, and he pulled her to him.

"Thank the gods," he said, holding her tight, the ash flaking away from her lithe body.

Ceridwen's eyes went wide, and she tensed, pushing him away from her. "What are you doing?" she demanded. There was a fiery intensity in her gaze that he did not at first comprehend, but her ire became all too clear as she snatched up her staff from the ground and struggled to stand.

"Eve and Danny, we have to help them."

"Of course," he agreed, guilt searing his heart and mind as he helped her to her feet. "Let's bring this conflict to an end."

Ceridwen shot him a wounding gaze filled with disappointment and anger. Emotion had clouded his judgment, and he had much to answer for, but the lives of their comrades took precedence. The Fey sorceress moved away from him, blue fire dancing around her eyes and from the ice sphere atop her staff, leaving him to stand alone and to ponder the repercussions of his actions.

Or lack thereof.

EVE wiped a trickle of blood from her mouth, smearing a crimson band across her face that she was sure looked like war paint. *That's appropriate,* she thought, preparing to have another go at the thrashing monstrosity. For this was most certainly war.

Danny had managed to grapple with two of the Hydra's heads at once, squeezing their necks in his arms, forcing their hissing jaws closed. Again and again he struck their hideous, spade-shaped faces. The exposed leathery flesh of his body was covered in bloody bites, and Eve could see that his ferocity was starting to wane. They had to end this quickly, before they all ran out of energy and wound up as Hydra food.

Eve sprang at the many-headed beast. One head hung limply from the thick trunk of the Hydra's body, blood dripping from its open maw, the first real casualty of their teamwork. She landed atop the monster's back, digging her claws into the nearest wavering neck, feeling the skin at last pop, blood gushing out from the wound as the Hydra wailed in agony. Eve brought her mouth down to the steaming geyser, swallowing gouts of the monster's blood in an attempt to replenish her strength.

The blood tasted like shit, but she felt revitalized. Uttering a deep, throaty laugh, she bit into the throat of the dying head, through thick skin, muscle and bone, finally tearing the head from the body. The creature bucked violently and Eve lost her grip, falling hard to the dusty ground. Danny had lost his hold on the other heads, and he leapt back as they snapped at him.

Eve still held a severed Hydra head and proudly showed it to Danny before tossing it away.

"Don't know if that was such a good idea," he said breathlessly, looking back at the beast.

She began to ask what he meant, when suddenly she understood. The muscular stump was writhing in the air, the scaly flesh of the monster beginning to morph. And suddenly, from the stump, there emerged another head, growing quickly.

"Did you know it could do that?" she asked him, tensing to throw herself at the monster yet again.

"Saw it in some movie once." Danny explained, not taking his eyes from the hissing beast. He was breaking away a layer of solidified Hydra ash that had collected on his arm and chest. "Thought they'd just made it up. Guess not."

"Thanks for sharing," Eve said. "I really appreciate the intel."

There were nine heads again, and she wasn't quite sure how much longer she and the kid could keep this up. The Hydra was taking stock of its prey again, careful, heads weaving around, preparing to strike.

Eve was about to lunge again when a familiar voice boomed through the ashen forest.

"Hold!" Ceridwen cried, her staff raised above her head. A storm of electricity churned around the sphere of ice at the top of the staff.

Eve felt the air crackle. "Back up!" she shouted at Danny, just as a bolt of lightning tore through the heavens, cleaving the sky as it descended to Earth to strike the Hydra. The monster shook with the power of the storm as the lightning surged through it, smoke rising from the soil beneath. Eve and Danny were thrown backward, hair singed, skin prickling.

Danny rubbed his eyes as he regained his feet. "Damn. I guess Ceridwen's okay."

Eve knew otherwise. Danny had been momentarily blinded by the brightness of the lightning, but Eve saw the elemental sorceress crumple to the ground, like a marionette with severed strings.

The Hydra, its skin blackened and charred, yet far from dead, reared up from the ground, parts of its serpentine form still smoldering with fire. Nine mouths screamed out its rage, surging forward to continue its attack.

"Come on!" Eve cried out as a head bent forward, mouth agape. "What does it take to kill this thing?" She took hold of its upper and lower jaw as it struck, preventing it from biting her.

The other heads had driven Danny to the ground, and he was snapping off fangs and gouging eyes, trying to keep himself from being bitten in two, doing whatever he had to just to keep himself alive.

A thick, noxious cloud of ash plumed from the mouth of the Hydra as Eve struggled, the substance clinging to her face, momentarily blinding her. She let go of the monster's head, throwing herself back and away, bouncing off what could only have been the side of the Range Rover. She tumbled to the ground, clawing at the hardening ash on her face, tearing most of it away before it could solidify.

Eve watched in horror as the blackened body of the Hydra loomed above Danny, each of its heads preparing to strike at the boy. She attempted to get to her feet, but excruciating pain exploded in her side, and she was driven again to her knees.

She could only watch as the Hydra's heads dipped and Danny's hands rose instinctively to protect his face. But then something happened that at first Eve could not begin to explain. The Hydra's attack was stopped.

No, she thought, watching carefully, *not stopped, slowed down.* As though in the space around the demon boy and the Hydra, time itself had become disoriented.

"Amazing," she said, ignoring the grinding of broken ribs in her side, and getting up from the ground. Conan Doyle and Ceridwen strode side by side toward the monster, their hands extended, trails of sizzling magickal force leaking from the tips of their fingers. Their faces were etched with strain and focus.

"Eve, if you wouldn't mind, this is far from easy," Conan Doyle said, a slight tremble in his voice. "Kill it."

"Haven't you been paying attention?" she asked. "That's what Danny and I have been trying to do, no help from you."

Conan Doyle grimaced, turning his gaze briefly to a broken tree limb on the ground. "The branch," he began. Fat beads of sweat had begun to collect on his brow from the strain of the spell that had slowed time. "Use it to pierce the Hydra's heart. Much like yourself, it's the only way the monster can be . . ."

His voice trailed off, but she had the information she needed. Eve raced to grab the branch, then ran at the monstrosity that still towered over the boy. Whatever magic they had used, it only affected those who were in the vicinity when it was cast. But the Hydra and Danny would not be slowed like this for long.

"This is going to hurt you a lot more than it does me," Eve said as she placed her hand against the charred scales of the monster's breast, feeling for the pulse of its heart.

Eve found what she was looking for. With all the unnatural strength she could muster, the vampire plunged the jagged end of the makeshift spear through the creature's chest and into its heart.

She found the act strangely liberating.

The Hydra shrieked in agony out of all of its mouths, a

chorus of anguish so profound that Eve was almost moved to pity.

Almost.

When it crashed to the ground, throwing up volcanic ash in clouds that spread in concentric circles around it, she strode over to the monster and kicked it. "It wasn't ever gonna be me in the dust, ugly. Not today."

7

ASH clouded the sun above the petrified forest. The breeze blowing across the island of Lesbos would soon clear away what had not already clung to the skeletal trees or blanketed the ground. In the moments following the death of the Hydra, Conan Doyle concerned himself with the well-being of his associates. All of them were injured, yet Danny and Eve healed quickly.

"Let me have a look," he said to Ceridwen.

She had sustained several long gashes on her right side. But even as he tried to see to her wounds he could feel a wave of cold emanating from her hands where she touched her scored flesh. Ice formed on her skin.

"I'll be fine," she said, curtly at first, and then she caught herself and her features became gentler. "Truly. I will be fine. See to the others. Or better yet, see to Gull. He and his friends weren't very much help, were they?"

Conan Doyle smiled bitterly. "Did you expect them to be?"

"Son of a bitch!" Danny snarled.

Through the drifting, settling ash, Conan Doyle saw the demon boy striding toward him with Eve at his side. Sunlight shone down in patches but the bit of magick Gull had taught Eve to protect herself was holding up for the moment. At least that had not been false.

"What is it?" Ceridwen asked, moving toward them in concern, wincing at the pain in her side.

Conan Doyle did not have to ask, but he awaited the answer to the question in any case. Eve spun around, her arms wide, taking in the entire dead, petrified landscape around them.

"They're gone!" she said.

"Bastards!" Danny added for punctuation.

Eve laughed humorlessly. "Can you believe these guys? Drag us all the way out here to get answers and instead we get to fight the Hydra! And now they're gone! Took off while we were trying to stay alive. We have been so completely punked."

Conan Doyle did not know the term, but its meaning was clear. He only nodded. Rather than respond he set off toward the place he had last seen Gull, Hawkins, and Jezebel.

"Arthur?" Ceridwen called.

Lost in concentration, he barely heard her. He had an idea but wanted confirmation. The ash continued to settle, drifting, and he wiped it from his eyes as he circumnavigated the corpse of the Hydra. He would have to see to it before they left, some spell to disintegrate it, perhaps, so that it was only more ash in the petrified forest. Certainly he had no intention of reburying it.

Beyond the monster's corpse he strode a hundred yards farther to a place where the dead trees formed a kind of natural circle. Or, rather, it appeared natural. Conan Doyle knew better. In the rough center of that circle was a hole in the ground. Ash coated the earth, but Conan Doyle fell to his knees there and plunged his hands into the hole, sifting ash and digging a bit deeper.

He drew out a human skull.

Ceridwen, Eve, and Danny had followed him at a distance, observing. Now the demon boy swore aloud once more.

"So this is the grave of that dude? Forceps or whatever?"

Conan Doyle held the skull up. "This is human. Ancient, but human. The father of the Gorgons was not human."

"Then whose grave is this?" Eve asked. "What the hell was Gull up to here?"

He raised his eyebrows and stood, tossing the skull back into the ash. "I should think that much would be obvious, my dear. Some time in the past . . . perhaps as early as the very beginning of the Third Age of Man . . . the Hydra was buried here to guard this grave, to destroy anyone who came in search of it. My old friend Mr. Gull availed himself of our services as bodyguards. He simply did so without informing us."

"Bodyguards?" Eve snarled. "More like bait."

"As you wish," Conan Doyle acknowledged. His attention was still not fully on the conversation. He scanned the ground, eyeing the fresh ash as he began to walk away from the grave. Silently he counted paces in his mind, paused to glance deeper into the petrified forest, then crouched and plucked from the ground an object that at first appeared to be just a stone beneath the ash.

"No offense, Mr. Doyle, but you don't seem nearly as pissed off about this as I'd like you to be," Danny said. "I mean, what now?"

Ceridwen sketched a symbol in the air, and a gust of wind scoured the stone in Doyle's hand clean of ash. Beneath it was a familiar box whose sides were etched with sigils as old as human civilization.

Conan Doyle turned his face up to the sky. Now that the ash had cleared he enjoyed the warmth of the sun. The back of his neck was sticky with sweat, however, and that he could not abide. He longed for a luxury hotel room with a decent shower.

"He's not as upset as you are, Danny," Ceridwen said in her lilting Fey voice, "because he knew this was going to happen."

Eve snickered darkly. "Of course you did. Of course you did! Fuck!"

Danny shook his head. "I don't get it. If you knew, why did we even come?"

Conan Doyle frowned and spun on his heel to stare at the boy in consternation. "Daniel, I'm disappointed. How else was I to discover what Gull had in mind? Now, at least, we know where to begin."

"We do?" Danny replied, throwing up his hands. "Maybe you do, but I'm like totally lost."

Eve put a hand on his shoulder, smiling now, her own anger and the last of her bloodlust leaving her. "Doyle's never lost."

"Well," Conan Doyle said, allowing himself a small swell of pride. "Never is awfully strong. Rarely, then. I'll accept that much." He cradled the Divination Box in one hand, and with the other he reached out and let his fingers brush Ceridwen's hand. When she allowed his touch to linger, he felt a wave of satisfaction. Though his concentration had been elsewhere, part of his mind had been with her. He glanced at her, and she nodded, her eyes gentle.

"Go on," she urged. "I'm curious."

Conan Doyle glanced deeper into the petrified forest. "Well, to begin, they had another vehicle waiting for them not far from here, well aware that they would be leaving us behind and that they would unlikely be able to reach the Range Rover."   •

"Okay, but what about the grave?" Danny urged.

"Do you know the story of Orpheus?"

The demon boy nodded. "I think so. Something about saving his girlfriend from Hell. Mom used to watch *Xena*."

"Hades," Eve said quietly. She kept glancing at the open grave as though its nearness disturbed her.

"Hades. Whatever. Greek Hell," Danny muttered. "Okay, go on."

Conan Doyle turned to Ceridwen. She was unlikely to know any of what he was about to explain, and it seemed most important to him that she understand what was happening.

"Orpheus was the son of Calliope and Oeagrus. Some of the myths say his father was Apollo, but no matter. He was the greatest musician written about in the Greek mythology. His voice could soothe wild animals and lure the trees to dance. He appears in the story of Jason and the Argonauts, but that is not the greatest myth of Orpheus. For his story is intrinsically tied to love.

"His wife, Eurydice, died of a serpent's bite, and Orpheus was so stricken with grief that he would not accept her death. He descended into the underworld and sang to Hades himself, his songs so beautiful that the lord of that terrible realm agreed to allow Eurydice her freedom. But not without condition. Hades instructed Orpheus that Eurydice must follow him to the surface and that he must not look back. But the agony of being unable to see her, to know for certain that Hades had kept his word, was too much for Orpheus, and at the last moment he did turn, and Eurydice was drawn down into Hades' realm once more.

"Orpheus grieved for the rest of his days, and his songs of mourning made the heavens weep. Yet his luck did not improve. The Maenads were female followers of Dionysus, women who would dance in praise of their god and become so frenzied that they would lose control of themselves. When Orpheus refused to admire them, to lust for them, because grief still clouded his heart, they attacked him and tore him to pieces."

Danny visibly flinched. "Damn, I don't remember that point being on *Xena*."

"Nice," Eve whispered.

Ceridwen only frowned, troubled, and said nothing.

Conan Doyle took a breath, glancing at them each in turn. "The Olympians were so furious with the Maenads that they turned them into trees." His gaze surveyed the petrified forest. "And as for Orpheus . . . they threw his head into a river, and the river fed the ocean, and in time his head came to rest on the shore of the island of Lesbos."

Only the wind broke the silence. They stared at him. Danny shook his head.

"No way."

"You're saying—"

Conan Doyle waved them to quiet. "Indeed. I believe the skull in that grave to be that of Orpheus. Gull had need of it, and used us as a diversion to appropriate it."

"But he left it behind," Ceridwen said.

"Because he found out what he wanted," Conan Doyle explained. "The ash all around the grave, even beneath our feet now, is wet." He plucked at the knees of his pants, which were damp. "The girl, Jezebel, is a weather witch. We have seen her work this magick already. She made it rain here, just in this place."

"I am so not following this," Danny sighed, reaching up to scratch the flaking leathery skin around his horns. "Wake me up when we get to the ass-kicking part."

Eve thumped him on the arm. For once, Conan Doyle approved.

"Why would she need to make it rain?" Eve asked. "Come on, seriously. Every second you take enlightening the terminally dense here is another second between us and them. Assuming we do want to catch up to them?"

"Oh, we do," Conan Doyle assured her. "But I'll attempt to be brief."

"Far too late for that," Ceridwen noted, violet eyes flashing in the sun.

"I've told you of Gull's work with ancient magicks. Dark magicks that no one in their right mind would ever work for fear of how it might taint them. He sacrificed his face for that power, and other things as well, I should think. One of the rituals he practices allows him to . . . borrow the voices of the dead. If he drinks rainwater from the mouth of a corpse, he can speak in its voice."

"That is hideous," Ceridwen whispered. "Desecrating the dead in such a way."

"But useful at times, I'm sure," Conan Doyle conceded. "For instance, if you wanted to open the gates to the ancient underworld, to the home of whatever might remain in that realm from before the dawn of the Third Age of Man, and you knew that—"

"The voice of Orpheus," Eve said. "This is just too much. You're saying this guy can speak in the voice of Orpheus now, and that's somehow the key to some ancient netherworld."

Conan Doyle sighed. "Precisely. But more than that, Gull will be able to *sing* in Orpheus's voice. And few will be able to resist him."

"What the hell does he want in the netherworld?" Danny asked.

The four of them stood there in the midst of the petrified forest, the sun beating down on them, and Conan Doyle raised the Divination Box in his hand.

"That, I do not know. But I have no doubt we will soon discover the answer, and to our misfortune. Gull might have left this behind because he expected me to follow. Or he might simply have flung it away now that he needed it no longer, so arrogant that he could not conceive of my being able to use it."

Ceridwen reached for the box and raised it up, studying it in the sunlight. "But won't you need some piece of Gull? Something of his flesh?"

"Not necessarily flesh. And not Gull, either." He withdrew from his pocket a lock of hair bound with red string. Red hair. "From Jezebel. With this, we can locate her. And when we find her, we find Gull."

"And when did you collect *that* little sample?" Eve asked, arching an eyebrow.

"Last night, while she slept, I gathered it from her hairbrush." Conan Doyle turned from them and started toward the Range Rover. "Come. I've got to prepare the Divination Box, and then we'll see where we are headed next."

They followed, but as they did, Danny spoke up. Though he had the face of a demon, the hideous visage of some hellish thing, there was still somehow something of a human teenager in his expression. At times this phenomenon was comical. At others, it was chilling.

"Hold up. So Mr. Doyle had this all figured from the start, right? All of it."

"Not all," Eve said, striding along, plucking at the tears in her clothing, clearly more displeased with the damage to her outfit than anything else. "He took the girl's hair as a contingency. Probably one of a hundred backup plans he's got in his head. And as for Orpheus, he only just figured that out since all of this happened, and even now he's not completely sure."

Conan Doyle paused at the Range Rover with his hand on the door. He turned and regarded his three companions. Ceridwen came to him, standing intimately close. It made his heart light to have her near, but he refused to let it affect him now. His love for her had almost cost them dearly in this fight, and he would not allow it again.

"Is that true, Arthur? Are you unsure?"

"On the contrary. I'm entirely certain for any number of reasons, not the least of which being that there's nothing else in that grave. Only the head. And when I held it . . . it seemed to hum."

Conan Doyle climbed into the Range Rover but paused before he shut the door. He leaned out again.

"Eve. Danny. A small favor, if you will?"

They had been about to get into the vehicle but now waited, eyeing him curiously.

"I'm going to deal with what's left of the Hydra. Before I do, could I trouble you to go back and remove its teeth and bring them to me?"

Eve frowned. "Do I even ask?"

Danny seemed thoughtful for a moment, searching his

mind for something familiar, for the story. Conan Doyle saw
the process, saw the moment when the demon boy's eyes lit
up with realization. He had remembered. He grinned at
Conan Doyle.

"The Hydra's teeth. That just rocks." The boy bumped
Eve affectionately. "Come on. You're going to love this. I'll
tell you the story while we work."

Conan Doyle nodded and slid back into the Range
Rover's seat. Ceridwen climbed in beside him. Together
they began to work with the Divination Box, and all the
while his curiosity ate at him.

*What are you after, Nigel? What could be so vital to you
that you would dare disturb the tomb of an entire age?*

THE blue sky over Athens had deepened to a rich indigo,
and a hint of the moon was visible above the Acropolis.
Tourists walked the long path down the hill from the
Parthenon, surrendering at last to exhaustion after a long day
exploring the city. On their way down, none of them glanced
up into the darkening sky, but even if they had they would
not have been able to see the ghost of Dr. Graves as he
floated back the way they had come, an errant cloud in the
shape of a man.

As night crept across the city, Dr. Graves looked up at the
outline of the Parthenon silhouetted in the dark and was
humbled by its beauty. *This is a ghost*, he thought. *You,
Leonard, are merely an afterthought. An echo.*

Graves had first visited Athens in 1927. His memories of
the Acropolis were what brought him there tonight. In those
days he had been a living, breathing man, a thing of flesh
and blood. Now he was a wisp of smoke, nothing more. Yet
even then he had sensed the ancient soul of this place, all the
lives and cultures that had thrived and died there, all the
souls that had cried out to their gods for succor. The destruction the Venetians had wrought. The blood that had
been spilled upon the stone and earth of that hill. If there

was a better place for him to go and try to commune with the phantoms of Athens, he could not imagine it.

The strange part was that in those days of flesh and blood and adventure he had not believed in such things. He had told himself that what he felt was merely awe and respect for the achievements of that ancient society. But that had been foolish. The specters of ancient Greece still lingered atop the Acropolis.

Now Graves cursed himself for waiting so long to come here. It had seemed sensible to begin with the Gorgon's victims, those fragile humans whose lives had been snuffed when she had turned them to stone. He had spent hours trying to follow the paths of the Gorgon's victims into the afterlife. The passing of their souls had left a kind of ethereal residue, but it had grown fainter as he followed it, and Graves had found himself lost in the swirling gray white nothing of the spirit world that existed just beyond the reach of human senses. Athens had many ghosts, contentious spirits whose awareness had crumbled over the ages so that they were little more than imprints, repeating the same arguments with long dead relatives or raving about the injustice of their death. There were those who had died far more recently, but they were disoriented by the cacophony and chaos and were little help to him.

There would be no help from that quarter. He needed a place that was a locus for the city's most ancient spirits, those powerful enough to maintain their hold on Athens and on their minds. Ghosts that had been here long before the population had exploded, during a simpler time.

The ghosts of antiquity, he thought, propelling his ectoplasmic, weightless form through the air, rising up the hillside toward the Parthenon. Their presence had been strong even when he was just a man. He hoped that now, three-quarters of a century later, they were still cogent and aware.

Olive trees lined either side of the path beneath him. The last of the tourists straggled down from the hill even as the phantom came in sight of the Propylaea, the ancient gateway with its colonnades of Doric columns to the east and west and the rows of thick, proud Ionic columns on either side of the central stair and corridor, holding up nothing but the sky. Spirits were propelled through the tangible world by force of will alone. This was one of the facts of the new science he had studied ever since he had become a part of it. And yet Dr. Graves slipped more rapidly through the veil of night without even realizing he had quickened. He moved above the Propylaea and then paused abruptly, hanging in the air, staring at the majesty of the Parthenon, the temple built to honor the virgin goddess Athena upon her defeat of Poseidon, with whom she had warred for the patronage of the city.

Perikles himself had initiated the construction of the temple in the fifth century B.C. It had been a Byzantine church, a Latin church, and a Muslim mosque in the centuries that had passed since then. When Graves had last been on the broken, bleached ground atop the Acropolis, the Parthenon had been a terrible sight; never having recovered from an explosion that had destroyed part of the temple when the Venetians laid siege, attempting to wrest control of the city from the Turks. Then that thieving bastard Lord Elgin had stolen so much of the sculptural decoration of the place and shipped it back to London to the British Museum. Leonard Graves had spent time on archaeological digs in Greece, and though it had been more than one hundred years since Elgin's crime, the mistrust he had found among the Greeks had saddened him. But he could not blame them. That was what happened when an ignorant fool stole national treasures. He ruined it for everyone else.

Some of the sculptures remained, but the place truly was a ghost of its original glory. Even so, he was pleased to discover upon closer inspection, drifting on air currents toward the eight-columned face of the temple, that restoration was under way and appeared to have been going on for decades. Barriers were in place that would keep tourists out. And as he alighted upon the marble stairs and then passed between two of those columns and into the massive central chamber he was surrounded by scaffolding.

He felt he could almost hear the chants of the cult of Athena, could almost see them gathered there around her statue. The dust of history coated everything, both in the physical world and the ethereal one.

"Hello?" he called, standing in the center of the chamber, looking up through the collapsed ceiling at the night sky as the stars began to appear.

The ghosts came like the stars, materializing one by one in the darkness of the temple, between columns and beneath scaffolding. Some floated above him, others crouched on the marble beams around the edges of the chamber. Graves said nothing as they scrutinized him, most of them faceless shades, so long dead that they had forgotten their own images and could no longer form the details of their fleshly appearances. Some were in the helmets and garb of Grecian warriors, others in the robes of priestesses of Athena.

Yet for all of the cultures that had lived and died upon the Acropolis, the ghosts of the Parthenon seemed to number only the most ancient. Only the Greeks. Graves wondered if all of the other ghosts, the Turks and Venetians and the rest, had all been driven out.

At length one of the ghosts drifted toward him. Dr. Graves could not see if it was male or female, for this specter was little more than an upper torso clad in a robe and the rough shape of a human head. It had no face. Neither eyes nor mouth. When it spoke the words seemed to manifest upon the air much like the spirits themselves. Leonard Graves had been dead more than half a century. The ancient dead could not harm him—as far as he knew—and yet he felt a rippling chill pass through him as he heard this voice out of the ancient world.

"You are not welcome here."

The words were in another language, an ancient form of Greek, but such barriers meant little to the dead. Like other ghosts, Dr. Graves could draw the meaning of the words from the ether itself. From the substance of the spiritual realm, a tapestry woven from the souls of humanity throughout the ages.

"I apologize for the intrusion," Graves said quickly, for he had been schooled in many things during his life, diplomacy among them. "I will stay only a moment and then leave you to your peace."

The faceless dead laughed at him. Their spokesman tilted his head to one side, and the words came again, yet now Graves wondered if it was he speaking or if this was the voice of the collective.

"There is no peace here while the world treads upon this ground and admires the temple of Athena as nothing more than a relic. It would be better if it were nothing more than dust. Perhaps then we could move on."

Graves nodded, hoping he projected sympathy. He began to speak again, but was interrupted.

"And you will leave when you are instructed to do so. Or you will never leave. We shall see to that."

Fear rippled through his spectral form again, and Graves bowed his head and began to withdraw. "My apologies again. I merely thought that if the Gorgon had desecrated this temple with her presence, you might tell me."

"Wait."

Dr. Graves forced himself not to smile as he paused and glanced around. The gathered dead drifted closer, some of them emerging from among the columns and forming a tighter circle around him. There was a flicker of identity across the face of the spokesman ghost, but then it was gone.

"What do you intend for Medusa?"

"Medusa?" Graves repeated, mouth dry. So it was true. Not just a Gorgon, but the hideous monster of legend. "Only to stop her from killing anyone else."

There was a susurrus of whispers on the ethereal plane, the voices of dozens, perhaps hundreds of ghosts speaking all at once. He heard them as a single sound, the hushed noise of the wind through a cornfield. Then all at once it ceased.

The faceless spokesman slid closer to him, staring at him with no eyes, speaking to him with no lips.

"She has been here. We sent her away."

Graves nodded. "There are too many people who might see her."

"Fool!" the voice in the ether snapped. The faceless ghosts swirled closer, and Graves shivered with the cold of tombs millennia old. *"We would never allow Phorcys's tainted spawn within these walls. It would be the gravest insult to the goddess."*

"Of course," Graves agreed, moving backward toward the entrance. "If only I knew where to find her, I could be sure she would never be able to insult the goddess again."

Once more the temple was filled with that ripple of whispers.

"She hides among the dead, those who were ancient before the first stone of the temple was laid."

CLAY was behind the wheel of the car. Squire had to set up a rig to reach the pedals, and they didn't have time for such foolishness. The goblin sat in the passenger seat, still wearing his silly cap. Clay gripped the steering wheel and drove down Ermou Street, careful at each intersection. The Greek way of handling such things was to honk the horn as one approached a cross-street. Whoever beeped first had the right of way. But if two cars blared their horns simultaneously, an accident was almost inevitable.

They had followed a small map Yannis had given them. It had been simple enough to find the Monastiraki train station, despite the torn up roads. The city seemed dotted with dozens of places where the streets were being improved, and others where they were in terrible disrepair.

"Not far now," Graves said.

Clay glanced in the rearview mirror. The ghost was visible there, manifesting in the backseat. In the darkness of the night, with only the glow from the dashboard and what light came in from the buildings that lined the street, Graves seemed almost solid.

"You can feel it?" Clay asked.

Dr. Graves nodded. "Like a winter storm coming on."

"Yeah, good for you, Casper," Squire muttered, shaking the map in his hand. "That's great and all but, hello, map?"

The hobgoblin had his booted feet up on the dashboard. Clay shot him a sidelong glare. Squire had his uses, but often the annoyance outweighed them.

"Focus on the task at hand," Clay told him. "We're going to have to be very quiet. It may go badly for us if we cannot take her by stealth."

"What, I'm not quiet? I'm the fuckin' soul of quiet."

Clay sighed.

"I doubt the Gorgon's stare will affect you, Clay. You are infinitely malleable," Dr. Graves said, his voice like a cold breeze in the car.

Clay shuddered.

"I don't like guessing," the shapeshifter replied. "You're dead. And Conan Doyle made it clear hobgoblins were immune to certain curses. But I'm not sure in my case, so let's just take it slowly. And"—he glanced again at Squire—"be quiet."

The hobgoblin grinned. "My middle name."

The cemetery loomed up on their right, and above it a church whose domed roof seemed the color of rust in the moonlight. The Kerameikos was closed, of course, the gates locked. And somewhere inside, among ancient ruins of Greece that few tourists and fewer Athenians ever bothered to visit, among graves and aboveground crypts and crumbling markers, Medusa was supposed to have made her lair.

"Are you certain of this?" Clay asked as he pulled the car to the curb. Dr. Graves's eyes seemed yellow in the dark. Clay parked and killed the engine, turning around to face the ghost.

"She hides among the dead," the phantom adventurer said. "Those who were ancient before the first stone of the temple was laid. That's how they told it to me. The corpses of Athenians were buried here for more than a thousand years, as far back as the twelfth century B.C. Nowhere else in the city fills that bill. It's an ancient place with far less human traffic than anywhere else in Athens."

"A good hiding spot," Squire said, peering through his window. "Nice and homey. Let's go."

He started to open his door, and Clay grabbed his wrist. Squire twisted around to face him. Clay smiled and pulled the foolish cap from the goblin's head.

"Quietly," he said. "Graves makes no noise. I'm going in on cat feet. If Medusa hears us coming, it'll be you who gives us away. Please don't."

Squire put one hand over his heart. "You wound me, buddy. To the core. And I heard you the first fifty friggin' times."

The hobgoblin popped his door and stepped out, closing it gently behind him. Clay glanced back at the ghost in the rear seat.

"What do you think?" the shapeshifter asked.

Dr. Graves raised an eyebrow. "I think there's a reason we're not all going in together," he said, and then he rose up through the roof of the car, passing right through fabric and metal as though it weren't there at all.

Clay climbed out, pocketed the keys, took one look around, and then he *changed*. The feeling was not precisely painful, but it was often unpleasant. When he transformed into a creature smaller than himself, it was not as though he was being physically compacted, crushed down to size, but rather as though a part of him was draining away to some other place.

Fur pushed through his skin. His bones popped and re-shaped and shrunk. His ears perked up. His rough tongue darted out, and he twitched his whiskers, tail waving behind him. On cat feet, fur the color of copper with a white streak along one ear, Clay darted to the gate of the cemetery and right through grating meant to keep humans out.

Graves was likely already inside, and Squire was nowhere to be seen. Clay assumed he had simply melded with the shadows outside the cemetery and emerged from some dark place within. The cat trotted across the brittle grass among the tombs.

The hunt had begun.

Kerameikos hardly looked like a cemetery at all. The tombs were mostly ancient stone arranged in long, low walls, and many of the markers were simple columns. If not for the dead, it might have been an intriguing collection of ancient ruins, something that had crumbled away to nothing but those walls and the patches of grass and bare earth around them. But the names on the markers gave the place away.

Clay twitched his tail and paused on the edge of a low wall, lifting his cat-nose to the night breeze, whiskers twitching. A scent had caught his attention, yet he was certain it was not Medusa's. Something else was here as well. Watchful, he leaped down from the wall and trotted behind a tree. In addition to ancient stones, the boneyard was filled with trees. Yet they were sparse, nowhere growing close enough to be considered a wood. And though their branches were not bare, there was something about the way they twisted at odd angles, stretching upward, that gave them a skeletal aspect.

The cat darted silently across a scrubby stretch of grass and then paused once more, crouching behind a short stone wall. He sniffed the air, purring in quiet curiosity. His rough tongue tasted the wind. Beyond that low wall was an enormous whitewashed stone monument topped with a marble statue of a bull. In the moonshadow beneath that bull's heavy belly, Squire appeared, sliding from the deepest dark into the gray night, like a newborn from its mother's womb.

The hobgoblin clutched the marble legs of the bull and poked his head out from beneath it, surveying as much of the cemetery as he could see from that vantage point. He saw the cat and nodded solemnly toward Clay, then slipped into the moonshadow again and was gone. The entire thing had taken only seconds and been executed with more stealth than Clay would ever have given the hobgoblin credit for. It was not that he had never worked with Squire before, but that the goblin behaved like such a buffoon so often that it was easy to forget how competent he was in the worst situations.

The shapeshifter did not bother searching the sky or the treetops for Dr. Graves. The ghost would have made himself invisible on all spectrums. There was no telling how acute Medusa's senses were.

Beyond the marble bull was a small hill, and Clay discovered a narrow path among shrubs and trees. Claws scratching hardscrabble earth, the cat slipped between two shrubs and made an alternate trail for himself, moving up the hill parallel to the footpath. His ears twitched, and he arched his back, barely able to keep from hissing. Wings fluttered, and several birds burst from a nearby tree. Clay could not be sure if they had become skittish because of his presence, or if something else had spooked them.

A shudder passed through his feline form, and his hackles went up. Something wasn't right here. Some presence was fouling this place.

The Gorgon. It has to be. If anything else was here, she would have killed it.

At the top of the hill Clay moved beneath the shrubs back onto the main path and paused there. The wind died in that very same moment. No sound reached him save the distant noises of the city around the cemetery. On a broad stretch of hard-baked ground from which more of those skeletal-finger trees reached for the night sky, there were perhaps two dozen stone crypts spread across the hilltop. They were small, barely larger than an ordinary coffin, and at first glance it seemed they had been arrayed there with no thought to symmetry, as if a random wind had scattered them across the hill. Clay paused, staring at them, and after a moment realized he had missed the organization of the stone coffins. They formed a rough circle, not unlike the standing stones found all over the United Kingdom.

The lid was off the largest of the crypts. Beside it was a pair of dead rabbits. Clay stepped out of hiding at the top of the path and started to creep toward the circle of stone coffins. As he reached the nearest of them, his ears twitched again and he heard a sound. A wet, slick, sucking sound. And then a crack of bone.

The cat peered around the corner, fur brushing stone, and spied the open crypt with its lid slid off and propped on the ground. The copper scent of blood was in the air, and he saw the red that stained the rabbits' pelts. As he watched, a handful of tiny bones flew up out of the coffin into the moonlight and landed in the dirt. A low hiss came from within, and something shifted and gleamed in the dark. A serpent slid its head over the stone rim, as though saddened at the discarding of the bones. A second and third followed. Clay froze, unsure if he could be seen but unwilling to make a single motion that might give him away.

The serpents receded, and the sounds of sucking and gnawing began again.

Clay hesitated for a moment. As a shapeshifter, he could read living things, could replicate any human, any animal, any creature who ever lived. Almost. He focused for a moment on the horror that lay in hideous repose within that stone coffin gnawing on the bones of rabbits, and he knew with certainty that he could not take *that* shape. It was a mystery for another day, but he suspected it had to do with her appearance being the result of a curse and not something crafted by the Maker.

The cat slipped from one stone coffin to the next. If he tried to rush across the circle, he might well give himself away. Instead he moved on to the next, and then the next, swift but silent. Within two coffins' distance, he paused again. There was the crunch of small bones snapping, followed by the most intoxicatingly female sigh he had ever heard. Clay froze. There came the sound of shifting limbs from within that large stone coffin. Still the cat stayed out of sight.

The moonlight threw a shadow past the coffin behind which he was hiding. It was tall and full-breasted, and atop its head a nest of shadow vipers coiled. The cat's hackles went up again, and Clay forced himself not to hiss at the shadow on the ground, so close. There came a wet crack, and in his mind he could practically see the remains of a rabbit shattering against the very crypt he hid behind. The shadow ducked down, perhaps snatching up one of the other dead rabbits, and then retreated. He listened to the sound of Medusa settling once more into the coffin.

Ears pricked forward, the cat prowled to the next crypt. The next one along the circle was his destination. Something shifted in the darkness now, and it did not come from ahead of him, but behind.

Clay turned, tail twitching, and scanned the cemetery and the branches of the strange grove of trees that surrounded this circle of the dead. All was still. The leaves hung seemingly lifeless, no wind at all to disturb them. Still the cat let its gaze linger a moment. Then, out of his peripheral vision, he saw something else move. Twisting to the right, he saw a patch of moonshadow beneath a distant monument give birth to Squire. The hobgoblin crawled carefully, silently onto the ground. His eyes gleamed in the dark. When he spotted the cat, the gnarled little man stood into a crouch and nodded slowly. He tapped the side of his nose, indicating that it had led him to this spot. The cat curled its tail around and used it to point at the open crypt. Squire took a step forward, and Clay shook his feline head. For once the hobgoblin did as he was told and remained still.

As he crept across the ten-foot expanse that separated his hiding place from Medusa's lair, the cat darted a glance all around, on guard. Something else was here. He was certain of it. A ripple in the air at the center of the circle of crypts caught his eye, and he saw the ghost of Dr. Graves taking shape. *Excellent.* If he could grab Medusa from behind to avoid her stare, he ought to be able to choke or beat her unconscious. If not, Graves and Squire were there to help him immobilize her.

Her. Not a monster anymore. Not after hearing that sigh. No matter how hideous she was, no matter how insane her curse had made her, there was still a part of her that was the sensuously beautiful creature she had once been.

This thought was still echoing in Clay's mind as he willed himself to change once more. Not a human. Not a cat. Not a monster, this time. He transformed into his natural body—or the one with which he was most intimate—a seven-foot-tall, hairless man, whose flesh was his namesake. Clay. Lined with cracks, cool and dry. And strong.

With uncanny swiftness he crossed the last five feet to the stone coffin and reached for Medusa.

An earsplitting, almost musical whistle split the night.

The sound disturbed her, and even as Clay reached for the Gorgon, Medusa dropped the rabbit she had been gnawing on and erupted from the crypt. The nest of serpents on her head hissed in chorus and lunged at him, snapping, even as Medusa turned toward the sound of the whistle . . . toward Clay.

He did not have a chance to avert his eyes.

Clay heard Squire shout in alarm and saw Dr. Graves's spectral form flying down at the Gorgon, even as he felt paralysis take hold. Horror blossomed within him. He was malleable, ever-changing, ever in motion. But now he froze, solid, unable to move or change.

No longer clay, but stone.

8

THE fishing boat rocked beneath his feet, and Conan Doyle was surprised by how quickly he regained his sea legs. His mind briefly flashed back to his military service during the Boer Wars, when he had traveled to South Africa across turbulent seas on a British steamer. It had been years since he had thought of that part of his life, but he did not often ruminate on his more mundane existence, before his supposed death. *Memory is such an odd device of the mind,* Doyle mused, gazing out over the emerald green waters, *stimulated by the most random things.*

The winds blowing off the waters of the Ionian Sea were invigorating after the long day of travel from the island of Lesbos, and he greedily filled his lungs with the rejuvenating Mediterranean air. It wasn't the rest his body craved, but it would have to do.

Conan Doyle turned to look at the weathered fisherman in the wheelhouse behind him. He had found him in a small tavern at the bay of Marmari. While his companions waited outside to avoid arousing any unwanted suspicions, the mage had gone in alone to hire a boat. All the fishing boats were in for the day, and none of the seamen present would even entertain the thought of taking their crafts out again, especially at the request of a foreigner—and an Englishman to boot.

He had reached the point where he was seriously considering using magick to manipulate one of their minds, when Danny had grown tired of waiting and came in to find him. The appearance of the boy had cast a pall of silence over the establishment. Even though his head was covered with the hood of his sweatshirt, in such close confines it was impossible for them not to recognize that the boy was not normal. His eyes, his teeth, his skin . . . The atmosphere of the tavern had grown immediately hostile, and Conan Doyle had decided that it would be best for them to leave at once.

Now the captain returned Conan Doyle's gaze, yellow eyes glinting like polished gold in the last rays of the setting sun. *A kindred spirit,* he had called himself.

He had intercepted Conan Doyle and his group at the rear of the tavern, introducing himself as Captain Lycaon. Conan Doyle had sensed immediately that there something not quite human about the fisherman—something unnatural, but there seemed no malice in him, no duplicity. If he was an agent of Gull's, well, that was the risk.

The captain smiled now through the wheelhouse window as he piloted the boat, and Conan Doyle could not help but notice again that there were far too many teeth in the man's mouth. He doubted that Captain Lycaon smiled much around his fellow fisherman, or even that he had much contact with their like at all, other than to occasionally partake of some refreshment in the same establishment.

Kindred spirits. Lycaon said that it was Danny who had changed his mind, that he had sensed their kinship and would never have forgiven himself for not helping one of his own. Conan Doyle had considered asking the old man for his story, but decided against it, choosing instead to simply offer their destination.

"We'll need passage along the coast to Cape Matapan—or Cape Taenarus as it used to be called."

The old man had nodded slowly, removing a pipe from his back pocket, preparing to smoke.

"Let me guess," he had said between puffs, the sweet smell of his tobacco causing Conan Doyle to crave the relaxing pleasures of his own briar pipe. "It's the Ayil Asomati caves you seek."

"Precisely."

Lycaon spoke with a strange accent, not Greek, or anything else familiar, but with the hint of the Mediterranean in it nevertheless. "At night I hear the call of the caves sighing upon the winds, and they ask me if I am ready to lay down and sleep my last, but I tell them that it is not yet my time, that there are still many fish to catch, and much ouzo to drink."

"Will you take us then?" Conan Doyle had asked after a moment of silence during which the old captain puffed on his pipe, seeming to listen for the sounds of the caves.

"When would you like to leave?"

"Immediately."

They were on their way in a matter of minutes.

Now upon their journey, Conan Doyle took stock of his Menagerie. At the back of the boat Eve, Danny, and Ceridwen sat, enjoying a moment of respite before the next phase of their mission. They were tired and could have used some time to rest and regroup, but Gull had a healthy lead on them, and if they had any thought of catching up to him and his Wicked, they could not afford to tarry even for a moment.

Eve must have felt his eyes on her, for she glanced up, brows knitted in consternation. She rose to her feet and strode toward him, tugging at her torn leather coat, which was stained with her dried blood.

"I'm going to stink like fish for days," she complained, the wind whipping her hair around her sculpted features.

Conan Doyle always marveled at her beauty. Here she was only hours after battling a Hydra to the death, and she looked as though she could have stepped from the pages of *Vogue*.

"You don't smell of fish," he assured her. "Blood, yes, but not fish."

Eve stared at him then, dark, almond-shaped eyes boring into his own. "Are you all right?" she asked. There was empathy in her gaze, but a steely judgment as well. "Back on Lesbos, with the Hydra, you were a little off your game."

"I was momentarily distracted." His concern over Ceridwen's injuries had left him embarrassed and a bit ashamed. Matters of the heart needed to be set aside when dealing with conflicts of this magnitude. "I assure you it will not happen again."

Eve slowly nodded. Sometimes she seemed so very modern, so young, and at other times her gaze revealed the profoundness of her age, and an ancient wisdom lay within. "That's good to hear. Danny and I almost got our asses handed to us today."

Conan Doyle glared at her, leaving no doubt that the conversation was over.

She put up her hands in defense. "It had to be said."

The boat's engine cut off, and Conan Doyle watched as Captain Lycaon emerged from the wheelhouse. The old man was smoking his pipe again and said nothing as he pointed to the promontory that was gradually coming into view as they rounded the headland from Cape Matapan, the southernmost point of continental Greece.

Danny and Ceridwen had joined them, each peering out into the darkness for a glimpse of their destination.

"Is that it?" Danny asked. "I don't get it. Why do you think Gull wanted to go there? It's just a big cliff."

Ocean-blue cloak fluttering in the wind, Ceridwen extended her arm, fingers splayed, feeling the emanations from the great stone projection. "So much more than that," she said in a voice tinged with foreboding. "So much more than is obvious."

Eve made clicking noises with her mouth as she placed

her hands on her slender hips. "Isn't that always the way," she said, giving Conan Doyle a quick look from the corner of her eye.

The high rocky formation loomed above them, and Conan Doyle moved to the front of the boat for a better view, searching for the area that was rumored to be an entrance to the Underworld. The Ayil Asomati caves were the most famous of Hades' ventilation shafts, favored by mortals on quests.

Captain Lycaon joined him. "I'll get you as close as I can," he said, eyeing the towering rock formation as he suckled the end of his pipe. "But you'll need a raft, if you're planning on climbing to the caves."

"Bring us as far as you dare, Captain," Conan Doyle ordered. "We'll make do from there."

The sound began as a distant warble, and Conan Doyle at first mistook it as the cry of some lonely night bird. It was a song, perhaps one of the most beautiful he had ever heard, and it was coming from somewhere on the cliffs of the promontory.

"Look!" Eve called, distracting him from the unearthly tune.

Conan Doyle followed her gaze, again enveloped in the overpowering beauty of the song, and saw three figures standing on one of the small ledges jutting out from the promontory. It was Gull and his people, and the deformed sorcerer was using his damnable gift to sing in the voice of Orpheus.

They were closer now, and Conan Doyle could make out the words of the song in the language of time long past. Plaintively it asked for the entrance to the Underworld to be revealed.

"It's beautiful," Captain Lycaon whispered, and Conan Doyle saw that the old seaman was crying.

As he looked back toward the promontory, he realized that it was not only they who had been affected by the song of Orpheus. Conan Doyle watched transfixed as two towering gates of solid rock parted in the face of the mountainous cliff.

The Underworld.

CLAY is falling.

Deeper and deeper he plummets into the darkness within himself, the oblivion into which he has been cast by the gaze of Medusa. After a while, he finds himself comforted by the darkness surrounding him, the desire to escape slowly draining from him.

He wonders if this was how Medusa's other victims had felt? Suddenly trapped within themselves, gradually losing the will to be anything but stone.

For a brief moment he again struggles against the sucking pull of the abyss, but to little avail. He is drowning in shadow, the ebony pitch attempting to work its way into his mouth and nose. It wants to be inside him—to consume him. It wants him to forget that he ever existed.

And it almost succeeds, but then he hears Eve's voice, as he had that day they lunched on Newbury Street. "Do you remember?" she had asked, a longing in her voice that made his heart break.

And he does. He remembered then—and he remembers now, and his unremitting fall into oblivion is slowed by the recollection. Memories flash before him, curtains of darkness are savagely torn aside. Clay recalls a murk deeper and darker than the one that now envelops him, but it lasts for only a brief instant, before it is banished by the brightest flashes—the light of creation. And the inky black is replaced by entire constellations.

Creation. *It is his first conscious memory.*

The memories give him buoyancy, and he begins to ascend.

Clay remembers the hands of the Creator, molding and shaping him—preparing him to take on the forms of the wondrous life that would inhabit these new worlds. He is the imagination of God made malleable flesh.

He is the Clay of life, and God was his sculptor.

Oh, the creatures he had become. Clay remembers each and every one as he climbs up from the darkness, suddenly able to resist the pull of the depths. He tries to alter his form, there in the dark, to become something more acclimated to swimming in the sea of black, but realizes that he has no shape here, that he is nothing more than conscious thought.

To be only one thing, unable to change . . . the idea fills him with a powerful fear, and Clay remembers another time when he felt this afraid.

The Creator had been finished with him. Every form of life that was, and would ever be, had been molded from his being. God's masterpiece of creation was complete. And he was cast aside, left to wander the new and glorious world that he had helped to define, forgotten and alone.

Alone.

But he survived. He thrived and became a part of the world, found a purpose for himself. Clay feels the darkness take hold again, its pull given strength by his despair, and he fights against it, finding strength in the knowledge that he found his own way in the world. A life shaped not by the Creator's hands, but by his own intent.

The shadow's hold upon him slips away, and he surges upward. He is not merely refuse left over from the Supreme Being's master plan, he is needed. Clay will not squander the potential of the life he had made.

He is not cold, lifeless stone.

He is the substance of creation.

He is Clay.

HIS eyes were first to change.

In one instant he was blind to the world around him, and the next his vision was restored, the stone crust over his eyes flaking away. Clay gazed around the Kerameikos Cemetery, not sure how long he had spent in his petrified state. The confrontation was still going on.

Squire darted in and out of the shadows, keeping Medusa off guard, as Graves hovered above the scene, fashioning a net from the ectoplasm that made up his body. *Interesting*, Clay thought, but he wasn't convinced their plan would succeed. They needed his help.

The eyes were but the first step. Clay exerted his will over his body, forcing away the shell of rock that now enveloped his form. The enchantment of Medusa's accursed gaze fought against him, not wanting to relinquish its hold, but he was so much more than mere flesh and blood, and its grip on him shattered. His flesh had fought the curse from the moment he had begun to succumb to it, and now he forced every atom of his form to return to life from stone death, leaving only a sheath of rock around him. That sheath popped and snapped like melting ice on a frozen lake during the first days of spring, and it fell away from his body in large chunks to litter the ground.

"Heads up, honey!" Clay heard Squire cry out.

He turned just in time to see the hobgoblin emerge from a patch of shadow cast by a section of ancient stone wall. Squire threw himself at Medusa's legs, and, as she fell forward, Graves silently swooped down, dropping the shimmering net of ghostly material over her.

Clay willed himself to move, ignoring the stiffness in his joints and the burning aches in his muscles as he ran across the burial ground to join his comrades.

"Nice to see you up and around," Squire said, moving out of his path.

Clay dropped to his knees, throwing the weight of his body on top of the Gorgon, who thrashed beneath the ectoplasmic net. "Give me a hand here," he called to the goblin. Medusa was strong, incredibly so, and was trying to maneuver her body to again affect him with her petrifying gaze.

Sorry, not this time.

He instinctively shifted the configuration of his face, his

eyes receding into the flesh to be replaced with highly sensitive sensory stalks that picked up on vibration and the shifting of air currents no matter how minute.

"Holy shit, I think I dated your sister back in seventy-five," Squire sniggered, even as he attempted to hold down Medusa's thrashing legs.

"Maybe you should hold off on the commentary and sedate the Gorgon. Just a suggestion," Clay said, even as he struggled to keep Medusa down.

Squire grimaced. "Wait, so now you're funny all of a sudden?"

"Sedate her?" he heard Graves ask from above them. "Why on earth would we want to sedate her?" The ghost drifted closer, and Clay glanced at him, and through his translucent form. "The Gorgon must be dealt with as we would any other monster. She must be destroyed."

Clay understood exactly what the ghost was saying, but something deep inside him did not agree. Medusa was ancient and had seen and experienced so much, he found it a tragedy to have to kill her. Yes, he knew she was a monster, but so was he, and that shared bond made it very difficult for him to end her life.

It was as if she sensed his hesitation—his weakness. Medusa twisted her body in such a way as to tear the ectoplasmic netting and free her hands. She shrieked like the damned, as she raked her clawed fingers across the dry, cracked flesh of Clay's face, ripping away one of his sensory stalks. The snakes atop her head hissed, writhing and striking out with equal savagery.

"Damn you!" Clay bellowed, recoiling from the injury, providing her the opportunity she sought. He was slow, still feeling the effects of her curse, and before he could recover, she had freed herself from the net, swatting Squire away as if he were an annoying insect.

"Graves!" Clay called out, the pain in his face beginning to subside, another stalk already growing.

It sounded like short claps of thunder, and Clay suddenly

realized what the ghost was doing. He had seen Graves do it before, summoning replicas of guns from his past, created from the substance of his body, shooting bullets of ectoplasm.

The gunfire came to an abrupt stop.

"Did you stop her?" Clay asked, the stalks on his face moving about in the air attempting to locate the doctor's ghostly shape.

"No," he said. "She obviously knows this cemetery far better than we."

"Beautiful. Then we lost her—again," Squire muttered, picking himself up from the ground where Medusa had thrown him. One arm hung limply from its socket, longer than its counterpart, and Clay watched as the goblin casually reached out with the uninjured arm to roughly yank it back into place. He winced at the popping sound that accompanied the movement.

"That's better," the hobgoblin sighed, moving the restored arm, checking its mobility.

"We have not lost our quarry," Dr. Graves said, floating down to join them, the white of his shirt and his dark suspenders and trousers equally transparent, as if he had been superimposed upon the cemetery.

"What do you mean?" Clay asked. With a thought, he replaced the writhing sensory organs on his face with eyes.

Graves gazed off into the cemetery and beyond. "I hit her at least once," he said, holding up a ghostly pistol that shimmered in the darkness, threatening to become insubstantial. "The bullets are made from my life-stuff," he explained. "She is carrying a piece of me inside her—as if I've been brought along for the trip."

Squire smiled, pointing a gnarled, stubby finger at Graves. "You da man," he said with a wink. "So what are we waitin' for?" He rubbed his hands together eagerly. "Let's go finish off this critter."

"No," Clay said.

"No?" Squire repeated incredulously. "What, are we

gonna let ole snake head rampage through the streets of Greece turning everyone into decorative lawn ornaments? If you ask me, that brain inside your coconut is still made out of rock."

Clay shook his head. "I didn't mean we weren't going after her. We're just not going to kill her."

His comrades stared at him.

"We're going to take her alive."

IN the ancient language of the elements, Ceridwen thanked the waters of the Ionian for their assistance. On the face of that promontory, atop a ledge perhaps one hundred feet above the water, the cliff had opened like massive stone doors, the gates to the Underworld. Conan Doyle had charged her with finding the fastest way to that ledge. His only criteria was to do it before Gull's cajoling spell wore off, and the stone doors slammed shut again.

From the deck of Captain Lycaon's boat she'd looked up at the entrance in the rock face and pondered the puzzle. She thought about conjuring a traveling wind, but determined that their number was too great and that the amount of time needed for the proper enchantment was out of the question.

She'd felt Conan Doyle's anxious eyes on her as the others bid the good captain farewell.

"We must be going now, Ceridwen," he had urged, and she had looked down over the side of their transport and suddenly had known how they would reach the Underworld entrance.

She had approached the side of the boat and thrust her staff into the emerald waters, asking for its assistance. At first the Ionian was sluggish to respond, but soon it warmed to her request, pleased to know that the Fey—who had once wandered this world at will—still existed. The sea had obliged Ceridwen, and the waters encircling the boat began to bubble and churn, and the air grew increasingly colder.

A bridge, she'd whispered in the language of the sea, *my companions and I need a bridge.*

In response, a swirling waterspout had surged up and out of the body of the ocean, bending and twisting to connect the sea to the rocky face of the promontory. The air grew steadily colder, and colder still, and the once-fluid ocean waters became solid in the sudden, magical chill. A bridge of ice was formed.

"Impressive, my dear," Conan Doyle said, a twinkle in his eyes.

Ceridwen felt a flush on her pale cheeks. "Quickly now." She urged them on as they scrambled over the side of the fishing boat and began their ascent toward the opening in the cliff face.

"I'm almost tempted to go with you," Captain Lycaon said as she went over the side, the last to begin the climb. He stood at the rail, watching, eyes filled with wonder. The man was trembling, but she doubted that it had anything to do with the cold she had summoned. "But I fear that should I enter that place, I would not be allowed to leave."

"This is not a journey for the likes of you, good Captain," Ceridwen said, balancing on the ice. "Go back to the life you have made and leave matters of the Underworld to others."

Captain Lycaon bid them all farewell, and they continued across the frozen bridge that would bring them to the land of the dead.

Frost crunched beneath the sole of Conan Doyle's leather walking boots. He turned to see how the others progressed. Eve appeared to be having the most difficulty, struggling to maintain her footing, but he had little compassion for her. Before leaving Boston he had instructed her on the significance of a good walking shoe, but she had ignored him as usual, preferring to wear a high-heeled Italian boot.

Eve was indeed a slave to fashion.

"Quickly now," he encouraged. "I have no idea how long Gull's enchantment will remain over the opening, we must get inside before the doors return to their previous state."

"An ice bridge," he heard Eve grumble from behind. "Couldn't have made something a little less dangerous. An ice ladder maybe?"

"If you want, you can hold on to my shoulder," Danny suggested. "My sneakers give me pretty good traction."

"Thanks, kid," she said sarcastically. "That way when one of us slips and goes over the side we'll have company on the way down."

The demon boy laughed out loud, and Conan Doyle was again reminded of how young Danny Ferrick actually was, and how well he was adjusting to the new life into which his metamorphosis had thrust him.

"Hey, I think I see some fish frozen in here," the boy said, dropping to his knees and brushing the frost away from the path.

Eve was attempting to make her way around the boy as Ceridwen patiently waited for him.

"Daniel, please," Conan Doyle said. "What did I just say about quickening our pace?"

The boy lifted his head, embarrassed, and quickly got to his feet. "Sorry. This whole frozen ocean thing is just so cool."

A loud crack ricocheted through the air, and Conan Doyle felt a powerful vibration pass through the icy surface beneath his feet. He glanced at Ceridwen, troubled.

"Risk of the gates closing is not the only reason we should quicken our pace," she said, placing a hand against Danny's back, urging him forward. "The ocean's natural state is volatile. The spell will not hold it for long."

Another loud crack, followed by a succession of smaller, more muted pops, erupted. The frost on the bridge had begun to melt, making the surface more slippery. Conan Doyle concentrated on his footing, not daring to slow his progress now to check on the others. He trusted they would be moving with both caution and alacrity as well. The cave was just ahead, a thick, less-than-welcoming sulfurous stench exuding from the yawning gates.

There came a low, unmistakable grinding that Conan Doyle knew came not from the melting ice beneath their feet, but from the stone doors as they began to close.

"Blast it!" he yelled, trying to increase his speed. Instead he lost his footing and stumbled forward, hands sliding across the surface of melting ice. He was skidding toward the edge, when he felt his momentum arrested by a strong grip on his left ankle.

"No time for fun and games," Eve said, helping him to his feet with Danny's assistance. Jagged cracks splintered through the ice beneath them.

"Forget me!" Conan Doyle bellowed, shrugging off Eve and Danny. He pointed to the rock doors slowly swinging shut. "Stop them, or this has all been for nothing!"

Inspired by his words, Danny sprang forward and caught one of the stone doors, but it continued its inexorable progress, dragging him across the icy slick ground. Eve got a grip on the other door, planting her feet in the slush and pooling seawater. She managed to stop it from closing.

"What a pussy," she grunted to Danny. "Can't believe I'm stronger than you."

Danny repositioned his feet on the slick surface and hauled back upon his door. "Fuck . . . you," he snarled with exertion and, for a moment, succeeded in keeping his side open as well.

Conan Doyle reached the doorway, stopping to allow Ceridwen to pass. "After you, my dear,"

"Cut the gentlemanly bullshit, would you?" Eve grunted. "My arms are coming out of the sockets any second now."

"There's always time for manners, Eve," Conan Doyle chided, following the Fey sorceress into the darkness of the Underworld.

"What's the matter Eve?" Danny asked, his voice strained. "Door a little heavy for you?"

"It's a good thing I like you, kid," she said, letting go of her door and reaching across to grab Danny by the ear. The boy growled as she pulled him toward her, and the two tumbled to the ground in a heap upon the cave floor, as the twin doors slammed shut with a resounding echo.

Eve landed astride the demon boy and smiled down on him. She grabbed hold of the leathery flesh of his cheek and gave it a pinch. "I could have left you outside on the ledge," she said, crawling off of him. "And maybe you'll wish I had."

He smiled back as he climbed to his feet. She could feel him watching her as she wiped the dust and dirt from her pants. For effect, she took her time, then glanced up at him.

"Take a picture. It'll last longer."

Danny just scowled and made an obscene gesture. Eve laughed softly. She found it flattering, enjoyed the fact that even at her age she could still make the young ones sweaty.

Now she surveyed their surroundings. It was not as dark as she had expected. They were in a cave with a ceiling perhaps twenty feet high, but it grew wider and taller as it tunneled deeper into the rock, into the earth, and where the tunnel turned out of sight, a kind of orange glow illuminated the depths. A thick, rotten egg smell, riding on gusts of warm air, wafted out to greet them.

"That's nasty," Danny said, holding his nose and looking about. "Where's Mr. Doyle and Ceridwen?"

"Where do you think?" Eve asked, moving toward the orange glow. "Stink central. Where else would they be?"

The sides of the rounded cave walls were smooth and warm to the touch. The deeper they went into the widening tunnel, the warmer it became.

"It's hot in here," Danny commented from behind.

"Figured that out all by yourself?" Eve sniped, a feeling of unease beginning to creep through her.

The tunnel curved, descending toward what looked to be an exit into a much larger chamber beyond. Eve emerged from the tunnel and stopped dead in her tracks, overwhelmed by the sight before her. Danny kept right on walking, slamming into her back.

"What the fuck?" he uttered in astonishment, and she had to agree. *What the fuck, indeed.*

They stood on a ledge with a breathtaking view over a valley—a landscape that could have given the Grand Canyon a run for its money—but where the canyon was breathtaking in its majesty, this place filled Eve with a creeping dread that made her bones ache and her stomach churn. Every muscle in her body screamed for her to run away.

"Ah, I see that you've finally decided to join us," came a voice, and Eve nearly jumped out of her skin. Conan Doyle appeared from the shadows to the left, with Ceridwen trailing behind. He wiped moisture from his brow with a white handkerchief. "I was beginning to think that you hadn't made it."

Eve gazed once more out over the hellish landscape. "And, boy, am I glad I did."

"Come now, Eve," Conan Doyle said as he joined her. "What did you expect from the Underworld? Rolling fields of grass? Apple orchards? Rose bushes, perhaps? It isn't supposed to be Eden, my dear."

His last comment was like a jab in the ribs, and Eve gave him a hard look. Conan Doyle was well aware of how sensitive she was about her early days and often used such references to help her to focus, but this time it only made her angry. This was the sort of place she expected to end up in for what she had done. The ultimate punishment for her sins.

"So where are we, really?" Danny asked, moving past her, closer to the edge. "Is this really it? Really the Underworld?"

"Close enough," Doyle said. He tucked his handkerchief back into his suit jacket pocket. "Think of a bubble, or better yet, a garbage can containing the refuse of another age, a sanctuary away from a world that has mostly forgotten that this age had ever truly existed." He stopped suddenly and looked around, cocking his head slightly to one side as if listening.

"What is it?" Eve asked.

They were all looking around now.

"It's nothing," he said, turning away. "There's a path over here that will take us down," he said, and started in that direction, clearly expecting them to follow.

Eve's upper lip curled back. "Goody."

Silently, they descended deeper into the Underworld, Doyle, Ceridwen, Danny, then Eve. The walls themselves seemed to glow with an otherworldly light, as though fire blazed on the other side of each stone surface, and it was burning through in spots. The sulfurous smell came and went on the strange winds of that place. The terrain was awful, and they had to be cautious, for the stony ground was pitted with soft places, where the rock would suck like a quicksand mouth as they stepped past.

Hideously twisted things flew along the roof of the cave, but they blended so well it was difficult to determine their size. They seemed harmless enough, though their eyes glowed white, and Eve wondered what they fed on here. There was little other sign of life, either current or past, though they came once to a long stretch of dusty plain at the base of a craggy hill where calcified bodies jutted from the ground as though they had fallen there in death long, long ago, and sediment had settled around them.

Those whose mummified skulls were exposed had their jaws open as though they had died screaming.

After a while Eve stopped thinking about leaving and started to wonder what Nigel Gull and his people could possibly want in a place like this.

"So what do you think, Doyle?" she asked, breaking the silence. "Why are we here? What's Gull up to?"

The landscape had grown even bleaker. Smoldering rock, skeletal trees twisted and gnarled, dead for what looked like centuries, but she guessed it was probably longer than that. *Much longer.*

Other than the twisted things that had flown by, they were the only signs of life in this place.

"I gave up trying to figure out Nigel Gull a long time ago," Conan Doyle said as he helped Ceridwen circumvent a large, black boulder that blocked their path. The Faerie sorceress had been doing her best to cover it, but Eve noted a falter in her step. Her skin was pale and marbled with blue veins, but there was a greenish tint to her flesh now, and her eyes seemed somewhat disoriented. Ceridwen looked decidedly unwell. Eve wondered if it was an effect of the Underworld and made a mental note to watch Ceridwen's back if things got wild.

Conan Doyle was looking around again. "I sense something here. Something other than Gull's passing, something oddly . . . familiar."

Danny had continued on the path and was half a dozen or so feet ahead of them, bounding down the rocky slope as if he were some kind of mountain goat.

"Hey, kid," Eve called out, the bad vibes getting to her. "Wait up."

He disappeared around a bend and was lost from sight.

"Fucking kid," she grumbled, and Conan Doyle smiled.

"Boys will be boys," he said, putting his arm around the ailing Ceridwen and continuing their descent.

Upon a narrow plateau, Eve paused to ask if the elemental was all right, but her question was interrupted by a chilling scream. Danny bolted out from behind the cover of some large rocks, a look of absolute terror on his usually fearsome demonic features.

"Run!" he shouted, on the verge of hysteria as he scrambled up the sloping path toward them.

From what? she wanted to ask, but never got the opportunity, because her question was answered when she saw that he was being chased.

It was the biggest dog she had ever seen, about the size of an elephant, scrabbling across the rocks in hot pursuit of the boy. Its ferocious growl sounded like the rumbling of a diesel engine.

It had three heads, each of them snapping after Danny, hungry for a piece of him.

THE large black cat stared at Julia Ferrick from the middle step in front of Conan Doyle's brownstone, its wide, jade eyes assessing her as she began to climb the stairs. She didn't remember Mr. Doyle having a cat, so assumed it belonged to one of the neighbors.

"Hey, kitty," she said offhandedly as she placed the shopping bag she was carrying at her feet and began to fish through her pocketbook for the key that Dr. Graves had given her.

The cat continued to watch her with curious eyes. She found the key and pulled it from her bag.

"Got it," she said, showing it to the animal. "Are you going to let me by?" she asked the cat.

It studied her, extending its neck to sniff at her pants leg, as if considering her question. It looked up into her eyes again, meowed once, and left its perch, joining three other cats of various sizes and colors that had mysteriously appeared at the bottom of the steps.

Julia found it odd and rather disconcerting the way they were watching her as she slid the key into the lock. She glanced over her shoulder to make sure the cats weren't ready to follow her, then quickly slipped into the house.

The inside was eerily quiet.

"Hello?" she called out, knowing no one was home, but wanting to be sure. The only sound was the ticking of a grandfather clock in a hallway off the foyer.

Danny had asked her to bring a few of his favorite CDs, DVDs, and books the next time she was in the neighborhood. She had gone to see her therapist in Cambridge earlier that morning and decided she would stop in, so that his things would be waiting for him when he returned from wherever it was he had gone.

She thought about her son quite a bit these days. *What*

had Mr. Doyle called him? she thought, climbing the stairs to her son's room. *A changeling?* A demon baby switched with a human child. It was the most insane thing she had ever heard, but the facts were all there. She remembered her child the way he had been before the onset of puberty, before the disturbing physical changes, and wanted to cry.

Julia thought that she had gotten beyond all this, surprised that she even had any tears left, but there they were. She wished she could talk with her therapist about it all, but of course, that was out of the question.

She stopped on the stairs and took a deep breath, composing herself. No matter what he was, she still loved her Danny. He was still the child she had raised and loved with all her heart for sixteen years.

It's like if he was gay . . . but different. Really different.

Julia set the bag of his things down as she entered his room on the second floor and breathed in the scent of him. Since beginning to change, her son had started to give off a strange aroma, a heavy musty scent not too far removed from the smoky smell of a wood-burning stove. His sweatshirt was on the floor at the foot of the bed, and she bent down to pick it up, instinctively folding it and crossing the room to place it on the edge of the bed. She wondered where he was and if he was safe. She felt a certain peace knowing that Dr. Graves had promised to look after him, and smiled at the thought of the man. He was good for her son, despite the fact that he was . . . what he was. Dr. Graves knew how to put her fears at ease, and because of that she had developed quite a fondness for him.

Julia picked up the shopping bag and placed it on Danny's bed, wanting him to see that she had brought his things, to know that she was thinking of him. *Always thinking of him.* Then she left the room, closing the door gently behind her, and headed down the stairs to the foyer. She had just placed her hand on the crystal doorknob, when she heard the sound.

A strange thumping noise came from the hall closet.

Julia held her breath, her chest aching with fear. She knew she should leave, maybe call the police, but found herself strangely drawn to the sound.

What the hell are you doing? An inner voice screamed as she slowly reached for the knob. Again she heard the noise, and immediately pulled her hand back, only to slowly reach out again.

She would never have dreamed of doing such a thing before Arthur Conan Doyle and his strange companions had come into her life. It had to be their influence on her, that's the only way she could explain it. The metal knob was cold to the touch and she counted to five before tearing open the door with an ear-splitting scream.

Squire cowered in the corner of the closet, covering his face as if attacked by a flock of angry birds. "Jesus, Mary, and Joseph! You just about made me soil my boxers."

Julia's heart threatened to burst through her ribcage. "What the hell are you doing in the closet?" she asked, not liking the sound of her voice, pitched high from fear and the adrenaline coursing through her body. "I thought you were all away on some mission."

Squire turned away from her and immediately began to rummage through the floor of the closet. "We are," he said, dropping to his knees. "But I need a couple of things from here before we continue with our business in Greece."

She was going to ask how he had gotten there, but remembered something about the goblin using shadows to travel in, and decided that she didn't need to know anything more.

"If I was a titanium mesh net where would I be?" he asked himself, disappearing beneath a curtain of Doyle's long winter coats.

"You're in Greece?" she asked, immediately curious. "What does Danny think of that? He's always wanted to travel and—"

"He ain't with us," Squire said, potato-shaped head popping out from beneath the dark overcoats. "He's with Mr. Doyle, Ceridwen, and Eve."

A knot immediately began to twist in her stomach. "You mean Leonard . . . Dr. Graves isn't with him?"

Squire shook his head. "Nope, Casper's with me." He disappeared again underneath the coats. "Titanium mesh net, titanium mesh net, titanium mesh net."

Danny's in perfectly good hands, she thought to herself. *Sure, Leonard is elsewhere, but he still has Mr. Doyle, Eve, and Ceridwen to look after him. There's no reason to worry.*

Is there?

"Got it!" Squire yelled. He crawled out from the bottom of the closet hauling a thick net of what appeared to be woven metal. "I knew I'd left it around here somewhere," he said, a victorious smile gracing his grotesque features.

"So do you know if he's okay?" she asked, trying to keep the panic from her voice.

Squire shrugged. "Couldn't tell ya, babe. The kid could be pushin' up daisies for all I know." The goblin laughed uproariously. "Just kiddin', I'm sure he's fine. I wouldn't worry."

Too late for that, she thought, immediately picturing herself on a plane to Greece, traveling to identify the body of her son killed doing God knew what.

"Hey, listen," Squire said, bending down to again go to the back of the closet. "I gotta get back to work. It was nice chattin' with you. If I see the kid, I'll let him know you were asking for him."

With those words, he was gone, disappearing inside a patch of shadow, like a rabbit going down into its hole. Julia could do nothing but stare into the closet, mouth agape. Closing the closet door, she stood in the foyer, her mind a jumble. The thought of going home to her empty house, to sit and wait by the phone until Danny got back and finally got around to calling her was not appealing in the least.

She was going to wait for him to return.

Julia Ferrick left the foyer and walked into Mr. Doyle's study, going straight for the liquor cabinet. She was going to need all the help she could to keep her wits about her.

She found the scotch and poured herself a double.

9

A terrible malaise had fallen upon Ceridwen. Her body shivered with weakness, and her vision was clouded as though cataracts veiled her eyes. Yet she refused to allow Arthur to see how this transition to the Underworld was affecting her. Faerie was her home, and her relationship with the elements there, with nature, was nearly symbiotic. If her life did not precisely depend on that rapport, her health could certainly be affected by it. Traveling from Faerie to Arthur's world—the Blight—was not difficult. For millennia, the two realms had been connected, and their natures were not dissimilar, their elemental forces kin to one another, sisters, in a way.

This horrid place was merely a distant cousin, and a withered, sickly, and malevolent cousin at that. Cut off from the elements of the Blight, she was weakened, and though she could feel the elements of this place all around her, they did not welcome her. Nor did she relish their touch. In truth, the moment she had entered the Underworld the flame had snuffed out at the center of the ice sphere atop her staff, and then the ice had begun to melt.

It was good to her now only as a walking stick. Though Arthur had seen that she was unsteady, Ceridwen did her best to put her weight on the staff rather than entirely upon him. He would have danger enough to combat without worrying overmuch about her.

That had been her concern during their initial descent into the Underworld, and the moment she heard Danny Ferrick scream, it became reality. When the demon boy crested the ridge ahead, the look of terror etched on his face forced Ceridwen to summon all of the strength and courage remaining to her.

It was precious little preparation for the sight that confronted her next. The three-headed dog scrabbled up the rocks in pursuit, grunting, eyes glistening crimson in the gloom. The weight of its three heads ought to have thrown off its balance, but its body was wide and built for that burden, and it was agile enough. The hound came to an abrupt halt the moment it saw that its prey was not alone.

"Cerberus," Conan Doyle whispered at her side, obviously in awe of the gigantic beast that now regarded them with three sets of crimson eyes. Other than those few odd flutterings in the cave above them, it was the first real sign of life they'd seen since passing beyond the gates, but judging by the stink that radiated from the hound, she wondered if it was truly alive at all. The great dog reeked of death and decay, and she could see spots where the flesh was missing, exposing stringy sinew and yellow bone.

Danny ran toward Eve. She marched forward to meet him, the bottom of her brown leather coat flapping behind her in a sudden gust of sulfurous air from below.

"Stop running," the vampire snapped.

The demon boy brought himself up short upon her command, moving to her side quickly, though his expression was dubious. "Do you not *see* the dog?"

"Yeah. And me without a really big newspaper," Eve sneered. "There's nowhere to run, kid. The only way to live is to win."

They all remained perfectly still, allowing the dog to familiarize itself with their scents. It continued to growl threateningly as each of its heads paused to study them individually. Ceridwen assumed that now that it had more than one target, it was assessing their vulnerability, deciding which of them it would try to catch and eat first.

Then its growl turned to a high-pitched whine, and it tensed upon its haunches, its hackles rising as it prepared to attack. She had already noted the fragile wall to the right of the dog, where it crouched on the ridge of steps leading up from the floor of the Underworld. Without a further thought she put her own pain and illness aside and began to call upon the elemental forces. Cut off from the elements of Faerie, or even the Blight, she was forced to tap into the elements of the Underworld.

Ceridwen screamed. Unimaginable pain wracked her body as the ugly nature of that realm fought her, for this was a place of death, and it cared not for the requests of the living. Then, abruptly, tainted brackish water spun in a circle around the top of her staff and solidified into ice, and a sickly yellow flame sparked to life within. She cried out once again, her muscles tightening painfully as the connection was made, as the filth and death of the Underworld seeped into her flesh and bone. A putrid orange light crackled around her staff, and then elemental fire surged from the icy sphere atop it and struck at the cave wall.

A portion of the wall shattered, and thousands of pounds of stone crashed down onto the ridge . . . but too late. Cerberus bounded toward them as the rock wall fell harmlessly behind it. There was an ancient, empty hunger in the hound's eyes.

Nausea roiled in Ceridwen's belly as she tried to summon the elements once more, but she was met with painful resistance. She slumped to the ground, sapped of strength, watching helplessly as Conan Doyle lunged forward to meet the giant dog's attack.

"Heeeyahhhh!" he cried out, advancing toward the beast.

Cerberus paused, crouching low to the ground. But Conan Doyle showed no fear, glaring into its eyes.

"Back off, you damned fool!" Eve shouted, sprinting to his side.

Conan Doyle risked a quick glance toward the vampiress and the dog sensed its opportunity. With a snarl that came not only from each throat but from deep in their shared chest, Cerberus sprang at him. Ceridwen wanted to close her eyes, but she could not look away.

The mage was a man of quiet dignity and propriety, but in battle, he was fearsome indeed. He seemed almost to transform, bracing himself in a warrior's pose, his right hand burning like the sun. He met the attack head-on and plunged his blazing fist into one of Cerberus's open mouths. The other two heads cried in agony, but the one assaulted by the magickal fire burned horribly from within, its eyes boiling from their sockets as the flesh and fur of its wide, heavy head burned away to reveal its flaming skull.

Conan Doyle stumbled away from the beast, clutching his wrist and staring at his own smoldering hand in obvious pain. The spell had been a weapon of incredible power, and there was always danger in magick. He had burned himself badly.

But Cerberus was not going to give him time to recover. Its injuries were horrid to see, but the two surviving heads were driven only to greater madness. They frothed at their mouths, a yellow foam that stank worse than the beast itself. Where its body was dessicated and the bone and muscle showed through, fresh blood and pus flowed as it shook in fury. It had been deciding which of them to rend and tear, but now Conan Doyle was its only target.

"Arthur!" Ceridwen cried, damning herself for her weakness even as she summoned the strength to stand. She would be too late.

But Eve was there.

She pushed Conan Doyle out of harm's way as the remaining two heads, driven to the brink of madness, lunged for him with utter ferocity. One of the still functioning heads snapped its jaws closed on Eve's shoulder, and she roared in pain, baring long fangs. She spun and pummeled its snout, but Cerberus flipped back its head, shaking her like a rag doll. Eve's flailing feet caught the still smoldering third head, and it exploded in a shower of blackened bone and red burning embers.

Danny was right behind her. The demon boy ran at Cerberus and leaped into the air with uncanny strength. He launched himself at the hound and sank his claws into its side. Where its flesh was rotting away, Danny began to tear at Cerberus. Blood and pus drooled out onto its fur as he tore strips of decaying flesh. Then he reached inside and clutched a yellowed rib. The bone snapped off in his hands.

Eve screamed as Cerberus bit down harder on her, shaking her still. Her own blood splattered the ground like scarlet rain.

Ceridwen climbed to her feet, ignoring the creeping numbness that permeated her body. She picked up her staff and stumbled forward. The growling of the dog's heads and the screaming and cursing from Eve echoed through the cave.

"I can't risk hitting them," Conan Doyle screamed over the ruckus, his hand again radiating an unearthly light, his body trembling with the effort.

"We've only just begun this. We'll not die now," Ceridwen replied. Mustering all her remaining strength, she brought the heel of her foot down on her staff, breaking the end so it now tapered to a jagged point. She hefted the broken staff and threw it like a javelin with all her strength, willing the wood—the only bit of nature from her own world in this horrid place—to fly true.

The spear pierced the thick muscle of the dog's chest. The head holding Eve opened its jaws to yelp in pain, flinging her limp and bloody form into a broken heap at the edge of the ridge.

Ceridwen and Conan Doyle ran to Eve, but Cerberus was already on the move, the remains of Ceridwen's staff protruding from its chest. Conan Doyle sketched a pattern into the air, and from it a spiral of blue light erupted, rocketing at Cerberus. Danny still clung to its side, tearing at its flesh, but he was not in the immediate line of fire. The hound was badly injured, but it still moved with uncanny speed and dodged that magickal attack, thundering toward them.

"Take her," Conan Doyle ordered, moving between the women and the slavering monstrosity.

Ceridwen grabbed Eve beneath the arms and began to pull her away from the edge. She could hear Conan Doyle's melodious voice beginning a new incantation when another sound filled the air.

Screaming.

"Enough! That's just enough of that shit!" Danny Ferrick screamed.

Tearing into Cerberus's body, he climbed the hound as though to saddle it, then he grappled with one of its heads, gouging at its eyes, scooping one of them out. The hound bucked and threw him forward. Danny landed, rolling, and then rose again. He screamed, shaking as he confronted the dog with such ferocity that it paused and took a step back. Danny seemed to be in the grip of madness.

"I'm not afraid of you!" the boy bellowed, then threw himself at the hound, claws flying, tearing and rending and pummeling its remaining heads, driving the animal back.

"Daniel, be careful!" Ceridwen called out as the boy rammed his new horns into the belly of the beast.

Cerberus reared up on its hind legs, attempting to use its front paws to repel its relentless attacker, but to little avail. Danny drove it back farther and farther until there was no longer any place left for them to go.

And Ceridwen watched in horror as the two tumbled backward over the edge of the ridge, disappearing into the Underworld below.

TUMBLING down the rocky cliff, Danny tried to use Cerberus's disgusting body as a shield, tucking himself close to the putrid, matted fur so that the beast could take the brunt of the damage. They crashed again and again into the cliff, and with each jarring impact, Danny did his best to twist around to keep Cerberus between himself and the jagged outcroppings of rock. Then their painful journey came to an abrupt end with a whimper from the hound and the splintering of bones inside it. An enormous rib bone shot up through it, nearly impaling Danny, just before the impact sent him sprawling across the ground. He rolled, grunting in pain with each bump, and at last came to rest against the trunk of a gigantic tree.

Danny lay there for a while, looking up into the skeletal branches and strangely shaped leaves that decorated them, until a flow of warm blood into his eyes obscured his vision. With a trembling hand he wiped away the blood, and slowly pushed himself into a sitting position.

Cerberus was lying in a heap among the rocks across from him. It didn't look as though the multiheaded dog had been as lucky as Danny.

Serves you right, you piece of shit, he thought, still feeling a trace of the terror he'd felt when he had first unknowingly trod upon the sleeping monstrosity. Danny didn't like dogs much; ever since his loser father had brought him a dog not too long after his parents had split. It was a mutt from the local animal shelter. All the thing did was bark, poop, and piss all over the house. It hadn't lived with him and his mother for very long. When he thought of dogs, all he could think of was his father, and how the only thing the prick *hadn't* done to his mom was shit and piss all over the house. The bastard had all the bases covered when he'd brought that dog to live with them.

His body felt like one big open wound, damp with his own blood, every movement met with white-hot agony. But Danny figured he'd gotten off lucky. He was surprised that the damage wasn't worse, considering how far he had fallen. He looked at his arms and, for a brief moment, was thankful for the changes he'd been undergoing, as he grew into his true self. Yes, there were scrapes and some bloody gashes, but he was alive, and he was sure he wouldn't have survived that fall if he'd been a normal teenager.

Danny heard his name being called from someplace far above and gazed up to see the tiny shapes of his companions as they made their way down the cliff toward him. He climbed to his feet, checking out his legs, making sure that nothing had been broken.

"Down here!" he called up to them, hands cupped over his mouth.

Danny could see that Doyle and Ceridwen were helping Eve. He hoped that she was all right. Between the fight with the Hydra and now this, she had been taking quite a beating lately, and he wasn't sure if she was as durable as he was. Ceridwen, at least, seemed a little better. She'd been drag-assing back in the tunnels and he'd thought she was just going to pass out or something.

As the others made their descent, he took the opportunity to look around. It was a cruel place, rocky, with strange, skeletal trees rising up out of the gray dirt like the hands of some animated corpse. Even though the air was still, the strangely shaped leaves rustled, producing an odd grating sound.

Weird, he thought. Danny began to look more closely at what he believed to be leaves, but the sudden sound of growling distracted him.

The boy turned, stunned to see the giant dog stalking toward him on wobbly legs. Cerberus hadn't been killed in the fall after all. Huge chunks of its flesh were missing, and exposed muscle and bone glinted wetly through the various rips and gashes.

"Give it up," he told the dog as it slowly moved closer.

The animal continued to growl, bloody strings of saliva dripping from its two remaining mouths. Danny glanced in the direction of his friends, but they were not close enough to lend him a hand. It looked as though he was going to have to deal with this problem on his own.

"Last chance," he told the animal. "Just get the hell out of here, and we'll call it even."

Cerberus continued its inexorable advance.

"All right," Danny said, reaching up to break away a limb from one of the skeletal trees. The branch came away with a loud snap, followed by a metallic rustling from the weird leaves.

He turned back to face the dog and saw that the animal had stopped. "Changing your mind?" he asked, a snarling smile on his face.

Cerberus seemed to have forgotten about him, its two remaining heads looking around as the sounds from the trees began to intensify. Its ears had gone flat against its blocky skulls, and Danny thought that he heard at least one of the heads whimpering.

What now?

The dog seemed afraid, and even though he would have liked to think it was because of him, something told him that really wasn't the case.

Suddenly, Danny realized that the leaves weren't leaves at all. He watched in awe as the shapes dangling from the trees began to drop, unfurling sleek, angular wings just before hitting the ground and gliding back into the air.

"Son of a bitch," he whispered in awe, as the strange birds filled the air, their bodies catching the muted light of the Underworld, their feathers like tarnished metal. As he watched them dip and dart about, he trawled his knowledge of mythology, gained mostly from television, for the identity of these strange, metallic creatures.

One of the birds flew past his face, the side of its wing gently glancing his cheek, and he recoiled from its touch. His hand came away from his face covered in fresh blood. *Wait. I remember. Birds, but with metal razors for feathers, some shit like that. Something to do with Hercules.*

The swarming birds cried out, their strange song reminding him of the shriek of a rusty screen door, only much louder. They were agitated, maybe picking up on the vibes from him and Cerberus. Most flew in a shrieking cluster above them, but they were starting to dip lower, single members of the flock dropping down from the sky, razor-sharp wings coming dangerously close.

From the corner of his eye he saw Cerberus leaving, its heads and body tucked low to the ground as it began to trot. The flock apparently didn't care for the dog's sudden movement. Their grating cries grew louder, and more of them glided down from the sky, the touch of their wings slicing into the rotting, broken flesh of the hound. Danny could hear the giant dog yelping in pain as it fled across the barren landscape, shrieking birds in pursuit.

Then Cerberus fell, and the birds swarmed him. Even at that distance, Danny could hear the dog whimpering, and he almost felt bad.

Almost.

Most of the razor birds had left with Cerberus, and Danny used the opportunity hurry to the cliff to meet his friends. They were almost to the bottom.

"You all right?" Eve asked weakly. "You look like total shit." She smiled at him then, and he knew that she was okay, despite the fact that she was covered in drying blood.

"You guys might want to hurry," he said, looking back over his shoulder. Only one or two of the birds were visible in the dark gloom of the cavernous sky. Most of them were still savaging Cerberus, and perhaps they would roost there for a time.

"What now, Daniel?" Conan Doyle sounded a bit exasperated.

"I think we're okay." He reached out to help Eve with the final step to the Underworld floor. "But there were these crazy birds made of metal and—"

"Stymphalia," Conan Doyle interrupted.

"Whatever," Danny agreed. "They're nasty shits."

Conan Doyle nodded as he removed his handkerchief from his pocket and wiped the sweat from his brow. Both Eve and Ceridwen were sitting on the rocks at the bottom of the cliff path. Eve was already starting to look better, but now that he could see more clearly, Danny wished he could say the same about Ceridwen. The Faerie sorceress sat with her face buried in her hands. She might have gotten her second wind before, but it seemed like she had just about used it up.

Danny caught Conan Doyle's eye. "Is she okay?"

The mage nodded, going to her side and putting a gentle hand on her arm. "This place seems to be having a debilitating effect." Danny noticed an uncharacteristic touch of concern in the man's voice.

Ceridwen leaned her head back against his chest and looked up into his eyes. "Don't be concerned," she told them, all the while speaking directly to Conan Doyle. "Give me a chance to acclimate myself, and I'm sure I'll be fine."

Eve was up now, walking around, stretching her legs. But Danny saw her freeze in midstep, and she turned toward him. "Hey, kid. Your friends are back."

She gestured with her chin to a rocky hill, where at least a dozen Stymphalia perched, watching them silently. More fluttered down from the sky with a metallic clatter.

CONAN Doyle frowned as he watched Eve and Danny in the twisted landscape of this new level of the Underworld. They were gesturing to one another, but for the moment seemed in no danger. He turned his attention once more to Ceridwen with an ache in his heart that only resonated more deeply when he caught her gazing at him. Something was happening here, between them. The caution, the resentment, the echo of the past was being stripped away.

It frightened him. He had caused her so much pain before that he knew he ought to keep her at arm's length. But Conan Doyle did not know if even he had the strength for that. Particularly not now. Her normally pale skin was starting to turn an unhealthy gray, and it looked as though she were having a difficult time staying awake.

"I'm sorry," he said.

Ceridwen smiled weakly. "For what? This is not your doing, Arthur. You spend far too much time blaming yourself for things not in your control."

"If I had known this damnable place would have such an effect on you, I would have—"

"You would have done exactly as you have done." The sorceress cut him off. "I am not the focus of this mission." She stood and moved to him, reminding him of an old woman who had sat too long in a cold winter chill. "Drive your concerns for me from your mind," she said, placing the palm of her hand against his face, her cool touch providing a moment's respite from the heat of the Underworld. "Stopping Nigel Gull should be your focus."

He took her into his arms then, and he could not stop himself. In the tongue of the Faerie he whispered to her. *"For so long I had lost my heart. So many years that I stopped noticing it was gone. But now I have found it again, and the fear of losing it weighs heavily upon me."*

Ceridwen pulled away and placed a hand on his chest, searching for the beat of his heart. Finding it, she smiled and was about to speak when a screeching din filled the air.

"Lord, what now?" Doyle muttered as he turned to see Eve and Danny walking backward toward them.

Beyond them, a flock of screeching, razor-winged birds filled the sky.

The Stymphalia had returned.

Conan Doyle and Ceridwen moved as best they could to meet Eve and Danny. The four of them gathered there on that hellish plain, and gazed at the glittering, screeching cloud coming toward them.

"Wish I knew what pissed them off so bad," Danny said.

Conan Doyle did not have time dwell on the question. The angry flock was quickly descending, and he had to act if he and his charges were to survive the onslaught.

He took hold of Ceridwen's hand. "Lend me what strength you have to spare." The sorceress nodded, gripping his fingers tightly, and he felt a surge of power flow into his body.

"Is this it?" Eve asked, panic in her tone as the birds wailed above them. "We're going to drive them off by joining hands and singing 'Give Peace a Chance'?"

"Eve," Conan Doyle snarled. "Stay close, and do shut up."

He attempted to blot out the sounds of the angry Stymphalian Birds, concentrating on a spell of protection. Where normally such a spell would flow from his lips, immediately providing the protection they so desperately needed, Conan Doyle found that his familiar magicks were not inclined to work efficiently in the Underworld. Even with Ceridwen's strength added to his, the task of summoning a shield was exhausting and quite painful.

The birds unleashed their first wave, the more ferocious of their number diving down to touch razor-sharp feathers to delicate flesh.

"Doyle!" he heard Eve snap. "We're waiting."

The birds' cries were louder, more frenzied. He flinched as one flew past his arm, slicing through the material of his suit coat and the shirt beneath. He could feel the warmth of his own blood trickling down his arm.

"We're going to be cut to fucking ribbons!" Danny yelled, and Conan Doyle sensed that the boy was about to bolt.

"Stay where you are," he commanded, feeling the troublesome magick begin to bend to his wishes.

The air around them hummed as the enchantment began to coalesce into the shield he had cast. The Stymphalia collided with the crackling sphere, their metal bodies falling to the ground in an explosion of cold, white sparks. It took everything Conan Doyle had—and what Ceridwen was continuing to give him—to maintain the bubble of magickal force. He wasn't sure how long he could hold it.

The birds grew even more furious, descending in a ravening cluster, a blizzard of razor blades. Doyle and his companions were blind to the world outside as sparks exploded in the air around their protective sphere with the relentless onslaught. Conan Doyle felt Ceridwen's grip begin to weaken and glanced over to see his woman struggling to stay upright.

"Hold on, love. Hold on."

The sphere began to waver, and one of the Stymphalia managed to break through. Conan Doyle cried as the bird landed atop his head, sinking its needle-like beak into his scalp.

Eve was the first to react, swatting the animal to the ground and stamping on it with the heel of her boot.

"My thanks, Eve," he gasped, a warm stream of blood from his scalp tickling the back of his neck.

Ceridwen fell to her knees, her pale flesh tinted more green than ever. She had given all she could, but it still was not enough. The magickal sphere of protection threatened to buckle.

"Eve, I want you to listen to me," Conan Doyle said through gritted teeth. "I can't keep this up much longer. When the sphere falls, I want you and Danny to take Ceridwen and run. I'm certain that there are caves nearby where you can find shelter and hold off any further attack."

"What about you?" she asked. "Don't even think about telling me you plan to stay here because—"

"I will hold them off so you can get a healthy head start. Please, when my magick fails, take Ceridwen and Danny away from here."

Eve came around to face him. There was rage and a hint of fear on her beautiful yet tired features. "What the hell is wrong with you?" she screamed, the birds outside riled even more by her display of anger. "You're an arch mage for Christ's sake, and you're going to allow some metal fucking birds to end your life?!"

Conan Doyle shook his head sadly. "My magick is not working as it should here. The power in this place is different, more ancient. Ceri cannot wield the elements of this place as she should. They are not eager to be tamed, they fight her at every turn. And the magick is similar. Unfamiliar to me."

He looked into her eyes and saw that she was speechless, a rarity for her. Then Eve nodded. "I'll get them out. But then I'm coming back for you."

He was weakening far faster then he would have imagined. All they had were moments, and he looked to see that they were ready. Eve held Ceridwen in her arms, and Conan Doyle's heart was wrenched by how frail the sorceress looked.

The magick fought to slip away from him, and he fell to his knees, straining to hold on to his control. The Stymphalian Birds continued to swarm around the sphere, screeching excitedly, as if they knew that their dogged patience was about to be rewarded. But then, above their cries of savagery, Arthur Conan Doyle heard something else.

A voice raised in song.

The magickal shielding fell away with a fleeting whisper, but somehow they remained safe.

"Should we be running?" Eve asked, warily watching the swarm of razor-feathered birds that flew above their heads.

"Listen," Conan Doyle said.

The song grew louder, stronger, and he could just about make out the words. Its message was one of peace and serenity, and it was sung in a language that even the Stymphalia could understand. Where the sky had once been filled with winged death, it was now suddenly clear, the razor birds darting into the distant shadows of the cavern, convinced to be elsewhere. Conan Doyle could still hear their screeching cries, but they were far away now.

And though the threat had been dispersed, the song continued to fill the air, and Conan Doyle watched as Nigel Gull, singing out gloriously in the voice of Orpheus, approached, his Wicked following like obedient dogs at his heels.

•　　•　　•

"HELLO, Arthur," Gull said. He could not help but smile. To see Conan Doyle so helpless, it was absolutely priceless.

"Nigel. I suppose we owe you a bit of thanks."

Gull waved his words away. "Not at all, old friend. You were in a fix, and I was happy to oblige. Would you not do the same for me?"

"Of course they would have," Hawkins agreed.

Jezebel giggled, biting at a fingernail with her dainty mouth.

Conan Doyle remained silent, ignoring the commentary, and turned to check the condition of his people. Despite his words, Gull wondered if the man would have left him and his operatives to the mercies of the razor birds had the situation been reversed. For in truth he would not himself have bothered with saving Sir Arthur and his Menagerie if he did not still need something from them. He would have quite enjoyed watching them all die horribly.

Gull watched as Conan Doyle took Ceridwen from Eve's arms and laid her upon the ground. He caught the demon boy watching him with a steely, untrusting gaze. *This is one to watch,* Gull thought, returning his attentions to Doyle and his lover.

"What seems to be the problem?" he asked with an attempt at concern. It was *so* difficult to muster.

"Nothing that leaving this place won't cure," Conan Doyle said as he rose from Ceridwen's side and stalked toward Gull. "Why are you here, Nigel? What purpose could you possibly have in this damnable place?"

Hawkins chuckled as he moved to stand beside his employer. "The old man knows you well, sir," he said with a sneer. "Type of bloke thinks he's smarter than all the rest. Two steps ahead of everyone else."

Conan Doyle barely acknowledged the silver-haired man, his eyes boring into Gull. "Why?" he asked again.

Nigel gazed around at the black, gnarled trees that grew

sparsely across the charcoal gray earth of this place. There were other landscapes here—the terrain changed almost constantly as one traveled through the Underworld—but this place was almost pretty in comparison. "There is something I need, here. Something that will help me gain a prize I've long been denied."

Conan Doyle laughed disdainfully, and it took all the self-control that Gull could muster to not slap the condescending smirk from his face.

"What is it now, Nigel?" the mage asked. "What forbidden treasure has tempted you beyond the limits of rational thinking this time?"

Gull wanted to tell him. To explain that there was no ancient book or scroll, or object of power to sell to the highest bidder. Instead, he swallowed painfully, the dry air of the Underworld making his throat ache, and stepped closer to the man who had insulted him so.

"Matters of the heart, dear boy," he whispered, leaning forward slightly so that Conan Doyle was sure to hear. "Matters of the heart."

Conan Doyle's face screwed up in confusion, and Gull was certain that the infuriating man wanted to know more, but Gull's patience was gone and they had to move on.

"What the devil are you talking about man, matters of the—"

Gull raised a misshapen hand to silence him. "I've said enough and wasted too much time with you." He scanned the skies of the forbidden world. "In case you haven't noticed, this can be quite a dangerous place, and to stay put for too long can mean your demise."

His stare locked with Conan Doyle's. "We have to leave."

"And where are *we* going?" his adversary asked grimly, straightening his jacket as though he could look presentable down in this ancient hell.

Gull cleared his throat, preparing to once again sing. "You're not going anywhere. I require only Eve."

Alarm flashed in Conan Doyle's eyes, and a crackle of golden light flared from his fingertips, but Gull would have no such resistance. He sang out a single note in the voice of Orpheus, freezing the Menagerie where they stood. Conan Doyle gritted his teeth, attempting to fight the paralyzing command of that song, but to no avail.

Gull paused to rest his vocal cords, gesturing toward Eve. "This way, dear lady. We have an appointment with the Erinyes."

Hatred burning in her eyes, fighting the movement of every muscle, Eve stepped away from her friends.

"I'll kill you for this, you know," she said, showing Nigel her fangs, and he sang several soft notes that sapped away all her aggression.

I'm sure you would, he thought. *But I'm not fool enough to give you the chance.*

Then he looked at Jezebel and Hawkins. "Take her," he ordered. The girl took one arm, and the man the other, and they led Eve away. Gull returned his attentions to Conan Doyle and the remainder of his team. "I want to say a proper good-bye."

"Will you kill us, Nigel?" Conan Doyle asked, swaying on his feet, still under the sway of the Orpheus song. Ceridwen moaned on the ground behind him, the demon boy kneeling by her side.

"What do you take me for?" Gull asked, feigning horror. "We have far too much history for that." Again, he looked to the dark, ocher skies of the Underworld, and filling his lungs, sang out a lilting verse, long and powerful. A song of summoning. "I cannot kill you, Arthur, but this place . . ."

Gull cocked his head, listening for a particular sound and found it. It was the sound of flapping wings far off in the distance—but growing closer.

He smiled, turned on his heel, and left them to die.

10

SQUIRE scurried along the shadowpaths.

To others it was only darkness, but to the hobgoblin it was a vast network of tunnels leading to any place on the planet, and even beyond, where the slimmest touch of shadow was the means to travel great distances. All shadows were connected, and Squire knew their secrets well. He jogged through the dark, instinct guiding him toward his destination.

In his mind, he began to review the list of items Clay had asked him to bring from the brownstone. He stopped for a moment, removing the bundled titanium netting from his shoulder and dropping it to the shadowpath. "Let's see," he grumbled. "Got the netting, of course. Can't catch a beastie without a good net."

He picked up a small box and opened it to reveal a clear, glass vial. He took the container from its case and admired the milky fluid inside. *A whole lot of South American tree frogs gave up their skin to produce this bottle a' bad business. Should knock'er on her ass.*

The hobgoblin put the narcotic back into its protective case and turned his attentions to the tranquilizer rifle. Normally he would have preferred weapons with a more archaic flavor—knives, swords, crossbows, axes—but in this case he was willing to bend a bit. From what he could see, the rifle was in good working order, and he slipped it back under the netting until it was needed.

Then he caught sight of the brightly colored Skittles package. "There you are," he said with an enormous grin, snatching up the package of candy. "Come to Papa." He tore open the package with his teeth, tilted his head back and dumped most of the candies into his open maw.

"Oh that's good," he grumbled, as the multiple flavors exploded in his mouth. "It's been too long." He tried to remember the last time he had satisfied his nasty sweet tooth. Close to two days, probably a record.

He was in the midst of a euphoric sugar rush when he thought he heard Clay's voice. Squire paused in the stillness of the shadows, gooey wad of sour candy in his cheek.

" . . . *ire hurry up, damn it!*"

It was Clay all right. "Shit," the goblin muttered beneath his breath, pouring the rest of the Skittles into his mouth and gathering his things. He tossed the candy wrapper and hauled the net filled with stuff over his shoulder, trudging down the appropriate shadowpath.

He knew by the ruckus wafting into the ocean of darkness that he had reached his destination. The exit was a small one, a tight squeeze, but that didn't matter to a hobgoblin.

Squire forced his way into the opening, bones bending to accommodate the tiny space. The cool touch of shadow clung to his flesh as he emerged from an oval-shaped patch of shadow thrown by a cast iron trash barrel: first his head, followed by his short, muscular body. It was kind of like being born, minus the death of his mother and the attempts of the midwife to kill him, but there was no time for sweet nostalgia. He hauled the netting out of the pool with a grunt.

The hobgoblin quickly scanned his surroundings, searching for his friends, but found only bad news instead. What they had feared had happened. He was at a train station, squatting beneath a glass overhang that would have protected him from the elements if necessary, and where commuters, tourists, and the like should have been awaiting a train, there were now only cold statues of stone.

"Damn it," he hissed, throwing the net over his shoulder and moving out from beneath the overhang. Squire scanned the area, his sharp eyes taking in every inch of the place. *Where the hell are Clay and Graves?* he thought, carefully moving around the poor saps who had simply been waiting for a train when Medusa decided to pass through town.

"You see a big guy that can change himself into monsters?" Squire asked a large man who had been frozen to stone as he looked up from his morning newspaper. "He had a ghost with him."

And all was eerily silent.

Until the mastodon came crashing through a wall at the far end of the platform, destroying a mosaic depicting famous Athenian landmarks.

"Never mind," Squire told the stone man. "I think I found him."

THE attack had come without warning.

Clay and Graves had been in pursuit of the fleeing Medusa, hopeful that she would steer clear of the more populated locales. But the Gorgon seemed not to consider her surroundings, intent only upon her destination. Clay had grown certain of that. Following her path, it was obvious to him that she moved with purpose, as though she knew exactly where she wanted to be.

Like she's following a trail.

That trail had taken her to the Theseum train station on the west side of Athens, at the beginning of the rush hour commute. She moved with incredible speed, slinking along the city streets near the edge of the train station, reminding Clay of a sidewinder snake, slithering across the desert. They'd almost lost track of her a few times, but Graves had always managed to find her, sensing the ectoplasmic piece of himself still imbedded inside her.

They tried their best to catch up, hoping to stop her before she reached the station, but Medusa only moved faster, as if spurred on by some unknown lure. Squire would have muttered something rude under his breath, some obvious joke about the monster needing to catch a train. The thought, though foolish, rang true. Why else come to a train station? Clay dropped to all fours, flesh shifting, bones reknitting, all in a single instant so that by the time he hit the ground the fur had sprouted on his body and his tail whipped behind him. He needed speed. As a cheetah, now, his claws tore at the ground, and he sprinted into the station.

Medusa had already climbed the stone steps up onto the platform, and he could hear the screams of those who had caught sight of her.

They didn't scream for long.

The cheetah bounded up the station steps, and above the final cries of Medusa's victims, he heard a sound that filled him with dread.

The hiss of a train as it pulled away.

He sprang onto the platform, just in time to catch sight of Medusa leaping onto the last car of the departing train. Clay watched in horror as the Gorgon tore off a door with a shriek of metal and tossed it aside. Then she disappeared inside, that nest of snakes upon her head coiling excitedly.

"Damn it!" Clay snarled even as his flesh altered again and he stood upright, unfolding into the body of a man. Already the deaths of those at the train station weighed on his conscience, but now there was the train. He tried not to wonder how many passengers were aboard.

The air shimmered beside him, and Dr. Graves appeared, phantom guns drawn. His shirt cuffs were rolled up, and through his transparent form, Clay could see the X where his suspenders criss-crossed his back like bandoliers. He had always cut a heroic figure, but just then there was nothing heroic about the dread etched upon the spectral features of Leonard Graves.

"We have to catch that train," the ghost said. "I can do it, but you'll need real speed."

Clay swore under his breath. He nodded, and his flesh began to flow once more, becoming malleable . . . but he never completed the change. A figure clad entirely in black appeared from among the stone people on the platform and let fly with a throwing blade. Clay turned, but not fast enough, and the thin blade bit deeply into his shoulder. He tried to shift back to his more human state, but was wracked with an excruciating pain that radiated from the wound. In a form between cat and man, he leaned forward and tore the blade from his flesh with his mouth, tossing it to the ground. His own blood glinted off the strange sigils etched on its surface. He heard his attacker laughing, the sound of joy muffled by a cherubic mask. The effect of that childlike mask on the killer's face was profoundly unsettling.

Blasts of ectoplasmic gunfire filled the air, and Clay watched Graves descend upon their foe.

The baby-faced figure danced among the gunfire, eluding the phantom bullets with a disturbing grace, and as he moved, Clay saw that he had taken a cylindrical canister from a pouch on his belt and was spreading its grainy contents in a circle below the ghost's floating form.

"Graves!" Clay warned, but it was too late. The ghostly adventurer began to scream, his normally translucent form, beginning to fade.

"What have you done to him?" Clay growled, finally able to take on his natural, earthen form, but only for an instant. He was eager to show their attacker that he had messed with the wrong people.

The figure in black let loose with another blade, this one sticking in the center of Clay's orange, cracked flesh. He tore it away with a snarl and ran toward the assassin. In his mind he saw the image of a powerful silverback gorilla, and willed his body to become it. Again he was stricken with an incredible bolt of pain, driving him to his knees.

He glanced up at the dwindling form of Dr. Graves. "The dirt," the ghost moaned. "It's from my grave . . . it binds me . . . calls me back there."

Another throwing knife pierced Clay's flesh and the masked man giggled. He was playing with them. Enraged, Clay forced his protesting flesh to assume the shape of the gorilla and lunged at their attacker. The man tried to avoid him, but this time Clay was faster, knocking him savagely to the ground. He roared, tossing back his head and shrieking to the heavens, his fists beating on his broad chest.

"We've underestimated you," the man said. His voice from beneath the disturbing cherub mask was a dry whisper, like the rustling of leaves. "Thought the knives would have shut you down by now."

The silverback brought its arms down upon the man's chest as though they were clubs. The man made not a sound as he was pummeled. Clay reared back, staring down at the body of his attacker. The man looked like a broken rag doll, arms and legs askew, the eerie baby-doll face looking up at the pale, blue Athenian sky.

The places where Clay had been stabbed burned as if touched by acid, and he looked away from his foe for an instant to check on Graves. The ghost was gone, only the circle of earth upon the ground remained.

"Finished with me already?" the whispering voice said mockingly, and before Clay could react, the man was up from the ground and had climbed upon his back, locking himself in place with his legs and arms about the gorilla's throat.

Impossible. He was dead. Bones shattered.

Clay roared, hurling himself to the side, thrashing about in an attempt to dislodge his attacker. He considered changing his shape again, to become something even more powerful. For a moment, he hesitated, the memory of the awful pain giving him pause. The knives were imbued with some sort of sorcery, a spell meant to prevent him from changing his shape. Whoever this guy was, he knew things about Conan Doyle's Menagerie, ways to stop them. Ways to kill them.

Another knife bit into the thick muscle of his shoulder blade, and the silverback roared. He reached over his shoulder, powerful arms attempting to pull his attacker from his back, but could not do it. The man was stuck like a tick on a dog.

Clay threw himself to the ground, rolling across the train platform, crashing into the stone bodies of Medusa's victims. The bodies toppled to the ground, crumbling into pieces, but still the man in black held tight.

His thoughts raced. He had to do something.

"Squire, hurry up, damn it!" he bellowed, directing his voice to the nearest patch of shadows though he doubted it was possible for the little bastard to hear him. If there was any time that they could have used the hobgoblin's assistance, it was now.

As he rolled across the hard ground of the station, the image of another animal filled his mind—something big. And his body began to change. Clay quivered and shook. The pain was unbelievable, and for an instant it almost stopped him.

Almost.

The silverback was gone now, replaced with body of a mastodon, and Clay tossed its huge head back, tusks gleaming, and blew a triumphant blast through his trunk. The pain had infected his entire form, it was absolute agony retaining the shape, and the intensity of what he was experiencing drove him wild.

The huge beast thrashed its mighty body from side to side. Clay could still feel the man clinging to his back, almost as if he had burrowed beneath his flesh. Blinded by agony and rage, he surged forward with no concern as to what was in his path.

The huge beast plowed through the back of the decorative mosaic wall, shattering it to rubble, and for an instant he felt the man's grip on him lessen. Sensing an opportunity, Clay pitched its massive head forward. The assassin was flung from his back, and upon striking the ground rolled to his feet, seemingly unfazed. He held more of those enchanted throwing knives in his hands.

"This should do it," he hissed from behind his cherub's mask.

The assassin lifted a hand, about to fling more blades. Clay braced for the savage bite of those knives . . . but then his attacker's head snapped viciously backward. He staggered, daggers dropping from his gloved hands to clatter upon the ground. His hand rose to weakly brush at an object protruding from one of the eyeholes in the cherub mask.

A tranquilizer dart had been shot into his right eye.

Clay watched with great satisfaction as the figure fell limply to the station floor, arms and legs twitching.

"Did you see that shot?" Squire hooted, rifle slung over his shoulder as he advanced across the platform.

The feeling gave out in the mastodon's legs, and Clay slumped to the ground. Bracing for pain, he transformed to his humanoid guise, flesh flowing once more. The process was excruciating, his body feeling as though it had been set afire from the inside.

"What the hell's wrong with you?" Squire asked, kneeling beside him.

Clay looked into the face of the hobgoblin, pleased for once to see the little man. "Didn't think you were that proficient with modern weaponry," he said as he tried to stand.

"Don't care for them really," Squire responded, hefting the rifle. "But it doesn't mean I can't shoot the balls off a blue jay at fifty yards."

Clay stumbled over to the circle of dirt. "We have to see about Graves," he said, falling to his knees before the circle. "He said that this dirt came from his grave, that it was calling him back to his body."

Squire nodded in understanding. "Old-fashioned binding

spell for wandering spirits," he explained. "At first they're bound within the circle and then slowly drawn back to their bodies where they're imprisoned until the sorcerer who cast the spell decides they can go free."

"That's where he is now?" Clay asked, searching the air above the dirt circle for a sign of the ghostly adventurer. "Back with his remains?"

The hobgoblin stepped closer to the circle. "If I'm remembering right, it can take a little while for the spell to kick into full gear, especially if the spirit has a particularly strong disposition." He rubbed away part of the circle with the toe of his shoe. "He may not be quite there yet."

The air above the broken circle shimmered and pulsed as Leonard Graves began to materialize. The ghost was not in the best of moods.

"Bastard!" he roared, the twin Colt 45s taking shape in his hands. "Where is that son of a bitch?"

"Whoa, Len. Where's your usual calm reserve? Be cool, pal," Squire said. "We took care of him for ya."

"He's down," Clay confirmed as he reached up to remove the last of the attacker's knives from his shoulder, hissing with pain as the dagger came loose. "But we still have to catch that train—"

"Where is he?" Graves interrupted, gliding through them, ghostly guns still in hands. "I want to see the assassin up close. I'm going to make sure he doesn't have any other tricks up his sleeve."

"What's the matter with you, Casper?" Squire chided as he turned around. "He's right th . . . oh shit."

The figure in black was gone.

"I remember the day when getting shot in the eye with a tranquilizer dart pretty much took you out of the picture," Squire said, walking over to check out where the body had lain. The dart lay upon the platform. "But I shouldn't be surprised."

"What are you talking about?" Clay asked, frustrated by

this latest turn. *Isn't anything going to go right on this mission?*

"Our mystery boy with the kewpie doll face mask is named Tassarian. A real nasty prick, let me tell you. Used to work for Conan Doyle's old pal Nigel Gull."

The goblin nudged the tranquilizer dart with his shoe. "Or at least he did until about twenty years ago, when I killed him."

GULL had left them to die.

In the voice of Orpheus he had compelled them to lie upon the ground and await an inevitable death. Now the sound of beating wings grew louder, and Conan Doyle winced at the horrid shrieks that filled the air in the distance, growing nearer by the moment.

"I can't move," Danny growled. The demon boy's tone was a mix of rage and panic. "If those razor birds come back for us, we're screwed."

"It is not the Stymphalian Birds whose cries you hear," Conan Doyle said, forcing the words from his throat. Gull had not commanded them to silence, but even so any action that was not part of his instruction was difficult.

"It's not?" Danny asked with a spark of hope.

"No. I'm afraid it is something far worse." Conan Doyle wracked his brain, desperately trying to think of a spell or incantation that could counter the power of Orpheus.

"Worse?" Danny said. "*Worse?* Now I'm *really* worried."

Conan Doyle managed to roll onto his back, gazing up at the misty sky of the vast underground cavern. The ceiling was so high that the true height of it was impossible to discern. "Sarcasm will do nothing to help us, boy. If that's all you can contribute, I'd appreciate it if you would hold your tongue."

"Dude," Danny exclaimed. "There's a good chance we're about to die here. I think me being sarcastic is the least of our problems."

The shrieks were closer now.

"Gentlemen," Ceridwen scolded in a whisper, her face pressed to the ground. "Perhaps our energies could be put to better use, hmmm?"

Conan Doyle was glad to hear that she was conscious, but hardly thrilled that she would be awake to experience what would likely be a grisly fate. A succession of horribly shrill cries filled the air; eager wails of excitement from creatures that had at last found their prey.

The Harpies had found them.

Warm fetid air blasted the ground from the power of their wings, kicking up dirt and dust as they dropped from the sky. There were three of them. Their hideous, bird-like bodies reminded Conan Doyle of vultures, but with the heads of women. The Harpies roosted upon the rocks and perched there, gazing down on their prey. Conan Doyle could feel their hungry eyes on him, and smell the stench of death wafting from their feathered bodies.

Danny Ferrick began to whimper. "Oh shit. Oh shit. Oh shit. Oh shit. Oh shit. Oh shit."

"Control yourself, Daniel," Conan Doyle instructed, with all of the authority he could muster.

Oh shit, indeed.

The Harpies huddled together, strengthening the image of vultures. But vultures did not speak. *"What have we here, Sister Twilight?"* one of them asked in archaic Greek, its voice a terrible screech.

"I'm not sure, Sister Dark," replied a second.

"I think a tribute has been paid to us, sisters," said the last of the three. *"Oh yes, I think the one whose beautiful song we heard has bestowed this honor of fresh meat."*

"Come now, Sister Dusk," said Twilight. *"Why would one who sang so beautifully wish to pay us tribute?"*

"Are we not beautiful as well?" Dusk replied.

As the other Harpies agreed, Conan Doyle frowned. He was skilled in linguistics, particularly ancient languages, but he should not have been able to understand them so well.

Curious, he glanced sidelong at the demon boy. "Daniel," he whispered. "Can you understand these creatures' speech?"

"Yeah, but I wish I didn't. If they're gonna eat us I wish they'd just do it and get it over with, their voices are like fingernails on a damn blackboard."

Fascinating, Doyle mused. It was as if the Underworld were somehow accepting them, bestowing upon them an understanding of the ancient language of myth. They were becoming part of this place. It made certain things easier, but somehow he found it very unsettling as well to wonder what else it might mean. This was something that he would need to look into later . . . if there was a later for them.

"An offering perhaps," Sister Dark suggested. *"For safe passage across the land. As Charon takes payment for passage across the Styx, this is our due for allowing them to cross the land unhindered."*

"An interesting theory," said Twilight, reaching up with a talon to scratch the side of her head. The Harpy's hair was long and gray, matted with filth. *"But I'm not sure that—"*

Conan Doyle cleared his throat. He could understand the Harpies. Could they understand him? "If you would like to know why we have been left here, good sisters, all you need do is ask."

The creatures exchanged glances and then fluttered down from their perch on the rocks. They alighted upon the ground, another cloud of black dust roiling beneath them.

"Look, sisters, the carrion speaks," Twilight said, bending forward to take a closer look. *"Do you have answers for us, tender morsel? Do you know the reason why you have been abandoned here?"*

Conan Doyle could feel Gull's spell weakening slightly, and was able to sit up. The Harpies recoiled, baring razor-sharp teeth and hissing in warning.

"Just stretching, my dears. No cause for concern." He wanted them as calm and complacent as possible, in case an opportunity to escape should present itself. Danny was moving about more freely also, as was Ceridwen.

"My belly rumbles for food," Dusk shrieked. *"You will explain why you are here immediately—or go down our gullets with questions unanswered. Soon I will be too hungry to care."*

"Of course, of course," Doyle answered. "Let me see." He raised a hand to stroke his mustache. "Where to begin?"

The Harpies leaned closer, eager to hear his tale. Their feathers were stained and matted with the dried blood of previous meals, the smell wafting off their bodies sickening.

"We are here, my compatriots and I, because we were betrayed."

Twilight cocked her head to one side, intrigued. *"The one whose voice sang the most lovely of songs, was he the purveyor of this betrayal?"*

Conan Doyle nodded. "Sadly, yes," he explained. "He acquired, by magicks most foul, the voice of Orpheus, and has used its persuasive capability to steal away one of our group, and to order us to stay to meet our fate at your mercy."

"Horrible," Twilight hissed.

"Terrible," said Dark, with a disgusted shake of her head.

"Appalling," Dusk interjected for the sake of unity with her sisters. *"It is enough to weaken the already precarious trust we have in those that we so tentatively call friend."*

Dark and Twilight turned their attentions to their sister, obviously taken aback by her words.

"Your trust in us is precarious, darling sister?" Twilight asked, ire in her tone.

Dusk shook her head furiously. *"No, no. Do not misconstrue. I speak of friends, not dearest family."*

Then Dark flapped her wings in agitation. *"And what friends do you have in this misbegotten place but us? Can you tell me this?"*

Like the electricity in the air before a thunderstorm, Conan Doyle sensed it growing around him, raising gooseflesh on his arms. He frowned deeply and glanced around, trying not to draw the Harpies' attention. Someone was using magick. He glanced toward Ceridwen, her regal features in profile. She was conscious and sitting up, but he could tell that she was in no condition to attempt a spell of any kind, and Danny was not capable of such a feat.

Then who?

The Harpies were being manipulated, a spell had been cast to foment hostility among them. Their argument was reaching a fevered pitch, and they had begun to scream at one another, their talons digging into the dry, rocky earth as they grew more agitated.

"And what of you, Twilight?" Dark shrieked, spittle flying. *"Do you mistrust me as well? Am I the last to know how you two really feel about me?"*

Twilight flapped her powerful wings, stirring up clouds of dirt. *"I have had suspicions about the two of you for quite some time,"* she snarled. *"When were you going to do it? As I slept? Helpless while in the embrace of dream? I should have known."*

Conan Doyle caught Danny's eye as the sisters continued their tirade against one another. The demon boy slid closer to him.

"What the hell's going on?"

The mage managed to stand. The effect of Orpheus's voice was indeed wearing off, and he helped Ceridwen to her feet as well. "I'll explain later." He reached down to haul Danny up. "But now might be a good time to get as far away from here as possible."

The Harpies did not even notice them getting to their feet and moving away. The sisters were totally engrossed in one another, blind to anything other than their heated squabble about betrayal and mistrust.

"I'll see you both dead!" Twilight raged, and the ugly beast spread her wings, lifted off the ground several feet, and then descended upon her sisters, curved black talons tearing at them savagely.

Dusk and Dark responded with equal fury, their

screeches of outrage filling the air as they attacked each other with wanton abandon.

Potent magick, Conan Doyle thought as he watched the horrible creatures engage in their insane melee. As he and his companions made their escape, he scanned the cliffs surrounding them, but still could not find the source of the spell.

They were moving far slower than he would have liked, the residual effects of Gull's song still working on them, but they made progress nonetheless. The screams of the Harpies receded into the distance as they scrambled down an embankment into a gully.

In places the cavern ceilings were so high that moisture gathered in the eaves and swirled into clouds. As they traveled, they heard the sounds of distant oceans and the thunder of lumbering beasts as they made their way through tunnels and across barren plains of rock and cold, slippery moss.

In time they found themselves on rough terrain with uneven hills of craggy stone and outcroppings of rock that jutted up from the ground as though rammed through the earth from below. Some were small, little more than a scattering of blocks, and others were towers. It reminded Conan Doyle of the American Southwest, of the red rocks that were spread across sections of Arizona, among other places.

They weaved their way around the largest of these, following paths cut into the ground by the wind that scoured the stone. It was rough going, but at least they had left the Harpies far behind.

"So what happened with the sisters back there?" Danny asked. "Why'd they go all Jerry Springer on each other?"

"Magick happened to them," Conan Doyle explained. "A spell was cast that caused their already rabid emotions to run amok."

Ceridwen stopped and turned to look at him, her face cast in eerie shadows from the strange gloom of this place. "And did you cast this spell, Arthur?"

Before he could answer the wind brought a new scent to them. It was the smell of a campfire, and of cooking meat.

Conan Doyle didn't know how the others were responding to the drifting aroma, but his stomach was close to cramping, it was so empty. And like the cobra charmed by a tune, he found himself drawn toward the smell. They fell silent and walked quietly in between two tall stone outcroppings, which seemed part of a ridge of towers that loomed up on all sides of them now.

"Hey!" Danny said. "Is this a good idea?"

"Perhaps we should find out," Conan Doyle answered. At this point he had gone beyond caution, his sudden realization of hunger perhaps making him a tad careless. Beyond that was the simple fact that this was the direction Gull had taken Eve, and he was determined to retrieve her.

They saw the flicker of the campfire reflected on the stone thrusting up from the earth ahead. The smell of roasting meat was nearly overwhelming, and Conan Doyle could have sworn he heard the hissing sound of grease as it dripped into the fire.

It compelled him to move closer.

Their path among the stones twisted slightly, and around that bend was the prize that had drawn them like a moth to flame. Conan Doyle slowly, cautiously peered around the corner into an open area, a clearing in this forest of stone.

A giant sat upon a rock before a roaring fire, some sort of beast roasting over the hissing flames on a spit. The giant's back was to him, but Conan Doyle could see that he was powerfully proportioned. The hair cascading down his back was very long and curly, and he wore only a loincloth made from the fur of some animal.

Conan Doyle was unsure of how to proceed. He thought about clearing his throat to introduce himself and the others, but considering how friendly the other denizens of the Underworld had been, wasn't sure if this was the best course. His questions were answered for him when the huge man, sitting hunched before the fire, addressed him in a low, melodious voice.

"Welcome, strangers." The giant turned to face them from his rocky seat. "Step into my humble abode."

Ceridwen and Danny froze beside Conan Doyle as the giant fixed them in the stare of the single eye at the center of his broad, bearded face.

"You're just in time for dinner," said the Cyclops, and his lips spread wide in a ghastly smile.

11

THE Underworld was vast. And yet for all its size it seemed stifling and small, claustrophobic, and crowded.

Yeah, Danny Ferrick thought as he stared up at the one-eyed giant, the Cyclops, that leered hungrily down at him and his companions. *Crowded's exactly the fucking word.*

They had climbed over the ruins of ancient temples and trekked beneath the gaze of sentinel statuary. Fires burned in the walls. Every new tunnel, every change in the landscape, seemed to push them into the midst of another threat, into the lair of another monster. *Then Gull shows up, and it's like this was what the ugly bastard had intended all along,* that he wanted them to follow, that he needed Eve and had planned to take her. And he'd just *done* it, right under their goddamned noses, and there wasn't a thing they could do about it.

Danny was sick of it. The whole time down here he'd been wishing for a minute to breathe, for their trail to lead them somewhere there weren't ancient horrors lying in wait. Now he'd changed his mind. The Cyclops started to laugh, glaring at him and Ceridwen and Mr. Doyle with that big, damp, bloodshot eye, and Danny was never happier to meet up with something that wanted to kill him.

"Come, my friends—" the Cyclops began again, its voice like an earth tremor. The single horn that jutted up from its head gleamed in the blue light that misted off of Conan Doyle's hands.

"We're not your friends," Danny snarled.

With a grunt the demon boy leaped onto Conan Doyle's shoulders, then sprang to the top of a stone ridge that had earlier hid the monster from view. He heard the mage shout in protest, but Danny wasn't worried about hurting Conan Doyle. He wasn't any ordinary man and could take a bit of shoving around.

His claws dug into the stone, and he twisted his upper body, tensed to spring. The Cyclops blinked its one eye slowly, and the expression on its huge, leathery face was one of confusion and then amusement.

"What are you, young one? You have a Satyr's face, but I have never—"

Danny bared his razor teeth in a shout of frustration and rage and he sprang from the stone, powerful legs rocketing him at the giant monster's face. The beast's single eye went wide, and it tried to turn away. The demon boy shifted his body in midair. He had been lunging at the monster's face but managed now to land on the Cyclops's shoulder. Danny tore into the monster's back with the claws of his left hand, just to anchor himself, and with the right he gripped its throat, beginning to tear the thick hide there.

Ceridwen and Mr. Doyle were shouting, but Danny could not hear them. There was a red haze in his mind, a fury he had bottled up. If they were going to survive the Underworld, this was the way they were all going to have to fight. Brutally and without hesitation, without reserve.

The Cyclops roared and reached for him, one massive hand closing on Danny's head. He felt pressure on his own small horns and then his skull, as the monster began to crush it. Danny shot out his tongue, and its sharp tip punctured the skin of the Cyclops' palm. It flinched, withdrawing its hand long enough for him to reach out and grab thick handfuls of the thing's filthy, matted hair. He hauled himself quickly upward and wrapped his arms around the Cyclops' horn, his legs around its neck. He felt himself keenly aware of the glistening softness of the monster's single eye. Silent in his determination, he raised his right hand, flexed his clawed fingers, and swept them down toward the Cyclops' eye.

His hand froze.

Danny had just enough time to look at his fingers and see the white fire that blazed across his skin all the way up his arm before he was plucked from the Cyclops's back. His entire body went rigid. Danny hissed but could not even open his mouth; he tried to struggle but to no avail. Liquid white fire—cold enough to gnaw his bones—swept over him, and he hung there in the air like bait as the Cyclops turned toward him.

"Please accept our apologies," Conan Doyle said.

The Cyclops touched its shoulder and throat, holding up its fingers to examine the black blood Danny's attack had drawn. He glared at the demon boy, and Danny had never felt so vulnerable. *What are you doing, Conan Doyle? I'm a crunchy granola bar up here, as far as this thing's concerned.*

The one-eyed beast regarded him with a grimace as though it was trying to decide how to cook him. Then, slowly, Danny felt himself moving. Conan Doyle had caught him in a spell, a net of sorcerous fire, and now the mage drew him down to the stone floor of this Underworld cavern. When at last the spell dissipated, he looked around to see Conan Doyle taking a step nearer to the Cyclops. He was about to protest what the old guy had done when he felt Ceridwen's hand on his shoulder.

Danny glanced up at her and felt all his anger dissipate. Her eyes had that effect. Even weakened, she had that effect on him. The Fey sorceress was ethereally beautiful—his opposite in so many ways—and yet it was not just her beauty that soothed him, but the benevolence that exuded from her.

"What the hell—" he began.

Ceridwen placed a pale finger over his lips, and Danny hushed. Confused, but no longer angry, he turned to see what Conan Doyle was up to. The mage had both hands up, blue light still misting from his palms but making no movements the Cyclops might interpret as hostile.

"—apologies for my young friend," Conan Doyle said, speaking loudly so that the giant might hear him. "This place is new to us and unsettling. We have met only enemies here and have had to defend ourselves many times. I believe he'd come to think there could be no kindness in this place."

The mage glanced back at Ceridwen and Danny. The sorceress kept a firm hand on the demon boy's shoulder, and an unseen wind blew through that ancient ruined world, that endless catacomb, and her cloak fluttered against him.

Danny shrugged, glaring back at Conan Doyle. *What?* he thought defiantly.

When the mage spoke again, he kept his eyes on Danny. "We have to adjust our expectations now that we have met you. We cannot confuse a hospitable invitation with a heinous threat."

Conan Doyle let his gaze linger on Danny a moment longer, and the boy saw the mage sigh, chest rising and falling. Then Conan Doyle turned to the Cyclops again.

"My name is Arthur. My friends are Ceridwen and Daniel. Please forgive us, and accept our thanks for your gracious offer."

Throughout this apology the Cyclops had touched its throat and shoulder several times. The wounds had stopped bleeding. It did not even seem to be bothered by the cut he had made to its fingers, but Danny was not going to remind the monster either. Its single eye blinked, and it had a sour expression twisting up its ugly face.

For a long moment the Cyclops stared down at Conan Doyle. Its cooking fire crackled a hundred feet behind it, burning brightly, though the dead, black wood seemed to cry out as it surrendered to char and ember.

The monster looked at Danny, who flinched. He might have tried to defend himself, but Ceridwen held him fast.

"That was an interesting attack, with your tongue," she whispered.

With Eve he might have made a joke of it. Even with Ceridwen, had he been feeling bold. But as the Cyclops pushed Conan Doyle gently aside and took two long strides toward him, he could not have thought of a humorous retort if his life depended on it. His throat was dry. He ran his rough, sharp tongue across the backs of his teeth.

The Cyclops crouched in front of him like a man bending to scold a puppy. The monster extended one long finger with its cracked yellow nail and poked him. "That hurt," it said. "Don't do it again."

"I . . . I won't." It felt absurd, having this conversation. But it felt dangerous as well.

Then the Cyclops grinned and nodded. "Good. Are you hungry, little Satyr?"

And Danny realized that he was. The smell of meat cooking over the flames had his stomach growling. He glanced over at Conan Doyle, who nodded his encouragement, looking almost sinister in the shadows of this place.

"Um, well, yeah. I could eat."

"Excellent!" the Cyclops rumbled. "Come!"

He moved back to his fire and picked up a long shaft of wood—a tree branch to the rest of them, but little more than a stick to the monster—and began to cook once more. At the end of the branch was some kind of creature but it was only smoking meat and bone now, and Danny could not tell what it had once been. Nor did he want to know.

Ceridwen ushered him forward, and the two of them strode up beside Conan Doyle.

"That was a near thing, Daniel," the mage said, brushing fingers across his mustache, unconsciously straightening it. He glanced warily at the Cyclops.

Danny glanced at Ceridwen, then back to Mr. Doyle. "How did you know he wasn't going to eat us?"

Conan Doyle stared at him for a moment, then gestured up at the tall rock Danny had leaped from. "He seemed surprised when you attacked him. Mystified by it. Perhaps even a bit hurt. Before that, I confess his invitation to dinner did sound menacing to my ears. Even now, I'm not completely certain of his motives."

"I am," Ceridwen said. They both glanced at her, and she shook her head. "There's no cruelty in him. His kindness is genuine."

Danny wasn't convinced. Were farmers cruel to the turkeys before Thanksgiving? He didn't think so. But there was such certainty in the way Ceridwen spoke that he thought her reasoning was from more than just observation, that she had a sense about the Cyclops.

The one-eyed creature inhaled the aroma of his cooking and grunted appreciatively. "Are you coming, friends?"

"Yes, absolutely. Sorry for the delay." Conan Doyle nodded at them and started toward the Cyclops's cooking fire.

Danny stopped him. "Wait, one last thing. How does he know English?"

Conan Doyle frowned. "What are you talking about?"

Ceridwen smiled, her grave features lighting up with fond amusement. "Oh, I see. You were speaking with him and you thought . . . no, Danny. He wasn't speaking English. You were speaking Greek. Very old Greek."

"What? But I—"

"It isn't only you," Ceridwen told him. "It is happening to us all. When we first entered this place, it was draining me. Cut off from the nature of the world I know, with only the cruel, lifeless elements of the Underworld, I was weak. I've begun to regain my strength now, at least a little of it. And just as I adjust, as this place comes to think of us as—"

Danny scoffed. "A place can't think."

Ceridwen raised an eyebrow. "No? All right. If it's simpler, consider this. This is a place of magick. A place where the souls of the dead from the entire history of a grand empire came upon their death. Not all of them spoke the same language. Yet they had to understand this place and one another."

He felt sick. "So the Underworld is treating us like we're dead? Like we're, what, damned to this place?"

Conan Doyle put a hand on his shoulder. "Something like that."

Danny sighed and gave a small shrug. "I'm not gonna say I like the sound of that, but at least it makes sense. I was afraid it was just me."

"There are things about your nature and your parentage that are only beginning to reveal themselves," Conan Doyle said. "In this case, you're not the only one affected. But at a guess, it wouldn't surprise me to learn that you could have understood the language here even without the magick present. Demons are ancient. Ancestral memory for you will be different from that of ordinary humans. I've no doubt you may discover you speak dozens of languages. Or, perhaps"—and he looked thoughtful as he said this—"all of them."

"Holy shit," Danny whispered.

Conan Doyle smiled. "Yes."

He linked one arm beneath Ceridwen's as if they were strolling through the park and together they walked toward the Cyclops's fire. Danny hesitated only a moment before following.

"That smells wonderful, my enormous friend," Conan Doyle said. "Your hospitality is greatly appreciated."

As they sat on an outcropping of stone near the fire, the Cyclops grinned at them, obviously pleased with the unexpected pleasure of socialization in this place.

"The pleasure is mine, Arthur."

Ceridwen gazed up at the giant. "It saddens us that we will not be able to stay very long. One of our number has been stolen from us by vile enemies. We know only that our enemies seek the Erinyes, the Furies, and so we must seek them as well."

The Cyclops's single eye narrowed, and his expression was grim. He nodded heavily and regarded each of them in turn. "I am sorry you cannot stay. This is a bleak place, and it is not easy to find friends. I hope that we will meet again. You will eat your fill and be on your way. And while you eat, I will make a map for you, to show you the safest way. The Erinyes are very cruel, though. Not like me.

"They don't like visitors at all."

SQUIRE missed driving.

The train had left Athens headed due west toward Corinth, and there seemed no choice but to pursue it, pausing at each of its scheduled stops in dreadful hope that some catastrophe would have occurred to give them a clue as to Medusa's actions. How long could she go unnoticed, after all? Whatever part of Dr. Graves's spirit had tainted her when he had shot her with those bullets, Medusa had managed to extricate it. Perhaps she had pried out the spectral bullets. However she had done it, Graves could no longer track her.

They had to find another way. For now, following the train was the only solution. Their greatest concern was that she might throw herself from the train and disappear into the countryside or some village along the Aegean. There was also the possibility that they might actually overtake the train and manage to be waiting for it when it pulled into Corinth.

But with Clay behind the wheel, that seemed a distant hope. He drove like an old lady. Back home Squire had rigged Conan Doyle's limo with foot blocks on the brake and accelerator so his short legs could reach. He loved to drive . . . and he loved to drive fast. It was torture for him to sit in the passenger seat.

They had driven through Megara a while back. Now the road had swung far enough south that the blue-green shimmer of the Aegean was visible, like some ancient paradise beckoning them to abandon the modern world.

"It's beautiful, isn't it?" Clay said, glancing out his window.

"Absolutely. So nice that we have time to appreciate the wonders of the Mediterranean. For Christ's sake, just drive the fucking car! If you stop sightseeing, we might actually catch up to her."

He wanted something fried to eat. Onion rings, yeah, that would be perfect.

Clay gave him a sidelong glance, accelerating to a speed at which the car began to shudder. The shapeshifter grunted in amusement, but he wore a fond smile. "Don't take it out on me because you're too short to drive."

The ghost of Dr. Graves drifted forward from the backseat, moving his head between them and glancing at Squire. "Need I remind you, my friend, that you have the advantage of being solid?"

"Oh, so now we're trying to top each other's miseries? Next Captain Quint's gonna show us his shark bite."

But Graves was right. He liked being solid, and not just because it meant he could drive a car. There were a few other of his favorite things he needed flesh and bone to do. Eating was up there, but it wasn't number one. Much as he hated to admit it to himself, the ghost had given him some perspective.

Squire glanced at Clay again and grumbled. "Just drive."

The engine whined loudly, as though under the hood was not an ordinary car engine but something swapped out from a Honda motorcycle. Traffic was sparse, and for all of Squire's complaints, Clay was driving fast. The road hummed under the tires.

The hobgoblin reached out and clicked on the radio. He scanned the stations, finding a lot of static and too many voices speaking Greek. At one point he paused on a familiar song, Bruce Springsteen's "Born to Run," but the reception was for crap, fading in and out, sounding muffled and tinny, and he gave up, cursing.

"Greek radio," he muttered.

"Yeah," Clay agreed. "You don't get a lot of international pop stars out of Greece."

Squire snorted. "Exactly." The hobgoblin punched the radio off with a stubby, leathery finger.

"Well, gentlemen," said the ghost in the backseat, "as much as I hate to miss a moment of this scintillating conversation, I think I ought to check on the train's progress again."

Squire sighed and crossed his arms. "Yeah, well, I don't see you jumping in with the funny anecdotes, Doc. I need to get one of them Game Boys. Or, hey, either of you guys know Mad-Libs? What I wouldn't give for a Mad-Libs right now. I'm a riot with those things."

There was silence from the backseat. After a moment Squire frowned and twisted around to glance behind him, expecting to see the familiar features of Dr. Graves. Squire had to hand it to the guy, the 1940s adventurer look really worked for him. Tall, dark, and handsome, all that shit. Only problem was, he was too serious.

He was also gone.

"Son of a bitch," Squire muttered, shooting a glance at Clay behind the wheel. "Now that's just downright rude. Here I am talking and he just . . . poof!"

Clay nodded. "Ghosts do that."

"Fucking ghosts."

"Sometimes Leonard just needs to be on his own," Clay added. He reached up a hand and brushed back his brown hair, fingers pushing through the single, odd patch of white. It wasn't his real hair, or his real face for that matter, just the one he used the most often. Squire was not completely sure Clay had a *real* face, unless it was the formidable shape he often took in battle, the hairless, dried-earth creature that seemed made of actual clay.

"Still, he could have said something," Squire replied.

Graves had gone to check on the progress of the train eight or ten times already. They had agreed at the outset that he would not try to locate Medusa on the train, or to engage her. Clay could have shapeshifted into a falcon or something even faster on the wing and caught up with the train as well. If Squire knew where he was going along the shadowpaths he probably could have found the train—saving them all the trouble of traveling in this crappy car and the uncertainty of their pursuit of the Gorgon—but he'd never been aboard the train, and it was in motion, and it might have taken him ages to find the right shadow. Never mind that he'd have to carry along all of the nets and weapons he'd gathered to catch Medusa. And they had agreed it was wiser if they were together when they located her again.

It soured Squire's outlook considerably, knowing he was holding them back.

The road curved northward and soon they lost their view of the Aegean. Only then did Squire realize how much he had appreciated it. The sea was the only thing worth looking at from the road. Sure, they had seen little villages sprawled on either side of the highway, but there was not much chance to appreciate them while whipping past them at eighty miles per hour. The isthmus that connected Athens and its surroundings with the Peloponnese was a part of Greece that deserved a more casual approach. Squire would much rather have been meandering through seaside villages, sampling the local cuisine at each stop. At that moment a piece of spinach pie would have gone down very nicely.

But from the highway, and without the gleaming Aegean to remind them of their location, the landscape could have been a hundred other places.

Squire glanced at Clay. He was intent on the road, hands at ten o'clock and two o'clock, like the poster boy for driving school. But the shapeshifter's eyes kept moving, checking the rearview mirror. Every couple of minutes he would lean to one side and try to get a view of the sky out of his window. He wasn't looking for the ghost of Dr. Graves.

"He can't fly," Squire told him.

"Who?" Clay asked.

"Who? The guy who's got you so antsy. The reason none of us has been that talkative. Got you spooked, didn't he, with his dirt from the Doc's grave and whatever that thing was he did to you. Not only is he watching out for Medusa, protecting her, but he was expecting us."

For a long moment, Clay said nothing. Squire realized that he must really be a little spooked. That didn't sit well with the hobgoblin after all. Clay was . . . he didn't like to think about what and who Clay was. And if he was nervous—

"Hey, I killed the idiot once," Squire added. "We can do it again."

A car whipped by them on the highway doing nearly a hundred miles an hour, judging by how quickly it passed them. Neither of them bothered to comment. Clay gave Squire a sidelong glance.

"Over time I've learned that anybody who comes back to life after you kill them is usually much harder to finish off the second time around."

Squire rolled his eyes. "Yeah, yeah. You're a font of wisdom. I'm just saying he's maybe hard to kill, but that doesn't make him special."

"All right, then tell me about him. Tassarian. How did you kill him the first time?"

The hobgoblin grinned. He leaned back in his seat and put his boots up on the dashboard. "Now that's a memory I cherish."

They passed a small town to the north of the highway but he could see nothing more than the sides of buildings and cars going by on the roads. It had been twenty years— more—but his recollections were crystal clear.

"Used to be, every couple of years Conan Doyle would send me on a little acquisition trip to buy—or, ah, otherwise get my mitts on—some ancient weapon or other. Some of 'em he wanted because they had special attributes, enchanted swords, an ensorcelled quiver of arrows, that kind of thing. Others he just had his eye on. Of course the ones he just wanted he wouldn't have me steal if they were in a museum. But the lion's share of these beauties are owned by private collectors who didn't come by them any more honestly than I did."

The car jittered over a section of cracked pavement, hitting a pothole that Clay did not even try to avoid. The shapeshifter glanced at Squire.

"That thing you're doing right now? It's called a tangent."

The hobgoblin shot him a gnarled middle finger. "Anyway, Tassarian worked for Nigel Gull. I'd met him a couple of times before that. Gull and Conan Doyle have history, obviously. Can't stand the sight of each other, but they keep tabs. Run in the same circles, too. So it was inevitable they'd bump into each other now and again. Especially with Conan Doyle looking for Sweetblood.

"Gull and Conan Doyle, they have a lot in common. Gull likes pretty, shiny, sharp things too.

"So I'd been in Europe for about three weeks on what was probably the most successful acquisitions trip I'd made. I had some sweet stuff. Rostini's Axe. The Helm of Kyth. Hunyadi's Daggers. This perfect longbow from Germany, inlaid with gold, with a bowstring made of ectoplasm. A blind man with no arms could hit a gnat's asshole with this thing.

"I'm in Prague in this little flat Conan Doyle rented for me for a month. I've got a whole room just laid out with these babies. I'd had a feeling a few times during my running around that somebody'd been keeping an eye on me. But Tassarian knows all that ninja bullshit, and I really didn't twig to him until I walked in on the guy trying to sneak off with an entire armory."

Squire shook his head. "Idiot."

Clay kept his foot on the accelerator. If anything he gave the car a little extra speed as he checked the rearview mirror again. "Okay," he said. "But how did you kill him?"

The hobgoblin laughed, thinking back on it. "Well, death and resurrection must have smartened him up some, 'cause that time he sure hadn't done his homework. I'm ugly, but I'm not stupid, and I'm pretty good with weapons. The moron came to steal my cache in the late afternoon. Maybe he got the whole shadow thing wrong, thinking he shouldn't try it at night. Or maybe he figured I was out for a walk, or asleep. I don't know.

"What I do know is, that time of day the shadows are nice and long. The sun coming in the windows threw huge distorted shadows off of every chair, bedpost, and friggin' doorknob. I had a couple seconds' surprise on Tassarian, and that was all I needed. I moved in and out of the shadows, kept out of his range, snuck up on him a dozen times. I must have hit him with every goddamn weapon in that room. Even broke the blade off one of Hunyadi's Daggers in the base of his skull. I killed the guy enough to snuff ten other guys. Just kept killing him until he actually laid down and didn't get up again."

Another mile of road went by in silence before Clay glanced over at him. "But Tassarian *did* get up again."

Squire shrugged. His gaze had drifted past Clay and out the driver's side window, where the Aegean had come back into view. It was distant, but there. He smiled. "Yep. Guess I'm going to have to kill him some more."

The hobgoblin glanced over to see Clay smile broadly . . . then the smile disappeared. Clay's eyes went wide, and his arms locked into place on the steering wheel.

"What the hell?" the shapeshifter snarled, even as he jerked the wheel to one side.

Squire turned his eyes back to the road. The ghost of Dr. Graves stood in the center of the highway, one hand on the butt of a phantom gun and the other raised to wave them to a halt.

The tires squealed as Clay cut the wheel too far.

Squire shot a hand out and grabbed the wheel, straightening it out. "Run him down. He's already a ghost!"

Clay slammed the brakes on, and the car slewed to one side as it shuddered to a halt on the shoulder of the highway. A car barreled past them, the driver laying on the horn.

Squire popped his door open and clambered out, scanning the road for Graves. "Where are you, Spooky? I'll wring your neck! What're you trying to do, give me a friggin' coronary?"

The ghost was nowhere in sight. Cursing under his breath, Squire turned and stared expectantly through the windshield at Clay, but the shapeshifter did not get out of the car. After a moment, the hobgoblin went to get back inside, only to find the transparent wisp of Graves's ghost in his seat. In the interplay of sunlight and the shadowed interior of the car, the specter was nearly invisible.

"I'm sorry if I startled you," Dr. Graves said.

"Sorry!" Squire sputtered. "You couldn't just have ghosted yourself back into the car like you did before?"

"I needed you to stop," the specter said. "We don't have a great deal of time."

Clay narrowed his eyes so tightly that his flesh seemed to alter with the expression. "Has Medusa left the train?"

"Oh, I'm almost certain she has. And we'd best hurry if we want to search before the authorities arrive. It's a matter of minutes, I expect."

Squire's head hurt. "Search what? You lost me, Doc."

The ghost seemed suddenly more solid, and the expression on his spectral features was bitter. "The wreckage, Squire. The train has derailed."

Dr. Graves pointed to the northeast, where several columns of dark smoke were pluming into the sky. The crash sight was two or three miles away from the highway, but he and Clay had been caught up in conversation and had not even noticed the smoke.

"Damn," the goblin whispered.

Dr. Graves floated right up through the roof of the car and hovered above it. "I think we ought to leave the car here for the moment. We'll reach the site faster by our own means."

"Agreed," Clay said. He put the car in drive and pulled farther onto the shoulder, then locked it up tight.

"Any survivors?" he asked, just before he transformed, his flesh popping and rippling as it diminished. In a handful of moments, Clay was gone, and a hawk hopped about the ground in his place.

Dr. Graves floated toward the crash site. "We'll find out soon enough," said the ghost.

Squire went to the shoulder of the road. Beyond it were only olive trees and open ground, with some power lines in the distance. Clay and Graves flew toward the pluming smoke, just a bird and this blur against the sky that looked more than a little like a jellyfish, distorting the light that passed through it.

"Don't wait up, guys," the hobgoblin muttered.

He went back to the car, glanced over his shoulder at the power lines, and then dove into the long shadow the vehicle cast on the shoulder of the road.

The darkness swallowed him. His senses spread out through the shadowpaths, fingers on Braille, and he began to run. A short time later he emerged from the shadow beneath an electrical tower. He did not step into the sun, but emerging from the darkness he still had to shield his eyes from the brightness of the day. A quick scan of the sky showed him that he was slightly ahead of the hawk and the ghost. Not far from him he saw the railroad tracks. The crash had happened perhaps a mile east. The smoke was thinner, now, wispy.

Like ghosts.

Squire gauged the distance to the crash and slipped back into the shadows. The darkness caressed him as he slipped along the path, feeling the various conduits all around him, touching the shadows intimately. He knew them.

Even so, he almost missed the path he wanted. It was so

dark that he did not notice it at first. Then he moved along it and let his instincts feel for the egress.

The hobgoblin slid from the shadows inside the wreckage of the train. The car was turned on its side, windows shattered and metal walls torn like paper. Seats had been ripped from their moorings. Squire breathed through his mouth, prepared for the wretched stench of blood and death.

But all he could smell was smoke and dust.

Confused, he looked around the wreckage. It took a moment for him to realize what he was seeing. There were no bodies. None of flesh and blood, at least.

Medusa had turned the passengers to stone.

The crash had reduced them to rubble.

THE River Styx did not crash and churn, no whitewater foamed its banks, yet it ran deeper than imaginable, fast and steady and inexorable in its strength. To attempt to swim its breadth would be foolhardy. Suicidal. And though Nigel Gull knew his soul was likely damned—whatever that really meant—he did not want to discover what would become of his spirit if his body was destroyed here in Hades' realm. There was the additional complication of Eve. Hawkins carried the vampire over one shoulder. The man was stronger than he looked, but no one was strong enough to swim the Styx, carrying one hundred and thirty odd pounds of dead weight.

They had to cross the Styx. And according to both myth and reality, there was only one way to do that.

"This is it, then, huh?" Jezebel asked.

Gull glanced at her. She looked so small, so young to him now, this teenaged girl who had left her whole world behind for him. He wanted to protect her. But there were other things he desired more.

"Yes, Jez. This is the Styx. It only gets worse from here. We've been descending all along, but once we cross the river it will not be a simple thing to get back." He fixed her in his gaze. "In truth, we may not come back at all."

A flicker of fear went across her face, but it disappeared quickly. "If you're going, Nigel, then so am I. What are we waiting for?"

Hawkins shifted Eve from one shoulder to both, spreading out the burden of her weight, and took a step past them, nearer the river's edge. "Isn't it obvious, love? The ferryman. We're waiting on the ferryman."

Gull nodded. "Charon."

Jezebel glanced past him and she flinched with a sharp intake of breath and pointed out across the water. "That would be him?"

A trickle of dread ran down Nigel Gull's back, and he shivered, even as he turned to gaze out over the river. In his long life the twisted mage had seen extraordinary things, impossible things. Hideous and terrifying things. They were in the Underworld now and were about to cross into the land of the dead. Yet the sight of that small craft skimming across the top of the river gave him a chill that made him feel very small, as though he were a child again.

This was no nameless demon, no Slavic bogeyman, no trickster spirit. This was Charon, a figure unique in myth. Not a god, not a man. Not a monster or a demon. Simply Charon, who carried the spirits of the dead to a land of endless nothing, a place of waiting, where waiting was the only destiny, and at the end there was only more waiting. Gull had always envisioned this ancient vision of Hell, left over from the Second Age of Man, as an asylum filled with muttering, ghostly madmen, their eyes darting to follow imaginary pests, their bodies rapt with anticipation of something, anything, that might happen *next*.

But there would never be a next.

Not on the other side of the Styx.

The fabric of human faith had created entirely new Hells, new spirit destinations, in this Third Age of Man. Gull had reasoned that very few crossed the river anymore.

Yet Charon frightened him. That eternal asylum frightened him.

The ceiling of the cavern was so high above it was lost to sight, and though there clearly was no sky there, no sun, still a strange illumination cast a dim gray light upon the river and its banks.

The boat moved swiftly toward shore. Gull felt he could not breathe, and both of his companions seemed equally unsettled. Hanging from the prow of the boat was a lantern whose jaundiced light shone upon the surface of that perhaps bottomless river. The current ran swift and deep, and yet the narrow launch was uninfluenced by its power. No sway or eddy nudged that vessel from its course.

In the rear of the craft stood a solitary figure in dark robes the color of river silt. If the ferryman had hands, they were lost within those robes and whatever grim countenance might be hidden beneath his voluminous hood, there was only darkness.

So entranced was Gull by the ferryman's progress that when the prow of the boat lightly touched the riverbank he flinched away as though he had been slapped. Jezebel watched him, gnawing her lower lip and twirling a lock of her hair in her fingers. Hawkins dumped Eve's inert body on the shore, her arms flopping onto the damp black soil. The vampire's eyes were wide and unseeing, but a glimpse of her heartened Gull's resolve. He thought of all the planning that had gone into this excursion.

He thought of Medusa.

Gull brought up a hand and ran the pads of his fingers lightly over the contortions of his face.

He turned toward the ferryman, and though a thin tendril of his dread remained, he ignored it.

"Charon, will you carry us?" Gull asked, and the river seemed to swallow his voice.

The ferryman was perhaps twenty feet away. Even this close no trace of a face could be seen beneath his hood. Charon was entirely still—as frozen in place as his craft—

master and vessel unmoved by ticking seconds or by the rush of the unfathomable river. It was as though they had ceased to exist for him, and Gull watched him for any sign of recognition. Even so, when it came he was startled.

Charon extended his right hand, palm up. The skin was gray, colorless, and as dry as parchment. There seemed on that flesh the seared imprints of a thousand thousand coins, the images on that currency pressed into the ferryman's very substance.

Gull hesitated.

The ferryman beckoned with his spindly fingers.

They were not dead. Not yet spirits. But apparently he was willing to deliver them to their destination. Perhaps with so few passengers Charon was not as discerning as he might once have been. Or perhaps the laws that governed this realm had withered away, just as the faith in old myths had, all of them losing their power.

"What are you waiting for?" Hawkins whispered.

Gull had never heard him afraid before. He glanced at the Englishman, saw Hawkins lick his lips. The man's hands were shaking. Gull nodded twice. They were his people, Hawkins and Jezebel. His agents. He had brought them here. He was the catalyst for everything that was happening, everything that would happen.

Jezebel came up beside Gull and slid her hand into his as though seeking protection. There was ice on her fingers. "Don't you still have the coin?"

"I have it," Gull said.

His throat was dry as he pulled the silver coin from his pocket. It had been struck in Mycenae in 1404 B.C. and bore the face of a ruler whose name had long since been lost to antiquity. Gull strode to the riverbank, hesitated a moment, and then waded in up to his knees. The water dragged at him, and he could feel it leeching vitality from him. He felt unsteady on his feet, and not merely from the powerful pull of the current.

He placed the coin in Charon's hand. The ferryman inclined his head, hood draping low, then that parchment hand disappeared once more within his robes. Charon again gazed at Gull, or so it appeared, though it was impossible to know for certain when his eyes were lost in shadow.

The ferryman extended his hand again, palm up, thin fingers scratching the air, demanding.

A flame of anger ignited in Nigel Gull's heart, burning away whatever trepidation remained.

"What is he doing?" Jezebel asked, coming to the river's edge. "You paid him."

"Good sodding question," Hawkins agreed. He grabbed the still form of Eve by the arm and dragged her across the muddy bank to join Jezebel. "You said you did the research, that that coin would get us all across."

"I did, and it should have," Gull said flatly.

"Wonderful," Hawkins muttered. "Maybe the price went up. Inflation in the Underworld. Have you got some spell that'll—"

"There isn't any magick I know that would force a being like this to cooperate," Gull interrupted, glaring at those thin fingers, at the coin scars on that palm. The latest was the imprint of the Mycenaean ruler, whoever he had been.

Jezebel hugged herself and shivered, staring forlornly at the stark figure of the ferryman, holding out that wretched hand expectantly. "What do we do now?"

The ferryman simply waited, ominous and forbidding. Their transaction had begun. There was no way to know what would happen if they did not conclude it, what he might do. A sudden wind rustled Jezebel's hair and caressed Gull's contorted features, but the ferryman's robes did not so much as shudder in the breeze. The river flowed. Charon remained motionless, implacable in his demand.

"Now?" Gull asked.

He reached beneath his coat and withdrew his pistol, a Robbins and Lawrence pepperbox. It was an original, made in 1849, a breech loader that carried five shots.

Gull put the first bullet squarely into the patch of darkness beneath Charon's hood. The report exploded out across the river and was lost to the vastness of the cavern above. The ferryman's head snapped back, but Gull kept firing. The second .31-caliber bullet struck Charon in the chest, as did the third. The fourth struck the ferryman's shoulder as he collapsed, spilling over the side of the boat.

He never fired the fifth round. Gull waded in to catch the creature—the myth—before he could slip into the water and be swept away. He holstered his weapon and drew out a khanjarli, a curved Indian dagger perfect for his purposes. He wrapped his arm around the ferryman's head, unwilling now to look at the face hidden beneath that hood, and plunged the dagger into Charon's throat, cutting flesh and muscle, grinding the blade against bone.

The ferryman's head tumbled from the hood and splashed into the river.

"Oh, for fuck's sake," Hawkins said, from up on the riverbank.

Nigel Gull let the body slip into the river. Even as he did so, the current caught the boat, and it began to float away. Gull caught the prow, the lantern swinging, throwing that sickly yellow light back and forth. At last he turned to look at his operatives, there on the shore. Both of them watched him wide-eyed, Hawkins still standing over the unconscious Eve, and Jezebel hugging herself even more fiercely than before.

"What do we do now?" he echoed, staring at the girl. "We bloody well improvise."

12

THERE was a forest in Hell.

Ceridwen knew that this ancient Underworld was not the equivalent of the Christian Hell, that it was a repository for all the dead souls of its age, not merely those considered damned. Yet its subterranean nature was enough to force comparisons to all Arthur had told her of damnation. Caverns and flame, barren landscape . . . and yet it was not entirely barren.

The Cyclops had engraved his map on stone. They could not possibly carry it, but Ceridwen had no trouble committing it to memory. Weakened as she was, she was still capable of that much at least. While the caverns continued to slope downward, luring them farther from the surface world, the Cyclops had suggested a quicker route to the River Styx, through the blackthorn forest. It was treacherous territory, a broad expanse of hard-packed earth from which grew grove after grove of twisted, unnatural trees. Their trunks and branches were thin and ebony black, ridged with dagger-sharp thorns.

Danny led the way through the blackthorns. Ceridwen had been hesitant at first. An elemental sorceress, she had a rapport with nature in Faerie, and had always taken for granted how easily she adapted to the nature of Arthur's world, the Blight. But here she was cut off. The environment was so unnatural that her innate connection to the world around her was disconnected here, and it sapped her strength.

She could not *feel* the trees. Could not touch or sense them. The blackthorn groves were to her like the ghost of a forest.

This was the path they must take. That knowledge had given her the strength to forge ahead, to ignore her trepidation and move among those deadly branches. Danny went first, his skin more durable than hers or Arthur's, and searched for the easiest passage. He blazed the trail and Ceridwen followed. Arthur brought up the rear in silence, but Ceridwen understood. Ever since they had descended he had been attempting to make sense of this place, to understand what Nigel Gull's purpose here was. Now that Eve had been taken, he was even more haunted. He prided himself on his powers of perception and observation. They were sorely tested here.

Ceridwen paused a moment and blinked. There were places in the Underworld where it was light enough to see easily, but here there were only shades of gray and sometimes the path among the trees was difficult to spy. She pushed back her linen hood, and it coiled around her throat. Where was the boy?

"Danny?" Ceridwen called.

A rustle of snapping thorns and branches came from just ahead of her. Startled, she took a step backward. Her tunic caught on a blackthorn tree, and the ocean-blue fabric tore as she tried to pull herself free. Her chest hurt as though a hole had been punched through it, this place where she ought to have felt the air and water and fire, where the trees ought to have whispered to her. She felt empty. Drained.

Yanking herself from the thorns was too great an effort. Ceridwen stumbled sideways and fell to her knees, thorns cutting the marbled white flesh of her arm. She swore, mewling in pain, hating the weakness in that noise.

"Ceri!" Arthur cried.

Then he was beside her, blue mist spilling from his eyes. Though he was being affected by the nature of this place, clearly it was not so debilitating for him. He crouched by her and held her arm, plucking out a thorn that had torn loose of its branch and stuck there. She stared at the wounds in her flesh as if the arm did not belong to her, amazed by the searing pain. They would heal quickly enough, even as weakened as she was, but the pain had come so suddenly, and it burned like a flame in her mind.

"I don't understand," she whispered.

Conan Doyle caressed her cheek, and she gazed at him a moment before he helped her up.

"What don't you understand?" he asked.

Before she could answer there came a crack of breaking branches and Danny emerged from the blackthorn trees just ahead. There were scratches on his dark, leathery skin and thorns had caught at his clothes. A branch dragged from one of his sneakers. Yet he seemed barely bothered by the prickers.

"Found us an easier path up ahead," he said, frowning as he saw Ceridwen's wounds. The demon boy glanced at Arthur. "Figured I'd clear you a trail to get there. The Cyclops turned out to be okay, but he's no thinker. Might be easy for him to stroll through here, but . . ." He shrugged and met Ceridwen's gaze. "You all right?"

"I will be," she said with an assurance she did not feel.

She rose to her feet with Arthur steadying her, took a deep breath of the dank air of the Underworld, and then together they continued on. He was by her side with one hand at the small of her back as they walked. Though Ceridwen did not really need the support, she did not break away. Down here in the blackthorn forest, in the midst of an ancient death realm, she was so far away from Faerie and from the Blight that the bruises he had once left on her heart seemed to mean very little. Despite his words, her pride had been preventing her from completely accepting that he still loved her, that perhaps his departure all those years ago from her world had been as difficult for him as it had been for her.

In this place the distance she had kept between them seemed foolish, and she cherished the closeness they had in those moments. With Arthur beside her, Ceridwen had hope that she would see the flourishing forests of Faerie again. Yet she could tell by the furrow of his brow and by the silence in which he had been traveling before that he did not take the same comfort from her, or could not, for some reason.

"You're thinking about Eve," she said.

Arthur nodded. "Of course." As he walked, the heavy coins in his pocket clinked together. The Cyclops had left them by his fire for a time and returned shortly with a massive handful of them, meant to pay the ferryman that would take them across the River Styx.

"Gull would not have taken her only to kill her," Ceridwen said, hoping to soothe him.

"That is not my concern. Eve has survived enemies far more ruthless than Nigel Gull."

Ceridwen did not like his tone. There was a faltering uncertainty in it that was unusual for Arthur, and it unnerved her. "What is it, then?"

He hesitated, his head inching to the left as if he sought some specter that lingered in his peripheral vision. After a moment his attention returned to her. Ahead of them, Danny paused and looked back, impatient to move on. It was not the blackthorn forest, Ceridwen was certain, that had him so anxious. The boy did not want to pause anywhere in this world for very long. There was no telling what might menace them next.

"Arthur?" she prodded, her voice lower.

The pressure of his hand upon her lower back increased, and they both quickened their pace. He glanced at her, and a small, apologetic smile appeared upon his face, only to quickly fade.

"There are two things, truly," he said, his voice an old man's rasp, no matter how young his body remained. "First, I have been attempting to deduce Gull's purpose in bringing Eve to the Erinyes."

"Have you been successful?" Ceridwen asked, ducking beneath a thorny branch that overhung their path, then moving carefully between a pair of trees uncomfortably close together.

"I have a theory."

Ceridwen reached up quickly in spite of her sapped strength and tugged him by the ear, just as her mother had done to get her attention when she was a tiny girl. Arthur blinked in surprise and stared at her.

"I hate when you do that," she said. "Speak all, or not at all."

Her once and perhaps future lover nodded. "My apologies." He rubbed his ear. "I have told you of my history with Nigel. Of our rivalry—or at least his view of it. He chose to study shadow magicks, dark powers of ancient times that would have been better left to molder in the tombs of dead gods."

Conan Doyle glanced around, apparently aware of the odd resonance of his words. He stroked his graying mustache with his free hand, and Ceridwen thought he might have shuddered.

"The cost for what he learned was his face. His features were deformed, twisted to reflect the deformity of spirit that resulted in his trafficking in such ugly sorceries. The Erinyes . . . the Furies, they have been called . . . might have the power to erase that taint, to undo the curse upon him."

Ceridwen shook her head. "I don't know. Do you really think Gull would do all of this just to be handsome again?"

"You didn't know him before. You did not see the change he underwent within and without. It would not surprise me."

"But why Eve?"

The ground had begun to slope down, and the blackthorn forest to thin. To either side distant mountains could be seen, cliffs that went up and up, but were really only the walls of the cavern, rising toward that unseen ceiling, that stone roof that separated this realm from any other.

Arthur paused and studied her a moment, taking her hands in his. Without preamble he raised her fingers to his lips and kissed them, just once. Ceridwen did nothing to stop him, nor did she protest. Conan Doyle took a deep breath, and then he turned to peer into the gloom, gaze hunting for Danny Ferrick and for the path ahead.

"This is not the Christian Hell. We've discussed that. But that does not mean that sinners go unpunished here. It is possible to be damned in the Underworld. And those sinners are given over to the Erinyes for their punishment. They are scourged for eternity—or for as long as this theological construct lasts, as long as the worship from the Second Age is not completely forgotten.

"If Gull wants something from the Erinyes, he'll need something to give them in exchange. What better than the ultimate sinner?"

"Eve," Ceridwen whispered.

Arthur nodded.

Ceridwen took a moment to process that. After a moment she took his hand and the two of them began walking again. They emerged from the blackthorn forest only to find Danny standing at the edge of a steep hill. They joined him there, and found themselves looking down on the broadest, swiftest river any of them had ever seen.

The Styx.

"All right," she said, staring at the river. "You said there were two things concerning you. What was the other?"

Arthur stiffened a bit. She glanced over and saw that his nostrils were flared and his eyes narrowed. He turned to her and gently pulled her into an embrace. Over his shoulder she saw Danny's eyes widen and the demon boy looked away. It felt awkward and yet startlingly good to be in Arthur's arms.

Part of her wanted to fight that feeling, but she surrendered to it. There were too many enemies down here. She felt his warm breath on her face as he whispered to her.

"Nigel and his agents are ahead of us with Eve. But I sense eyes upon us. Someone or something has been pacing us for quite a while, now. And we must assume this lurker in darkness is ill-intentioned. So be wary, Ceri. Be on guard."

CLAY did not even know the name of the village.

They had continued on foot, just as Medusa would have had to. She had been traveling due west on the train, and they knew that their chances of catching her now were slim. It was possible they would have to wait until she killed again. But logic dictated that if she were seeking out other ancient sites, she might well continue on to Corinth, and so they kept on in that direction, hoping to overtake her before she put too much distance between them.

If it became necessary to go back and fetch the car, that would mean they had given up hope of finding her today.

They walked along the train tracks, hurrying away so that the authorities arriving on the scene would not notice them. Side by side they set off to the west, toward the diminishing sunlight, as if they chased the day. Even Dr. Graves, who did not precisely walk, strode along intently, scanning the landscape on either side.

Six miles along the tracks they came to the village. The land to the north of the tracks sloped up into a low ridge of hills, and sprawled across them were dozens of whitewashed cottages that looked identical from a distance. Only as they set out from the tracks, finding the rutted road that led up into the village, did they begin to discover that each home had its own personality. Some had small gardens, others flags flying, and many of the structures were not homes at all, but proved upon closer inspections to be shops and restaurants.

Wooden doors, some that seemed centuries old, were set

into the faces of buildings, and wrought-iron railings ran along balconies that overhung narrow alleys that split off from the main road.

The road led up the hill, winding through the village. Cars were parked along the sides of the street, but they were empty.

The nameless village was eerily silent, save for the wind.

A short way up the road they found a restaurant with the windows shattered. The smells that came from the place were exquisite, enough to remind Clay how long it had been since he had eaten, and how much he would have relished the opportunity. The scent of moussaka would have lured him toward that place even without the broken glass.

"Oh, son of a bitch," Squire muttered as the hobgoblin stepped through the window frame and into the restaurant.

The ghost of Dr. Graves passed through the outer wall, immaterial.

By the time Clay entered—through the door—he knew what he would find. As he stood there in the shadowed interior of the place his skin rippled and changed. No reason to wear a human face here. There was no one to see him, no one to frighten.

Only stone. Only statues.

He had never felt so empty inside. Clay had been intent on the mission, had determined that they would capture Medusa, but he was rapidly losing the heart for it.

"We have got to stop this," he whispered, and he turned and left, his heavy earthen feet crunching broken glass. He had to duck to exit, now that he had taken on this form. The closest he had to a true shape—the shape made of clay, dry and cracked, yet malleable.

Out on the street he glanced up and down the hill. Now that he knew for certain what he was looking for, he saw them everywhere. In what was probably the village's only taxi, idling at the curb, there was a figure frozen behind the wheel. People had come out onto their balconies to find the source of whatever disruption they'd heard. Statues stood there now.

In store windows—what he saw were not mannequins.

Clay began to walk uphill, deeper into the village. The taxi was still running, and the moussaka was still fresh enough to give off that delicious aroma. How much farther ahead could she be? Could she have killed everyone in the village?

He began to run, not worrying about whether or not Graves or Squire could keep up with him.

At the top of the hill was an open park, a village square. Clay staggered as he entered it and nearly fell to his knees where the street had become cobblestones. He shook his head.

"No," he whispered.

There had been a festival going on. Some kind of celebration. Women in long dresses and headscarves gathered in groups of threes and fours. Children chased one another around the square. There was a circle of men who had been dancing, now forever frozen in the act, each of them having glanced over to see what had caused their wives and sisters and daughters to scream. The way they were situated, they all seemed to be staring right at Clay, at this monstrous earthen man who strode into the heart of their town.

Here, he thought, checking again the angle of the stone men's stares and his own location. *She stood right here.*

If he closed his eyes on a quiet night, somewhere near the heavens such as a mountaintop or the dome of a cathedral, he could almost remember what it felt like to be touched by the hand of God. In moments such as this, he did not want to. There was only darkness here, though the sun still shone on the horizon.

This is Your will? Clay thought, eyes pressed tightly closed. He shook his head and swore under his breath.

A cold sensation passed through him, and he turned to see the ghost of Dr. Graves beside him. The specter had a hand on his shoulder, and though Graves was insubstantial,

Clay could almost feel the weight of those fingers, the comfort of a friend.

"We will catch her," Graves assured him.

Beyond him, Clay saw Squire approaching. The shapeshifter shook his head.

"No. We won't." He looked at the ugly, contorted face of the misshapen little hobgoblin, but saw only the light of gentle grief in his eyes. "I'm sorry, Squire. Sorry I made you go back and get the nets and all the rest of the equipment to take her alive."

Once more he glanced around the square, met the stone gaze of two dozen men who died dancing, and who stared at him as though they expected him to avenge them.

"It's too late for that now."

Clay wandered away from them, needing a moment's peace. A moment's solace. At the far end of the square was a church. Heart torn by conflict, he forced himself to approach it, and then to step inside.

"All right, we're with ya, big guy," Squire said, hurrying after him with a scuffle of his weathered boots. "But how do we find her? We could search forever now and not get any closer than this. Hell, she could be in one of these houses, and we might never find her."

Dr. Graves crossed his arms and stood beside Squire. It was easy to see why he had been considered so formidable in life. The ghost wore a grim expression.

"We will search for her until we find her. I have eternity to look." The comment was meant to be halfway amusing, but there was simply too much melancholy in it.

Clay was barely listening. He had glanced back at his companions, but now he returned his attention to the church's interior. Candles burned inside. Clay's stomach churned. A warm breeze washed over him, causing the candles inside to flutter.

"We don't have to search anymore," he said.

"What're you talking about?" Squire asked.

Clay gestured for them to come forward, to see what he'd

seen. Sprawled just inside the entryway of the church was the corpse of an Orthodox priest, his robes spattered with blood, his limbs jutting out at odd, impossible angles. Broken. His face was black and swollen, and there were dozens of small puncture wounds on his cheeks, forehead, and throat. One of his eyes had been punctured as well and had dripped vitreous fluid like thick tears.

The ghost of Dr. Graves whispered past Clay, floating down beside the corpse as if he were kneeling. In the combination of the church's shadows and the light from the doorway, Graves seemed only partly there, a mirage. He shook his head, studying the body, then glanced up. Through him, Clay could still see the candles up on the altar.

"I don't understand," Dr. Graves said. "Why isn't he stone?"

Clay lumbered deeper into the church, his flesh flowing and bones popping as he walked. Wearing the face of the dead priest, he knelt by the corpse. He traced his fingers along the corpse's face, then reached up to his own eyes.

Once again he shifted his form, taking on the appearance of the man known back in New Orleans, and in Boston, and in other places around the world, as Clay Smith. Clay Smith, with a unique skill at solving murder. Not a detective, but often of help to police departments in whatever city he called home.

"He was blind," Clay said simply. "He could not see her, therefore her curse did not affect him. So she killed him, probably infuriated. The marks on his face—"

"Snakebites," Graves interrupted.

"Yeah," Clay said.

Squire strode across the small church, producing a stubby cigar from his pocket. He lit it from a candle and turned to face them.

"All right. But explain it to me. How come this means we don't have to go looking for her?"

Graves studied Clay a moment, then looked at the dead

priest, and finally gave his attention to Squire. "Our friend Mr. Clay has more than one talent, remember?"

Squire's face lit up and he puffed on the cigar. The hobgoblin gave a short cough and nodded eagerly. "Right, right. The thing. The . . . the ectoplasm trail, or whatever. But you couldn't see it before, because Medusa's victims were all stone. It wasn't working."

"No," Clay agreed. "It wasn't." He looked upon the dead priest with sorrow, but also with grave determination. The souls of murder victims haunted their killers for a time, perhaps with intent but more likely simply because their lives have ended so abruptly that they cling to whatever is nearest them when they die, afraid to go anywhere. To move on.

But the ghosts leave a trail, a kind of thin phantom line, a tendril that connected their ravaged bodies to their souls, no matter how far the souls traveled away from their husks. If he discovered the victim soon enough after death and he followed that link, that tendril, he could find the killer.

A faded pink mist clung to the dead priest, stretched like a rope out the front of the church and through the square, then farther up into the village. Into the hills.

Into the west.

"I've got her trail," Clay said. "It's only a matter of time, now."

HER bones ached.

Eve drifted slowly up into awareness, and though her eyes were still closed, her brow knitted in discomfort. She lay on her side already, her body rocking with some unknown rhythm, but now she pulled her legs up tight beneath her and shuddered with the cold. Her lips drew taut, pressed together, and then she shifted uncomfortably.

Her eyes fluttered lazily open, and she saw her hands, crossed at the wrists over her breasts. A thin sheen of crystal frost had formed on her flesh, and a chill mist swirled around her. The rocking motion continued, but only now did

Eve have the presence of mind to recognize that she was in a boat.

Memories stirred, and she remembered her circumstances. Rage washed over her, warming her icy blood, and her upper lip curled to bare her fangs even as she sat up. They were in a small boat, Eve at the prow. Nick Hawkins was nearest to her, smoking a cigarette, and the moment she was in motion he began to shift toward her, hands coming up in a defensive posture.

Eve was thousands of years faster.

She sprang at him, lunging through the mist and ignoring the sway of the craft or the rush of the water beneath it. Hawkins snarled, clenching his cigarette between his teeth, but he had neither the strength nor the swiftness to fight back. Eve clutched his throat with her left hand, the right gathering up the fabric of his jacket, and she drove him down beneath her. The back of his head struck the wooden floor of the boat with a solid thump. A guttural curse issued from his lips even as the impact knocked the wind from his lungs. Eve held him down as he bucked, attempting to throw her off, but she was too strong.

Her vision was far more than that of a human. Her eyes saw through gloom and mist with utter clarity, and when she looked up she saw every line in Nigel Gull's hideous features. He had been sitting behind Hawkins—beyond him the girl, Jezebel, had her hands in the water, somehow using her weather magic to propel the craft—and now Gull shifted forward, raising his hands. The old mage did not dare to stand in the small boat for fear they would all spill over into the frigid, rushing river.

"Not a fucking spark of magick on those fingers, asshole," Eve snarled, purposely flashing her fangs as she choked the man beneath her. "Or Hawkins loses his head."

Jezebel twisted around at the sound of Eve's voice, and her eyes went wide with alarm. "Nick," she said, her lips forming the name almost soundlessly.

The mist rolled across the water's surface, and the boat

knifed through it. Gull was half-crouched, hands still contorted as if frozen in the act of casting a spell. His ugliness was made worse when he smiled, as he did now.

"Let's not be hasty, pet," Gull said, lowering one hand to the bench below him in order to keep his balance.

Eve punctured Hawkins's skin with her fingernails. "Call me that again, you pompous prick, and I'll kill him just for fun, and to hell with what comes of it."

The smile disappeared from Gull's face. His nostrils flared, and the mist that swept past his face seemed also to swirl behind his eyes. The mage began to hum, the sound low and guttural.

"I don't think you want to do that, Eve," he sang in a voice that was not his own, the sweet tones of Orpheus. "You don't want to move at all, in fact."

She tried to fight the influence of that voice, her every muscle strained and burned with the struggle, but there was nothing she could do. The power of Orpheus's voice was too much. She felt her heart surrendering, her rage pacified, though in the dark depths of her mind her hatred still churned. A spark of panic ignited in her.

Once, long ago, she had been overpowered by a demon with the sweetest of voices. The memory seared her, and she did not want to allow it to take root, yet she seemed as helpless in her mind as in her flesh. Eve collapsed in the prow once more, on her back this time, forced to stare at the distended face of Nigel Gull and to see the mad light of triumph in his eyes.

"Mother of two races, hunter of two races, ancient as evil's kiss. Do you think I'd have you here with me without preparing to deal with you?" he sang to her.

The river rocked the craft, water sprayed over the side and dampened her face and hair, and Eve could only lie there with her eyes open as Gull sneered at her. In the rear of the boat, Jezebel smiled at her and then plunged her hands into the water again. The girl had paused in her propulsion of the vessel, and it had begun to be swept along with the

current, but now the boat rushed forward across the water
once more.

Hawkins sat up, his gunmetal eyes hard as he glared at
her. He reached up to touch his neck, and his fingers came
away bloody. With an unsettling laugh he licked his fingers
clean and then crabwalked forward so that he was looking
down upon Eve, prone and helpless.

"Just to be clear, I don't care what you are. Just another
sodding relic to me." He wrapped both hands around her
throat and began to squeeze. "You don't need to breathe, I
know that. But I'll wager you need your head attached to
your body, yeah? If Mr. Gull didn't need you . . . ah, but he
does." Now Hawkins grinned. "Might sample a taste of *your*
blood, next time, though. Play your little vampire game. So
mind your manners, leech."

The wood was rough beneath her. Eve smelled blood but
could not be certain if it was Hawkins's or her own. Beneath
that smell was another, one she was noticing for the very
first time. The stink of the dead. Not the rotting odor of fresh
death, but the dusty, brittle smell of the tomb. It lived in the
wood of the boat and drifted with the mist. This place was a
realm of the dead, and so it did not surprise her, but it served
to calm her. Though she had no desire to rest in the grave,
Eve had to remind herself from time to time that she was, in
essence, one of the dead. Creatures far more wretched than
Nick Hawkins had done far worse to her than he would ever
be able to conjure in his most depraved imagination.

Eve managed to sneer. But she would not give Hawkins
the pleasure of a response. Instead her gaze shifted beyond
him, to Gull. Focusing the entirety of her will, she managed
to force her lips to move.

"You . . . need me?" she rasped. "Why?"

The mage nodded slowly. "Indeed." He placed a hand
over his heart. "As to my purpose, I'm afraid you'd never
understand. All of this—" He gestured around him, taking
in Hawkins and Jezebel, the boat and the river, and the
netherworld beyond. "It's for love. I've orchestrated all of it

for the sake of a woman." His face stretched into that horrid smile again.

"I'm a romantic, you see."

Another spray of water came over the side, and Eve blinked it away. On her lips, the droplets had the salt tang of tears.

"What woman would have you?" she asked. It was becoming easier to speak, though she still could not move her limbs.

Gull gazed out across the river, all amusement gone from his eyes, leaving only a melancholy emptiness behind. "The most beautiful creature in all the ages."

"I hope she's worth it," Eve said. "The pain, I mean. Conan Doyle and the others—my friends—they'll be coming for you."

The ugly man raised an eyebrow and stared at her. "I'm prepared for them, as well. I know what Arthur is capable of. Do you think I'd underestimate him?"

Gull settled into the craft as though it were a throne. He gestured for Hawkins to join Jezebel in the aft of the boat. The slender man moved carefully past the mage, then Gull turned his attention to Eve again.

"Sit up," he commanded.

Jerking like a marionette, she complied. Somehow his instruction had freed her upper body, at least enough that she was able to glance around at the river.

"The Styx," Gull said. "And we come, momentarily, to the far shore."

Eve turned to see that he spoke the truth. They approached the bank of the river, where the ground seemed made not of soil but of cold, gray ash. She shot Gull a withering glare.

"You don't think Conan Doyle will find a way across?"

"Oh, I'm certain he will. I'd be terribly disappointed otherwise."

Only then did Eve notice the activity in the rear of that small, ancient craft. Jezebel still had her hands thrust into the water, surges of white foam jetting out behind them as she forced the river to propel them. But now Hawkins knelt beside her, one hand on her shoulder. Despite the chill of the mist and the river, beads of sweat had formed on his forehead.

Gull saw that she had noticed them.

"Mr. Hawkins is a psychometrist," the mage said. "You know that. But he is capable of more than simply reading images and emotions. With enough motivation and focus, he can also communicate them. Jezebel is *one* with the river. Through her, Hawkins is pouring hatred for Conan Doyle into every drop of water, tainting all of the Styx with the single, unrelenting thought that Arthur is the enemy and must be destroyed."

A knot of fear twisted Eve's gut. She had faith in Conan Doyle, but Gull seemed so confident . . .

Still, she did her best to hide her alarm. "Water? You expect the water to rise up and stop him?"

"Of course not," Gull replied. A sneer of satisfaction split his face. He dropped one hand over the side of the boat and let his fingers trail in the river. "Here there be monsters, my dear Eve. Here there be monsters."

13

THOUGH only in small measures, Ceridwen could indeed feel that she was growing stronger. The deeper they progressed into the Underworld, the more acclimated she became to the nightmarish place. The process was equal parts relief and concern. Although glad to be regaining her strength, she had to wonder the cost. Already she had begun to feel a certain, disturbing sense of belonging, the simplest thought of returning to the land of the living filling her with uneasiness. What that meant, she did not know. But it troubled her deeply.

They had reached the shores of the swiftly flowing Styx and were awaiting the ferryman to take them across. Danny and Conan Doyle stood at the river's edge.

"Where is he?" Danny asked, attempting unsuccessfully to skip a stone across the river's turbulent surface. "The Cyclops dude said that Charon'd just show up after we got here." He threw another stone, waiting for Conan Doyle's reply.

Arthur remained silent, staring out over the Styx, trying to see through the thick, undulating clouds of gray vapor. Ceridwen did not like the expression on his face.

"An excellent question." Conan Doyle turned his gaze

from the river to the black sand of the shore. The sand had been disturbed. There was no doubt that Gull and his operatives, along with captive Eve, had arrived first. He removed one of the two gold coins the Cyclops had provided them to pay Charon and began to play with it, dexterously rolling it back and forth across the knuckles of his hand. It was a trick he had learned from Harry Houdini, a friend from long ago.

"What have you done now, Gull?" Conan Doyle whispered, lost in thought as the coin danced atop his hand.

As if in response to his query, the Underworld answered.

Ceridwen could feel it in the elements around her— from the granules of sand beneath her feet, to the mournful whistling of the wind that caused the skeletal branches of the trees along the shore to click and clatter. The Underworld was attempting to speak to them, and only she had the ability to hear.

She closed her eyes and listened. Then she wandered across the sand, closer to Conan Doyle and the boy, closer to the river's edge.

Conan Doyle watched her as she approached. "What troubles you, Ceridwen?"

She did not respond, his voice added to the cacophony of the elements as they attempted to communicate. The river was the loudest voice of all, and she found herself drawn to its flow. This was the place from which the answer would come: the Styx, eager to share with her what had transpired. Ceridwen squatted down at the shore and extended her hand toward the hellish waters.

"No!" Danny yelped, his alarm cutting through the static inside her head, and she looked up into a face wracked with worry.

"I don't think you want to do that." He turned his nervous gaze out over the water. "There's something . . . not right about it."

Conan Doyle had moved closer as well, and she tried to

assuage their fears with a smile. Then she gently touched her fingertips to the agitated water.

Ceridwen and the River Styx were one. Her body went rigid, her mind filling with rapid-fire images detailing what had come to pass, what the river had seen. Most of it was monotony, the ferryman in his launch and its countless journeys, transporting the dead to their final destination. Faces flashed across her mind, wan and bewildered. *So many faces.* But then her mind's eye settled upon the most recent passengers, including the twisted, ugly visage of Nigel Gull. Ceridwen witnessed what had transpired from the river's point of view, as though she were looking up from beneath the water. Gull had committed a terrible crime, a most foul act. Ceridwen saw the murder of Charon, saw Gull set his body adrift upon the river.

She drew her hand from the water with a gasp, stumbling into Conan Doyle's waiting arms, the violence seared into her mind.

"I told her not to touch it," she heard Danny say, concern in his voice. "What did it do?"

Ceridwen opened her eyes and looked up at them, pulling back from Arthur's embrace. "The ferryman is not coming. Gull and his people were here with Eve no more than two hours ago," she said, seeing the ghastly image reenacted in the theater of her mind. She closed her eyes and shuddered even though the temperature was oppressively hot.

"What has he done?" Conan Doyle asked, eyes stormy beneath salt-and-pepper brows.

"He's killed Charon," she said, trying to force the images from her mind. "And they've taken his boat across on their own."

Conan Doyle clenched his fists in anger, turning his back upon them and walking away. She understood his frustration. Their enemy was besting them at every turn. This was not something to which Arthur Conan Doyle was accustomed.

"So we're screwed, then. Game over," Danny muttered. "How do we help Eve now?"

"Arthur?" Ceridwen called. He was standing with his back to them at the edge of a forest of black, skeletal trees, again lost in thought, but this time she suspected she knew what occupied his mind. It was the way he eyed the copse of trees that gave his thoughts away.

The sorceress was far from Faerie, far from anything the Fey might think of as nature, but she had begun to establish a rapport with what passed for the elements of this barren place. Her strength was returning. Her magick as well, though tainted now by the Underworld. Yet Arthur did not know that. He must have sensed that communicating with the elements here was not as debilitating for her. He had, after all, only just witnessed her forging a bond with the River Styx. But he could not know how far she had adjusted.

This is a test for him in a way, she thought. Conan Doyle was a man of both thought and action, and he prided himself on practicality. What must be done, he would often say, must be done, and damn the consequences. Yet in their battle with the Hydra, his fear for her had caused him to become distracted, endangering the lives of the others and the success of their mission. He had promised it would never happen again.

But here was a similar situation. *Will he ask it of me when he knows it will cause me pain?*

Ceridwen was about to take that responsibility from him, when Conan Doyle turned to face her. The steely look on his face told her all she needed to know.

"Gull has thwarted us for the last time," he announced, walking toward her. "These trees," he motioned to them with a wave of his hand. "We have no time to build a raft, nor anything to lash them together. You must coerce them into taking on the shape of something we can use to get across." He walked past her to stand again at the river's edge, gazing out over its broad expanse. "We must act with haste."

Danny strode angrily toward him, his features more demonic than ever. "What is wrong with you? You know she can't do that. This place is bad for her. Using magick here hurts her. It's obvious you don't give a shit about people when it comes to getting what you need, but I figured if there was anyone, it'd be—"

Conan Doyle turned and glared at him, nostrils flaring, and the boy was silenced. Ceridwen wanted to speak up for him, but if they were going to survive, they would have to rely on one another. Part of that was working out their own conflicts.

"Have you given Eve up for dead, then?" Conan Doyle asked, every word a dagger. "Abandoned her to her fate?"

"Of course not," Danny growled.

"Nor have I. Whatever Gull's intentions here, they are likely sinister. Even if they were not, he has manipulated us throughout this fiasco, and now Eve's life is in the balance. I ask what is required, nothing more."

When Conan Doyle spun to face Ceridwen again, Danny seemed about to argue, but then fell silent once more. The sorceress did not blame him. Arthur was correct. In truth, she was relieved that he had chosen their purpose over her comfort.

"Can you do this?" he asked.

And how could she deny him?

THEY walked upon a surface of bones.

From a perilous mountain path, they had descended into a broad expanse of what Eve at first believed to be limestone. But as they grew closer, she had begun to see pieces of dry, yellow bone scattered on the dirt. In a matter of minutes, no matter where her foot fell, the soles of her Italian leather boots landed atop the remains of something that had once been alive. Some of the bones were human, yes. She recognized those readily enough. But from what she could see there were bones there belonging to just about everything in creation.

"Am I the only one who's a little freaked out by this?" Eve asked, turning to face her captors.

"It's the bloody Underworld," Hawkins snarled. "What do you expect, a field of poppies?" He reached out, placed the flat of his hand against her back, and shoved. "Keep moving."

Eve stumbled, still under the sway of Nigel Gull's magick, then turned to look into Hawkins's eyes. She prided herself on the way she evolved with the world, but in her were all the women she had ever been, all the ages she had lived, and now in her fury she fell back on the Eve of another era.

"Mark me," she said. "You may do your best to forget who it is you trifle with, but I shall not forget. I have bred legions of monsters, and slain even more. Your bones will join these others beneath my feet before long. One way, Mr. Hawkins, or another."

Hawkins tried to smile to show her that he was not bothered by her words, but he could not quite manage it. Instead he gestured as if to push her again, but she was already turning to forge ahead. The path gradually angled upward as they approached a hill. Eve wondered what new thrills the Underworld had in store for them on the other side.

Calmer, now, she shook off the remnants of the past, summoning the sardonic swagger that had become so much a part of her survival as an immortal. Eve glanced over her shoulder at Gull.

"So, are we there yet? I'm bored."

Gull was walking with Jezebel, a protective arm around her waist. There was something untoward about the intimacy between them. The mage was not her father, but regardless Jezebel was still only a girl. Even if there was nothing sexual there, still it was troubling. Jezebel was powerful, and with her red hair and green eyes, and her sensuality, stunning. But she was so obviously broken inside, clamoring for Gull's approval. And he twisted her around with his words just the same way he wrought magick with his contorted fingers.

Throughout their trek, Jezebel had grown quieter, and now she appeared to be a little shaky, perhaps not really digging the whole bone carpet thing.

"Damn, the girl doesn't look well. Maybe she's just realizing what I figured out the second we arrived. This is a place the wandering souls go. The damned, right? I figure we all belong here. It's like coming home. Can't be easy on the kid."

Jezebel shuddered at her words.

"Shut your mouth," Hawkins barked, but he did not touch her. "D'we need this, Nigel? Think I liked her better when she couldn't talk."

"That will be enough of that, Hawkins," Gull said casually, as though they were all just taking a pleasant Sunday stroll through the park.

They reached the base of the hill, the bone path leading upward, and Eve again considered what awaited them on the other side. Jezebel stopped to rest for a moment, taking a seat on an enormous skull that could only have belonged to something monstrous.

"In answer to your question, Eve, I would wager that we are close," the hideous sorcerer said. He stroked Jezebel's hair as if he were calming a nervous house pet.

She leaned into him, closing her eyes, lost in his attentions. "I think I would like to go home now," she whispered in a tiny, little girl's voice that trembled on the brink of tears.

"There, there, pretty Jez," Gull comforted, continuing to stroke her fiery red hair. "It won't be long now."

Eve didn't like the sound of that and wondered where she fit into the mage's plans. Throughout her time as his prisoner she had fought against the enchantments placed upon her, but she was still incapable of directing her own actions. Eve would be free. Of that, she had no doubt. A moment would come when she would have the opportunity to free herself, and then she would kill them all. She would need patience, however, but Eve had lived almost forever and had learned patience very well indeed.

"Won't be long until what?" she asked Nigel, as she squatted to the bone floor and retrieved the skull of what could have been a crow. She used its beak to clean away some of the grime that had collected beneath her fingernails—a manicure was definitely in her foreseeable future. She looked up into the sorcerer's eyes, the only part of his body that hadn't been twisted by magick. "C'mon, Gull, the suspense is killing me."

"We'd best hurry, then. You'll need to survive at least until we can deliver you." Gull smiled, and it was wretched to see. The mage hauled a dozy Jezebel from her seat. "On your feet now, girl," he commanded, no longer sounding quite so fatherly. "We have places to be."

Jezebel did as she was told, hugging her body as if cold.

"Hawkins, see to her," Gull instructed, and the man moved to stand beside the girl, ushering her gently along.

The sorcerer moved toward Eve, gesturing for her to begin the climb up over the rise. She didn't care for the implications of his words, but they came as no surprise. He had kidnapped her for some reason, and she doubted that her scintillating conversational skills had anything to do with it. Eve had difficulty maintaining her footing on the shifting slope, and she used her hands to pull herself along. The pieces of bone were sharp, but the pain kept her focused.

Gull had begun to climb as well, eagerly matching her progress, his breathing becoming labored as they neared the top, perhaps more from anticipation than exertion. Eve found herself increasing her pace, eager to reach the summit before her captor.

"Last one to the top is a deformed fucking freak," she snarled. "Aw, too late." She went up over the rise . . .

And froze. After all she had seen in her excruciatingly long lifetime, she had never seen anything quite like the sight that greeted them over the top of that hill.

Gull joined her, fury twisting his features all the more horribly. "There were times when I actually felt a sense of guilt over what I was going to do with you. But now I believe . . ." Then he, too, stopped and gasped.

"Just when you think you've seen it all," Eve said, eyes riveted to the valley below her.

The body of a giant lay splayed upon the valley floor, so enormous that it covered much of the valley. The corpse was larger than an aircraft carrier, large enough that a small town could have been built atop it. And *corpse* was the word. The giant was quite dead, of that she had no doubt, and had been dead for some time by the look of him. Desiccated skin hung loose and leathery from its monstrous skeleton. A wispy fog floated above the enormous cadaver, the smell blowing up from the valley on a breeze ripe with the stench of rot.

Jezebel started to cough and gag, the stink of the decaying giant nearly making her sick.

"It all seems to have a certain logic now," Gull said wistfully, the overwhelming stench seeming to have no effect on him. "The disorder and degeneration—the chaos."

"Someone you know?" Eve asked, bringing a hand to her nose. As the mist above the great corpse shifted in the breeze, she began to notice the details of its attire. The giant wore pitted bronze armor, tarnished green with the passage of time.

"In a sense. Think about it, temptress. One of your experience ought to be able to put the pieces together. Who can this be, a god so large that the Underworld itself is almost too small for him?" Gull asked, a hint of awe in his voice.

Eve couldn't wrap her brain around the concept. *How is it even possible? How is it possible for a god to end up this way?*

"Hades," Gull said in a reverent whisper. "What sad fate has befallen you?"

When Eve began to descend the steep hill toward that extraordinary sight it was not only the voice of Orpheus and Gull's command that drove her. She had to see it, this magnificent panorama of death, so enormous that she could barely contain the fact of it in her mind.

"So, if the Lord of the Underworld is dead," she rasped, "then who's running the show down here?"

Gull did not look at her as he spoke, his eyes fixed upon the dead god before them. *"Turning and turning in the widening gyre,"* he muttered. *"The falcon cannot hear the falconer; Things fall apart; the center cannot hold; Mere anarchy is loosed upon the world."*

"When you start quoting Yeats, I'm guessing that's code for you don't have a fucking clue," she said, careful not to lose her footing on the slippery slope.

The closer they got, the more details she took in. The craftsmanship of the god's armor was some of the most beautiful and intricate ornamentation she had ever seen. But what would one expect for a lord of the abyss? Hades' face was a shrieking death mask, the withered flesh pulled tight against his skull. Strange birds whose feathers seemed to glint like metal in the faint light of the Underworld flew out of the god's gaping maw in a shrieking flock as they approached, but her eyes were drawn to something else.

"Look at his throat," Eve said, staring at the dry, curling slash that had been cut across the leathery skin of Hades' neck.

The ground in that valley was a black, fine soil, but on the acreage around the desiccated head of the dead god the earth was stained a deep burgundy. Though there were trees and other plant life familiar to the Underworld growing about the vastness of the deceased, Eve could see that nothing grew where the dead lord's blood had flowed.

"All of the detritus of Greek myth had retreated here when their era came to a close. It was their only hope at survival," Gull explained, glancing at an awestruck Hawkins and a giddily grinning Jezebel. "They ought to have built a paradise down here to rival Olympus. Instead, they died, and the place fell to ruin. Entropy. The center could not hold. I wondered what could have happened to cause such chaos here." Gull spoke slowly, mesmerized by the sight before him. "I never imagined that it could have begun with the murder of Hades himself."

Who has the power to murder a god? Again Eve struggled with the inconceivable.

Hawkins trotted several steps ahead of them, trying to get a closer look at the wound, himself now a tiny figure dwarfed by the sprawling, rotting cadaver.

"Not murder," Hawkins said, and they all stared at him. Soldier, spy, and assassin, he was well schooled in murder. "Look in his hand. He's holding a knife. I don't think he was murdered at all, I think the poor bugger offed himself."

Eve looked at the dead god Hades, really looked at him; how he lay prostrate upon the floor of the valley, his mouth agape as if attempting to call to his brethren in Olympus above, and she knew that Hawkins's words were true. Hades had taken his own life.

The closer they progressed, the more foul the stench of decay was becoming, almost palpable in its intensity. Eve found that even she was becoming affected, hacking and coughing with the others. And since she really had no need to, she made a conscious effort to halt her breathing.

That's better.

Gull was gasping, a twisted hand placed flat against his chest. He had stopped his descent and was trying to catch his breath. Hawkins tied a handkerchief behind his head, covering his face, and Jezebel appeared to be fighting the urge to vomit. Despite the revelation that loomed ahead of them, the sublime nature of the thing and the thoughts of divinity and history that it demanded, the two hovered around Gull protectively.

There they were, perfectly helpless. Eve could have

killed them all with ease, if not for the voice of Orpheus. Trapped by Gull's magick, she could do nothing but wait for them to get their shit together.

The sorcerer finally caught his breath and pulled Jezebel to him. "Wind," he said, between gasps of the tainted air. "We need wind to take this foul odor away."

Her eyes were watering badly, trailing black mascara down her flushed cheeks like war paint. "I don't know if I can."

"You must, sweet Jezebel." And despite his use of that endearment, his tone was clear. It was a command, with consequences if she disobeyed.

She nodded slowly, and took a deep breath punctuated by a cough.

Hawkins sidled up beside her. "Sometime today," he snarled, his voice muffled by the cloth about his face.

The two normally seemed so solicitous of one another—particularly Hawkins of the girl—but it was clear now that their camaraderie was a shallow thing. Scratch it deeply enough, and there was nothing underneath. Jezebel looked at Hawkins with teary, hate-filled eyes as he walked away.

"Proceed," Gull commanded, his breathing becoming more labored.

Eve wondered if the power of Orpheus would still hold should Gull be rendered unconscious. But it was too much to hope for. Jezebel closed her eyes, reaching down deep to call upon whatever mojo she commanded. Her hair whipped around her face in a wind that was not natural, and she winced. The process looked painful, and for a minute it seemed she wasn't going to pull it off, but the girl hung tough. Whatever it was that she was summoning was fighting her, and her body began to twitch and spasm, beads of perspiration breaking out on her brow.

Eve almost felt sorry for the little witch, but then thought better of it.

The girl fell to her knees with a gasp, and raising her arms, she turned her face to the ceiling of the Underworld.

Lightning snaked from her fingertips and eyes, erupting into the oppressive atmosphere. The wind swirled around them, growing in intensity, and then shifted in a single direction, a gale that swept the noxious fumes of the god's decay away from them.

Jezebel slumped to the ground, curling up in a tight little ball. "I did it," she said over and over again in that little girl's voice.

Hawkins yanked down the mask from his face and gave the girl a round of applause. "Now that didn't hurt too bad, did it?" he asked as he bent down to help her up from the ground. "About time you earned your keep."

The man was begging to die, and as soon as she was able, Eve would oblige him.

Gull took a large gulp of purified air into his lungs. "Much better."

They descended farther into the valley in silence, the body of the fallen god looming larger and larger. They passed through small patches of skeletal wood and scrub brush. Jezebel's manipulation of the wind had done the job for the most part, but the closer they got the harder the wind had to work to keep the stench from overwhelming them again. The rot had left gaping holes in the flesh, exposing muscle, sinew, and bone.

At last, they stood before it, marveling at its enormity.

"So is this it? Have we arrived?" Eve asked, interrupting their reverie. "Or are we going to have to go around this rotting carcass to get to where we're supposed to be?"

Gull fixed her in a steely gaze. "I think I've had just about enough of you."

She was about to reply, but he stopped her with a word. "Silence."

Eve had no choice but to obey.

"Now drop to your knees."

Once more she was forced to comply, and Eve found herself kneeling upon the damp earth before the body of the fallen Hades. Gull looked her over, then licked his thumb, reaching out to her face to rub away some blemish of grime that had stained her cheek. With his long, twisted fingers he combed the hair from her face, then stepped back and again studied her appearance.

"I guess that will have to suffice," he said. Gull looked to the god's corpse. "The misery of the dead calls out from here. I can feel it. This is their place. It is no wonder Hades chose this valley in which to spill his blood."

Gull walked away from Eve then, toward Hawkins and Jezebel. "I would advise you to step back, my friends. I've no idea how they will react to our presence."

How who will react?

The Wicked did as they were told, leaving Gull to stand before the rotting corpse alone. The dark mage raised his arms, and in the booming voice of Orpheus, sang out. Although the song was sung in an ancient language that she had never known, Eve understood the words perfectly. It was a song of summoning, a song that called for the attentions of three sisters—Tisiphone, Alekto, and Megaera. They were the Erinyes—the Furies of legend. He sang of an offering, something to satisfy their unquenchable desire to see the guilty suffer for their sins.

In a sweeping motion he gestured toward Eve, and the suspicion she had been nursing was revealed to be truth. *She* was his offering. Gull finished his beckoning song, hanging his head and resting his voice as he waited for their response.

He didn't wait very long.

From one of the rotting wounds in the side of the corpse, a decaying hole perhaps fifty feet up the side of Hades' rib cage, Eve saw the first hint of movement.

"What have you brought to us?" came a voice that issued from within that corpse, a voice that made the hair at the back of Eve's neck stand on end. It was a voice devoid of warmth or emotion, a voice that promised only cruelty.

"Come out, dear sisters, and see," Gull sang, the enticing nature of his borrowed voice certain to draw them from hiding.

Eve's eyes grew wide as the Erinyes emerged from the ragged hole in the side of the dead god, three sisters clad in robes of darkness. They eagerly clambered down the side of the great corpse to claim their prize.

A 5 Ceridwen calmed the normally torrential currents of the Styx, Conan Doyle and Danny rowed the magickally crafted raft through the dark water. Conan Doyle kept an eye on Ceridwen, who sat at the edge of the raft with one hand trailing in the fearsome waters. He watched as her mouth moved, words softer than a whisper escaping, as she attempted to bond with the elemental force of the river. The fact that they were actually making progress across the Styx was evidence that Ceridwen was succeeding.

Conan Doyle was worried about her connecting with a world usually reserved for the dead. Though she appeared to have regained nearly all of her vigor, he did not care for the distant look in her eyes, a look that hinted that the despair of the Underworld had touched her deeply. He feared what would happen when it came time to leave.

"How's she doing?" Danny asked, paddling with all his might.

The boy had removed what remained of his tattered T-shirt and his muscles strained as he rowed. The demon's flesh was continuing to evolve, growing more leathery, thicker, darker. There were blotches of color on his back that reminded the sorcerer of the burned orange of fall leaves on Beacon Hill.

"She's doing fine," he responded, marveling at the youth's tenacity. *To think that mere months ago he was living as a typical teenager, totally unaware of his true nature.* He was proud of Daniel Ferrick. A normal youth his age would have been driven to the brink of insanity on more than one occasion with what the boy had witnessed in recent days. He was indeed a welcome addition to the Menagerie.

"And you?" Conan Doyle asked, his arms burning with exertion.

"I'm good," the boy said between puffs of air. "Getting a little tired, but I think I can hold out until we get to the other side. How are you doing?" The boy smiled, exposing sharp-looking teeth. There was a mischievous twinkle in his eyes. "Hanging in there, old-timer?"

He didn't care for the boy's lack of respect, but considering what they had been through, he decided to let it slide. "Don't concern yourself, boy," he stressed, staring straight ahead, attempting to pierce the shifting gray vapor that hung over the river to the other side. They had to be getting closer. "Focus on staying alive."

Danny laughed and continued to paddle. The thick shroud of mist parted momentarily, and something caught Conan Doyle's attention. He set his makeshift oar down on the raft and climbed to his feet.

"What is it?" Danny asked. "Are we close?"

"Stop rowing," Conan Doyle ordered. His eyes had found the spot again, only to have his line of sight obscured by the drifting vapor. "There's something in the water ahead."

Danny did as he was told, placing his oar down and getting to his feet. He peered over the side of the raft. "We're still moving."

Conan Doyle saw that the boy was right. They were being drawn toward the area where he had seen movement on the water. "Ceridwen," he called, looking over his shoulder.

She had removed her hand from the water and was clutching it to her chest, a look of shock on her face. "There are things in the river," she whispered. "Things that hate us quite ferociously. And they mean us harm."

"Holy shit. Take a look at that." Danny pointed out across the water.

A whirlpool had formed in the Styx, a swirling maelstrom that was inexorably drawing them closer.

"Charybdis," Ceridwen said, and Conan Doyle saw that her hand was immersed in the water again. "The whirlpool is alive. I don't understand how, but it's a living thing. It's called Charybdis."

Danny couldn't take his eyes from the spiraling vortex. "Why does it hate us? What the hell did we do this time? Oh man I hate this shit!"

Gull, Conan Doyle thought. Somehow, his old adversary was responsible.

"It believes we've come to do it harm . . ." Ceridwen began, her eyes wide and her expression dreamlike as she extracted the information from the turgid water. "It has been told that we've come to separate it from its mate."

"Who told it that?" Danny asked. He had picked up his oar and was attempting to paddle the raft away from the maelstrom, but to no avail. "Was it Gull?" His voice was on the brink of hysteria. "It was that ugly fuck, wasn't it?"

They drew toward the dark, sucking center of the whirlpool. The raft began to rock, and Conan Doyle and Danny were driven to their knees. Water surged up over them, soaking their clothes.

"Is there any way you can ask the river currents to pull us from the whirlpool's grasp?" Conan Doyle shouted at Ceridwen over the roaring water, trying to clear his vision to have the comfort of the sight of her.

She looked up at him with eyes barely focused. "I'm trying," she croaked, shaking her head in the negative. "But Charybdis is too strong."

It tore at him to see her so helpless, but there was nothing he could do. If they were to survive, all of their power and guile would have to be brought into play. He reached within himself, drawing upon the magick that resided there. Conan Doyle expected excruciating pain, but found only the slightest discomfort. Just as the nature of this place was adjusting to Ceridwen, the laws of magick were growing accustomed to him. He didn't like that at all, but at the moment he was more concerned with Charybdis.

Conan Doyle raised a hand above his head and sketched at the air. A sphere of dark blue energy coalesced around his fingers, and then a lance of magick thrust across the river, causing a wall of water to erupt beneath it as it passed. It was a powerful enchantment meant to disrupt magick, to short-circuit the supernatural. Again and again he summoned that spell, and cast it out across the river to strike at the heart of the swirling water. The river began to froth and steam, and a strange sound, the cries of some ethereal beast in pain, rose up from the water to fill the air.

The raft rocked upon the choppy water as the vortex started to falter, and from the corner of his eye Conan Doyle saw Ceridwen pitch to one side, coming dangerously close to falling from the raft. He scrambled to her, pulling the sorceress closer to him.

"I have you," he told her as a wave of exhaustion passed over him.

"I think we beat it," he heard Danny say excitedly, and he looked to see that the boy was standing at the raft's edge, peering into the slowly calming waters. The raft was again at the mercy of the river's natural flow.

Ceridwen was shaking off her stupor, trying to talk, but her voice was so soft that he could not hear. He bent his ear down close, attempting to decipher her whispering words.

"Charybdis," she began. "Charybdis is no—"

"Charybdis is gone," he said, pulling her close in an attempt to comfort.

Her violet eyes flashed angrily as she pushed herself out of his arms, shaking her head from side to side.

"No," she said, her voice stronger. "Charybdis is not . . . alone."

He recalled her words from before; that they had come to separate Charybdis from its mate.

Its mate.

The water in front of them began to bubble and churn, and again their raft was tossed about.

"What now?" Danny shrieked, losing his balance and collapsing.

Something exploded up from the depths, its skin catching the strange light of the hellish place, glistening with all the colors of the rainbow. Conan Doyle was reminded of a rainbow trout, but this was no mere fish.

Scylla, the mate of Charybdis, surged up from the bubbling black waters of the Styx, her voice raised in a scream of rage over what they had wrought upon her consort.

Once she had been a beautiful sea nymph, loved by Zeus and Poseidon in turn, until twisted by the jealousy of Circe into something monstrous. If one looked closely enough, past the slick, greasy skin and thick appendages that grew like tumors from her body, one could see that this had once been a creature of beauty, but that had been so long ago that Conan Doyle doubted even Scylla remembered.

The river beast surged toward them in a spray of water. Scylla grabbed the front of the makeshift raft in large, webbed hands, tipping it forward. Holding Ceridwen tightly in his arms, Conan Doyle dug his fingers into the wood, halting his slide toward the enraged beast.

"Hold on!" he cried out to Danny, but the boy's clawing hands could not find purchase, and he began to slide toward the monster.

Her tentacles darted at him with incredible speed, almost as if they had a sentience all their own. Conan Doyle watched in horror as the tapered ends of those appendages split open to reveal snarling faces, needle-toothed jaws snapping in horror.

Is there no end to the nightmares of this place? Conan Doyle thought as he plucked a spell from his memory. He thrust out his hand and began to utter the incantation.

The blast that streamed from his fingertips struck Scylla square in the chest and seared her flesh black. With an ear-piercing scream she dove beneath the water to recover.

Danny struggled to climb back up onto the raft, and Conan Doyle was forced to leave Ceridwen's side to assist him.

"Take my hand, boy," he cried, extending his arm.

"What the fuck is up with this place!" the boy yelled, hauling himself out of the water with Conan Doyle's help, and back up onto the raft. "Does everything have to have multiple heads and a serious mad on for us?"

"It does appear that way, doesn't it?" Conan Doyle sighed, taking a moment to catch his breath now that Danny was safe.

The waters of the Styx were becoming agitated again. He was about to tell the boy to hold on, when he heard Ceridwen's cry of warning, and he turned just in time to see the elemental sorceress standing, her hands crackling with unrestrained power as she prepared to defend them.

"That attack will come from beneath us!" she cried out just as the raft was struck from below.

Then they were airborne, the raft propelled up and out of the water by the savagery of the attack. The raft was destroyed, reduced to wreckage floating upon the turbulent waters of the River Styx. Conan Doyle broke the surface, spitting the foul tasting water from his mouth. Its taste was like nothing he had ever experienced before, and it stirred memories of times and events best left forgotten. Times of sorrow. The water wanted him to surrender, to give himself over entirely to the flow and pull of the river.

But Sir Arthur Conan Doyle would never surrender.

Shrugging off the influence of the river he began to search for Ceridwen and Danny in the choppy waters. In the distance he saw something upon the undulating surface, and relief surged through him as he realized it was Danny, clutching Ceridwen with one arm and with the other clinging to a section of their decimated raft.

Swimming against the current, he went to them.

"I think she might have hit her head on something," Danny shouted over the rush of the river.

Conan Doyle helped him with Ceridwen. The sorceress

had a gash on her temple, and she moaned fitfully as she struggled to regain consciousness.

"We have to get to shore," the demon boy said, his eyes wild as he searched the waters for any sign of further attack. "I can't freakin' stand this anymore."

Conan Doyle could offer nothing to allay the boy's fears. They were being carried by the current, not near enough the bank to swim, only the wreckage of the raft keeping them above water. Conan Doyle racked his brain for a way to the other side.

Then he saw Danny's eyes go wide with fear.

"Something just touched my . . . " The demon boy gasped, but never finished as he was yanked beneath the surface of the water.

"Danny!" Conan Doyle cried, illuminating one of his hands and plunging it down into the river. But he could see nothing in the darkness.

The boy was gone.

The water began to churn again, and he readied himself for the conflict. Ceridwen was barely conscious so he could not depend on her for assistance. As he clung to a piece of raft, keeping his love from sliding beneath the river's cold embrace, Conan Doyle brought forth a spell of defense and held it at the ready.

The turbulent waters exploded, and the monstrous Scylla reared up from beneath the Styx, shrieking like the damnable thing she was.

But there was something wrong. Scylla was not attacking. She was fending off an attack.

Bobbing upon the roiling waters, Conan Doyle looked on in astonishment as Daniel Ferrick clung to the body of the raging sea monster. The lunatic savagery of his demonic birthright had overcome him, and there was nothing human about him now. His yellow eyes gleamed as he tore away chunks of the monster's flesh with his claws and needle-teeth in a bloody frenzy of violence.

The river churned as though attuned with Scylla's pain.

It took everything Conan Doyle had to keep himself and Ceridwen above the raging waters. Scylla dove repeatedly beneath the surface and exploded upward in an attempt to loosen the hold of her attacker, but to no avail. Danny held fast, rending her flesh with wanton abandon.

The last thing Conan Doyle saw before succumbing to the pull of the Styx was the monster Scylla beckoning to the heavens as the demon boy dug into her chest with his claws, hunting for her heart. Scylla screamed as if pleading to the gods that had cursed her for mercy.

14

THE shipyard stank of fish. Squire wrinkled his nose as he ambled among the dry-docked fishing boats. Some of them were obviously being repaired or repainted, and one or two seemed to be in the midst of a patchwork reconstruction using the remains of several others. The majority were rusting or rotting hulks that had been abandoned long ago, their paint flaked off so completely that they appeared ancient. From the awful odor, it seemed like one of those old wrecks—or perhaps one of the boats under repair—still had a hull filled with the catch of the day.

If the day was a week ago, he thought.

The smell was ferocious, and he breathed through his mouth. It might have come from the boats themselves, from the sea seeping into the wood, or maybe it was just that stench that sometimes came off the sea at low tide. But something about it made Squire reasonably sure it was local. Either there was a trawler-net full of rotting fish nearby, or something had crawled up out of the ocean and died. Maybe a lot of somethings.

The night was humid, and even the breeze off the Mediterranean was hot. They were farther south now, Medusa's trail having led them to the coast and then southward, passing through several small villages and at last to this place. *Marina* would be far too rich a word for it, and *dock* was not nearly descriptive enough. There was a dock where local fisherman brought in their catch, but that didn't account for the ships under repair or the ones that had been abandoned. It was like some nautical junkyard occupied by dedicated fishermen who wouldn't give up on a boat until it was beyond repair . . . but from the look of things, whoever these fishermen were, they had paid little attention to the upkeep of their vessels until things went horribly wrong.

Squire licked his lips, wishing he had a thick, sugary glass of ouzo to relax him. What he liked best about the Greek liqueur was that it was sort of like getting drunk on melted candy.

The evening sky was a blue-black, and the darkness seemed to nestle within the shipyard in graded hues, an evening shadow in one place and an utter, inky black in others. It was almost as though the place had something to hide and the night was its conspirator. Squire paid it no mind. Natural or otherwise, he was intimately familiar with the dark. The shadows were *his* conspirators.

He whistled an old Frank Sinatra song, "Summer Wind," and turned seaward, passing through an opening between two skeletal boats, one of which appeared to have once been put to military use. As he moved nearer the Mediterranean there were fewer wrecks and more ships under repair, propped up on scaffolding or hoisted off the ground with ropes and pulleys. A pulley clanked against the side of a boat, and Squire paused, frowning, but he did not turn to see the source of the sound.

The wind was strong, but enough to sway the heavy apparatus?

He continued on until he emerged from among the ships. A wide, rutted path separated the shipyard from the docks—wide enough for a car or truck to pass through—and beyond that was the Mediterranean. Whitecaps churned atop the waves, whipped by the wind and the night. Squire had always thought the sea was a nocturnal animal, only truly coming to life after dark. Scientists talked about the pull of the moon, but he felt it was more than that.

The masts of fishing boats swayed on the horizon. Smaller boats were tied up at the docks, silent but scarred with the wounds of their history, of hard work and rough seas. The smell of dead fish receded as he crossed the span of rutted earth between shipyard and dock, and he breathed more deeply of the moist, heated air. It had started to blunt even his prodigious appetite, and he was pleased to be away from the stink.

Squire thought smoking was a filthy habit. Except, of course, on the rare occasions when he felt like having a stogie. He reached into the inner pocket of his coat, fingers pushing past the steel razor he kept there, and withdrew a fat Cuban cigar. *Fidel. Hell of a guy,* he thought.

"Gonna have to commandeer one of these," he muttered aloud, scanning the sea again, evaluating the fishing boats. He didn't want a trawler. The speed on one of those old, choking things would have driven him apeshit. There was one that looked like it might actually be a charter boat, kept up nicely, outfitted for the sort of thing where businessmen paid to go out and have someone bait their hooks, and reel the fish in, and all they had to do was hold a rod for a few hours in between. But it probably had a decent engine.

Sails were okay for a backup plan, but the hobgoblin didn't trust them. And he wasn't all that enthused about the physical exertion they required.

It didn't hurt that the charter-looking boat probably had a galley full of food.

He used his sharp thumbnail to pop the end off of the cigar and clenched it in his teeth. A quick check of his pockets produced a lighter. It was always extraordinary what a hobgoblin might find in his pockets that hadn't been there moments before. It was a bit of magick luck, and Squire thought it was about the best quality a guy could be born with, even better than a startling endowment. Or close, at least.

The lighter flared in his hand, and he puffed on the cigar. The tip glowed in the dark as he slipped the lighter back into his pocket. Impatience was part of his personality, so it was difficult to relax there at the edge of the sea. He smoked the cigar, his exhalations pluming in the air, and he sighed. Squire had his heart set on that boat.

With his incredible gift, Clay had been following Medusa's trail south from Corinth.

"What the hell does it look like?" Squire had asked him.

"Chewing gum," Clay had replied. Then, after the hobgoblin had shot him a hard look, he had shrugged. "It does, in a way. Like bubble gum that someone has chewed and started to stretch out to an impossible length."

Weird shit, Squire thought now. But it worked. He and Graves had followed Clay, and Clay had followed this invisible ghost-line that connected victim and killer. It had led them here, but unfortunately it didn't stop here. The ectoplasmic trail that Clay was following stretched out across the water, which meant Medusa had left in a boat. She could probably swim, but even a creature of myth couldn't stay afloat forever. Given her curse, the only way the ugly thing could have left the shore was with the help of someone else.

Squire chuckled under his breath and took another draw on the cigar that was almost a sigh. He snorted the smoke out through his nostrils and chewed on the end a bit, rolling it in his teeth. As he did so he walked a bit closer to the docks. There were nighttime shadows down there, the moonlight throwing the space beneath and beside the dock in a darker shadow than seemed natural.

"Seriously," he said. "How stupid do you think we are?"

Even as he spoke, he turned, knowing he was swifter than any opponent would guess a creature so truncated might be. His right hand thrust inside his jacket, and he pulled, snaps tearing fabric, brandishing the flail he had retrieved from Conan Doyle's armory. Nineteenth-century Indian, the weapon was little more than an iron bar with two long chains attached to one end, a heavy metal ball dangling from each chain.

Squire had the flail swinging even before he was certain of his opponent's location. But his eyes were used to shadow, and he saw Tassarian immediately. The resurrected assassin was all in black, and a veil was drawn across his face beneath his sunken eyes. Tassarian moved with such swiftness and precision that Squire could not have evaded him.

It mattered little.

The walking corpse was a master of weapons, but so was Squire. Tassarian's great advantage had been surprise.

Tonight, he had lost that advantage.

Squire swung the flail, darting toward the killer. Tassarian tried to block the attack—it would have been impossible for even him to dodge—but the iron balls struck his face, cracking his cheek as the chains wrapped around his arm. The dead man grunted and started to reach his free hand up to try to extricate himself.

"No chance, dumbass," Squire barked, cigar still clenched between his teeth.

He cracked the flail like a whip, snapping the bones in Tassarian's arm with a loud pop. From the thin scabbard clipped to the back of his pants the hobgoblin drew an ornate, seventeenth-century Italian stiletto. He tugged Tassarian toward him. The assassin used the momentum to attack. Leather rustled as Tassarian shot a kick at Squire's head. The dead man underestimated him again. Squire stepped in closer, hauled on the flail's handle to use Tassarian's own broken arm to block the kick. The dead assassin hissed in pain even as he stumbled, off balance from the conflicting momentum of the kick and the twist of his arm.

Squire jammed the stiletto into Tassarian's left eye. The blade plunged through the orbit and into the skull with a wet, sucking sound, spiking into the dead man's brain.

But the killer was already dead. He shot his hand out, fist

striking Squire's chest hard enough to have killed a human. The hobgoblin staggered backward, losing his grip on the handle of the flail. Tassarian took two steps nearer to him, silently glaring with his remaining eye. The dead man plucked the antique stiletto from the ruined eye, blood and white fluid dribbling out of the socket. With the black mask covering his face, his expression was unreadable. He snatched the end of the flail with his good hand and began to unravel it, ready to use it.

"I wish we had time to really make a night of this," Squire said, smiling, twisted lips pulling up into a sneer. He'd kept the cigar between his teeth through all of this, and now he took a long puff on it, stoking the embers at its tip. "You got the drop on us last time. Hurt us. It'd be nice to take our time. But we've got places to go. People to see."

Tassarian barely reacted at first. Then the dead man dropped into a defensive stance, head tilted to listen to the night around him. Squire did not even bother attacking him, but watched as Tassarian spun around to see the ghost of Dr. Graves shimmering into existence just behind him, phantom guns drawn. The assassin swung the flail, but it passed right through the specter, and Graves pulled his triggers. Ghost bullets punched through Tassarian's dead flesh, and he jerked several times, staggering, forced backward.

Clay was waiting. He darted forward, a small, sleek Persian cat, but the air rippled above him as he ran, and by the time he reached Tassarian, he had transformed into a massive Bengal tiger. It shed the night like water as it grew, and then Clay leaped at Tassarian. Dr. Graves shot the killer again, and the dead man danced as the tiger fell on him, tearing his left arm from its socket with a single swipe from its massive paws.

The hobgoblin and the ghost watched as Clay tore Tassarian to pieces and scattered them throughout the shipyard and the docks. Squire would have liked to linger over the killing, but they had no time. Even the twenty minutes the task consumed was too long.

When they had stolen the boat Squire had been eyeing, Graves took the helm and Clay stared southward, still following the ectoplasmic trail Medusa's last victim had left behind.

Squire stood at the back of the boat, Tassarian's crushed skull in his hands. He waited until they were several miles farther down the coast before tossing it into the Mediterranean. It bobbed on their wake several times before slipping beneath the surface.

"This time stay dead, you prick."

EVE had walked the Earth a thousand times, had witnessed the birth of religions and the death of empires. She had studied the worship of civilization and tracked her vampiric offspring through the mythology of every region of the world. She knew precisely what these women were.

Women. The word itself was entirely insufficient.

The Kindly Ones. The Madnesses. Potniae. Praxidikae. They were the Furies, the Erinyes, and though she herself was ancient and cruel in her fashion, Eve could only stare at them in terrible wonder. The sisters had emerged from the gaping hole in the corpse of suicidal Hades, the armored remains of a god the size of a small town. They had crawled headfirst toward the ground, talons hooked into the rotting flesh of the lord of the Underworld, and then dropped the rest of the way, landing with uncanny lightness and ease.

Megaera, Tisiphone, and Alekto. But though they did not look precisely alike, Eve could not tell them apart. The myths had not described them in detail, of course, for who might have gotten close enough to tell such tales and returned from this place to do so? Which had made her wonder, in that moment, if this was to be the end for her as well.

The Erinyes were far taller than any ordinary women, thin and elegant, their features regal and beautiful. They were cloaked in strange garments, sheer and torn, that barely hid the pale flesh beneath. They had no armor, yet there was nothing vulnerable about them. They moved with a grace and power that was intimidating, yet they seemed cautious as well, not coming directly at their prey.

Each held a whip in her hand, barbed all along its length, and the whips seemed to twist of their own accord with the menace of deadly serpents. When Eve heard the hissing sound she assumed that it issued from the whips, and only as the sisters drew nearer did she see the tiny snakes nesting in the dark hair of the Furies.

Blood streaked their faces in vertical stripes like macabre war paint. It took Eve several moments to realize the sisters were actually weeping blood. Their eyes were red orbs too large for their thin features, and another part of their myth came to her, then. Gaea had been enraged at Ouranos, the Earth furious with the Sky, and she enlisted the aid of her son Cronos. Cronos attacked Ouranos, wounding him, and from the blood that was spilled, the Erinyes were born.

Born of blood.

"Erinyes!" Nigel Gull called as the women strode across the black, dead soil of the Underworld toward them. "Eumenides, please accept our obeisance and lend me your ears."

The mage turned his misshapen face toward Hawkins, who nodded quickly and knelt, his weight puffing black dust around him. Jezebel gazed at the sisters as though she were a foundling at last discovering her true family. Her eyes were bright with hope, and she ran her tongue over her lips, a tentative smile on her face. The Erinyes trailed their whips in the black dust, barbs dragging on the ground, and the things moved and darted with their own life. Jezebel followed the movement of the whips.

"It's you," she whispered, and the words carried to Eve. "It's really you."

Eve pitied the girl.

Gull put a large hand on Jezebel's shoulder and forced her down. She turned a fiery glance upon him, but then realized what he wanted and she nodded, chagrined, and knelt quickly, the mage falling to his knees beside her.

"Down," Gull demanded.

The four of them were on their knees as Tisiphone, Megaera, and Alekto came nearer. The ethereally sheer cloaks that draped their forms moved, like their whips, of their own accord. Now that she was on her knees, Eve heard more than just the hiss of the tiny serpents twined in the sisters' hair. There was another sound.

A chorus of weeping and cries of despair.

Eve pushed her fingers in the fine, black sand beneath her, eyes downcast. Her heart felt vulnerable to attack, and she imagined herself becoming part of that dead land's soil. What would grow in her, she wondered? What deathless sapling would take root in her ancient dust?

She thought for a moment that the weeping was that of the Erinyes, the source of the bloody tears upon their cheeks. But there were too many voices by far, some sounding very distant and muffled and others a whisper in her ear, so nearby that they seemed almost to brush past her.

Just at the upper edge of her vision she saw one of the sisters step in front of her, the hem of the Fury's cloak swaying. Eve would have tumbled backward then, tried to leap up to her feet and protect herself, but the voice of Orpheus controlled her. Thus far the Erinyes seemed to be studying their visitors, curiosity drawing them slowly closer. But the air of sorrow that emanated from them was stifling, smothering Eve. *Where are their victims?* she wondered. *Where are the damned of Hades's netherworld?*

The voices grew louder. Eve blinked, and then she knew. She understood. Her gaze narrowed, and she focused on the hem of the punisher's cloak. The fabric was unlike anything she had ever seen, shifting and unstable as though woven of mist . . . but even as she studied it Eve knew it was neither fabric nor mist. There were faces in the texture of the cloaks of the Erinyes, with eyes and mouths open wide in cries of agony and endless despair. Damnation.

Fingers that seared her flesh with a touch lifted her chin so that she was looking up into the Fury's face, and then she saw those eyes, and she knew they were not really eyes at all. They were tiny pools of blood that spilled like tears, and yet though the creatures' faces were streaked, not a drop fell.

Eve tore her gaze away. Now that the thing had touched her, she felt some of Gull's control lift. Eyes narrowed, muscles tensing, she turned to discover what he had done. The mage wore a hideous grin where he knelt on the ground with his operatives. Hawkins had his eyes downcast, but he breathed evenly. Jezebel was still gazing at the Erinyes in adoration. A sickly golden light crackled around Gull's hands but he kept them crossed before him, as though he was kneeling for some sort of prayer service. Which Eve realized he was.

What the fuck are you waiting for, Gull? she thought. *They're just going to kill us. You did all of this, planned the whole thing, just for this?*

"Eumenides, will you hear my plea?" the mage said at last, and when he raised his chin and looked up at them, his eyes glowed with the same strange light as his hands.

They drifted toward him, then, all three moving like ghosts to encircle him, and as they gazed down upon Gull, Eve felt the oddest mix of relief and disappointment. She watched the twitching and slithering ends of those barbed whips and she felt . . . loss.

What are you, an idiot? You don't want anything to do with these things. They'll rip you open.

Her gaze was drawn again to their cloaks, and she had to force herself to look away, to concentrate on the Erinyes themselves and the way they glared down at Gull, ignoring even the worshipful Jezebel.

"We are those who walk in darkness," announced the one who stood directly in front of Gull. She dragged her whip slowly upward, and it coiled itself around the mage's throat. *"Speak."*

That sickly golden light sparked and danced in his eyes,

and he stared up at her. Hawkins muttered something at his side, some curse, but Gull seemed not to notice. He seemed more hideous than ever in that moment, for Eve saw something in his face that made her realize he had not been lying earlier. His expression was one of utter desperation. He had said he had orchestrated all of this because of love.

"Oh, shit," she whispered.

It was true.

"Those who walk in darkness," the mage echoed, "I am called Nigel Gull. Even for such as you, who have seen the ugliest in humanity, the most abominable fiends, the twisted and the damned, you can see I am cursed."

He ran a hand in front of his face, illuminating the folds of his skin with that golden light. For the first time, Eve felt a measure of sympathy for him, but it was fleeting. From what she knew he had always been a monster and had been given the face to look the part.

"But it is not for my sake that I come to you."

One of the Erinyes had turned from Gull to gaze down on Jezebel. The girl looked so very eager as the punisher, the purveyor of madness, reached down to stroke her hair and caress her face. The terrible, beautiful creature took a fistful of Jezebel's hair and pulled the girl toward her, turning back to Gull and dragging Jezebel behind her. The girl submitted willingly to this treatment, and Eve winced.

What did you ever do, she thought, *that you feel you deserve this?*

"You appeal to us for her?" asked the Fury who had spoken.

Gull shook his head. "The girl's my . . . ally." He nodded toward Hawkins. "As is the gentleman. They are in my service. It's not for either of them that I've come to you, but for the heart of my heart, for one whose curse is even graver than my own. To heal her, I must have you weep, Eumenides. I must have the tears of the Furies."

The sister who held his throat with her whip tightened it

so that the barbs cut him, and Gull hissed in chorus with the serpents in her hair.

"We weep for all sinners, even as we punish them. The dead and damned come to us, and we give them what they have longed for. Correction. Pain. Retribution."

Eve remembered the tales of the Erinyes. As long as there were sinners in the world, it was supposed that they could not be banished . . . and yet here they were, banished along with all the other relics of Olympian myth, hidden away to survive the birth of a New Age. Even so, they were terrible, and Gull was a fool to think he could coerce them.

Unless . . . coercion was unnecessary.

"Fuck." Eve hung her head again, understanding at last. So she did not see Gull respond, but she heard his every word.

"The goddess Athena placed a curse upon my love, upon Medusa," the mage said, his deep voice creeping up Eve's spine. "Only your forgiveness will release her. In exchange for that forgiveness, for your tears, I offer you the greatest prize the Third Age of Man has to offer. I bring you the woman who damned the entire human race twice over, who stained Adam's bloodline with sin, who laid down with demons. Give me what I desire, and you shall have the ultimate sinner to put to the lash."

The hesitation before the Erinyes spoke was eternal damnation all its own. When they spoke, it was all three, in unison.

"Eve," they said, and there was pleasure in their voices.

Then the one who had been speaking with Gull continued. *"There is a bargain to be struck. But not here. Enter our home, the caverns of the damned, the halls of torment. There, we will speak of Gorgons."*

The whip cracked the air.

Eve lurched to her feet, struggling against Gull's control. Her muscles were slow and pained, but they obeyed, and she staggered away. The whip caught her around the neck, barbs digging into flesh, and the punisher pulled Eve off her feet.

The creature turned, dead souls crying out in unending sorrow from the fabric of her cloaks, and dragged Eve behind her, tearing out the vampire's throat as the Erinyes returned to their home.

Inside the gigantic corpse of the lord of the Underworld.

I C Y currents tugged at Ceridwen, wrapping her in a shroud of her own cloak. For just a moment—or perhaps a handful of moments, not enough to steal her life—she had lost consciousness in the water. The Styx raged around her, pulling at her limbs, caressing her, as though the spirits of the river were fighting one another to claim her.

She awoke choking, drowning, but then her violet eyes snapped open, and she flailed her arms, kicked her legs, righting herself in the water. Ceridwen closed her mouth and swallowed the water that was in her throat, mind racing, blackness threatening the edges of her thoughts as her lungs cried for breath.

Arthur.

That was her only thought.

Her hands were empty, so she thrust out her right hand, and bright orange fire—unaffected by the river's rush—arced from her fingers. This was no ordinary fire. It traveled through the water, darting in a lightning path, until it found her broken elemental staff being dragged along the river bottom by the current. Tendrils of sorcerous fire gripped the staff and drew it to her. Before it even reached her grip she was gazing around her in the water again, fighting the current, swimming.

Scylla and Charybdis hated Arthur. In its way, the river hated him as well. Ceridwen had no idea how Gull had accomplished this, but that was a question for later. For now, she could use it. In the past when she had traveled from Faerie to the Blight, it had taken time for her to adjust. But despite the corruption of the human world, its soil and air, its water and vegetation, were not so different from Faerie.

The Underworld was something else entirely. Dark and twisted, things grew that should have been dead. Lifeless, terrible things that somehow thrived. Her bond with the elements had withered upon her descent into this nether realm, but she had become acclimated to it. It sickened her, yet now she embraced it, for it was her only hope.

If the River Styx hated Arthur, and she could touch the river, commune with it . . .

Ceridwen stopped fighting the current, let herself be swept by it. The water was all around her, and now her body shimmered with a dusky light. The river hated Arthur, which meant it was aware of his presence . . . she touched the water, and she searched for him.

There. At the riverbank, but deep beneath the surface, dragged along the edge and dashed against rock and black earth. Arthur.

The fire that glowed within the icy sphere atop her staff flared once. Ceridwen had hesitated to connect too fully with this world, but now she mustered all of her elemental magick. The current changed direction around her, the water grasping her and propelling her toward the riverbank. She rose to the surface, and she burst up into the air to take several deep breaths, caught a glimpse of the strange sky, the cavern ceiling so high it could not be seen in the gloom.

Then she willed the river to drag her under again. It curled around her, swept her to where Arthur drifted. She saw him kick feebly, trying to swim to the surface. Weak, but he was alive. His hands reached upward, and she grabbed his wrists, and though the river hated him, she forced the water to propel them both upward.

The Styx erupted in a spout of water that tossed them onto the riverbank. Ceridwen struck the ground hard, and for a moment she could only lay there, catching her breath. Her chest hurt as if there was something broken inside, and she prayed it was only her need for air. She heard Arthur coughing beside her with a wheezy rasp, but he was alive.

She turned her head, forced herself onto her hands and

knees and crawled to him. Finally she knelt and put a hand on his back as he caught his breath, and then he fell into her arms and she held him, simply held him, the way they had done so very long ago, when it hadn't taken the threat of death to make them see what they were to each other.

"Ceri . . ." he began.

"Sssh, no, Arthur." She pushed damp locks of hair away from his forehead so that she could kiss him there.

Then she stiffened and turned toward the River Styx. Her people were known for their passions in love and war, but not for their sense of family. Nevertheless, they were fiercely loyal, and she had been ingrained with that loyalty all of her life.

Arthur saw her alarm, and then his eyes mirrored her own concern. He sat up painfully, and they rose side by side.

"Danny?" he said.

Ceridwen shook her head. "I . . . I didn't see him. I could only think of you, and . . . the river let me find you. Gull did something, but . . . I'm not even sure if I could—"

Then she was moving, running toward the water's edge. She had to try at least to locate Danny Ferrick. The boy had sacrificed himself trying to save them. Ceridwen could do no less if there was a chance he might still be alive.

"Ceri, wait!" Arthur shouted. She turned to see him pointing back up the river. "Look!"

Out on the rushing river a section of the water was white with the undulations beneath. She had no time to act before the Styx erupted and the sea monster, Scylla, shot up from its flow, letting loose with a shriek that caused her to clap her hands over her ears and stagger backward. It swayed and rocked in the air, shaking and continuing to shriek as its heads swung about.

Then it spotted Ceridwen and Arthur on the bank. It reared up, whipping back and forth in a frenzy, maddened with rage.

Arthur came up beside her and raised his hands. Ceridwen lifted her staff, but she knew that they were both depleted. She wondered if they would be able to summon enough energy to destroy the monstrosity.

One final time Scylla shrieked.

Its belly swelled, inflating quickly. The thing's jaws opened, but this time its scream was of silent agony. Scylla's flesh tore, ripped open from within, and a gore-covered figure emerged from its viscera.

Danny Ferrick leaped into the river and hit the water with a splash only seconds before Scylla toppled in after him. Unmoving, the giant beast floated half above and half below the water, and the current began to drag it away.

When Danny climbed from the water, Ceridwen and Arthur ran to him. He was hunched over, unsmiling, horns gleaming wet, and his eyes glowed a perilous red. The boy had never looked more like a demon. There was so much of Hell in his eyes that they stopped a few steps away, regarding him warily.

"Oh, man," Danny said, shaking his head and then reaching up to cover his face. "That just totally sucked."

Ceridwen smiled and went to him, pulling him into her embrace.

"Thank you," she said.

Danny shrugged, wildness in his eyes. "Any time. This is why we're here, right? All in all, I'd rather be watching TV. But if we don't do the dirty work, there won't be any TV. So, I figure, we do what we've gotta do."

Arthur clapped a hand on the boy's shoulder, a bemused smile on his face. "So, you're fighting monsters and traversing the netherworld to make the world safe for television?"

"Pretty much."

"Well," Conan Doyle said, "as long as you have your priorities straight."

15

THEIR time in the Underworld had been a parade of the astonishing, a mind-boggling series of sights and experiences unlike any they had previously experienced. Conan Doyle had come to believe he had grown numb to it, that there was nothing left that could surprise him. Now, standing on a hill of bones, gazing down on the sprawling corpse of Hades, the mage realized how wrong he had been.

"Y'know what?" Danny asked beside him, breathing through his mouth to avoid the horrendous stench of decay that permeated the air. "I've had enough. I'm going home."

Ceridwen moved up next to the boy and placed a comforting arm about his shoulders. Conan Doyle knew the Fey were sensitive to the emotional states of others. She could feel Danny's turmoil and was attempting to calm him. That was good, for he himself had no time for such mollycoddling. One of his Menagerie was in grave danger, and he would move Heaven, Earth, and the Underworld itself to get her back.

"You don't mean that," Conan Doyle said, as he started down the slope toward the enormous corpse. "What about Eve? Do you want to leave her here?"

"Eve can handle herself," Danny replied, but Conan Doyle could hear little conviction in his tone.

He stopped his descent and turned to look at Danny and Ceridwen, who were still standing on the crest of the hill of bones. "But she will not have to, for we are going to assist her."

Danny shook his horned head. "No way. I can't do it anymore, it's just too much." He gestured toward the body of Hades in the black soil valley below. "Do you see that?" he asked, his voice growing higher with panic. "It's a giant fucking dead guy!"

The boy turned, and for a moment Conan Doyle thought he was about to walk away, but he spun around to reiterate his point. "It's been one thing after another since coming here—since hooking up with you."

"And you've become a welcome part of our motley tribe," Ceridwen said, as she calmly stroked the back of his head.

Danny quickly stepped away from her touch. "I'm sorry, I just can't."

There was a tremble in the boy's voice, and Conan Doyle was certain that he was about to cry. *This will not do, not at all.*

"You asked for this, boy," he said coldly. "You *begged* to be a part of it."

The boy squatted and buried his face in his hands. "I know, I know, and there's a part of me that's starting to get used to it." Danny laughed, raising his head. There were tears in his yellow eyes. "Can you believe that? I'm sixteen years old, and I'm starting to get used to this shit. When we're in the middle of it, the blood and monsters and shit, there's a part of me that even likes it. Do you have any idea how much that scares me?"

"Get hold of yourself, Daniel," Conan Doyle snapped. "Are you not part of my team, of my Menagerie?"

Danny wiped his nose with the back of his hand. "It's just that . . . I was inside the belly of a fucking sea monster . . .

and now this." He again gestured to the corpse that filled the valley below, the remains of a god. "I just don't know if—"

"Damn you, boy! Answer the question!" Conan Doyle bellowed. "Are you not a part of my Menagerie?"

The young demon looked as though he'd been struck, rocking back slightly on his haunches, and then his expression began to change. Conan Doyle recognized the anger, which was exactly the response he was hoping to get.

"Did you hear me, Daniel Ferrick?" he continued. "Or was my question lost in the sound of your pathetic blubbering?"

The youth rose to his feet, and Conan Doyle could have sworn he saw a flicker of crimson flame erupt from his eyes.

"No, I heard you just fine," Danny growled. "And, yes, I am part of your fucking Menagerie."

"Excellent," Conan Doyle said, reaching up to casually stroke his mustache. "Now follow. We'll see this through. Eve would sacrifice immortal life for any of us. You've never served in the military, Daniel, but still you should understand. We don't leave one of our own behind. Not ever." The mage turned and continued down the hill, off of the bone-strewn hill and onto the fine black soil of the valley.

Danny pushed past him, quickening his step. "What're we waiting for?" he growled. "The sooner we find Eve, the faster we can get out of here."

Ceridwen fell into stride beside Conan Doyle, one hand raised, stirring the wind so that the air, thick with the stench of decay, was more breathable. He had noticed that after the shattering of her elemental staff, she had somehow repaired it using the dark, corrupt wood of the Underworld. She had summoned the roots and made the trees do her bidding in building a raft for them to cross the Styx, and it was clear she had established a rapport with the elements of this place.

"Are you two coming?" the demon boy called.

"We're right behind you," Conan Doyle said, taking Ceridwen's arm. "Every step of the way."

•   •   •

CERIDWEN stood before the body of the fallen god and marveled at its enormity. From inside the great, decaying corpse there came faint sounds of life. Her gaze traveled over the incredible sight of the dead giant, rotting remains whose breadth was greater than all but the largest villages of Faerie.

Conan Doyle stood on her left, Danny on her right, all of them awed into silence until the demon boy shook his head, swore under his breath, and began to utter a mad little laugh.

"What do you think happened to him?" Danny asked. "By the looks of his throat, I'm guessing shaving accident."

She ought to have been reassured that the boy's twisted sense of humor had returned, but there was that lunatic edge to it that only made Ceridwen more concerned for him. She gazed down at the dark, powdery earth beneath her feet, then knelt and pushed the tips of her fingers into the tainted soil, gasping at the images flooding her mind. Conan Doyle joined her, and she took hold of his proffered hand as she tried to sort through the tainted memories of earth.

"Hades took his own life," she said, withdrawing her hand from the soil. She wiped her fingers on the hem of her cloak. "He knew it was only a matter of time before they were forgotten, and without the memory of the mortal world, they would cease to be." The very ground was saturated with the melancholy of the gods, and it threatened to overwhelm her. "The constant thought of it drove Hades mad, and he slit his own throat with a dagger that was a gift to him from his beloved Persephone."

"I'd slit my throat if I had to live here, too," Danny muttered to himself, still gazing in disbelief at the remains of the god.

Conan Doyle still held Ceridwen's hand and gave it a gentle squeeze. "And Eve? Can you sense anything of her?"

Ceridwen nodded, dredging up that particular piece of imagery from the countless others shown to her. She saw the hideous Gull and his followers, and she saw Eve, kneeling before the vengeful Furies. "Yes, they were here," she gasped. "As were the Erinyes. They've all gone inside."

She turned her gaze to one of the many ragged, rotting holes in the corpse of Hades, where strange, mournful sounds continued to waft out from within. *They live there,* she thought. *Not only the Furies, but others as well. The dead. The damned.* The gigantic corpse was like a city of death.

Danny only laughed. "We're going *in there*? Of course we are!"

T HE rotting flesh of the god was stiff with rigor, but tore with enough pressure, releasing the nauseating stink of decay. Conan Doyle was surprised to find how simple it was to climb Hades' corpse. Only the stench was a deterrent. They scaled the mountainous corpse to one of the larger gashes at the rib cage and slipped inside, walking on wounded flesh that seemed to have moved from putrefaction to petrification. Inside, the corpse was so dry it seemed almost mummified.

Conan Doyle led them within and found that pathways had been constructed of repurposed flesh and bone. There were chambers and tunnels, and quickly enough they found a makeshift bridge fashioned out of a rib bone. Conan Doyle crossed that bridge, and the others quickly followed. It was like they had entered another world. Within the corpse it was dark, but what looked to be stars twinkled from the ceiling above, suspended in a velvety black sky, illuminating the strange landscape with the faint hint of twilight.

"They can't be stars," Danny said, squinting up at the ceiling. "We're inside a body . . ."

The demon boy's voice trailed off, arousing Conan Doyle's curiosity. "What is it, Danny?" he asked, looking up as well, but unable to penetrate the inky black.

Ceridwen raised her hand, blue-green light springing to

life at her fingers as she attempted to illuminate the darkness above, but it was impenetrable.

"Those aren't stars," Danny said with a slow shake of his head. "They're eyes."

Conan Doyle squinted, but it was obvious that the youth's recent demonic metamorphosis had enhanced his night vision, for as much as he wanted to, he could still see nothing.

"The entire roof, or whatever it is . . . it's covered in bodies, thousands of bodies, and they're watching us." Danny shuddered, looking quickly away.

"The spirits of those being punished by the Furies," Ceridwen said thoughtfully. "I saw it when I was tethered to the soil. The Erinyes built their lair here, transformed Hades' remains into a palace of suffering for those condemned to their ministrations."

Danny looked up at the ceiling again, unable to take his eyes from it. "It's . . . it's horrible," he whispered. "Their mouths are all moving—they're reaching out for somebody to help them." He sounded very young.

Conan Doyle put a hand on the boy's shoulder. "There's nothing we can do for those poor souls now. They're the ghosts of another age. But we can prevent Eve from sharing their fate."

This seemed to rally the boy's resolve, and they forged ahead, deeper into the body of the fallen god, the eyes of the damned lighting their way. There were strange formations of what first appeared to be rock on either side of the path they traveled. Upon closer examination, Conan Doyle discovered that it was not rock at all, but the ossified remains of what could only have once been other gods. They were huddled close, wearing masks of sadness and misery, draped over one another as if they had been commiserating when the end finally arrived. Minor deities and demigods, dressed in tarnished armor and wielding pitted swords and axes. They had inhabited the corpse of Hades at some point, who knew how many millennia before, and had died there, forgotten. Dozens of them. Hundreds.

The Children of Olympus.

And yet Conan Doyle could not help wondering what had happened to the others. Where were Zeus and Athena and Poseidon and their kin, the key figures of Greek mythology? Surely they were not these withered corpses whose remains had merged with the bones and dead flesh of Hades.

"This is where they fled," Ceridwen said, interrupting his musing as she reached out to brush her fingers across the remains of a dead god. She gasped, pulling her hand quickly away. "How horrible," she whispered, clutching the hand to her breast. "They are still alive—a spark of life still exists within these petrified shells."

"Come away," Conan Doyle said, taking her by the arm and leading her back onto the path. "They are echoes of the distant past. Relics. Their fate cannot be undone."

The demon boy hushed them, then, and Conan Doyle turned to see that he had moved ahead several yards. He was crouched with his head cocked, listening. When the mage and Ceridwen went to stand with him, they heard faint voices chanting in ritual, the words indistinguishable but growing louder.

They began to follow the voices. As they walked, the ground beneath their feet became soft and yielding, but not from rot, like the outer flesh of the corpse. It was as though they were walking across a carpet of thick moss. Conan Doyle wondered about it, but his musings were cut short as they reached a new passage. The sounds of voices were louder now, and he could distinguish that of Nigel Gull from the others. The sorcerer was pleading, begging in song that his petition be granted. The other voices, women's voices, made the hair at the back of Doyle's neck stand on end, and an icy chill run up and down his spine.

The fleshy passage opened up onto a ledge that looked out over an enormous chamber of dark, thickly muscled walls.

"The heart of Hades," Conan Doyle whispered to his companions, marveling at the sight.

The three knelt and carefully peered over the edge.

Below them Nigel Gull stood before three terrible creatures that could only have been the Furies. Hawkins and Jezebel knelt behind him in reverence to the sisters, their heads bowed, as if to look upon the Erinyes was to somehow incite their wrath. Eve stood obediently at Gull's side, the lash of one of the Erinyes wrapped around her throat like a leash. The twisted mage was using the voice he had stolen, the voice of Orpheus, to entice the sisters of night.

Conan Doyle felt Danny's hand tighten on his arm as they watched what was unfolding below. It was exactly as he had feared; Gull was giving Eve to the Furies, but for what he did not know. The hideous thing whose lash was wound about Eve's throat yanked upon the whip, pulling her violently to the ground. The Erinyes converged upon their prize, their pale, spidery hands fluttering excitedly about her prostrate form.

"Will you grant me my heartfelt plea, most revered Eumenides?" Gull sang out in a voice not his own.

Danny leaned close and whispered in Conan Doyle's ear. "We have to do something." The boy's grip on his arm grew harder. "We have to do something *now*."

Conan Doyle studied the scene below them. They could interrupt the ceremony, but then the mystery of Gull's request would not have been revealed.

And he needed to know. He needed to know what could drive a man to this.

"WILL you grant my plea, revered Eumenides?" Gull sang to the sisters of suffering.

The Erinyes were not an easy lot to read, and Gull wasn't sure how they would respond, but by the way they hovered around the vampire, he knew that his offer was at least tempting.

"It has been too long since last we punished a sinner such as this," one of the Furies proclaimed, leaning forward to sniff at Eve's hair, as one would take in the scent of an especially delicious meal.

"And long has the daughter of Phorcys and Keto suffered for her slight against the goddess Athena," said another of the three, her robes—made from the souls of the tortured— flowing eerily about her.

The Fury whose whip entwined the vampire's throat looked down upon her captive with eyes ripe with blood. *"You have done much to deserve punishment, lamia,"* she said, pulling Eve closer. *"Do you wish to stay with us? Do you wish to repent the sins you have perpetrated upon the Third Age of Man?"*

Eve looked up into the face of the Fury and smiled defiantly. "Can I have my own room?" she asked, and Gull cringed at her impertinence.

The sister of darkness smiled, seemingly unfazed by her lack of respect. *"I shall receive much gratification from your suffering,"* the Fury said as she bent forward to lay a gentle kiss upon the vampire's head.

"Tisiphone," she said, never taking her bloody orbs from her prize, *"give the heartsick magician what he so desperately desires."*

Gull felt his heart leap within his chest. His prayers had been answered at last. All that he had done in the name of love, all the lies and betrayals—it hadn't been for naught.

One of the Furies—Tisiphone—slowly glided toward him. *"In what shall you contain this valuable gift?"* she asked, hands as pale as alabaster folded delicately before her.

For a moment Gull was so overcome with gratitude that he did not understand the question.

"In what will you carry the tears of a Fury?" she screeched, infuriated by his silence.

His hands quickly went to his pocket, and he pulled out a glass vial, presenting it to Tisiphone.

"Open it," she commanded, and he immediately removed the stopper.

Tisiphone brought one of her long fingers up to her face, and with the nail, she poked at the bloody orb engorging the eye socket, enticing it to weep a single tear of crimson. Gull was there to catch the drop of blood, trapping it within the glass vial. The other Erinyes did the same, each in turn crying a lone tear for the sorcerer as payment for what he had brought to them.

"Would you like me to contribute to that?" Eve asked, still on her knees before the sisters. "I haven't taken a piss since getting to this fucking place."

Gull forced a smile as he gently pushed the stopper into the opening of the vial. "Thank you, but no," he replied. "I believe you've done more than enough for me."

He could not take his eyes from the container's contents, holding up his prize for all to see. He'd never experienced such elation before.

But the feeling was short lived.

"Nigel Gull!" thundered a voice from somewhere above, a voice he knew only too well.

"We have come for our friend," Arthur Conan Doyle proclaimed.

Gull watched as the Erinyes encircled their newest prize, their bloody eyes searching the chamber for these newly arrived enemies.

"By all means, Arthur," Gull replied, a twisted smile spreading across his malformed features. "Come down and take her."

THAT'S new, Eve thought, turning her head to watch as her allies leaped down into the chamber from a ledge somewhere above. It looked as though they were riding on a current of air. *Some hocus-pocus whipped up by Ceridwen,* she imagined.

The cavalry had arrived, but at that moment, with her

throat entwined with the barbed lash of Alekto, Eve had started to entertain the notion that perhaps this really was what she deserved. Kneeling before the Daughters of Night, she remembered the sins she had perpetrated upon the Third Age of Man and wondered if the punishment meted out by the Erinyes, or any higher authority, would ever be enough to absolve her. She doubted it, but was certain that the sisters were willing to give it a try.

Her past sifted through her memory, and she saw all of the sins she had to atone for, the betrayals and the debasements, the murders and the corruptions of the innocent. Eve had yearned for redemption so long that it no longer mattered if she achieved it. It was the quest that was her journey. Now, though, the recollections of her sins haunted her so profoundly that they sapped her strength.

As Conan Doyle strode toward Eve and her captors across the heart of Hades, she gazed up at him reluctantly, knowing he could never understand the part of her that wanted to surrender. Despite the Furies, Conan Doyle was undaunted, and he approached with his head high, Fey sorceress and demon changeling flanking him. The Furies closed ranks around her, protecting their latest acquisition from these would-be rescuers, whom they must have considered thieves.

"You're too late, Arthur," Gull called. "What's done is done. Eve is no longer your concern. She belongs to the Furies now."

Conan Doyle turned his attention briefly to the deformed mage, his eyes blazing with a suppressed fury. "She belongs to no one, you fool," he said through gritted teeth. "And she was most certainly not your property to trade away. I assure you, we will deal with that grievous error of judgment soon enough."

He looked back to the Furies and bowed his head in reverence. Danny and Ceridwen did the same. "But now I must speak with the Daughters of the Earth and Darkness."

Eve tried to stand, but the barbed whip wrapped about

her throat grew tighter, biting deeply, and she felt a fresh flow of blood cascade down her neck as she again dropped to her knees.

"There is nothing to say," Alekto declared. *"A contract was established, a transaction made. This sinner is our property now, to punish as we see fit."*

The other sisters nodded their agreement, the snakes that swam through the tresses of their hair hissing in agitation.

"Is there nothing we can do to change your mind?" Conan Doyle asked. There was sadness and sincerity in his voice, and Eve wished that she could muster the strength to tell him that she wasn't worth it, that she deserved to be left to their ministrations.

"A trade, perhaps?" he suggested. "Something that you might find of equal value and interest."

There was a flurry of movement as Gull surged toward the sisters. Eve saw a flicker of fear in his eyes.

"Don't listen to him," the dark mage warned. "He is not to be trusted."

All three Furies moved with terrible swiftness and precision, lashing out at Gull with their whips. Eve crumbled to the ground as Alekto's whip pulled away from her throat, tearing flesh, spilling more blood. The sisters attacked Gull, and the mage was driven to his knees, raising his hands to protect his malformed features. Each blow drew blood, but Gull did not cry out.

"We have heard enough from you, magician," the Furies said in unison, whips writhing menacingly on the ground only inches from the scarred and bleeding Gull. *"We will now hear what this other has to offer."*

With the touch of the Erinys's whip gone from her throat, Eve felt her strength returning, but the remembrances of sins that had blurred with the passage of time were still as fresh and raw as newly opened wounds. It was as if they had been committed only yesterday. Yet now her guilt and despair were fading. She had dedicated herself to making reparations for her sins, and yet the touch of Alekto's lash had brought all of her doubts and self-loathing to the surface. Rage began to burn away her regret and her longing for punishment.

Eve steeled herself, wondering what Conan Doyle was up to. The mage stood as though orating before a Victorian audience, holding the lapels of his coat with self-importance. It was a show, like the best snake oil salesmen had put on in their day.

"I propose that in exchange for our friend," the mage said. "We will leave the Underworld post haste, and you need never worry about us again."

Eve snarled, one corner of her mouth ticking up in amusement. She saw the Furies' confusion, the lashes of their whips writhing about on the floor of the chamber like the tails of angry tigers.

Tisiphone, who seemed to speak for the others when they weren't all speaking, slunk nearer to Conan Doyle and eyed him and his companions closely. Her talons hooked into claws. *"And how would we benefit from this barter?"*

Eve climbed to her feet, while Conan Doyle adjusted the sleeves of his jacket, as always, making himself presentable even in the most daunting of situations. Part of the show.

The sisters were distracted by his words and his manner and no longer noticed her.

To their peril.

"If you give me what I want," Conan Doyle explained. "There will be no reason for us to bring your rather gruesome domicile down around your ears."

And with those words, the mage nodded to Ceridwen, and both he and the Fey sorceress raised their hands into fists, blazing with magic, uncast spells and deadly enchantments. Gull called out a warning. Hawkins and Jezebel seemed at a loss, realizing they ought to do something but too overwhelmed to act.

"Do you understand this benefit now, sisters?" Conan Doyle asked as he extended his arms, bathing the interior walls of Hades' heart in eerie, dancing shadows.

"You dare threaten us in our lair?" Megaera shrieked.

The air crackled with the tension of impending violence, and Eve drank it in. Ever since she had been at Gull's mercy she had nurtured fantasies of vengeance, of wanton bloodshed and savagery the likes of which she had not indulged in for far too long. The guilt the Furies had wrought in her had stung her deeply, had torn open the oldest wounds in the world. And beneath her rage and her lust for revenge was the specter of her bloodlust. Eve was a vampire, the mother of all such creatures, and it had been far too long since she had satiated her hunger.

For once, she let the hunger and hatred take over. With a throaty growl, Eve sprang at Tisiphone, knocking aside her sisters. Fingers tearing at the creature's robes, at fabric woven from the souls of the tormented, Eve spun Tisiphone around to face her. A look of genuine surprise appeared on the Fury's face as Eve stared into her blood-swollen orbs.

"You picked the wrong pet, bitch," she growled, feeling her fangs slide out, razor sharp. "I'm nobody's doggy."

Eve hauled Tisiphone off the ground, rage and blood thirst driving her to madness. "This is for helping me remember what a vicious cunt I've been." And she brought her mouth down to the throat of the Fury, fangs plunging deeply into pale, alabaster flesh that reeked so pungently of misery.

Tisiphone wailed as she was driven to the ground by the ferocity of Eve's attack, an unearthly shriek of agony that caused the souls in her cloak to disperse, screaming themselves, ghosts fluttering like bats into the shadowed eaves of Hades' heart.

Conan Doyle had witnessed Eve's savagery countless times in their long relationship, often during the insanity of battle, but it never ceased to disturb him. The Erinys flailed beneath Eve's attack, her whip lashing repeatedly, tearing Eve's coat to shreds and scoring the flesh beneath, but to no avail. Eve rode the bucking myth, mouth firmly attached to her victim's throat.

The dying scream of the Fury was horrible, becoming

nearly unbearable as her remaining sisters joined in, filling the cavern with ear-splitting cries of shared anguish.

Then the chamber itself seemed to react, the ground starting to undulate as if something long dormant had been awakened by the sisters' plaintive wails.

Danny looked at Conan Doyle, panic in his eyes. "I don't even want to know."

The walls began to tremble. They had been dry, flaking, and chalky, but now they seemed damp and soft, very much like the floor. Conan Doyle was reminded of anatomy lessons at the University of Edinburgh and the first time he had seen the exposed musculature of a cadaver he would be dissecting. Hades' heart was the size of a cathedral, but now it became living muscle. It began to pulsate, emitting a rhythmic, near-deafening throb.

The heart of Hades had been made to beat again.

Ceridwen gripped his arm as the floor thrummed beneath their feet. Conan Doyle gazed across the chamber at Gull. He had scrambled away from the Furies and was consulting silently with Hawkins even as he cradled Jezebel in his arms. She had all but fainted, tears streaming down her face, red hair filthy and matted. The girl was falling apart. Hawkins was almost there himself from the look of it. The dapper Englishman was not so dapper now, his eyes wild as he spoke to Gull. For his part, the misshapen mage seemed at a loss for once in his godforsaken life, panic etched upon his grotesque features.

Obviously, whatever was happening now was not in any way part of Nigel's game plan.

"Come," Conan Doyle said, grabbing Ceridwen by the arm. The sorceress—his love—had been watching the surviving Furies, sickly green magick dancing from her fingertips. But the time for fighting was over. The time for retreat had arrived.

"Danny!" he snapped, gesturing to the demon boy, who was staring around at the beating heart of Hades with the same wild light he'd had in his eyes after he had killed

Scylla. He squatted on his haunches, ready to move. At the sound of his name, he looked up, alert.

"We came for Eve. Let's get her and go."

"That's the smartest thing you've said since I met you," the boy snarled.

Eve was still crouched over her prey.

Danny hurried toward her across the undulating floor of Hades's heart, but as the demon boy reached for her, she growled and batted his hand away with a bloody claw. She did not want her feast interrupted.

"Damn it! If I was carrying a rolled newspaper I'd slap you across the nose," Conan Doyle snapped. He and Ceridwen ran to Eve. The sorceress pulled the demon boy away and Conan Doyle himself let loose a tendril of crimson magick that swirled around Eve and pulled her from her victim. "Take your damnable head from the trough and let's go!"

Eve shook off his spell and landed on the pulsing ground several feet from her prey, fangs bared, her mouth and chin stained with gore. There was murder in her eyes, and Conan Doyle summoned a spell of defense in his thoughts, just in case.

"We're going now, Eve."

At first he wasn't sure if she even understood his words, but then he saw a glimmer of humanity return to her eyes.

"What a fucking rush," Eve whispered, burying her face in her hands. "Never fed on the blood of a deity before." She looked up at Conan Doyle, her eyes wide and radiant with a strange inner light. Then she smiled and wiped the drying blood from her mouth with the back of her hand.

"Potent. *Way* potent."

"I can only imagine," Conan Doyle responded, but before he could say anything more the voice of Nigel Gull interrupted.

"Look what she's done!" he screamed, and Conan Doyle turned to see the twisted little mage pacing around the fleshy chamber as it undulated and pulsed. "You've ruined everything!"

Hawkins swore at Gull, trying to lead him to one of the hollow blood vessels that would take them out of there. Jezebel was once more standing on her own, but she was a pitiful waif, stumbling after him, silently pleading.

Eve started toward Gull, but Conan Doyle grabbed her arm. Her bloodlust was sated, and the violence was gone from her eyes. "Survival is our only concern at the moment," he said.

With one last, longing look at Gull, she nodded. "Let's go."

Ceridwen lifted a glowing hand to illuminate their path. "This way," she said.

All four of them paused as the surviving Erinyes moved to block their path.

"You will go nowhere," Alekto and Megaera moaned in unison.

Hawkins had fallen in behind them, with Gull leading a muttering Jezebel by the hand.

"Oh, this is just lovely," Hawkins muttered.

"What do we do?" Danny asked.

Conan Doyle held Ceridwen's hand tightly, preparing to destroy the Furies. But then Gull's bitter laughter filled the chamber.

"Oh, dear Arthur, you've bollixed it all up for me now, haven't you, mate? So simple, it was. A bargain, nothing more. And you had to interfere. You couldn't just do your part."

As he raved, Conan Doyle turned to see what had set him off. There they were, the seven of them—intruders all—in the midst of Hades' pulsing, stinking heart. But beyond Hawkins and Jezebel, beyond the cursing, twisted shape of Nigel Gull, there were other figures. And now he saw what had prompted the dark mage's new tirade.

Gull's eyes narrowed with hatred, and his nostrils widened, snorting like a stallion's. "If your damned nobility keeps me from Medusa, I'll have your heart, you bastard. I'll have your heart."

But no one was listening to Gull anymore. On one side they were blocked by the surviving Furies. And now other creatures entered Hades's heart through pulsing arteries, gaunt, skeletal beings adorned in fabulous armor stained black by the passage of millennia. Conan Doyle had seen these creatures before, scattered about within the corpse of Hades, but in a far less animated state. Something had awakened the lesser gods and goddesses of ancient Greece.

"Another time, Nigel," he rasped.

"What the fuck is going on now?" Eve snarled.

Ceridwen's violet eyes flashed with light. "At a guess? You slaughtered a myth, my friend. You spilled the blood of the Erinyes, and it has set Hades' heart to beating again . . . and roused the dead gods who had made this place their tomb."

"Zombie gods," Danny said with a shake of his head. "Well, shit, it was only a matter of time."

Their numbers continuing to grow, the dead gods shambled closer. Many brandished ancient weaponry: swords, spears, battle-axes, and knives.

Resigned to whatever came next, Conan Doyle smiled sidelong at Eve. "This is another fine mess you've gotten us into."

She grunted. Not quite a laugh, but it would do. "Wasn't something I planned."

Gull pushed Conan Doyle out of the way, sputtering angrily at Eve. "You murdered one of the Furies! What did you expect?"

Eve stared at the creatures coming toward them and cocked her head to one side. It reminded Conan Doyle of a dog he'd owned in his youth, and how it would often tilt its head upon hearing something that he himself could not.

"No," Eve replied, shaking her head. "They're not attacking because of what I did, they're attacking because they're afraid."

"Afraid?" Gull exclaimed. "What in the name of bloody Christ could the resurrected gods be—"

"They're afraid that we'll take the treasure hidden outside this chamber. Afraid that we'll steal the treasure of Olympus."

Conan Doyle looked at her quizzically, his hand slowly rising to stroke his mustache. The dead gods moved closer and he listened to their mournful groans.

"I drank the blood of a deity, boys," Eve said. "I know all kinds of shit about this place now."

"The treasure of Olympus," Conan Doyle repeated, as he dropped his hands to his sides, allowing the magick through him. "How interesting. Who knows what wondrous things can be found here?"

"Oh, yeah, fantastic," Eve drawled, glancing back and forth between Alekto and Megaera on one side and the resurrected god-corpses on the other. "Lot of good it'll do us. I'll settle for not dying, thanks."

Eve hissed at Alekto. The Fury cracked her whip almost as though she was trying to herd them toward the dead gods. Eve caught it in her hand, the barbs ripping her flesh even as she yanked it from Alekto's hand. The Fury snarled at her, and the two began to face off against one another.

"You'd better have something up your sleeve, Doyle," the vampire snarled. "We can kill these bitches, but we'd need a small army to fight the undead of Olympus."

Conan Doyle slowly reached into his pocket, searching for something he had nearly forgotten. "A small army you say." He pulled his hand from his pocket to reveal the teeth. The Hydra's teeth.

"I believe I have just the thing."

THE ancients attacked as one, a single wave of shambling necrotic flesh, archaic weaponry and furious cries of indignation. The two surviving Furies urged the legion of reanimated corpses to slay the usurpers—to make them permanent residents of this hellish realm.

Eve was the first into the fray, lunging into the dead warriors and tearing at them. She punched a fist through the chest of the first to come near her and tore off the head of a second. Through shared desperation, Ceridwen and Gull joined forces, conjuring a cloud of crackling energy hungry for the desiccated flesh of the dead. Inspired by Eve's wanton violence, Danny Ferrick threw himself into the fray, many a decomposing god falling before his savagery. Hawkins proved himself deadly in hand-to-hand combat, shattering bones and crushing skulls with nothing but his hands. The girl, Jezebel, seemed to come truly awake and alive when at last the nightmare was about to swallow them. Her childlike qualities evaporated, and only the weather witch remained. Lightning crackled within Hades' heart, shattering gods and burning what remained of them.

All of it was merely to buy Conan Doyle time to bring his plan to fruition.

He knelt and dug his fingers into the ground, tearing away gobs of bleeding muscle. One by one he pressed the Hydra's long, sharp teeth into the flesh of the lord of the Underworld's heart. The legend called for them to be planted in the earth, but in this place, here was the soil, here was the ground. With a prayer to gods long passed from this plane of existence, he stood back from his chore.

"What have you done, sorcerer?" Megaera screeched, dropping down upon him like a hungry bird of prey. She landed on his back, her claws about his throat.

Conan Doyle surged up from his crouch, spinning around in hopes of dislodging the loathsome creature from her perch. The Erinys held tight, her powerful legs locked around his waist as the grip on his neck continued to tighten. He heard the agitated hiss of the snakes that lived in her hair.

He spun to see the battle in the chamber, and his hopes sank. The number of resurrected gods was growing, the corpses streaming into the chamber in endless numbers. His compatriots had to be growing tired, their sorceries and brute strength starting to wane.

"I feel your despair and sup upon it with glee," the Fury

cackled in his ear as her grip upon his throat tightened even further. *"Surrender yourself to me—do not delay the inevitable. For what you and your companions have done, your suffering will last for eternity."*

Doyle felt his legs begin to weaken. *It cannot end this way.* A crude spell of conflagration leaped to the forefront of his thoughts, and he brought it forward, feeling white-hot fire begin to swirl and grow in the palm of his hand.

"Surrender," the Fury hissed as he dropped to his knees, borne down by her weight.

Conan Doyle reached up behind him and placed the ball of fire into the creature's matted locks. "Never," he wheezed, hearing the whooshing sound of dry, ancient hair igniting and feeling the hold on his neck lessen.

The Erinys screamed, beating at her blazing head. Serpents, their bodies afire and smoldering, leaped from their burning nest to land on the ground, startling Conan Doyle with their number. He was preparing another spell, something that would reduce the foul beast to ashes, when, from within her robes, she produced her whip, and with blinding speed, cracked the lash.

The barbed, leathery tendril wound around his still-constricted throat, closing his breathing passage off entirely. Images of the wrongs he had committed during his long life flooded his mind.

"So much to be punished for," the Fury said, her burned and blackened visage grinning at him down the length of the whip.

She yanked Conan Doyle viciously forward, and he again stumbled to his knees. Sins of the past clouded his mind, making it difficult for him to concentrate. He grabbed hold of the barbed length of whip, using the pain in his bleeding hands to clear his addled brain. She was dragging him toward her, the sounds of battle in the background accompaniment to his struggle, inspiring him to fight on.

"Come to me, sinner," she hissed hungrily.

There were snakes all around her feet, but he noticed

something else. In the area where he had planted the Hydra's teeth, the fleshy earth was moving, startling the snakes and making them slither away. A geyser of blood squirted upward, and from Hades' very flesh there grew a soldier, brandishing a sword that looked to be forged from jagged bone.

Megaera spun to face her new foe, its body glistening with the blood that now pumped through the heart of Hades. She cried out for help from Alekto, and from the gods that had been called forth. But it was too late. The Hydra soldier brought his jagged blade of bone down through the thick muscle of her neck, sending her head spinning through the air before dropping to the floor.

Conan Doyle pulled the whip from around his neck, watching as more of the gore-covered soldiers climbed up from the fleshy earth. One soldier for every tooth, he observed, watching as they helped one another emerge from their birthing place. Before long they stood before him, fifty blood-drenched representations of man, their features unformed, mere holes for eyes and slits for mouths. They clutched their weapons of bone, waiting for the one who called them to life to proclaim his wishes.

"Fight," Conan Doyle cried, pointing to the battle being waged across the chamber. "Destroy these forgotten gods!"

The soldiers of the Hydra's teeth surged obediently forward, an unsettling, inhuman cry of war escaping their unformed lips.

16

GULL cut a swath of death through the resurrected gods, destructive magick spewing from one malformed hand, the gun that he had used to slay Charon firing from the other. And still they came at him, these once fabulous beings that had looked upon man from Olympus, manipulating the young race for their own amusement.

An emaciated, eight-foot-tall creature covered in silvery scales surged toward Gull, wielding a trident of gold. *One of the offspring of Poseidon,* he thought. *How sad that beings once so revered have come to this.* Gull fired a single shot into the god's bearded face, and the flesh and bone and stringy hair collapsed inward and blew out the back of his head.

In the moment he had bought himself, Gull checked his inside coat pocket for his prize, the treasure whose acquisition had caused all of this insanity. The blood of the Furies was still there, still safe. He had to leave this place soon. His goddess, his love, awaited the cure for her affliction. Medusa would finally understand that his love for her knew no bounds.

Another god, this one clad in the skins of animals, attempted to decapitate him with an enormous club, but Gull would not oblige him. The club-wielding god died squealing, an entropy spell swirling about his once mighty form, consuming what remained of his flesh.

Everywhere the sorcerer looked there was ferocious battle, and the dead continued to stream into the chamber. From the teeth of the Hydra, Conan Doyle had managed to conjure the assistance of a small army, and it seemed that the blood-slick soldiers had managed to buy them all some time. But Gull knew the dead would soon overwhelm them again.

He would have none of that.

Again, he patted his breast pocket, feeling the glass vial safely nestled there, and decided that now was the time to take his leave. He felt a momentary pang of guilt for deserting those who had begrudgingly become his allies, but there was too much at stake for him.

Through the sea of conflict, Gull saw an exit in a wall of the fleshy chamber, throbbing and pulsing not twelve feet away. Holstering his gun, he spoke an ancient incantation that would clear a path to the door and surround him in a field of dark and terrible magick. Killing magick. The gods who attempted to stop him died screaming, their bodies exploding into flames on contact with the shimmering aura that now protected him. Gull smiled as he reached the throbbing door, chancing a final, quick look over his shoulder before leaving.

"Nigel?" he heard a squeaky voice, ragged and full of panic.

And then he saw her, Jezebel, her clothing torn and stained with blood. There was a sad, sweet smile on the girl's face as she made her way across the battlefield toward him. Bursts of lightning leaped from her fingers, striking down any who attempted to block her path. He was her salvation, her oasis in this terrible sea of madness and violence—it had been that way since they met.

Gull remembered when he first found the girl, fourteen, shivering and wet, sitting at a campsite in the Sequoia National Park surrounded by the bodies of her family. Jezebel hadn't wanted to go camping at all. She loved them, but hated them at the same time, like so many girls her age. Spoiled and temperamental, in a fit of rage she had whipped the elements into a fury to match her own, calling the lightning down upon her mother and father, burning them black, scorching the earth around them. Her brother—whom she had despised—she pummeled to death with a rain of massive hailstones, so that what was left of him was unrecognizable pulp.

Nigel Gull had felt the presence of magick and tracked it to that place. In the aftermath, Jezebel had been shattered by guilt, attempting to use her power to kill herself. Gull had seen the lightning flash, darting fingers of fire into the forest again and again in the same spot. When he had come upon her, he saw it strike her once, twice, a third time, with no idea how many times it had struck before he arrived. The girl was weeping, the lightning not harming her at all, arcing around her, tearing up the ground in a circle around her.

Jezebel had been a troubled child, but also a talented one. One with potential. Gull had gone to her, risking the lightning himself, and though she had at first shrunken back from his hideous visage, when he had pulled her into his arms and whispered to her that it was going to be all right, that they could never have understood her but that he could help, she had relaxed into his embrace and sobbed uncontrollably. Eventually she had fallen asleep in his arms, and he had carried her out of the forest to his car, leaving the corpses behind.

They had been together ever since.

Now the immolation field that surrounded him crackled and hummed as Gull watched Jezebel make her way toward him. Her hair was whipping wildly around her in a wind of her own devising, and there was a desolation in her eyes, a hopelessness he had not seen since he had first discovered her. The jeans and barely-there T-shirt she wore were streaked with filth and torn in places. She had many cuts, but the worst was a slash on her right side from which streaks of blood had spilled down to saturate the leg of her pants, blackening the denim.

"Nigel, wait for me," she called, desperate.

Gull had become her protector as well as her employer, her unique talents and childlike view of the world serving him well on many occasions. Jezebel had been a tremendous asset.

Now she was merely a hindrance.

He could not afford to have her draw attention to his departure. She called his name again, and he could see the tears streaming freely down her face. Gull opened his arms as if to welcome her into their loving embrace. Jezebel quickened her pace, nearly falling as she navigated her way over the piles of dead gods, of bones and armor, that littered the floor. Gull almost felt a pang of guilt as she at last reached him, hungry for his arms to be about her—protecting her as he had done from the start.

The twisted mage closed his eyes just as she touched the immolation shield that protected him. Jezebel was unable to scream as her lovely body was consumed by a searing flash of supernatural light. He opened his eyes again, the image of her at that moment before her demise burned onto his retinas. He would miss Jezebel, and when this quest was done, he would tell his beloved Medusa of her sacrifice. Perhaps then he would shed a tear for her passing, but now, there wasn't time for sentimentality.

The exit quivered wetly behind him, and he ducked his head as he departed the chamber through the orifice. The shield of devastation waned and was gone, his strength nearly depleted. He would have to find a place to rest soon.

It was dark inside the passage, the stink reminding him of the London charnel houses from his youth. Gull carefully felt along the passage, the moist wall of flesh beneath his hand thrumming with life, or at least what passed for living in this infernal place.

"Going somewhere, Gull?" asked a voice from behind him.

Gull stopped, whispering a spell to illuminate his hand, and turned to see who had addressed him. The demon boy lurked in the shadows, his eyes glinting yellow in the faint light thrown by Gull's hand.

"Ah, Daniel, I was following one of the Erinyes and—"

The boy surged toward him. "Don't give me any of your shit," he growled, and Gull saw that something dangled from the boy's clutches. A head; the boy was holding the decapitated head of one of the gods he'd battled.

"Don't you take that tone with me, boy," Gull began, taking a step back. A spell that would have solidified the air around the youngster, suffocating him, danced upon the mage's lips, but the demon child was faster.

Danny charged, lashing out with the severed head, catching Gull across the face and knocking him to the ground. Nigel fumbled inside his coat for his gun, but the boy moved with frightening speed and was suddenly perched atop him. The demon gathered up the front of Gull's coat in his clawed hands, pulling him close.

"I saw what you did to Jezebel," he said, giving him a shake, eyes ablaze and mouth twisted in disgust. "How could you do it?" he spat. "How could you do something like that to one of your own team?"

Gull was still groggy from the blow to his face. "It was nothing personal," he slurred, attempting to pull his wits together enough to summon a spell to allow him to escape from the demon boy's clutches. "Just a sad fact of the job we do. Everyone is expendable."

The youth snarled with indignation and slammed Nigel hard against the ground before pulling him close again.

"You killed her," he spat, and flecks of spittle flew from the youth's fanged mouth to dapple his cheek.

Gull nodded in understanding. "She was drawing attention. She drew yours, didn't she? I should have been quicker. Even had I taken her with me, she would have slowed me down."

"Fucking piece of shit, I should bite out your throat right now."

"I only did what your beloved Conan Doyle would have done if faced with a similar dilemma," Gull said. "Do you really think he wouldn't gladly sacrifice any of his Menagerie to get what he wants?"

"Mr. Doyle would never . . ." Daniel started, rearing back, but then stopped midsentence, as if something in Nigel's words struck a chord of truth.

"Oh, he would, lad," Gull continued, a smile creeping across his twisted features. "But you keep on believing him, if it makes it easier for you to sleep at night."

The boy went wild, leaping up to drag him to his feet. "I don't need to hear anymore of your bogus bullshit," he screamed.

Gull reacted, sensing his opportunity. He bellowed a spell of incineration, thrusting his already illuminated hand into the boy's face. He cried out, but his grip did not lessen. The smell of burning flesh filled the stagnant air of the passage.

"Nice one," the demon boy said, the skin of his right cheek charred to black. "As if I wasn't pretty enough already."

The youth moved behind him, gripping his neck and pushing the twisted mage back toward Hades' heart, and the battle that still raged within.

"Got a little something you need to do before you go," the changeling growled in his ear. "And it involves that beautiful singing voice of yours."

"And if I won't oblige you?" Gull asked defiantly.

The boy tightened the grip upon his neck, one of his clawed fingernails breaking the skin. Gull felt the tickling sensation of his own blood as it ran down the side of his neck to his shoulder.

"Then I'll eat your heart."

"Fine," Gull responded, allowing himself to be maneuvered toward the doorway. "I just needed to know where we stand."

THE blood of long-dead gods was rank in her mouth, but Eve was beyond caring. She sprang at one of the resurrected and buried her fangs in its throat. With a savage growl, she pulled her head back, pulling flesh and muscle away, her face bathed in gouts of foul, black blood. Again and again the vampire slaughtered these minor gods, the foot soldiers of Olympus, avoiding their swords, spears, and axes, feasting on their rancid flesh and foul-tasting lifestuff, but still it wasn't enough. The dead continued their incessant march into the chamber. From the blood of the Fury she had feasted on, Eve had learned the names of each and every one of them, gods and demigods alike, and knew their sins as well. At that moment, they all shared a goal—to protect the treasures of Olympus at any cost.

The creatures born from the teeth of the Hydra were proving very helpful. She and her companions would have fallen to the deluge of the dead much sooner if not for their assistance. Quickly, she looked about the chamber. Ceridwen seemed to be holding her own, manipulating the elements of the Underworld to combat their relentless enemy. She wondered how much longer the Fey could keep it up. That fine-looking son of a bitch, Nick Hawkins was holding his own, not that she gave a shit.

Danny was nowhere to be found. That worried her.

She slammed her fist through the tattered remnants of the rib cage of a goddess, even as the tall, majestic creature tried to reach for her face. Eve tore her spine out through her chest.

Conan Doyle appeared at her side, as she spun around to face other enemies. A quartet of armored corpses were attempting to surround him, but Conan Doyle was not so easily taken. He wielded a pitted, ancient sword he must have taken from one of the fallen, but it was infused with a strange green fire that caused the dead gods to explode when they were cut by the blade. One after the other, he destroyed them.

"Enjoying yourself, Eve?" he asked, wearily.

"Oh, yeah, this might be the best field trip yet," Eve snarled, clawing at a black-eyed, hulking figure, spilling its viscera to the ground. "And to think, we owe it all to your buddy, Gull, and his hard-on for Medusa."

Conan Doyle muttered something beneath his breath, and the soft, fleshy ground beneath their enemies' feet turned to a bubbling, viscous fluid, swallowing six of the groaning, hideous dead before returning to its solid state.

"Gull and Medusa?" Conan Doyle asked, turning to her, a look of astonishment upon his blood-spattered face.

Eve twisted the head of an ancient god completely around with a loud, wet pop, tearing it from its roots. She rode the corpse to the ground and sprang up once more to fall in beside Conan Doyle. "That's what this is all about. I figured you'd have sussed it out by now. Gull's in love with Medusa and wants the tears of the Furies as some kind of cure to lift her curse. Ain't love grand?"

Conan Doyle uttered a disgusted laugh. "Oh, that's simply priceless."

A shrieking god clad in tarnished armor forced his way past the children of the Hydra's teeth, coming toward Conan Doyle with his spear lowered. Still deep in thought, the sorcerer did not seem to notice, and Eve moved to intercept the attack.

"Watch your—" she began, but a powerful hand wrapped around her ankle, sending her sprawling to the gore-soaked ground. One of her recent victims, it seemed, was not quite dead.

From the ground she watched it all unfold in slow motion, the spear-wielding zombie making his way toward Conan Doyle, and he turned slowly, too slowly. The spear was poised for the mage's heart, and there didn't seem to be much that could be done to prevent it from finding its mark.

Then she heard it, rising above the din, a song as beautiful as any ever sung in her eternal lifetime. She watched in wonder as the resurrected god fell to his knees, spear clattering at Conan Doyle's feet.

The scene was repeated all around the chamber as the song lifted through the air. The gods who had been stirred to battle by the cries of the Erinyes fell to their knees, enraptured by the voice of Orpheus.

Eve knew who was responsible, but was surprised that he had the decency to come to their aid.

Hawkins, the worse for wear and looking far less dapper, let loose a raucous cheer. He lifted a bloody battle-axe above his head as he watched his master step back into the vast cathedral of Hades' heart. Eve almost began to believe that the spirit of camaraderie had taken hold of Gull, but the dark mage stumbled over one of the hundreds of bodies that littered the floor, and she caught sight of the demon boy behind him. At first she did not recognize the hellish visage as the boy she'd grown so fond of. Danny was changing. Quickly.

Eve felt a wave of relief. The boy reached down to haul Gull back to his feet. He pushed Gull toward them.

"It's a good thing we decided to bring him, eh Arthur?"

Conan Doyle was looking about the room, distracted.

"Arthur?" she asked, catching his eye.

"Do you feel it?" he asked.

She shook her head. "Feel what?"

"Something familiar," he snapped, moving away toward an exit from the chamber. "Hold things here while I investigate."

CONAN Doyle had felt it on at least two other occasions since arriving in the Underworld, a presence of power not native to this death realm, a presence that brought about a tingling sensation at the back of his neck, and the disquiet-ing feeling that they were being watched, maybe herded in a certain direction. At first he'd chalked it up to his own, quite active paranoia, but each time he caught wind of it, his suspicions grew. He felt it now here within the corpse of Hades, a familiar electricity that drew him away from the safety provided by the voice of Orpheus to a passage that would lead him to the unknown beyond the chamber.

The feeling grew as he cautiously walked the winding path, the song of Orpheus growing fainter in the distance. As he rounded a bend, Conan Doyle stopped, a spell of de-fense ready as he saw a figure lying on its side in the path ahead. Cautiously he approached, studying the crumpled figure for any sign of movement.

Conan Doyle squatted down beside the body and was startled to see that it was the last of the Erinyes. She was quite dead, as were the snakes that had attempted to flee their host upon her demise. He rolled her onto her back and watched as a ghostly wisp of smoke trailed up from the fist-sized hole burnt into her chest. Conan Doyle reached down and touched the edges of the blackened wound, letting some of ash collect on his finger. He brought it to his nose and sniffed. It smelled of power.

An ancient and terrible magick had been unleashed upon the last of the Furies, a spell that he was certain had not been performed by any in his company, or even the enemy. By the acrid aroma of the residue, Conan Doyle knew this was magick of a darker nature, wielded with the utmost pre-cision, that could only be attributed to a sorcerer with enough knowledge and strength to master such fearsome power—an arch mage of the highest order and discipline.

He could think of only one such mage.

The Fury had been struck down before the entrance into another chamber, the passage having been at one time cov-ered in a thick membranous skin. The covering had been torn, and as he approached the rip, Conan Doyle could hear the sounds of movement from within the chamber beyond.

Stretching the opening wider, Conan Doyle forced his way into the room behind and gasped at what he saw. It was a workshop of sorts, but nothing like the hot, clanging place where Squire worked his weapons. This was not a workplace for hobgoblins or even members of the human race. This was the workshop of a god, a massive chamber cluttered with the enormous tools of the metalsmith and laden with gigantic swords and armor that had been crafted for the true gods of Olympus. No sword was smaller than Conan Doyle himself.

The mage stepped farther into the vast chamber, marveling at the sights before him; an intricately carved golden throne obviously meant for a king, a winged chariot, beautiful jewelry spilling from countless metal chests, weapons, and armor. There was animal statuary so wondrously sculpted that he could have sworn they were living breathing things. Everywhere Conan Doyle looked there was something so fantastic that it nearly took his breath away.

Once upon a time, this workshop had been the pride of Olympus, its fires forming the treasure of the gods. But like the Furies, the craftsman himself had relocated to the corpse city within the remains of Hades.

This was the workshop of Hephaestus, god of fire and patron of craftsmen. Not the most powerful god in the Greek pantheon, but among the most respected and best loved.

There came the sound of clatter and the mutter of an angry voice from deeper in the workshop, and Conan Doyle remembered that he was not alone. Cautiously he made his way closer. He could feel it again in the air, the familiar crackle of primordial forces reminding him that he was in the presence of awesome power.

He came around the gigantic bronze sculpture of a bull to see the figure of man dressed in a charcoal gray suit, as if he'd come from a wedding or maybe even a funeral. The man's back was to him, but Conan Doyle knew immediately who it was. It was as if the magick was saying his name over and over again.

Sanguedolce. Sweetblood. Sweetblood the mage.

"Lorenzo," Conan Doyle called out, but the man did not respond.

He continued to rummage about, grumbling beneath his breath as he furiously searched for something among the creations of Hephaestus.

"I should have known you had something to do with this," Conan Doyle said, cautiously approaching the man. "Gull couldn't have come up with anything quite this elaborate on his own."

Sweetblood slowly glanced up from Hephaestus's hoard. "Ah, Arthur," the mage said with the slightest hint of a smile. "It's about time you got here. I was beginning to worry."

Conan Doyle seethed. All of this, from beginning to end, had been a part of some scheme of Sweetblood's. Even Gull, the poor, mad, twisted bastard, had been manipulated. Sanguedolce had been his teacher and mentor in the mystic arts until the man's sudden disappearance in the early part of the twentieth century. Conan Doyle and Gull had both been his students. They knew better than anyone that Sweetblood was the most powerful mage in the world, but he was also cunning.

"What have you done, Lorenzo? What is it that you so desire that you had to orchestrate all of this?"

Sanguedolce waved off his inquiry, continuing to search. "Give me a hand, Arthur. I need you to help me find something." He picked up a bronze helmet, studied it momentarily, and then tossed it over his shoulder where it noisily clattered to the ground. "You're good at that, aren't you? Finding things that don't wish to be found?"

Conan Doyle fumed.

Sweetblood had secreted himself away in a hidden chamber, gone missing by choice, creating a magical chrysalis that would mask his power while he was entombed within. He claimed to have discovered a creature of unimaginable evil and power, out in the farthest reaches of space. The DemoGorgon. The evil had sensed him, had located him, and Sanguedolce claimed that his power would act like a beacon, drawing the DemoGorgon to Earth by its hunger to feed upon Sanguedolce's innate magick. The sorcerer had hidden in hopes that that unimaginable evil making its way across the universe would lose interest if his power were not there to entice it.

For the safety of the world, and all those who lived upon it, Sanguedolce had not wanted to be found. But Conan Doyle had done just that, searched for his former mentor and located him. The chrysalis had been shattered in the process, the mage was released from his self-imposed confinement, and now, according to Sweetblood, his power was drawing the voracious DemoGorgon ever closer.

Conan Doyle knew Sweetblood blamed him, and he accepted some of the responsibility. But if the arrogant bastard had bothered to inform his students, they might have avoided the doom that now seemed inevitable.

"Since your revival, I've made frequent attempts to contact you, to discuss the impending threat and to apologize for my misunderstanding of your—"

"Misunderstanding?" Sanguedolce interrupted. "Is that what you're calling it?" He moved away from a wall stacked with crates overflowing with golden chains. "An evil the likes of which this world has never seen moving inexorably toward the planet because of your . . . *misunderstanding.*"

The last word rolled off his tongue with disdain.

Conan Doyle longed to lash out against the his former teacher, to remind him that his own pursuits of forbidden power had been what had captured the attentions of the DemoGorgon in the first place, but he held his tongue. Now was not the time.

"What are you searching for, Lorenzo?" he asked again.

Sweetblood had returned to his objective, carefully moving about the room, delving into every nook and cranny. "Use your head, Arthur. What in Heaven's name could I want here? With the DemoGorgon on the way, what might be useful to me if I want to create something, a weapon, anything that might prove useful in combating it?"

Conan Doyle understood. Even before his question had left his lips, he had come to the answer. The idea of it made him catch his breath. "You've come for the Forge of Hephaestus. All of this has been about the Forge, about fighting the DemoGorgon."

"Don't worry," Sanguedolce said, laughing softly. "It's not some sudden noble urge. When the evil comes, it is going to come after me first. If I can destroy it, the salvaging of this pitiable, corrupted world will be only a byproduct."

He focused now on a particular section of bare wall, oddly free from clutter. "What have we here?" he asked, laying the flat of his hand against the wall—all muscle and membrane—tilting his head to one side as if listening. "Yes," the arch mage hissed, stepping back away from the wall and extending his arms. "This might very well be it."

Sweetblood weaved a pattern in the air, and it took crackling, sparkling form. The pattern seared itself into the wall, and it fell away to dust, disintegrating in an instant. There was a room hidden on the other side.

"No secrets can remain hidden forever," Sanguedolce said with a twinkle in his icy blue eyes. "We've learned that, haven't we, Arthur?"

Something moved swiftly within the darkness of the hidden chamber, and Conan Doyle reacted instinctively, leaping across the room to tackle Sanguedolce, knocking him to the ground.

"Have you lost your—" The arch mage began just as the sword blade swung out from the darkness, cleaving the space where Sanguedolce had just stood.

"If the Forge is as valuable as you say," Conan Doyle

said, climbing from atop his mentor. "Only a fool would assume it's been left unguarded."

The creature that emerged from the hole in that wall was at least ten feet high. It was a warrior, but not of flesh and blood. Not of bone and sinew. The guardian of the Forge was fashioned from bronze, a mechanical man, and he wielded an enormous sword. Fire from Hephaestus's Forge burned in the empty hollows of its eyes and mouth.

The creation of Hephaestus turned its head and let out a battle cry very much like rending metal, launching its attack upon them. The automaton moved stiffly, and Conan Doyle wondered whether the wondrous device wasn't feeling the effects of time's cruel passage.

Conan Doyle ducked beneath a swipe of the sword's blade and dove at a pile of weaponry, hoping to find something to stave off the bronze robot's attack. He needed a moment to collect his thoughts, to summon a spell that would destroy the guardian. The blade he raised was little more than a dagger to the gods, but it made an unwieldy sword for an ordinary man. He managed to lift a piece of unfinished armor plating and use it as a crude shield, blocking the bronze guardian's sword as it come down toward him. The force of the blow nearly drove him to his knees. Conan Doyle lashed out with his own blade, hacking away at the metal man with little effect.

The guardian's attack was relentless, and Conan Doyle could barely gather his thoughts enough to strike back. It was all he could do to defend himself. Magick was his only hope. When next the automaton raised his sword, Conan Doyle found the opportunity to unleash his spell.

The guardian roared, fiery sparks spilling from the sides of its open mouth as it brought the blade down again. Conan Doyle dropped his own weapon and raised his hand, shouting the final words of the incantation. The air bent and distorted as invisible power jumped the distance between them, and then the ancient machine was blasted backward into the many, carefully balanced crates of jewelry. The wooden boxes teetered and swayed, tumbling down upon Hephaestus's bronze sentry, burying him beneath a deluge of handcrafted baubles.

Dust undisturbed for countless millennia billowed in the air, and Conan Doyle squinted through the roiling haze for a sign of his foe. As the dust began to settle, he saw that the guardian had been buried beneath the avalanche; only a bronze hand sticking out from the rubble.

Conan Doyle dropped his makeshift shield onto a nearby pile of assorted weaponry and glanced about for Sanguedolce.

The bronze automaton erupted up from the wreckage, tossing it aside as if it were no more bothersome than collected raindrops.

The guardian reached for him, its large, segmented fingers closing in a vise-like grip upon his shoulders and neck. Conan Doyle gasped. Explosions of color danced before his eyes as his brain cried out for oxygen, and he feebly struggled to wrench those fingers from his throat.

A resounding clap of thunder filled the room, and Conan Doyle dropped heavily, painfully to the ground, precious gulps of air filling his greedy lungs. As his vision cleared, he saw that the mechanical man still loomed above him, arms extended, segmented fingers bent into claws, but now something was missing. Stunned, Conan Doyle gazed at the empty space above the mechanical sentry's shoulders where it's head had been. All that remained was a jagged, smoking stump.

Conan Doyle picked himself up, rubbing the feeling back into his neck.

"Quickly now, man," he heard Sanguedolce call, and he glanced up sharply to find the arch mage standing at the ragged entrance. His hand still glowed white from the forces he had just released against the guardian of the Forge, and he gestured for Conan Doyle to join him.

"I'm going to require your assistance if we're to take the Forge from the Underworld."

Conan Doyle stumbled toward the hole blown into the chamber. "Are you certain this is wise?"

Sanguedolce stood before a towering object made from blocks of stone that could only have been the Forge of Hephaestus. A pulsing orange glow like a miniature sun still burned from within the belly of the stone furnace, and Conan Doyle could feel its blistering heat on his face. There was something about the Forge, something that made him feel afraid. He could see by the expression on his former master's face that he was not alone in these feelings.

"No, I'm not," Sweetblood confessed. "But I don't believe we have any choice."

17

THE drape of night still hung heavy across the sky when Clay rode into Sparta, but the eastern horizon was tinted indigo, just the barest hint that dawn would soon arrive. Squire sat behind him on the battered motorcycle they had taken from an alley near the docks where they made landfall. Dr. Graves had wanted to leave compensation, or a note for the owner. Clay had dismissed the suggestion as impractical. They had no way of knowing if the owner would ever find the money.

"Besides," Squire had snorted. "We're hunting a monster. It's not like we're the friggin' Justice League."

Now Graves flew overhead, a silhouette barely visible against the night sky, and only to those who were looking. Clay maneuvered the motorcycle through the streets of Sparta with Squire clinging to the bike behind him and the forbidding shapes of the mountains looming in the distance. The nearer they had come to Sparta, the quieter they became. Even Squire had fallen silent now, with the dawn approaching. Clay wondered if he was simply tired or if he somehow sensed that they were at last gaining ground on their prey.

Medusa had stopped running. He assumed she needed to

rest, because he doubted that this was her final destination. Clay clutched the handlebars of the motorcycle and focused on the tendril of ectoplasmic energy that stretched out ahead of him, the soul trail left by the passing of the monster and the spectral remnant of the last human she had slain. He had hunted many killers in his long existence, and when he drew near to them he was always aware.

He could feel the murder in her heart.

The motorcycle's roar shattered the predawn quiet, grinding the air even as its tires bit the road. It was as though Sparta itself slumbered and the engine startled it awake.

They passed a decrepit hotel and a café, then came to a crossroads where Clay brought the bike to a halt, engine grumbling, struggling to spring forward once more. Squire continued his recent silence, and Clay wondered if the hobgoblin had somehow fallen asleep while straddling the motorcycle.

"What is it?" whispered the voice of Dr. Graves.

Clay glanced to his left and saw the ghost hovering there, a golden tint to his spectral form, as though the sunrise tinted not only the eastern sky but the adventurer's wandering soul.

"We're going to have to get off and walk soon. I don't want the engine to give us away."

Graves nodded once. "At your discretion."

Clay revved the engine and turned right. The road took them up into the hills, toward Sparta's own acropolis. In the bustle of the day, Clay thought there must have been a great deal of traffic on these streets, but at this hour the only vehicles they passed were trucks he assumed were on their way to make early deliveries. Otherwise the city seemed abandoned.

For long minutes he navigated the motorcycle in pursuit of that ectoplasmic thread, moving farther and farther from the populated center of the city. At the base of the hill upon which was the Spartan acropolis, Clay pulled the motorcycle off the road and into a small gulley that ran along beside the pavement.

"Thank goodness," Squire grunted as he dismounted the bike with some difficulty. "My balls couldn't have survived another mile."

Clay couldn't help it. He laughed. They had ridden fast and hard, daring disaster on every curve, and he had felt the tension of their hunt. Now they must be more cautious than ever, stealthy yet savage. The moment was not without trepidation. For perhaps the first time since he had known the hobgoblin, Clay found that Squire's humor was precisely what he needed. All the time Squire had been silent he must have been gritting his teeth in pain.

"Oh, sure, laugh it up. I don't see you walking like John Wayne." Squire staggered stiffly away, walking off his discomfort.

Dr. Graves alighted upon the ground several feet away. The ghost seemed barely an echo, almost entirely insubstantial. If Clay looked away, or tried to see the specter in his peripheral vision, he thought he might not be able to see Graves at all.

"You seem . . . less, somehow," Clay said. "Why is that?"

The pinpoint lights in the ghost's bottomless eyes glowed more brightly, and he narrowed his gaze. There was a tightness to his expression that belied the camaraderie that was usually between them.

"The night is ending. Dawn is near. Spirits are . . . *thinnest* then. I could manifest completely, but it takes more effort. I thought I ought to save that effort for Medusa."

Clay nodded. "I meant no offense."

Graves waved him off. "I took none. It just saddens me." The ghost rippled in the darkness as though in the breeze and turned to look up the hill. "She's up there, is she? On the acropolis?"

"No." Clay pointed to the west. "The soul-tether leads this way, around the base. My guess is our destination is on the other side."

The ghost drifted for several yards in the direction Clay had pointed and then seemed to realize what he was doing. With obvious purpose, Graves began to walk rather than float.

"Shall we?" he asked, glancing back.

Squire had gone the wrong way, but he had not strayed far. The hobgoblin had been watching them and now came strolling back, his gait no longer awkward. "Game time, huh?"

Clay laid the motorcycle down in the gulley, hoping to come back for it. "Yeah. And I don't know if we're going to get another shot at this, so—"

Squire bristled. "You think I'm some amateur?"

"Not at all." Clay shook his head for emphasis. "Not at all. You're Hell in a skirmish. But you get carried away sometimes, get loud. You like to talk."

The hobgoblin took a deep breath and let it out. "Not a sound. We'll get her. Greece is nice, but I'm through with the scenic tour. We end it here."

Clay looked at him a moment longer, and then the two of them set off after Dr. Graves, the ghost visible only in silhouette against the indigo of the horizon. A glimmer of gold had appeared in the east, now, as though the edge of the night had begun to kindle into flame.

THE corpse of Hades had become its own Hell, a city of damnation within the vaster Underworld. The Furies had tortured souls for an eternity in their lair, and the suffering screamed through the vast hollow caverns of Hades' chest. The anguish in the very texture of the air was tangible and oppressive, and now it seemed to close in around Ceridwen so that she felt the weight of this darkest of realms fully for the first time.

A warrior sorceress of Faerie, a Princess of the Fey, she was tainted by this place.

She had to escape.

"Come," she said, grabbing Eve's arm.

Still nearly feral, the blood of gods staining her fangs and chin, the vampire spun on her, snarling. Then her face softened.

"Eve, we must go now."

They had made their way back along the path that had taken them to Hades' heart and now stood within sight of one of the dead god's ribs, the massive bones that arced up the sides of the flesh city, columns that supported the dark heavens of this Hell. Even here the upper reaches of the cadaver's roof were not visible, the sky too dark to see.

A wind of ancient screams blew past them and out through the gaping wound in the side of the suicidal god's corpse. Eve had slain one of the Erinyes, murdered part of the fabric of the mythology that had sifted down from the earliest age of the world. The myths and legends, the soul debris of that primeval time, had not so much woken as twitched in the midst of its death throes. The ghosts of gods and the lingering specter of a thousand years of worship had felt the slaughter of one of the Kindly Ones, and had lashed back. Like a tornado of retribution, the grandeur of a bygone age had risen against them. It might subside, but Ceridwen did not believe it would do so before they were all dead, before blood had been spilled in exchange for the blood of Tisiphone of the Erinyes.

Once more she urged Eve toward the way out of Hades' corpse. It would take ages to return to the surface world—to Conan Doyle's world of Blight—but Ceridwen did not want to think about how they would manage the journey. She only wanted to be moving.

"We can't. We have to wait for Doyle," Eve said, eyes narrowed in anger and doubt.

Ceridwen bared her own teeth, aware that her ire could be just as terrible as Eve's if pushed. "Arthur left us to face some task he felt he had to confront alone. If his life were ebbing, I would know. If his heart were breaking, I would know. I *feel* him, woman, every moment of my life. How can you think I would leave him here? He will follow, and the best we can do to aid him is get ourselves to the exit from this blasted place so that he does not have to concern himself with our escape."

Eve stared at her, eyes gleaming yellow in the strange darklight of the Furies' Hell.

In the midst of Hades' heart there was a battle raging. Gigantic figures of metal and leather armor, supported only by bones and spirit-wraiths, the mad ghosts of the Greek gods, were battling with an army of swift, brutal soldiers grown from the ivory teeth of the Hydra.

Danny Ferrick had saved them all, forcing Nigel Gull to sing in the voice of Orpheus. Even now the demon boy was by Gull's side, and he no longer looked so much like a boy. It pained Ceridwen to see his transformation, but Danny was all demon now. The hatred in his eyes and the way his black-red skin glistened made him monstrous and terrifying, even more so than his horns or claws. He seemed to have grown during their time in the Underworld, his chest broader, his arms thicker and more powerful. It occurred to her that perhaps he had been tainted by this place just as she had been, and she hoped that both of them could somehow be cleansed.

But Ceridwen had little faith that either of them would ever be the same.

The changeling was clearly ready to kill Gull if he stopped singing. The voice of Orpheus rang sweetly through the Underworld, cutting through even the ancient cries of the damned. But Gull could not sing forever. The towering, shambling gods had ceased their battle. Even the Hydra's children had stopped attacking the dead things, the shades of gods.

Ceridwen gestured for Eve to look at Gull. The sorcerer's twisted face—as misshapen as his soul—showed the strain of his effort, and his eyes revealed his fear of Danny. Somehow, once controlled by Orpheus's song, the demon boy had become immune to it, and Gull had not bothered to try it on Eve and Ceridwen.

The girl, Jezebel, was dead, leaving Gull with only Hawkins as an ally, and the cold man with his colder eyes seemed only to want to survive, now that things had gone so terribly wrong.

"We've got to go," Ceridwen insisted.

Eve stared a moment longer at Danny, Gull, and Hawkins, and then she nodded.

"All right. But we don't go back out through the gates of this place without Arthur."

Ceridwen moved so swiftly that Eve could not stop her. Her fingers tangled in the vampire's hair and she gripped it painfully tight, even as she sent tendrils of ice racing down over Eve's face.

"We are allies, sometimes friends," Ceridwen said. "But question my loyalty once more, and one of us will die."

Eve slapped her hand away, fangs lengthening again. She hissed softly, held Ceridwen's gaze, then turned away.

"Danny! We're going!" Eve snapped.

The demon boy looked as though he wanted to argue, but then his gaze shifted from Eve to Ceridwen and back again, and instead he nodded once. He grabbed Nigel Gull and propelled the mage toward the wound in Hades' side. The skin around that gaping wound was ossified, insects and strange creatures fossilized in the dead god's flesh.

Ceridwen led the way, leaping from the dizzying height of the exit toward the black ashen earth below. She drew a wind beneath her as she fell, and landed easily. Before she could even turn, Eve dropped to the ground beside her, striking hard and rolling, kicking up ebony dust on impact.

Both of them turned to watch Danny climbing down the exterior of the unimaginably huge body, plunging his claws into the dead flesh and scrambling downward as though he was a spider. For a moment Ceridwen was surprised he had left Gull and Hawkins to find their own way down, but then she realized that the mage and his operative needed to flee this place just as quickly as she and her allies did. Emerging through the wound, Gull grabbed Hawkins by the hand, his mouth still open, the voice of Orpheus still flowing sweetly from his throat. Tentacles of blue-black fire wrapped around them, then shot toward the ground like lightning, carrying them down to stand only a few feet from Ceridwen and Eve.

Hawkins's expression had changed. He pulled away from Gull with a rictus of horror contorting his face.

"You right bastard!" he snarled. "You fucking killed her!"

Gull had no chance to argue. He had chosen Hawkins not only for his various psychic skills, but also for his murderous talents. When the man had touched Gull, he had learned who was responsible for Jezebel's fate. Now Hawkins backhanded Gull, driving him to the ground with a pair of quick jabs to the throat and gut. The mage had no time even to summon a spell to defend himself before Hawkins launched a kick at his head.

"Son of a bitch! All Jez wanted was someone to be loyal to, someone to make her feel like there was such a thing as family. She would have done anything for you, and you threw her away like some gutter whore!"

Hawkins kicked Gull twice more in the head, then in the arms as the mage tried to block the attack.

Eve and Ceridwen ran at them, but Danny reached them first. He had been spider-walking down from the wound when it began. Now he leaped from the side of Hades' corpse and somersaulted through the air, snapping his feet out at the last moment so that he crashed into Hawkins with a sort of dropkick that sent the silver-haired man tumbling across the black, blasted earth.

"What the hell are you doing, you moron?" Danny thundered, his voice no longer his own, but coming from some darker realm. "You've killed us all, assclown. You've goddamn killed us all."

For a moment, Ceridwen did not really understand. Then she heard the screams of angry gods from inside the corpse of Hades, and the ground beneath them began to rumble, and the entire wall behind them—the wall that was body of the king of the Underworld—began to tear in places, new wounds being ripped open in a handful of places along its length.

The ghosts of the gods were marching once more.

Hawkins had crushed Nigel Gull's throat with one of his blows.

The voice of Orpheus had been silenced.

Eve grabbed Ceridwen by the wrist.

"Run."

ON the southern slope of the Spartan acropolis the land leveled out and rough, grassy terrain gave way to forest. Between hill and forest was a pit bordered by stone. For just a moment, as Dr. Graves came around the side of the hill and first caught sight of the place, he saw its ghost. Once upon a time the ruin had been a theater, and imprinted upon the very air itself was the ancient shape of the thing. Though he himself was a specter, they were different sorts of ghosts, and so he saw it only fleetingly before the image gave way to the modern reality. Granite walls were crumbled, the marble stage was only partially revealed, the rest buried beneath the earth as though the theater was growing up organically from the ground. The rows and rows of seating—where thousands of people had once sat enraptured—were eroded by time, but echoed silently with the laughter and cheers of audiences who had been dead two thousand years or more.

In the deeper darkness of an alcove—almost a bunker—that had been created long ago by the collapse of a section of the wall, something shifted, moving swiftly and fluidly. If Medusa had come to this place to rest, she had managed little of it.

Graves moved away from the ruins, backtracking around the hill.

Clay and Squire were moving swiftly but quietly toward

him, their mismatched sizes almost absurd, and yet their approach was formidable. Dr. Graves caught the shapeshifter's eye and held an insubstantial finger to his lips, shushing them both.

The ghost reached down to the holsters he wore and drew phantom guns with nary a whisper. There was no leather and no metal, after all. Only the hush of the afterlife.

He moved swiftly, then, no longer bothering to pretend at walking. He sped around the base of the hill, floating several inches above the ground. He willed himself to fade so that he was nothing more than a ripple in the air and did not even hesitate as the ruins of the theater came into sight. He rushed past the tumbled down outer walls, past the colonnade, and then down into the pit, passing over the remains of the rows and staircases. Nearly as quick as thought, he swept down into the theater, hovering above the cracked marble stage, and from the lair Medusa had chosen, he heard the hissing of the snakes upon her head.

The snakes fell silent.

They had sensed something, or their mistress had.

But Dr. Graves was swift, and Medusa had no time to prepare. She had found herself a cave of sorts, but what she thought was a hideaway had proven not a place to hide, but a trap.

She lunged from it, snakes erupting into a chorus of hisses, and her fingers curled into claws as she glared around the ruin searching for her attacker. The monster relied upon her curse, upon her gaze. Had Graves been flesh and blood he doubted even invisibility would have saved him from her power. But he had been tested already. Medusa could do nothing to him.

Time to find out if the opposite was also true.

Leonard Graves was dead. That did not mean he felt no fear. Trepidation passed through him in that moment the way that a breeze moved the trees of a willow. It *swayed* him, but he would not let it stop him.

Medusa was hideous, her flesh somehow reptilian green

and corpse gray at the same time. Her mouth was stretched open as though in some silent scream and long, needle, serpent fangs jutted from within. Her eyes were black, recessed into her face as though they hid in the cave of her skull, yet there was a liquid darkness to them, as though they did not so much see as flow within. She moved in tiny bursts and flinches, a predatory thing, aware of her surroundings. She darted halfway across the stretch of marble, paused, head tilted to one side, and then she turned and looked right at him.

Graves was a ghost. A wandering soul. If he chose not to be seen there ought to have been no way for her to notice him.

But she had.

When he fired those phantom guns it was not to keep her from escaping him, but to keep her coming any nearer. Gunshots echoed out over the ancient ruins of the theater as a new drama began to unfold. The spectral weapons jumped in his hands, ghost bullets seared the world of the living, intruding upon it. Medusa attempted to dodge, but the first bullet caught her through the shoulder. The Gorgon screamed, and black blood spattered white marble. The second struck her beneath the left breast. The third shot missed, but the fourth grazed Medusa's head, shearing off one of the serpents that grew from her scalp.

Faced with an enemy capable not only of resisting her cursed gaze but of hurting her, making her bleed, Medusa fled. She darted across the stage and leaped into the crumbling stone seating area. Graves felt almost sorry for this creature, so exposed now that she had discovered herself vulnerable. But then he remembered the dead, the vast forests of human statues, of those stone effigies of her murderous progress across Greece. He swept across the theater in pursuit, phantom guns clutched tightly in his hands.

Medusa scrambled across several rows to a grand stone staircase that would take her out toward the forest behind the theater. Once in the trees, she might easily elude him.

Clay came down from the sky with the screech of a night bird. He was an enormous white owl. Medusa turned to defend herself, claws slashing skyward, snakes snapping at the air. Her own scream tore across the sky, and Graves thought that if the ghosts of ancients lingered here, she would have woken them. The last time they had clashed, the Gorgon had turned Clay to stone. Now he took no chances. Even as he dropped down toward her, he changed shape. Medusa lashed out at the owl, but the owl was no longer there. Instead, he was a hummingbird, darting past her face. Then, in the space between heartbeats, he became a Bengal tiger, massive paws crushing ancient stone to powder beneath his tread. Clay sprang at her. Medusa reached for the tiger, prepared to fight it. One of her hands closed on its forepaw . . .

An octopus sprawled across gray stone, suffocating even as its tentacles wrapped around the Gorgon, crushing her. One of those tentacles wrapped around her throat, but Clay could not retain that form for long without endangering his own life.

Warping the air and light around him, he changed again, to the biggest mountain gorilla Graves had ever seen. Medusa had been taken entirely off guard. Now she at last got her claws into him, slashing his face and chest. Clay let out the thundering cry of the gorilla and grabbed her by the throat. Serpent hair darted down and bit his hands, even as he raised her above his head and then hurled her with all of his strength at the stone stairs. There came the crunch of breaking bone.

Medusa flipped onto her belly, managed to reach her hands and knees, preparing to stand in spite of her injuries.

Now that Clay was out of the line of fire, Graves shot her again. Two bullets struck her, one in the leg and another in the pelvis. She crumbled to her knees.

From the massive shadow cast by the lumbering gorilla, Squire emerged. The hobgoblin had retrieved the net they had planned to use for Medusa, and now he hopped forward, agile and brutal, and cast it over her. Squire swore loudly as he kicked the Gorgon, trapping her in the net. The snakes on her head hissed at him, and the goblin hissed back.

Medusa thrashed against the net, trying to break free.

Clay, Squire, and Graves rushed to encircle her so that she could not escape. What she had become was not entirely her fault, but Medusa was a true monster.

She had to die.

A shrieking filled the Underworld, whipping around Eve and her companions on a tornado wind. The anguish of dead Olympus, the bitter sorrow and resentment of dead gods, echoed through the vastness of that death realm. Ghost-warriors, the armored remains of ancient gods, tore free of their mass grave within the enormous corpse of Hades. Others forced themselves up from the black soot underfoot, rising from the ground where they had once fallen and been forgotten.

But there were more.

On the wind.

Those without bones, without armor or any other remains, simply soared through the air, many of them not attacking so much as taking the opportunity to give voice to their pain, and their madness. They screamed, those spirits, and where they flew and twisted around Eve, their touch scoured her flesh like rough stone. These were no ordinary spirits.

She had Ceridwen by the wrist, and the two had begun to run up the long, steep hill that led back the way they'd come. But Eve glanced over her shoulder and saw that Danny was hauling Nigel Gull off the ground.

"Shit," she snarled.

As Danny got Gull to his feet, Nick Hawkins stood gaping like a fool at the gods in the midst of their resurrection. The nearest had been female once, and carried a quiver of arrows across her back. She was nearly out of the ground, and Hawkins seemed unable to tear his gaze from her.

Eve raced back down to them. "What the fuck are you doing? Just leave them."

Gull was bleeding from a broken nose and a gash in his cheek, and his eyes were glazed and disoriented. The demon boy got one of the mage's arms around him and started hustling him toward where Ceridwen stood up on the black-earth hill.

"He's still got serious mojo, even without the voice. We might need him," Danny said.

Eve stared at him stupidly for a moment. Of course he was right. "Shit," she snarled.

Someone started screaming behind her, in a voice that sounded like a little girl's. She spun, claws out, to see that in the moment she was focused on Danny, the resurrected archer had reached Hawkins and was driving him down to the ground, throwing up a low mist of black dust. The goddess of the hunt snatched an arrow from her quiver with skeletal fingers and plunged its sharpened tip through Hawkins's left eye. He twitched twice, and then lay still.

"Just my fucking luck," Eve muttered. She had been wanting to kill Hawkins since a few seconds after they'd met, and she felt cheated.

A trio of screaming ghosts whipped around her, spinning her, scraping her arms and face. Eve swore and snarled, but could not harm them. The others—the ones solid enough to tear apart—were scrambling nearer, but there were too many of them. Far too many.

She raced to Danny, and they held Gull between them, hurrying toward Ceridwen. As they half-dragged the mage up the hill, Eve saw Ceridwen's eyes begin to glow blue. A weird kind of steam issued from them, and then Ceridwen raised both of her hands. Eve felt a wave of frigid air blast past her, and the screams of the disembodied gods were silenced. She glanced behind her and saw several of the giant, armored corpses freeze, ice forming upon them. One tumbled and shattered in the black dust.

Nigel Gull, still staggering along with her and Danny's aid, began to chuckle dryly. When he spoke, his voice was a tortured rasp.

"We're all buggered now," he said. "They'll take us one by one. No way any of us are getting out of here. It's too far."

Eve fought the urge to shatter his chest with her fist and rip his heart out. She glanced over at Danny past the burden they shared and saw in his eyes that the words had cut him deeply. They did not slow him down, however. The demon boy hurried Gull along more quickly.

They had almost reached Ceridwen when the Fey sorceress pointed down the hill past them. She shouted something, but the howl of dead voices had returned, and Eve could not hear her. Spirits spun around her again. Danny lashed out at one but his claws passed right through it. Eve was less interested in these things than in whatever had drawn Ceridwen's attention.

She turned again.

The dead gods were marching after them up the hill, gathering nearer together now, an army of brokenhearted myths out to take vengeance for the spilled blood of one of their own. They trod upon the shattered-ice bones of their fallen comrades and upon the skulls and helms of others still trying to drag themselves from the ground. Most of them were minor gods and demigods, certainly, but she suspected that among them were some of the children of Zeus, the royalty of Olympus, withered and deteriorated until they were impossible to tell from their lesser relations.

Sad, dead, murderous things.

But it was not the gods that had caught Ceridwen's attention so completely. Beyond them, fire had burst up through the chest of Hades' corpse. Broken bits of the god's rib cage jutted from the hole the fire had made, and flames danced around the bone, charring it, sending swirls of smoke skyward.

Rising up through that blazing wound in a sphere of crackling flame was Arthur Conan Doyle. And he was not alone.

"Sanguedolce," Eve snarled, and the name was a curse upon her lips.

The master sorcerer and his former pupil hovered in the air within that fiery sphere, and between them was an enormous metal cauldron filled with gold-and-orange fire—the purest fire she had ever seen.

Ceridwen took several steps back down the hill, crackling with power, her eyes leaking that same frigid blue mist. As she passed them, Danny, Eve, and Gull all turned with her, staring at the sphere of fire as it rose up above the corpse of Hades as though it were the sun in this ever-night world. Even the shades of the dead gods down on that black field turned and looked up at them as the sphere began to move, burning the air around it. It hurtled toward the place where Eve and the others stood.

Beside her, she heard Gull mutter under her breath. "Ah, now I see, Lorenzo. I've been your fool."

"What's that?" Danny Ferrick demanded.

Gull snickered. "Sweetblood told me what I needed to break Medusa's curse, but he never worried if I would succeed. It didn't matter. I used Conan Doyle and all of you as my distraction to slip past Cerberus into the Underworld. Lorenzo used us all to focus the gods' attention so that he could claim the Forge of Hephaestus. Mad, brilliant bastard."

"So, basically, he fucked you over the way you fucked everyone else," Danny snarled. "Swell."

Eve was only half listening by then. She wanted to know more about the Forge of Hephaestus, about exactly what was going on here, but there wasn't time. The dead of Olympus were distracted for the moment, but it would not last.

The shrieking ghosts tore through the air, converging on that flaming sphere. They darted at it, battering themselves against it with a crackle and pop like insects swarming around a light. Spectral hands tore at the fabric of the thing, tearing strips of flame away with a ravenous frenzy.

"That can't be good," Eve whispered.

Beneath her feet the ground began to tremble, and then to shake. It buckled and heaved, and Eve was thrown down, tumbling once end over end on the slope before stopping herself. The entire hill rocked, and she looked around, finally overwhelmed by her frustration and fear. Rage overcame her once more, bloodlust taking her heart, fangs extruding sharply, and hands hooking into claws. She glanced around and saw Danny had also fallen and was crouched on the hill like an animal. Ceridwen floated on air currents that she drew around her, cloak whipping around her.

Nigel Gull was unmoved. Purple-black light coiled around him like a nest of ebony serpents and held him aloft. His nose still bled and his hideous countenance was distorted by a look of such malice that Eve shuddered. How much of his disorientation had been an act she did not know, but he had recovered.

"What now?" Danny roared.

Sweetblood and Conan Doyle hit the ground nearby with such force that she felt sure they would be killed. The fiery sphere was like a meteor, burning right into the soil of this hellish landscape. But when the black dust settled and the glow of the fire dimmed, the two of them stood on either side of the Forge, unharmed. It was enormous, at least five feet high and six wide. There was no way to remove it from here without magic, and yet the two mages seemed prepared to lift it.

"Ceridwen!" Conan Doyle shouted. "Come here! Quickly!"

Under other circumstances, the Fey would have snapped his neck for speaking to her like that. But now Ceridwen raced across the still-trembling ground toward her lover and the Forge. The hill heaved again, and this time Ceridwen did fall.

There came a thunderous crack unlike anything they had heard before, and Eve whipped her head around to look down the hill once more. The dead gods were on the march again, most of them managing to stay on their feet despite the buckling and shaking of the ground. Then, in their midst, the black soil erupted with a giant, skeletal fist easily as large as the Forge of Hephaestus. Parts of that broad, hellish plain collapsed, and minor gods disappeared into the yawning maw that appeared in the earth.

The gigantic, withered corpse that drew itself from the ground then still had some flesh attached to its face, and white whiskers on its chin. Its eye sockets were dark, empty holes out of which squirming white things tumbled as it rose, maggots the size of men. When its other arm burst up out of the earth, Eve saw that it had an axe in its hand whose double-edged blade was the length of an automobile.

Eve had felt true fear, terror for herself, only a handful of times since she had become immortal. After what she had suffered, few things could frighten her. Now a single bloody tear raced down her cheek, and she shook her head, speechless. She wiped the tear from her face and stumbled across the shaking ground to grab Danny by the shoulder and propel him after Ceridwen.

"What now, Eve?" he shouted. "What do we do now?"

"I don't know!" she snapped.

Danny stared for a moment at the gigantic corpse. Eve could not help doing the same. Beyond the first one, another head had begun to emerge, a cracked skull with one eye still intact, gleaming golden in the shadowed land. The dead gods that had attacked them thus far were only the foot soldiers. These others . . . they were the children of Titans.

Eve ran with Danny, the two of them rolling from side to side as though they were aboard a ship. Gull followed, whisking through the air, though now the blood flowed even more freely from his nose, and she could see the strain even this minimal magic was placing upon him.

Ceridwen was already at the Forge, and she was shouting at Sanguedolce. "I can't do it! Never with so many, and not here. My magick isn't the same! This place isn't the same."

Sweetblood only glared at her and then gestured to Conan Doyle to indicate that the problem was his to solve.

"We'll help you, Ceri," he said as Eve, Danny, and Gull gathered with the others around the Forge. "We can feed the strength to you, give you whatever you need, but it's a kind of magick none of us have. The spell must come from your fingers, your lips."

It was difficult to hear above the cracking of the ground and the screaming of the vengeful dead. Ceridwen did not bother to put her reply into words. She looked at Conan Doyle a moment and then reached out a hand to him. He took it, their fingers twining together. Eve had never seen Conan Doyle so pale, the circles beneath his eyes so dark. He looked drained. But when he touched Ceridwen, they both seemed to brighten with the contact, to come alive again.

Ceridwen nodded.

Conan Doyle turned to Gull. "Come, Nigel. You're needed."

"Good thing we didn't kill him, then," Eve snarled.

Danny was in a crouch, one hand on the ground to steady himself. He glared up at Eve. "Does this mean we're getting out of here?"

She didn't even dare look back down the hill. "Let's hope."

Ceridwen raised her hands above her head. The air seemed to flow to her fingertips and then down her arms, caressing her, swirling around her, beginning a kind of whirlwind current. Her body shook with the effort and blue light sparked between her fingers. Eve shivered with the icy chill that gathered around her, the temperature dropping rapidly. The Fey sorceress moved her lips in silent supplication to the elements themselves.

Conan Doyle took one hand. Gull took her other hand. Both had once been students of Lorenzo Sanguedolce, and now Sweetblood himself stepped behind Ceridwen and—with one hand on the Forge of Hephaestus—placed the other on the sorceress's back.

Only then did Eve understand what they were doing. She dropped into a crouch beside Danny and grabbed his hand, then reached out and clutched the back of Conan Doyle's jacket.

Danny was staring past her at the dead gods, at the two ancient Titans that were emerging from the dust of history and myth. He barely acknowledged her touch, his yellow eyes gleaming.

Thunder boomed, shattering the air with such force that Eve winced at the pain in her ears. She glanced up at Ceridwen, but the Fey was deep into the summoning of her spell. The thunder had not been her doing.

Lightning lit up the Netherworld as though sunshine had broken through into the land of the dead. It flashed, accompanied by more thunder, and then came a series of bolts that burned the air and blinded her. Eve turned to search for the source, and it took a moment for her eyes to adjust.

Beyond Hades a tower had exploded from the ground, a huge silhouette, a monument. The next bolt of lightning streaked upward from the top of that tower, and she saw that it was not some structure at all, but a hand. With lightning searing the sky, erupting from its fingers.

Zeus.

"Doyle! Ceri! Get us out of here now!" Eve cried.

But even as she bellowed those words, they were stolen by the wind that had begun to embrace them all. The traveling wind. It whistled around her ears, grasping at her body, blinding her to her surroundings. It was a storm, summoned by Ceridwen and powered by Conan Doyle, Gull, and their former teacher.

A traveling wind unlike any ever summoned before.

It picked Eve up off of the ground. She tightened her grip on Danny's hand and tried to see his face. In the midst of the whirlwind she saw only the cruel gleam of his demon's eyes. Then she was hurtling through the air, propelled by the currents, moving with the storm, wondering where in this realm of death and suffering the traveling wind would take her.

18

IN the grip of magick and wind, spun and blinded by the white-gray spell-storm, Conan Doyle held tightly to Ceridwen's hand. He had traveled with her like this before, during the Twilight Wars, but this was different. There was a dark tint to the winds, a texture to them as though the black soil of the netherworld had been drawn into them and now scoured his flesh like a desert sandstorm. And there was a smell, an unpleasant odor that was carried on the wind. It might have been the Forge of Hephaestus, the stink of brimstone, he knew. But Conan Doyle thought that it was something else, some part of Ceridwen's magick tainted by the fact that she was drawing on the nature of this place, the elements of the Underworld.

Or perhaps it's just Gull, and the poison that lingers in his magick, even after all of these years. His curse.

His eyes watered, demanding that he close them, but he refused. Though he only managed to keep them slightly open, Conan Doyle despised surrendering control, even to Ceridwen, and if the situation demanded it, at the very least he wanted to see where he was going. Not that there was much to see. The winds howled, rushing him forward. He gripped Ceridwen's fingers more tightly.

Then his feet touched stone. The traveling wind subsided too quickly, giving them no chance to halt their momentum, and Conan Doyle stumbled forward, dropping to one knee. Only Ceridwen's grip on his hand kept him from sprawling across the floor of the cavern. But his love was the only one who alighted gracefully. Danny and Eve struck the ground hard, tumbling painfully but rising uncannily fast.

Gull staggered several steps and then dropped onto his hands and knees, blood dripping from his broken nose. He trembled weakly for a moment before getting ahold of himself.

Conan Doyle glanced around. The traveling wind had brought them as far as it could, within this hellish world. They were at the mouth of the tunnel through which they had entered, perhaps thirty feet wide and forty high. In comparison to the vastness they had seen, it was narrow. It was ordinary. He looked back the way they had come, and only then did he see Sweetblood. Conan Doyle had been wrong to think only Ceridwen had managed to alight with any grace. Lorenzo Sanguedolce stood casually in the tunnel beside the massive Forge of Hephaestus. It gave off light and a strange heat that lent a warmth to the body without searing the skin.

Puppets, Conan Doyle thought. *We're all puppets.*

He strode to Sweetblood, and the mage raised a single eyebrow, regarding him coolly.

"I know the threat this world faces," he told his former mentor. "We would all have aided you. You could simply have asked."

Sanguedolce's nostrils flared. "It would have gone far more smoothly had the temptress not slain Tisiphone. I might have come and gone with none the wiser. That would have been best. As for your help, I have no need of it. When the time comes to face the DemoGorgon, perhaps you can serve again as you did this past day, as a distraction. As fodder, to buy me time for the real battle."

Conan Doyle was a gentleman, but in his life he had also

been a soldier. Yet neither of those facets of his spirit could summon a response to Sweetblood's appalling arrogance. They were all silent, each of them having heard the exchange. Ceridwen, Gull, and even smartmouthed Danny Ferrick, all stared at Sweetblood in amazement and distaste.

Eve was frozen by her shock for only a moment. Then she launched herself across the cave. "You cocky motherfucker! You'd still be back there being Zeus's fucking chew toy if it weren't for Ceridwen. This thing, the DemoGorgon, it's you the Big Evil is coming for, right? I say we just make you dead, and then it'll ignore us again."

She sprang at him, murder on her face. Sanguedolce put one hand on the Forge of Hephaestus and simply gestured with the other, and Eve was engulfed in flames. Her scream could have wrung tears from the damned.

Conan Doyle leaped between Sweetblood and Eve, his hands clenched into fists that crackled with swirling golden light.

"That's enough, Lorenzo. You've done far more than enough damage by now."

Ceridwen raced to Eve's side, fingers sketching the air, and Conan Doyle felt the superheated air drop eighty degrees in an instant. The flames that had momentarily touched Eve's flesh were snuffed and frost formed on her charred skin and scorched hair.

Danny tensed to spring, but Conan Doyle gestured for him to stay back. The demon obeyed, but with obvious reluctance.

Sweetblood smiled at Conan Doyle. "That's right, Arthur. Call your pets to heel. As for it being enough, I concur. We've all gotten what we wanted. Or, at least, what we needed."

His gaze shifted, and Conan Doyle glanced over to see what had drawn Sanguedolce's attention. It was Gull, who sat on the stone floor of the cavern with a glass vial of blood held up in his fingers, staring at it as though it were the world's largest diamond and he could study its facets.

Eve wasn't so easily distracted. Her skin would heal, but she would still feel the pain. Enough so that she abandoned the colloquial jargon that was so much a part of her modern persona. "Hear me, o' man," she snarled, baring fangs that gleamed in counterpoint to the blackness of her charred flesh. "There shall be a reckoning."

Sweetblood sneered. "Oh, yes. But you won't even be on the battlefield by then, dear one. This is so far above you—"

"Shut the fuck up."

The words came from Danny, but it was clear from his tone that they were spoken not in anger, but in fear. All eyes turned to him. The demon boy had walked deeper into the tunnel, just past the place where the Forge of Hephaestus sat, burning. Now Danny turned to take them all in with a glance, his yellow eyes wide.

"Do you hear that?"

Conan Doyle narrowed his gaze, peering down into the tunnel. He could see nothing save the same orange glow that had greeted them upon their arrival here. But Eve had left off her rage at Lorenzo, and she stepped past him to join Danny.

"Screaming," she said, her voice low. Then she turned toward Conan Doyle. "The ghosts are coming. The dead gods, the ones that are nothing but spirit now, they're coming after us."

Behind him, Nigel Gull laughed. "Or perhaps they simply want *out*."

Conan Doyle swore under his breath. If the dead gods escaped the Underworld, there would be catastrophe and slaughter. The specters were bad enough, but he suspected that they would not come alone.

The Underworld was another realm, a twist of the fabric of reality away from the world of Conan Doyle's birth. A barrier existed between dimensions, as it always did, but magick could open a portal or build a bridge. The portal between the Underworld and his own world was represented physically by two enormous stone doors, or gates.

He turned toward them now, glancing up at their height. "We've got to get them open. Now."

"No more voice of Orpheus," Danny muttered.

"We've wasted time," Conan Doyle snapped, glaring at Sanguedolce. "Come, Lorenzo. The gates must be opened, and then closed again once we are on the other side."

The cave floor trembled slightly beneath their feet. The distant wailing of anguished spirits came along the tunnel, audible at last to the rest of them, and growing louder by the moment. Sanguedolce turned and caressed the Forge of Hephaestus.

"Damn it, man! You didn't come in here without an exit plan!"

The ground shook so violently that Conan Doyle staggered backward. Ceridwen steadied him and then leaned on him herself. The cave split, a crack splintering across the floor and widening moment by moment, each time with a sound not unlike the profound snapping that came up from deep ice melting.

Conan Doyle glanced down the tunnel again. Nothing was in sight yet, not monsters or resurrected gods, but it was a matter of moments, he knew.

"Come on!" Danny snarled.

Eve held on to him.

Sweetblood shrugged. "My magick could free us. That was my plan. But there is a faster way." He pointed at Ceridwen. In the gloom of the cave her own slim, angular features seemed almost ghostly. "She is tied to the elements, to nature. The gates are of this world, and of that. All she must do is commune with the elements of our own realm, and the doors will open for her."

Conan Doyle nodded, then spun on Ceridwen. "Go. Do it."

She shook her head, confused. The cave shook harder, debris and dust falling down from the roof above them. "I don't know if . . . I've had to adjust to the nature of this place. I am not certain if—"

Nigel Gull choked his hoarse laughter again.

Eve rushed across to Ceridwen, grabbed her arm and propelled her the last few feet to the massive crack that went up toward the roof showing the seam between the doors. "Just fucking do it. No time for doubts, princess. Get us out of here."

The ground shook again, and Eve went to her knees. Ceridwen braced herself against the stone gates, her hands on either side of the seam. Conan Doyle held his breath as he watched her trembling not from outside stimuli, but from within. Her eyes lit up with a familiar blue glow, and they began to change color. Green and fiery red and white-gray and at last, night-black.

Black mist leaked from the edges of her eyes. Purple-black energy began to glow around her hands, spreading up her arms. It was tainted magick, the same hideous shade as he had seen Gull wield from time to time, but this was the base elemental nature of this place. Ceridwen was in tune with it, sharing her nature with it.

She screamed in anguish and disgust and threw her head back, her eyes oily black, her mouth gaping open. The gates in front of her began to glow with that bruise-black energy.

"Ceri!" Conan Doyle shouted. He ran at her, reaching for her.

His wrist was caught in an iron grip, and he spun, raising his free hand to attack, a spell coming to his lips. Then he saw that it was Danny who had grabbed him.

"We've got to get outta here and get the door closed from the other side," the boy said. "You know that. Maybe you should focus on keeping us alive in the meantime."

His fangs were longer, now, and the horns had grown during their time in the Underworld. Danny looked more the demon than ever, and yet in his voice he was still the boy, unsure of himself, trying his best to face up to the horrors that he had thrown himself into, to the truth of who and what he was. Conan Doyle had let his emotions interfere with rational thought for a moment, and he was ashamed of himself.

Ceridwen screamed again, but he turned his back on her. "Come, then. Let's buy her the time she needs."

With a crash, the ground shook again. Sweetblood stood beside the Forge, his entire body engulfed in a crimson flame, staring back along the tunnel. Eve grabbed Gull by his jacket and hauled him to his feet.

"Get up, asshole. We might need you."

Conan Doyle stood beside Danny, and while Ceridwen was busy trying to get them out, the five of them rode the cracking, undulating stone floor of the cave and waited for the hordes of resurrected myths to attack. The shrieks of disembodied gods grew louder, whipping with the wind through the tunnel, and Conan Doyle narrowed his eyes as he realized that they weren't just voices anymore.

He could see them.

Like heat distortion above the blacktop on a July day, they obscured the view of the far end of the tunnel, where it turned to the left and downward. The spirits had just appeared, but they were swift, streaking toward the gates with malicious momentum. From this distance and in the gloom he could not make them out as distinct from one another. Instead they were a wave of spectral hatred, flowing upward.

The tunnel shook again. Debris showered down from above. A shard of rock struck Conan Doyle on his left cheek and cut him. He hissed with pain and put a hand to his face, glanced down a moment to see the blood on his hand, and only when he had looked up did he see the shadow that had begun to obscure the orange glow at the far end of the tunnel. A massive, skeletal hand and a battle-axe. The shadow moved and in a moment had blocked all light from that direction.

The dead gods still shrieked, hurtling up the tunnel at them, but he could not see them any longer. The only light came from the Forge and from the magick crackling around

Sweetblood's body and Conan Doyle's own hands. And from behind . . .

A blinding flash of blue lit up his peripheral vision, illuminating them all in stark silhouette. So bright was the light that it shone deep into the tunnel, and for just a moment Conan Doyle saw the specters of gods screaming nearer, perhaps a hundred yards away now, and deeper, the march of an army of bones. With that image still imprinted on his retinas he spun in search of the source of that bright flash.

Ceridwen shuddered as though she were having a seizure, hands pressed against the high stone doors ablaze with purple-black light that flowed like mercury over her upper arms and spilled like cloud-tears from her eyes. The doors themselves radiated that same magick so that it seemed to be seeping from the stone rather than flowing from Ceridwen. But that dark glow had diminished somewhat, and the color was lightened by the bright blue light that blazed in the crack between the doors. It swirled with shades of blue, ice and sky and river, all shifting in the pure, brilliant glow that seemed only to grow.

In tendrils, the elemental magick of Earth slipped through into the Underworld and ran across the inside of those enormous doors, the gates of the Underworld. Like lightning it leaped through the seam and touched Ceridwen, merging with the black energy that consumed her, tinting the color of her eyes and the magick she summoned. Through the clash of light and magick, he saw that Ceridwen was weeping, but there was a beatific smile on her lips.

Swirls of blue light slipped into the dark field around her, and she was thrown back, away from the doors. Ceridwen fell to her knees amidst a shower of debris from the ceiling of the cave. Sparks of conflicting colors danced in her eyes and from her fingertips.

"Arthur!" Sweetblood shouted.

But he did not turn, this time. All the dead of Olympus might be upon them in a moment, and he would not leave Ceridwen to suffer alone. He ran to her side, stepping over a splintering crack that raced along the tunnel floor, and he knelt by her.

Reached for her.

Ceridwen glanced up at him. Her chest was heaving, and her face drawn, sickly. The elements of two dimensions warred in her, and the conflict was churning inside her.

"Arthur," she said. "Time to go home."

She staggered to her feet, reached out her right hand, which was swathed only in pure blue light. Though the light in her eyes was still tainted, she had managed to summon a connection that was devoid of the netherworld's darkness. Ceridwen touched the doors.

They blew outward as though a hurricane had slammed into them, and the light of dawn over the Mediterranean spilled in. Conan Doyle saw the sea churning far below, and relief washed over him. Despite the peril they still faced he felt a smile stretch his lips . . . and then Ceridwen collapsed.

"No!" the mage shouted, reaching to catch her before she could tumble to the stone floor.

With her in his arms he turned to call for the others, even as the ghosts overtook them. Their screams were so loud that spikes of pain shot through the sides of his head. Vicious spirits spun in the air, several of them reaching for Eve, lashing at her. Where they battered against her, the charred flesh of her arms and face was scraped away.

"Oh, you bastards!" she snarled.

Conan Doyle held out a hand, and an arc of green, ethereal light leaped from his fingers. When it touched the ghosts, they all ceased their screaming, stopped their swooping attacks. Danny had been about to defend himself when the spirits that had been diving at him began to drift aimlessly.

"Come!" Conan Doyle shouted. "They're mesmerized, but it will only last a moment! Danny, take Gull."

The demon boy snarled and leaped over to grab hold of Nigel Gull. They joined Eve, and the three began to run toward Conan Doyle, where he stood with Ceridwen by the yawning gates of the Underworld.

Sweetblood still burned with crimson flame. He stood beside the Forge of Hephaestus facing the march of the dead. Conan Doyle had bewildered only a small number of the ghosts, the first to reach them, and now the others were focusing their attention on Sanguedolce.

"Lorenzo!" Conan Doyle shouted. "We must close the gates!"

The arch mage glanced over his shoulder, a sly grin on his face, as though this were the most enjoyment he had experienced in quite some time. Then he raised both hands, fingers contorted in a pattern Conan Doyle had never seen before, and he screamed as though he had been run through with a saber. Crimson fire erupted from not only his hands but his entire body, spikes of it thrusting outward to skewer each of the dozens of spectral gods that surrounded him.

They had been shrieking in rage before. Now they cried out in agony, were engulfed in that same red flame, and one by one they winked out, snuffed from existence.

Sweetblood touched a hand to the Forge, and it levitated off of the ground. He turned to face Conan Doyle. "Go, you fool! What are you waiting for?"

With that, Conan Doyle turned with Ceridwen and, supporting her, hurried out of the Underworld and into the morning light of his own world. They stepped onto the ledge below the massive stone doors and then leaped out into the air, floating the twenty or thirty yards down onto the narrow, rocky shore. Then they stumbled into the water together, knee-deep in the blue-green Mediterranean. Eve, Danny and Gull were not far away . . . the vampire still healing, and fortunately still under the influence of the spell Gull had given her to protect her from the sun.

The roars of rage and cries of anguish from the open doors echoed out across the water. The ground even here shook, and loose stones tumbled down into the sea. Then, with a crash, the sound was cut off. The shaking of the earth subsided.

Conan Doyle spun to see Sweetblood hovering in front of the cliff face, the Forge of Hephaestus floating in the air behind him. The doors had been slammed closed. The arch mage had a single finger out, and the fire that poured from his body was sealing the gates, leaving only molten rock where any entrance might have been.

But once more his attention was torn away from the crisis at hand. Ceridwen fell to her knees in the water, waves washing around her, and began to vomit. Black bile spilled from her mouth and dripped from her nose. Purple tears slid from her eyes.

"Ceridwen," Doyle whispered, and he dropped to his knees in the water beside her. "Are you all right?"

A foolish question, but it meant something else, of course. Not was she all right, but was she going to be. Ceridwen nodded, trying to catch her breath, marble complexion somehow even more pale, if that were possible. She bucked and vomited again, hyperventilating between heaves. Her hands slipped out from under her, and she dunked face-first into the water, but the black, unearthly stuff she had thrown up had already dissipated.

When Conan Doyle drew her up from the sea, the waves still washing over her, there was a kind of relief in her eyes, and now at last he realized what had been different about her complexion. Blue veins ran beneath her skin, lightly visible beneath the whiteness of her flesh. They had been more numerous and darker when she had first emerged from the Underworld.

"Is she all right?"

Conan Doyle flinched as he heard Eve's voice. He glanced up and saw the concern on her face, and he nodded. "I think so, yes."

Eve smiled, the expression cracking the still burned flesh, and she sat down in the water herself. Some of the charred skin was flaking off to reveal new, pink skin beneath, already healing.

Strands of seaweed had begun to wrap themselves around Ceridwen's arms and legs, but they were not attacking her. The sea was caressing her. Nature was welcoming her back. This was not her home, not the way that Faerie was, but this place her people called the Blight was far more natural to her, its elements far more familiar. She could speak to them, rely on them, and they on her.

When he looked once more upon Ceridwen's face, she was smiling.

"Uh, Mr. Doyle?" Danny called from the rocky shore.

Conan Doyle turned and looked at him. The demon boy stood with Nigel Gull, who seemed to have almost recovered from his injuries. Recovered his dignity at least. He stood with his arms crossed, as though he were impatient for them to conclude their business. It took Conan Doyle a moment to realize why it seemed as though something was missing from the scene.

The cliff behind them was just a cliff, now. Stone. Nothing more. The ground had ceased all shaking.

But Sweetblood was gone.

"I didn't even see him go," Danny offered, shrugging in apology.

Conan Doyle threw his arms up. "Gone. Of course he is. Slip in, use the lot of us as his bloody chessmen, and then disappear before the dust can clear, no regrets, no recriminations. *Bastard.*"

He was stoking the fire of his rage, preparing for a proper rant, when Ceridwen reached up from the water and took his hand. Conan Doyle glanced down at her and saw that she was smiling fondly at him. His brow creased in a frown, and he turned to Eve, who had waded out a short way into the sea so that now only her head was above water. Charred flesh drifted around her, washed away by the surf.

Eve cocked her head to one side. "We survived. He played us, yeah. But we made it out of there. Shit like this, well, let's just say whenever the ennui of being immortal starts to get to me, it's good therapy to have to fight for your life."

Conan Doyle pushed his fingers through his hair and then flattened his mustache. He smoothed his jacket, trying to bring some order back to his immediate surroundings. When he spoke, he let his gaze drift to Nigel Gull, who was wiping drying blood from his face with his untucked shirttail. Gull had seemed defeated, deflated, before they escaped. Now he stood as tall as ever, a dark gleam in his eyes and a sneer set into that ugly face.

"We survived, yes," Conan Doyle confirmed, glaring at Gull. "But I wonder if we would have been so fortunate if Sweetblood did not think there might come a day when we might be useful to him again."

Gull snorted laughter, a fresh trickle of blood spilling from his left nostril. "Come on, old boy, do you really believe Lorenzo ever actually needs anyone."

Danny spun and marched toward Gull, then poked him in the chest. "I'm so sick of you, dude. Talk to Mr. Doyle like that again and—"

Black light crackled in Gull's eyes, and that bruise-purple energy began to coalesce around his fingers as he made a fist. "Don't press your luck, boy. You caught me unaware before. I'm quite alert at the moment, I promise you."

The changeling laughed. "What are you going to do to me? Burn me? Kill me? I'm not afraid to die, I'm afraid to—"

He left off there, quite abruptly, and Conan Doyle frowned as he finished the sentence in his own mind. *I'm not afraid to die, I'm afraid to live.* It would be good to get Danny home, and soon. The boy had been through a great deal. He needed his mother's comfort, and the counsel of a soul more tender than Conan Doyle. Dr. Graves had formed a bond with Danny. After this adventure, that would surely be put to the test.

Ceridwen rose from the water. She still looked a bit wan,

but a certain peace had returned to her countenance. The way her cloak and tunic clung to her made Arthur's breath catch in his throat. All of his righteous ire evaporated in that instant, and suddenly he was as grateful to be alive as Eve was. They had survived.

He reached for her and, despite the presence of the others, held her close. Ceridwen smiled as their lips brushed together, and then he pressed his cheek against hers, knowing his stubble was rough on her skin, remembering that she had always liked that.

Survived.

"Well, it's been lovely, but I'm afraid I must be going," Gull announced.

Conan Doyle turned toward him, still holding Ceridwen. Eve was floating blissfully in the water and barely acknowledged him, but Danny gaped in astonishment and looked to Conan Doyle for support.

"Come on!" the boy said. "This guy totally played us. You're not going to just let him walk away?"

Gull raised an eyebrow. "Isn't he? We go back a ways, boy. And Sir Arthur was never the sort to slay a man in cold blood. It's one of the obvious distinctions between the two of us."

For just a moment longer, Conan Doyle held on to Ceridwen, gaining strength from her touch and her nearness. Then he pulled away from her and strode out of the surf up onto the narrow, rocky shore. Gull cocked his head and watched him curiously. There was no sign of fear in the man's countenance, but Conan Doyle had known him long enough to see a bit of trepidation in his eyes. Only once before had they tested their skills against each other in dire combat. The truth was, rested and ready, Gull might have had more raw power. He certainly had dark sorcery at his disposal that Conan Doyle did not. But like any other conflict, a magickal duel was equal parts strength and cunning, and despite his conniving ways, Arthur felt sure that he could best Gull if it came to that.

But he had no intention of dueling.

Still . . .

Conan Doyle stepped into the swing, slamming his fist into Gull's face with enough force that the other man staggered backward. One of his knuckles popped. He kept after Gull, driving a left into his abdomen, then a right, and even as the twisted mage tried to block, magick crackling around him, Conan Doyle struck him one final time with a blow to the chin that knocked him off of his feet. Gull fell onto a ridge of rocks and rolled over once, crying out with the impact.

Fuming, magick roiling around his hands and steaming from his eyes, his mouth pulled into a sneer that distorted his misshapen head even further, Gull pulled himself painfully from the ground, climbing to his feet.

Conan Doyle stepped up onto the rocks to glare down at Gull. "I am not the man you once knew. I *could* kill you, Nigel. Don't imagine I'd feel any compunction about that. I have the will, and the capacity. But I have been considering your sins ever since I discovered your intent. Others have done far worse for love. No matter how misguided, no matter what you nearly cost my friends, and me . . . I am inclined to accept that we have all been equally manipulated. You were as much a pawn as the rest of us were. For that alone, I will not prevent you from leaving. But after what you've done, what you risked, and the callous way in which you threw away the lives of your own associates . . . I could not allow you to depart without expressing my displeasure."

Gull strode several yards nearer to the cliff face, his back to Conan Doyle. He reached into his jacket and withdrew the vial of blood he had received from the Erinyes, the tears of the Furies. After examining it to make sure it was still intact, he glanced back at Conan Doyle, nostrils flaring.

"I shall not forget that indignity."

"Nor should you," Conan Doyle warned. "Nor should you."

Eve at last surfaced and emerged from the sea, water

spilling off of her ruined clothes. Whatever designer had fashioned them would have wept to see the way she wore them now. She strode up beside Conan Doyle, and Ceridwen joined him on the other side. Danny crouched on a nearby rock, more at rest in that position now, it seemed, than standing upright.

All four of them stared at Gull silently for a moment.

"Are you going to tell him now?" Eve asked.

Gull bristled. "Tell me what?"

Conan Doyle nodded once and let out a long breath. The magick Gull had been mustering had begun to dissipate. The time for war was over, for now.

"When the first of Medusa's victims turned up in Athens, I sent agents to investigate."

The realization of what that might mean was instantaneous. Gull's eyes widened, and he glanced about as though he might find some solution on the rocks. Then his gaze hardened again, and he glared at Conan Doyle and his companions.

"If she has been harmed—"

Conan Doyle raised an eyebrow. "She's killed who knows how many by now. I can almost assure you that if they've caught up to her, she has been harmed. You may have put us all through this for nothing, in the end. A bid to cure a monster. Yet you, if anyone, should know that it is not the face that makes a monster, but the heart.

"Still, we shall see."

The morning sun had long since stretched across the water and the shore. Conan Doyle left all of them standing on the rocks and walked up toward the cliff. An outcropping of rock jutted from the craggy face of the peninsula, and he stepped into the cool shadow it cast.

"Squire," he whispered into the shade. "Hear me."

☐N the marble stage of the ancient theater in the shadow of Sparta's acropolis, Clay let out a bellow that frightened birds from the trees of the nearby woods. The shapeshifter had taken the form of a mountain gorilla, and he felt the weight and the grim menace of the animal in his heart and soul. If he had a soul. Somehow he doubted that in the midst of fashioning his creations out of the Clay of Life, the Lord had seen fit to provide one for him. He was a tool, after all, not a being.

Yet if he had no soul, how else to explain the horror he felt so deeply within him at what Medusa had perpetrated. He thought of the hundreds who had been murdered just in the last twenty-four hours, and it kindled a need for vengeance in him. Life was a gift. Clay had taken lives, but he had spent far more time punishing those who had stolen that gift from others, making up for what he had done, and attempting to bring some justice to the world.

No, not for the world. Just for people. For the dead.

He thought about the children and spouses of the dead, the parents who would not even have a corpse to bury but instead a statue. Stone. And never an explanation for how such an atrocity could occur.

"She's trying to free herself!" Dr. Graves shouted.

The ghost darted through the air, morning light shining through him, and fired his phantom guns at the Gorgon as she struggled against the net Squire had thrown over her. The bullets made her jerk and twitch and bleed black, but they would not kill her.

Squire kicked her again.

But they weren't here to torture her. They were here to *end* her. And end the threat she represented.

With the lumbering gait of the mountain gorilla, Clay moved in. His form was so enormous that it cast a massive shadow across the ground, the darkness sweeping over Squire as he passed the hobgoblin. The shapeshifter reached down with his enormous hands and grabbed up fistfuls of net, drawing the sides together.

Medusa thrashed, attempting to tear herself free. One of her arms slipped loose, and Clay grabbed it, snapping the bones in her forearm. He drew her into an embrace. She whipped her head around, eyes scarlet and gleaming with hatred as she tried to turn him to stone. Clay had solved that problem before by constantly shifting his flesh and bone, never holding the same shape so she could not work her curse upon him again. Now he closed his eyes even as his body began to stiffen, and his every molecule fought the effects of her influence.

He squeezed her tightly. The snakes on her head poked through the holes in the net and darted out to bite him, snapping at his face, sinking fangs into his flesh, and sending venom shooting through him.

Clay tightened his hold on her and felt some of the bones in her chest give way. He drew in a breath and prepared to crush her, to snap her spine, to rip her in two if that was what it took to destroy the evil inside her.

"Hey!" Squire shouted.

The hobgoblin struck him on the arm. Clay was so entrenched in the gravity of his task that he did not respond. There was no levity in this. No pleasure in it.

Squire punched him in the leg. "Hey, dumbass!"

Clay turned his face away from Medusa, the serpents biting his right cheek and his neck in several places, through the fur of the gorilla. He opened his eyes and stared down at Squire, then at Graves behind him. The ghost wore a confused expression that was entirely unlike him.

"Cut the crap," the hobgoblin snapped. "Wrap the bitch up with a bow. Just caught a whisper from the boss. Apparently we're supposed to deliver her alive."

Clay had convinced himself that Medusa's death was necessary. Had felt her bones break in his grasp. The urge to finish her, to shatter them all, was powerful.

Now he growled, the words rumbling in his chest. "Deliver her where?"

•   •   •

THE island of Kithira was just south of the Peloponnese, a beautiful place with enormous Venetian influence mixed with the Aegean. Eve had been there once upon a time, before the Venetians, when the Barbary pirates still held sway over the place. But it wasn't Kithira she had suggested for their rendezvous. It was Andikithira, the tiny isle she still knew as Aigila, though no one had called it that in many an age. It lay twenty-eight miles south of Kithira, a dot in the Mediterranean, and though it was not unknown to world travelers, it was no tourist haven. For centuries the only tourists had been pirates, and even now the only ferry came but once a week.

It was there, beside a whitewashed church overlooking the glistening blue sea, that they waited that long afternoon.

She sipped from a glass of wine that had been homemade by the Koines family, who had been on Andikithira as long as the island had been above water, or so it seemed. The spell that Gull had placed on her to protect her from the sunlight would wear off. The ugly son of a bitch had told her as much. But she was going to take advantage of it while she could. If it hadn't been for the presence of Danny Ferrick— still a teenager despite his demonic nature—she would probably have stripped nude and lain in the sun, giving herself over to its rays and its warmth. Instead she made do with her wine and the white wall that ran along the edge of the steep hill that overlooked the small village below.

The church was at the peak, the village below, and beyond that, the blue-green sea, so soothing to her now. She would never forget the sight of the Mediterranean in that moment when the gates of the Underworld had blown open and they were free. If she'd had breath in her lungs, the sight would have stolen it away.

Her skin was almost entirely healed, save for some mottling on her face that would take some time to go away. That was where she had been burned the worst. A quick stop on Kithira, and she had purchased new clothes, including attire

for traveling, as well as an outfit for an afternoon in the sun:
black linen shorts and a white gauze embroidered shirt that
she had tied just below her breasts, and sandals. It had been
millennia since she'd had occasion to bother with sandals.

There was a picturesque bit of architecture at the edge of
the cliff. A sextet of arches, three on the bottom, two in the
middle, and one at the top. Inside of the top two tiers there
were bells. Church bells, to let the villagers know the time
for mass had come. But other than a low, singing whistle
produced by the wind up inside them, the bells were silent
this afternoon.

The others were all inside the church. Eve had no desire
to enter, and even if she had, she wouldn't have dared it.
There was no way to know what would become of her.
Conan Doyle, Ceridwen, and Danny had each come out to
join her briefly, but now all three of them were back inside
with Gull, making certain he did nothing to endanger them.

Never turn your back on a scorpion, she'd warned Conan
Doyle. She knew from experience, from years in the desert.
And Gull was a scorpion if she'd ever seen one.

So Eve lay on the wall and drank her wine alone and
waited for the afternoon sun to burn down into the ocean as
evening approached. She saw the dust rising from the passage of a truck through the village long before she could
make out the distinguishing features of the truck itself. Not
that it mattered. The island was small. There was only one
reason for anyone to drive a truck up the hill to the church
this afternoon. Only one.

Reluctantly she rose and padded across the bleached pebbles and scrub grass that surrounded the church. She
knocked twice, hard, on the massive wooden doors and then
stood back. Even as she waited for someone to answer she
heard the noise of the truck's engine.

With a clank, the doors were pulled open. Conan Doyle
gazed back at her from the shadows within. The cool darkness seemed to beckon to her, to promise her comfort and

safety, but she would return to the nighttime world soon enough.

"They're coming," she told him.

Conan Doyle nodded, then pulled the doors open wider and stood aside, glancing in at Nigel Gull. Ceridwen and Danny sat together near the front of the church, conspiratorially near, though they'd left off their conversation to look up and see what was transpiring. Gull sat in the rear, hands folded on his lap as though he were the most penitent soul who'd ever entered a place of worship. Even his eyes had changed, for when he looked up at the interruption, they were filled with hope and love and expectation.

For a moment the malformed mage seemed fixed to his chair. Then the sound of the engine grew louder—loud enough to be heard inside the church—and he rose and strode stiffly toward the doors. Eve stepped aside to let him pass. There would be no subterfuge from him now. His focus was on his heart's desire, nothing more and nothing less.

Just as Eve had seen Conan Doyle do so many times, Gull smoothed his jacket and shook out his cuffs, trying to make himself presentable. He reached into his pocket, and she knew he would be clutching the vial in his hand, hidden away. The tears of the Furies.

The truck came around the corner, a rough old thing, the sort of vehicle that might be used on a local farm or to go to market. There was a man driving—or at least, Clay, with the face of a man. The face he wore most often, when he gave his name as Clay Smith. Beside him the air shimmered, and she could almost make out another figure. Someone else might have thought it a trick of the light, but she knew it was Dr. Graves.

Squire rode in the back, ugly little fucker bouncing around back there. Eve surprised herself by being happy to see all three of them.

Clay tore gears up as he halted the lumbering vehicle and killed the engine. He climbed out, and even as he did he changed, shifting with effortless fluidity to his natural form, the tall, hairless man whose flesh was cracked, dry earth. The Clay of God.

"You want a hand?" Squire asked.

"Couldn't hurt," Clay replied, as he hefted a burden from the back of the truck. A body, wrapped in chains, a leather hood covering its head, not unlike the sort of thing a falconer used to keep his bird calm.

Grinning, Squire began to applaud. "Come on," he said, glancing over at Eve. "Give the big guy a hand."

Eve scowled at him. Squire blew her a kiss, then hopped out of the truck. But he did not approach. He only leaned against the side of the vehicle and watched. Something was to unfold here, and he did not want to be a part of it. She saw a look of distaste flicker across his face, and then his sardonic grin returned.

Clay carried Medusa over his shoulder, reaching back to cinch the straps on her hood tightly as he strode toward the church. She did not struggle. Perhaps, like a hooded falcon, she was waiting for her moment to strike. When he had reached Gull and Conan Doyle, Clay slipped her off of him and let her fall to the ground. A moan of pain came, muffled, from beneath the hood.

"What have you done to her?" Gull demanded, kneeling by Medusa and glaring up at Clay.

His upper lip curled in hatred and disgust. "A few broken bones. Far less than she deserved." Clay looked at Conan Doyle. "Are you sure this is the right thing to do."

"No," Conan Doyle confessed, startling Eve with his honesty. "But it's what we're doing." Then he stepped up beside Gull and looked down at Medusa. "Do not remove her hood entirely until the curse is—"

"I am not a fool!" Gull snarled, rounding on him.

But then Conan Doyle seemed forgotten. Eve watched as Gull summoned a spell, sketching his fingers in the air, and the chains fell away, pooling around her on the ground.

"It is I, fair one," Gull whispered, the words eddying on

the breeze. "Come. Take my hand, rise and let the curse be broken."

Eve took a step back and tensed, waiting for Medusa to lash out in attack, prepared to stop her if she did. Conan Doyle did not move, but Eve could see a soft blue glow around his hands and feel the electric charge in the air around him that only came from magick. He was ready as well.

Medusa stood. Eve could hear hissing beneath the Gorgon's hood, and now that she looked closely, she saw the leather shifting, almost undulating with the presence of the serpents on the monster's head.

Gull put a hand behind her, touched the small of her back. Medusa flinched, and Eve twitched in response, ready to move.

"It's me," Gull whispered. "It's Nigel."

Then Medusa surrendered to him, sliding her taloned hands around behind him and pressing herself into him, molding her body to Gull's and laying her head on his shoulder like any young lover might do.

There was silence at the top of that hill. Even the wind seemed to hold its breath.

Gull reached into his pocket and produced the vial. He held it up in front of her face as though she could see it. Though that was impossible, of course, she sensed it somehow, for she froze, and her head tilted back as though she could inhale that blood. Eve wondered if it was the magick in that vial, the forgiveness, the power of ancient myth that Medusa sensed, or if it was simply the scent of blood that had caught her attention.

The mage did not seem so ugly in that moment when he reached up and uncapped the vial, then loosened Medusa's hood. Eve tensed again, worried that he would pull it off, but instead Gull only raised it high enough to reveal her mouth, the pale flesh and needle fangs and the forked tongue of the accursed Gorgon.

"Drink," he said, pressing the vial into her hand.

Medusa hesitated only a moment before she lifted the vial and sucked its contents into her mouth. The bloody tears of the Furies disappeared into her hideous maw, and that forked tongue ran out into the vial, licking it clean.

The effect was almost instantaneous. Medusa did not collapse or even flinch. Instead the visible gray flesh at her chin became pink and healthy and her mouth was that of another creature entirely, with lush, full lips. Damp tears ran down her cheeks.

Before she had been cursed by Athena, Medusa had been the most beautiful creature in the world. Or so went the myth. Now, as she reached up to remove her hood—all of them watching in hushed fascination—Eve could believe it. Her eyes were wide with joy, her lips trembling with emotion. She held her hands up and studied the long, elegant fingers, then ran her palms over her lissome shape. At last she reached up to touch her face, and even as she did she spun, looking at them each in turn. She was awestruck and lost in a blissful rapture. It was written in her every expression, her every movement.

"My darling. You are free, now. Your curse is ended. After an eternity, your beauty is returned to—"

His voice had given her focus for the first time. Medusa turned and looked at Nigel Gull, this twisted mage who had risked all for her, and she recoiled at his appearance. Her beauty was marred by the revulsion that curled her upper lip and narrowed her gaze as she took a step back from him.

Medusa was free of her curse, but Gull was still stricken by his own. The handsome countenance he had sacrificed for dark gifts of magick would never be his again. His misshapen features flinched now, stung by her reaction to him.

"Medusa?" he ventured, pitiful. Crushed.

When she spoke, the words were Greek, and so ancient that though Eve remembered the language, it took her a moment to translate in her mind.

"I am sorry," the Gorgon said. She reached up a perfect, slender hand, but fell short of caressing Gull's hideous features. The hand fell to her side. "I have despised my own face for so long . . . if I spent my days gazing at yours it would only remind me of the hell I have escaped. You have given me everything, but I cannot repay you. I cannot give you what you most desire in return."

At some point Danny and Ceridwen had come out of the church. Squire, Clay and Graves watched from their vantage point near the truck. Conan Doyle stood with Eve. And Gull was alone.

"What did she say?" Danny asked. "That language, what—"

"Ancient Greek," Conan Doyle explained. "But I don't know what—"

Nigel Gull understood, however. From the look on his face, it was clear that he understood all too well. All the light and hope had drained from his eyes, and there was only malice there once more. Any trace of the desire and love he had revealed was buried deep beneath the ugliness that was not only in his face, but in his heart. This was the cunning schemer who had betrayed them, who had used them, and who had discarded his own allies in the pursuit of his goal. This was the dark magician.

Oh, yes, he had understood Medusa perfectly.

Gull drew his antique pepperbox pistol from beneath his jacket, and shot her through the head.

Eve cried out, and Conan Doyle lunged for the weapon, but too late.

Medusa fell to the ground, blood spreading across the white pebbles of the drive.

Gull knocked Conan Doyle away, gave Medusa a final glance, and then a pool of bruise-purple energy gathered around his feet, and the ground swallowed him whole, the mage slipping down into some dark portal of his conjuring. Slipping away.

But as he went, Eve caught sight of his face, of the distant, hollow glaze in his eyes, and she knew that though he would escape them, he would never, ever be free.

EPILOGUE

ON the third floor of Arthur Conan Doyle's home in Louisburg Square was a bedroom with no bed. Shelves lined two of the walls, laden with maps and journals and artifacts from the life and career of Dr. Leonard Graves. There was no bed because dead men did not need to sleep. Instead, in addition to those shelves and a scattering of books the ghost of Dr. Graves had borrowed from Conan Doyle's library, there was an antique Victrola side by side with a CD player, old records and brand new discs. Graves was equally passionate about Robert Johnson and the latest modern day R&B songbird. He couldn't abide rap, though. He was just too old-fashioned.

Then there was his television. His DVD collection was extensive, racked in cabinets around his entertainment center. From time to time Conan Doyle or Clay might come up and take in a movie with him, relaxing in the comfortable chairs that decorated the room. They liked the old films just as much as he did.

Glorious black and white.

The curtains in the room were drawn, now, and familiar blue light gleamed from the television screen. Jimmy Stewart made his heartfelt plea in *Mr. Smith Goes to Washington*,

Columbia Pictures, eleven Academy Award nominations. If he focused enough, Graves could feel the solidness of the chair beneath him, even the texture of the fabric. He liked that, settling in to watch one of his movies. His Gabriella had been particularly fond of Jimmy Stewart. Despite the struggles they had faced because of their race, the hatred Dr. Graves had engendered in many quarters even as he gained respect and fame in others, he still recalled the era of his life as a kinder time, and the late actor seemed to embody that kindness.

Gabriella. A bittersweet smile touched his lips as the movie played on before his eyes. He could almost imagine her beside him still, though her spirit had long since gone on to a better place.

One day, they would be together again. He had made that vow a thousand times. But he was bound to this plane for the time being by the tragedy of his death. His murder. His assassination. Dr. Graves would not allow his specter to slip from the fleshly world to the ethereal plane until he had solved the mystery of his own death. Only then could he be with Gabriella again.

For now, he had his memories. And the movies she had loved so very much.

As he focused once more on feeling the fabric of the chair beneath him and let himself get back into the rhythm of the film, there came a knock at his door. Dr. Graves frowned. They had been back from Greece only a handful of hours, and had all agreed to get some rest. He did not sleep, but that did not mean he could not benefit from a period of relaxation.

The ghost floated up from the chair and then strode to the door. With focus, he grasped the knob and opened it.

Julia Ferrick stood in the hall, her features cast half in shadow by the dim illumination from the electric sconces on the walls.

"Dr. Graves," she began in a tremulous voice. Her forehead was creased in a frown. He did not fail to notice that she had either forgotten or chosen not to call him by his given name.

"Julia? What is it? Danny's all right?"

Graves had not seen the woman since their return, but he was not surprised that she had come so quickly. Her son had been cast into a situation of terrible danger. Of course she would rush to see him. But the ghost had assumed she would be pleased by his safe return.

"No," she whispered, swallowing visibly. "You've seen him. He's worse than ever. Those . . . horns. They're longer."

His heart ached for her. "Julia, we've discussed this. Daniel is what he is."

She nodded. "I know. It's just . . . where does it end?"

The ghost had no response for that.

"And you," she went on, her jaw set. "You said you'd watch out for him."

Dr. Graves blinked, and his spectral form rippled. "He was with Conan Doyle and Ceridwen. And Eve, as well. They were all watching over him."

Julia shook her head. "But I don't trust them. Any of them." She searched his eyes as though trying to locate something she thought she had seen before. "I trusted *you*."

"You *can* trust me. And you can trust the others as well. I had to be where I could do the most good. As did Daniel. But we're back. All of us in one piece."

"And what about the next time?"

The ghost met her gaze steadily. "No one can promise to return Daniel safely to you each time he leaves this house. When a crisis arises, when there is real evil to be faced, the outcome is always uncertain."

Julia stared at him. For a moment she reached out to touch him, mouth working as though searching for the words to express what she felt. It seemed to Graves as though she desperately wanted something from him then, some assurance, some solace, but he hesitated.

She shook her head, dropping her hand, and backed

away. Dr. Graves could only watch her recede down the hall and then descend the stairs. Somehow he felt more had passed between the two of them than he realized, that Julia's disappointment in him extended beyond her concern for her son. He did not quite understand, but it troubled him to have hurt her.

Dr. Graves found that he cared very deeply what Julia Ferrick's opinion of him might be.

And that troubled him as well.

CLAY stood in the kitchen of Conan Doyle's home, peeling an apple at the sink. He had been talking for quite some time in the living room with Squire, but the hobgoblin had gone to bed. Sleep called to him as well, but all he had wanted from the moment they had returned to Boston was a glass of ice water and a fresh apple. On the granite countertop, his water glass sweated drops of cool condensation, waiting for him. He made a small game of peeling the apple, attempting to take it all off in a single long strip. There was something calming about the process, the methodical nature of it.

"Hey."

The knife slipped, tearing the peel, and a long coil of it dropped into the sink. Clay felt a twinge of regret and smiled at the absurdness of it. He turned and watched Eve walk into the kitchen.

"Hey, yourself."

She came to the granite counter and took a long sip of his ice water. Clay uttered a soft, surprised laugh.

Eve grinned, toasting him with his own glass. "Sorry. It was just too tempting to resist."

If she heard the irony in that, she made no indication. Clay lifted the half-peeled apple. "You want some of this, too?"

A little piece of darkness flickered across her gaze and then was gone. "No. Thanks. This is just what I wanted."

Clay took another glass out of the cabinet for himself but went back to peeling his apple before filling it. Perhaps he ought to have been irked by Eve's presumption, but in truth he was glad she felt comfortable enough with him to just assume he wouldn't mind sharing. To be herself. There were very few people Eve could be herself with, and Clay understood what that was like. His life was the same.

Perhaps that made them friends. He would have liked to think so.

"Did Danny turn in?" he asked.

Eve nodded, but her smile went away. Though there was no romantic entanglement between them, Clay could not fail to appreciate her classic beauty. Her lips were lush and full, her eyes captivating, her raven hair perfectly framing and sometimes veiling her features. But Eve was never so beautiful as when the burden of worry lay heavily upon her.

"What is it?"

She shrugged, tossing her hair back, and took another long sip of ice water. They stood there across the counter from one another in silence a moment, Eve considering her words.

"I'm thinking you should talk to him."

"Me?" Clay asked. "Why? You're much closer to him. Ceridwen even more so."

Eve nodded. "Yeah. But he wants to talk about . . . about God. And evil. He's trying to figure some things out, Clay. I tried to tell him that it didn't matter what he was made of, where he came from, who his parents were. But the more we deal with things we call evil, and the more he has to look at himself in the mirror, the more he wonders, you know? He's still evolving. I think he's just afraid of what he might become."

Clay cut the last of the peel from his apple, but now he only held it in one hand, the knife in the other. He let the words sink in and then turned to face Eve.

"Maybe that's okay. Maybe he should be afraid."

• • • •

CONAN Doyle felt defeated.

He sat in the high-backed leather chair in his study, pipe clenched between his teeth, puffing slowly on it. The smoke swirled down into his lungs and drifted in twin streams from his nostrils. Normally he could let himself relax here, but nothing seemed able to calm his mind this night.

All of his Menagerie had returned from Greece alive. That was the only saving grace of this mission, as far as he was concerned. Medusa would no longer endanger the world, but though Clay and the others had been the ones to capture her, Gull had murdered her. Though they might have had to kill her anyway, the callousness of it had been unsettling.

Nigel Gull had used him, drawn him in, and now, at last, everything had gone horribly wrong for the mage. Once upon a time he had been a man of quiet strength and dignity, but his ambition had been stronger than his nobility. The dark magicks that had twisted his flesh had tainted him forever, but Nigel had never understood that. All he had understood was the power that they had granted him.

Conan Doyle wondered if Nigel understood, now.

He doubted it.

To all appearances, Gull was on his own now. Those he called his Wicked were dead. Tassarian for the second time. The girl Jezebel had been a tragic figure from the moment she crossed Conan Doyle's doorstep, doomed from the start, yet he would have saved her if he could have. Hawkins had been doomed as well. He had invited death constantly. It had only been a matter of who would play executioner.

But Gull might have other allies. Conan Doyle certainly had operatives that he kept in abeyance, old friends and acquaintances that could be called upon if the need arose.

Nigel Gull would be back.

At the moment, however, Gull was the least of his concerns. There was Danny Ferrick, who seemed too unstable for the work the Menagerie undertook, and yet who had nowhere else to go. He would have to adjust to what he was, or it would tear him apart. Then there was Dr. Graves. Conan Doyle had sworn to help the ghost solve his own murder, but thus far had been able to uncover precious little.

He knew he ought to concern himself with his allies. His friends. But such things seemed so small and petty in comparison to the threat of the DemoGorgon.

"There's nothing you can do."

Conan Doyle turned, broken from his reverie, to see Ceridwen standing in the open door of his study. Silhouetted in the light from the hall, she had never looked so beautiful, and his breath caught in his throat. His eyes watered from tobacco smoke in his lungs that he could not exhale.

The Fey princess had showered, her blond hair still glistening with water. She wore only a thin shift the same blue as a robin's egg, and the light from the hall caught the lines of her body through the translucent material. Lithe limbs, supple muscles, and the gentle, familiar curves that made him forget his heart was beating.

"Arthur?"

He blinked, the enchantment of her presence lifting, but only slightly.

"Yes?" Conan Doyle rasped.

Ceridwen entered the study, the fabric gliding over her body as she moved into the dim room. She crossed to the window, where the moonlight touched her as though it had longed to do so forever.

"You struggle with the rage you feel at Sanguedolce for having manipulated you. And the rest of us as well. But you resent him as well, because he belittles you at every turn."

Had anyone else spoken these words, he would have been affronted. Would have denied the truth of them, even to himself. To Ceridwen, he only nodded.

"He's a fool," Conan Doyle rasped. "His magick is so great that he believes himself omnipotent. No matter how powerful he is, if this DemoGorgon is what he claims, he will need all of the allies he can find."

Ceridwen crossed to him, then. She took his pipe from his hand and set it on its stand, then moved his chair away from the desk and slid down to sit before him. Arthur went to stop her, but she only smiled softly.

"In his own way, regardless of what he says, he is preparing to defend this world. When the time comes, we shall see if he rejects assistance." Ceridwen gathered his hands in hers and gazed up at him, and those violet eyes were all of the sustenance and comfort he had longed for. When he thought of the time they had lost, at what his stubbornness had cost them both, it crushed his heart.

"Meanwhile," she whispered, drawing herself upward, the fabric of her robe sliding over his hands, "you must focus yourself on matters at home. On the everyday darkness in this world, but also on the light. On the sunshine as well as the shadows. On your life, and the lives of this strange family you have gathered about you."

Her hands caressed his face, and Ceridwen climbed up onto the chair he sat in, kneeling so that she was astride him. Hope and joy and sadness swam in her eyes, and she trembled as she bent to kiss him. Their lips brushed only lightly at first, reacquainting themselves, and then she kissed him deep and long.

His heart had seemed to stop before, and now it beat with such speed and vigor he thought it would burst. His own hands trembled as they slid over her back, tracing her body from the softness of her hair to the extraordinary spot at the small of her back where his touch had always made her shiver.

"Meanwhile," she whispered, drawing her face back only inches from his, her profile illuminated in moonlight, her small breasts still pressed into him. "Focus on me."

Ceridwen began to undo the buttons of his shirt.

Arthur decided that, for this evening at least, the world would have to wait.